THE MEN
FROM
THE BOYS

THE MEN
FROM
THE BOYS

WILLIAM J. MANN

A DUTTON BOOK

DUTTON
Published by the Penguin Group
Penguin Books USA Inc., 375 Hudson Street,
New York, New York 10014, U.S.A.
Penguin Books Ltd, 27 Wrights Lane,
London W8 5TZ, England
Penguin Books Australia Ltd, Ringwood,
Victoria, Australia
Penguin Books Canada Ltd, 10 Alcorn Avenue,
Toronto, Ontario, Canada M4V 3B2
Penguin Books (N.Z.) Ltd, 182–190 Wairau Road,
Auckland 10, New Zealand

Penguin Books Ltd, Registered Offices:
Harmondsworth, Middlesex, England

First published by Dutton, an imprint of Dutton Signet,
a division of Penguin Books USA Inc.
Distributed in Canada by McClelland & Stewart Inc.

First Printing, June, 1997
10 9 8 7 6 5 4 3 2 1

Grateful acknowledgment is made to the following for permission to reprint from
previously published material:
"(I Never Promised You a) Rose Garden" by Joe South. Copyright © 1971. Published by
Lowery Music, Inc. Used by permission.
The Outermost House by Henry Beston. Copyright 1928, 1949, © 1956 by Henry Beston, ©
1977 by Elizabeth C. Beston. Reprinted by permission of Henry Holt & Co., Inc.

REGISTERED TRADEMARK—MARCA REGISTRADA

LIBRARY OF CONGRESS CATALOGING-IN-PUBLICATION DATA
Mann, William J.
     The men from the boys / William J. Mann.
        p.   cm.
     "A Dutton book."
     ISBN 0-525-94335-8 (acid-free)
     I. Title.
   PS3563.A53629M46   1997
   813'.54—dc21   97-3955
                                                                     CIP

Printed in the United States of America
Set in Janson Text
Designed by Leonard Telesca

PUBLISHER'S NOTE
This is a work of fiction. Names, characters, places, and incidents either are the products
of the author's imagination or are used fictitiously, and any resemblance to actual persons,
living or dead, events, or locales is entirely coincidental.

FOR TIM
AND, EVEN NOW,
FOR VICTOR

ACKNOWLEDGMENTS

Many people helped shape this book, persuading me of its worth and guiding it toward reality. In particular, I am indebted to those individuals who read and brought new insights into the developing manuscript: Christopher Bram, Michael Bronski, Lesléa Newman, Surina Khan, Jim Gemmel, Suzanne Lewis, Karen Bellavance-Grace, and Kelly Scannell. I am grateful not only for their sharp eyes, intelligent criticism, and constant demand for excellence but also for their sustaining friendship during this process. I want to acknowledge as well my deep gratitude to Dorothy Allison, who gave me invaluable early feedback and convinced me I wasn't a fraud.

Matthew Carnicelli provided the kind of encouragement and advice that an author dreams about from an editor. It has been a joy to work with him, and I thank him for believing in the book and its unique structure.

My agent, Malaga Baldi, has been a constant source of support. She is an untiring champion, a shrewd advocate, and a genuine friend.

Finally, I must thank my life partners. Tim Huber, as in everything else, provided unwavering love and support: material, financial, and emotional. A few words on an acknowledgments page can hardly express my gratitude and love for him. Without his belief in me, this book would not exist. Likewise, I can only offer humble thanks to Victor D'Lugin, a giant of a man who taught both Tim and me the meaning of unconditional love and support. His constructive criticism of early manuscripts helped fashion this novel, but even more important, his wit, wisdom, and unfailing devotion helped me navigate my life during the roller-coaster year of writing it. Even now—especially now—he continues to inspire.

TRICKS

Provincetown, June 1994

"Going tricking?" Javitz asked earlier tonight, in that voice that knows the answers to its own questions.

I just laughed.

Tricking. Such an odd little twist of a word. As if I would take one of these boys home with me and rather than sex I'd pull a rabbit out of a hat. As if we'd get to my door and I'd refuse to let him inside, turning instead with a maniacal grin to say, "Tricked ya!"

As if tricks were the antithesis of treats and not what they are: the caramel on the apple, the cinnamon in the bun, the cotton candy on the stick. Tricks are how we treat ourselves. Not that all tricks are always so delectable: some of mine have been the proverbial rocks in Charlie Brown's paper bag. But most of them have been sweet: Hershey's Kisses. Milky Ways. Almond Boys.

Tonight, it's his nipples that bewitch me from across the room, little pink cones in relief against sweat-dappled copper skin. The boy I am watching moves in a rhythm that repudiates the beat on the dance floor. He wears a vest but no shirt, a grin but no smile.

Summer is a time of random magic such as this, of surprising spirits conjured up between the sheets of my bed in a room overlooking Provincetown harbor. Here, strangers' kisses expose souls to me. The uneven scar on one boy's abdomen, the crinkles at the corners of another's eyes reveal more truths than I could ever discover in a more consistent lover.

It is the last summer in which I am to be young.

"Hi," the boy says to me, stroking his firm stomach idly. Little beads of sweat leave shimmering trails down the smooth brown flat plain. He can't be more than twenty-three.

"I've seen you around," he says. "You work up here?"

"No," I say, which is a lie. Mystery helps in this town—especially when you're no longer twenty-three. "But you do," I say. "A house-boy or a waiter?" I ask, knowing the options for a boy his age.

"A houseboy," he says.

And so the script stays on course, except for the brief flutter of my eyelids at that precise moment, when I find the eye of a man across the dance floor. My breath catches, and I worry that the houseboy notices. But he doesn't—of course not: he's deep into character. Acknowledging my distraction would be akin to an actor on stage responding to the laughter of the audience in the middle of a scene. He carries on, as is proper. But I stumble, drawn by a man across the room, a man I don't know, a man I thought was someone else.

I know no one here.

"What's your name?" the boy is asking.

I turn to face him. "Jeff. And yours?"

"Eduardo."

We shake hands. Our eyes hold.

And so another one.

Loving strangers is a heady mix of romance and reality, the sordid and the sublime. I have returned this summer for that mist of sweat across a boy's bronzed back, for the magic that happens when the two of us marry eyes across a dance floor and become forever young.

"Can I still get away with it?" I asked Javitz before setting out tonight.

He laughed. "Maybe for another year."

Once, Javitz and I were lovers, when my skin was soft and unmarked like the boy Eduardo's. That was before the little pinched lines began creeping around my eyes like the marks my mother used to make in the crust of her apple pies. My lover, Lloyd, tells me I'm being absurd, that at thirty-two I still have many years left to play. But he should talk: he with his monthly dosage of minoxidil and the tweezers he leaves behind on the sink surrounded by a scattering of his bristly gray hairs.

"Will we ever get to a point where we don't care?" I asked him not long ago. "Will we ever welcome the gray, disregard the wrinkles, skip the gym, eat that extra piece of chocolate cake?"

It is both lovely and terrifying to imagine: Lloyd and I, bald and fat, in matching reclining chairs, watching *Jeopardy!* side by side, finally free of the tyranny of youth.

Once, we were the boys of the moment, angry young men marching through the streets in black leather jackets covered with crack-and-peel slogans: "Act Up! Fight Back! Get Used to It!" Javitz and his generation, a decade older, had smiled indulgently at us. "Ah, youth," they would sigh. But how quickly our energy dissipated, how quickly boys are replaced. The hair on my head thins out, while in my ears it sprouts cocky as crabgrass. My body might be pumped from an afternoon in the gym, but one hundred crunches a day can no longer dispel gravity's influence on my waist.

"And then what?" I asked Javitz, replying to his comment about getting away with it for another year.

"I'll see you at Spiritus," was all he said.

That he will still join me there takes courage. Javitz is a tall, striking man with long, curly black hair and intense dark eyes. Once, when we were lovers, I thought he was the most handsome man in the world. Today, Javitz is forty-seven—a terribly old age for me to contemplate ever being. He's well known in Provincetown and back home in Boston, too. "A leading activist," one newspaper account called him, "an icon of the gay community." He was one of the engineers of the state's gay rights law; he helped get gay issues into the public high school curricula; he helped found ACT UP. But in front of Spiritus, the late-night cruisy pizza joint on Commercial Street, it's his loss of muscle tone that stands him out from the crowd, the predictable result of years of antivirals: shapeless calves, spindly arms. And not long ago he witnessed what happened to one man—near fifty, almost bald—who dared to assume he could still come out and play.

"Did you smile at me?" this man had asked, standing on the steps of the pizza joint, behind a cluster of boys in backward baseball caps.

"Sure," I offered.

"Are you trying to pick me up?" he asked.

I was taken aback. "No," I told him.

"No," he echoed, darkening. "Of course not." He slumped, like a tire slashed.

A boy beside me began to giggle. "They're going to find him washed up on shore in the morning," he whispered.

Growing old is not for sissies, so they say. But sissies *do* get older. All of us sissies here tonight, with the hot juice of youth pulsing through our veins. Some of us are already well on our way. Some of us are going to die long before our times. What does it matter, Javitz says. Get old or get AIDS: the end result is the same. Especially here, in this place: this place of sculpted pectorals and shaven torsos, heads thick with hair and bodies jumping with T cells. But the first wrinkle, or the first purple blotch on your leg, and you must accept the exile, a banishment that we rarely question, dismissing any who try.

"How old are you?" Eduardo is asking me now, the inevitable question.

"How old do you think?" My inevitable answer.

"Twenty-eight?" Last year, it probably would've been twenty-six, but it's good enough; it's what I want to hear.

"Around there," I lie. "And you?"

"Twenty-two," Eduardo responds.

Who has ever been twenty-two? I ask myself. Not me. Not ever. If I ever was, I don't remember. It was all such a long time ago, in a world very far away. And every summer, a new crop is twenty-two, standing at the cusp of the dance floor as if they were the first ones ever here.

"Do you want to dance?" Eduardo asks suddenly, as if it had just occurred to him, as if it were not merely part of the script, the way things are.

My line: "Sure."

And so we dance, the prelude to the sex I know will come, predicting the choreography in my bedroom just a short time from now: back and forth, round and round, up and down. We're all one big writhing mass of human flesh out here under the lights: male flesh, young flesh, raw bodies and sweat, humping together, wet luminescent backs sliding against each other, nudging shoulders, hands massaging chests where hard stubble sprouts like rough new grass, all of us pushing, shoving, grinding, grunting. I'm reminded of the time the bar threw an underwear party last summer. I came on the dance floor: hands in my Calvin Kleins, hands fighting each other for a turn, hands, hands, hands without faces, and I came onto the floor to prove I still could.

"So what is it that you do?" Eduardo shouts over the music. Another inescapable question. My answer will distance us. I'm no houseboy, no clerk at the scrimshaw shop.

"I'm a writer," I say.

Whenever I tell boys that I am a writer, they always respond in the same way. They appear to believe that this is significant, that they should somehow be impressed. "What do you write about?" they always ask in response, as Eduardo does now, a ridiculous question, one for which there is no answer. So I always say, as I do now:

"Whatever I can."

Eduardo smiles. He knows he can go no further. He's in over his head.

Was from the start.

Boston, January 1995

When I was a boy, my mother told me a riddle that terrified me. It went something like this: A girl is put in a room with no windows and only one door. That door is locked from the outside. There is nothing in the room with the girl but a radiator. Later, when they open the door, the girl is gone. What happened to the girl?

The answer: the radiator.

The radi *ate* her.

That riddle has come back to me now as I sit here on the edge of Javitz's hospital bed. He's been here for more than three weeks, straight through Christmas, fighting off the pneumonia we thought was whipped back in November. The snow outside is battering the windows like a flock of suicidal gulls. It's one of Boston's infamous snowstorms, the kind that slick roads within instants, that drop eighteen inches of snow in an hour.

I'm sitting here now, remembering that damn riddle, how the presence of a clinking, clanking radiator in a room terrified me for years, and then Javitz asks me about Spiro Agnew.

"Is he still alive?" he asks, watching the TV that's hooked up on the wall. The woman on CNN with the Barbra Streisand cross-eyes is talking about a bust of Agnew being placed in the rotunda of the Capitol.

"I guess so," I say. "They're giving him an honor."

Javitz makes a sour face. "He was a crook. You don't remember. You're too young."

"I remember watching Nixon resign," I protest. I was twelve, on summer vacation between seventh and eighth grade. My mother remained a die-hard supporter right to the bitter end. We both cried watching the resignation on the little black-and-white TV in the kitchen while she peeled potatoes for supper.

"You don't remember all the terrible things Nixon and Agnew did. Nobody seems to anymore. Nixon would've been as bad as Reagan on gays and AIDS and all that stuff. Maybe worse."

"How could anybody have been worse than Reagan?" I ask.

Javitz closes his eyes. "Luise Rainer was," he says. Talking about politics wears him out fast these days. "Especially in *The Good Earth*."

"I'll say," I laugh. "And they gave her *two* Oscars."

"Count 'em," he says.

"*Two*," we say in unison.

He takes a deep breath, eyes still closed. "We should do a Luise Rainer video festival this summer in Provincetown. What do you think?"

I consider it. Every summer for the last five years, Javitz, Lloyd, and I have rented a place in Provincetown, that little spit of sand at the end of Cape Cod farther away from the rest of the world than anywhere else. How we've managed to do this, I don't know—Javitz on his community-college faculty pay, Lloyd with his grad-school loans, me barely making enough income to pay taxes. But every year, each of us writes down on a slip of paper the top limit of what we can afford, and then we toss the slips together and add them up. Somehow this quirky little experiment in socialism has worked for us every time.

Once there, we rent old movies—our shared passion—and invite in the neighbors. A Dietrich night, a Cukor festival, a Liz Taylor cavalcade. But this year, with Javitz being sick, we haven't yet had a chance to find a place. Actually, I'm ambivalent about doing it

again, after everything that happened last summer, but I decide not
to bring that up now.

"All right," I concede. "But I can't imagine who'd come to see
Luise Rainer."

"Round up your little boys," he says, and his smirk looks even
more devious with his eyes closed. "We can tell them she was a
great actress. They'll believe anything."

"Almost," I correct him, and of course it's Eduardo we both
remember.

The snow blasts the windows again. Javitz is quiet for a while.
Then he says, "I wonder if Mrs. Maxwell is dead."

"Who's Mrs. Maxwell?"

"My third-grade teacher. She probably is. She was old when I
had her."

"Yeah," I agree, "she's probably dead."

This is Javitz's newest trick: thinking of someone for no apparent
reason, someone we met briefly years ago or some friend of his I've
never known, and wondering out loud if they're dead. Sometimes I
know; sometimes I don't.

Javitz thinks about death a lot, ever since he decided to leave
teaching after twenty-three years and go on disability. His T cells
had dropped to below one hundred, dangerous news not so long
ago, but who can say anymore? That's the thing these days: we know
less than we ever thought. Javitz's friend Ernie has *four*—not forty,
but *four* T cells—and he's been fine for over a year. Javitz's T's have
actually been rising, so I don't know why he thinks so much about
death. He isn't going to die, at least not soon. I sit here, thinking
about little girls trapped in rooms with malevolent radiators waiting
to gorge themselves on their flesh, and I know that yet again Javitz
will come home, and that this time he'll be able to do a little less
for himself than before. And then he'll get sick again and back here
we'll come and then home again—just as it has been for the last ten
years. The curse of the long-term survivor, Javitz calls it.

"Do you remember when we were at Hands Around the Capitol?" he asks. I nod. Of course I do. "I tricked with that guy. What
was his name?"

"James," I tell him.

"Oh, yeah. Is he dead?"

"How would I know?"

"I was just wondering." He closes his eyes. "Ask Lloyd. Maybe he knows. He tricked with him, too."

And he might very well. Lloyd stays in touch with his tricks, even falls in love with them a little bit. I could never understand that— at least, not before last summer. It's a dangerous game, falling in love with tricks. They can break your heart in a whole different way than a lover can.

Lloyd was supposed to come with me here tonight to Beth Israel to see Javitz, but he got beeped at the last minute. He's a psychologist for a crisis program over at Mass General. Mom always wanted my sister to grow up and marry a doctor; I beat her to it. "Tell Javitz for me," Lloyd said on his way out the door, "he better not die or anything when I'm not there."

Lloyd loves Javitz in a way I can't: free of guilt, free of a history that lingers between us. I envy that love. What must it be like, I wonder, when there's nothing that hangs around in the back of your mind like dirty socks in a closet, their existence unseen but their presence always known?

And Javitz loves Lloyd in a way impossible for me: free of doubt, free of competition. We're basically the same age, Lloyd and I, and in the gym we play silly little games: who can press the most weight, whose pecs stand out better beneath a white T-shirt, who gets the most looks from the boys. Yet neither of us would admit to playing such games or the seriousness with which we play them.

"You're thinking about Lloyd and what he told you that Sunday morning last month," Javitz says.

"No, I'm not," I lie.

"Jeff, you've got to stop being so afraid."

I react. "I'm not the one preoccupied with death."

He gives me a look, eyes wide and eyebrows up. Maybe he's right: why else has my mother's riddle—that damned radiator with the steaming fangs—come back to haunt me?

"You and Lloyd have been together for *six years*, Jeff. It's all right to be going through this."

"We're not 'going through' anything," I snap.

I wonder if Javitz ever thinks about what he and I might have been going through had *we* lasted six years. I met Javitz when I was just twenty-two, the same age as Eduardo, the boy I fell in love with last summer in Provincetown. Javitz was thirty-seven, just a little older than I am today. He seemed so *old* to me then: but old in a *good* way—a way these boys I trick with must see me. An older brother who's still young enough to fuck but old enough to explain what's going on. Before Javitz, all I had been looking for was a place to put my dick. Wide-eyed, eager, and horny, I was new to Boston, having arrived for my grad program in English at UMass with all the zest any boy feels upon his first move to a real city. I met Javitz at a reading by Allen Ginsberg, the very first poetry besides Dr. Seuss I'd ever heard read out loud. But what excited me more was the prospect of the boys who would undoubtedly show up. I wasn't disappointed. There were plenty of boys, but it was Javitz who caught my notice, Javitz with his long black hair and smoke-chewed laugh and the magnificent way he saw right into my terror.

"You there," he said, across the cheese and crackers. I raised my eyebrows questioningly. "Yes, *you*." He grinned. "You look as if you need someone to show you around."

I did, of course. We made a date for the next night. He took me to dinner at an Italian restaurant in the north end of Boston, with red and white checked tablecloths and carafes of red wine. He promised to show me gay Boston and, if I wanted, gay New York too, sometime. "Sure," I agreed, awestruck, sitting across the table from him. He knew so much, had been to so many places.

"How old are you?" he asked, sitting back in his chair.

"Twenty-two," I told him.

"*Twenty-two?* Who has ever been twenty-two?" he sighed grandly.

"You, I imagine," I said, trying to be cute. "Once."

It worked. He winked at me, and both of us were hooked. "So," he asked, next question: "Are you out?"

I lied, of course, and told him yes. Isn't it funny? No one's ever closeted when you ask them. But Javitz, as I was to discover, was a big-time activist, and he saw right through the cobwebs that shrouded my closet door.

We went back to his apartment, a third-floor space in Cambridge near Harvard Square, crammed with books on Plato, the Trojan Wars, and Billie Holiday. Javitz taught ancient history at one of the community colleges. He enjoyed teaching, he said, but activism was what he loved most. "Every once in a while some trick will try to impress me with his knowledge of the fall of the Roman Empire," he said. "I tell them: 'That happened fifteen hundred years ago. Did you vote in the last election?' "

He showed me pictures of the very first New York Gay Pride parade, pasted down in an old photo album with those little black corner holders. They revealed Javitz—back when he was still David Mark Javitz from the Bronx—in his big fuzzy Jewish Afro with peace signs dangling from around his neck. Later, he moved to Boston and became one of the heroes of the movement. In his scrapbook were clippings of demonstrations, of the passage of the gay rights law, quotes from David Javitz highlighted in yellow. One even had his photo (how much rounder his face was then) with the caption "Gay Activist Demands Change."

I remember when we all got together for the city's first ACT UP meeting. Talking about getting arrested made me nervous, but Javitz assured us all he'd gone to jail before. He'd been in anti-war protests during the sixties, he explained.

"I was in grade school during the sixties," an ACT UP boy with seven piercings through his nose teased.

"That's *your* misfortune," Javitz responded, unruffled.

He was fond of saying: "Youth is nothing but an instant in time, when we don't know what the fuck we're doing but we believe ever so earnestly in the importance of doing it."

He told me he'd tested positive just a few months before, one of the first to go for the test after it became available. He was also the first person I knowingly had sex with who had the virus. I was young. I don't remember any fear. Hot, healthy, horny. I'd read the pamphlets, been to the workshops. I knew my way around HIV. There was never any fucking with Javitz, not even with condoms. I rarely took the head of his dick into my mouth. When I did, it was a big occasion, one that he was grateful for but never expected. It was the mid-eighties. We all were so different then.

Right now, I can't remember why I broke up with Javitz. We

lasted not quite four years. I was twenty-six. He was forty-one. Maybe that was it. But it's hardly enough of an answer: we don't talk much about it, so maybe we'll never know.

"I wonder if I'll see Richard Nixon when I die," Javitz is wondering.

"Heaven wouldn't make much sense if you do," I reply. "Republican crooks and angry AIDS activists living together for eternity?"

That's when it hits me: why my mother's riddle has come back to me at this particular time. And why it so terrified me all those years ago. It didn't make any *sense*, and mothers were *supposed* to make sense. The riddle was utter nonsense, and that's ultimately why it scared me so.

I mean, if what happened to the girl was that the radi ate her—what is a "radi"? If that little syllable had some double meaning—slang for "rhinoceros" or something—it would have carried some logic that would have made the riddle much more clever. But "radi" means nothing, so how could a "radi" eat her?

Thus I had an image of this heinous radiator coming to life like some mad creature out of the late-night horror movie and devouring the poor girl. It would have strained against its bolts, finally breaking free, its hot iron elongating into claws. Then it would have loomed over the girl before consuming her in its steaming mouth.

But now, as I sit here and watch Javitz fall asleep, I think that the reason the riddle so frightened me was not so much the demonic radiator but the image of the girl being shut up in a room with no way to get out—abandoned, left to die, forgotten. They put her in there and left her all alone, defenseless, against that hellish radiator. And my mother had the nerve to ask: "What happened to the girl?"

Hah. As if she didn't know.

Provincetown, June 1994

"Aw, yeah, man."

His nipples taste salty. I test them with my teeth. Eduardo moans softly in appreciation. Rare that a boy's nipples should be so sensitive. Usually takes years.

He's stretched across my bed, still in his vest and shorts. I lick the hollow space between his taut pectorals: smooth warm skin, tasting bitterly of sunblock. He has a fit of passion: grabbing me from behind he pulls me down to his mouth. We kiss hard, clinking teeth, an accidental toast. He rolls over to straddle me and begins kneading my chest, playing top for as long as I let him.

Now his vest is on the floor and my shirt is gone, and we're kicking off our shoes. That's always the most awkward part: the shoes. Unlacing trendy boots—black Doc Martens on him, beige work boots on me—takes time, and pulling them off sweaty feet, with moist, unyielding socks, is work. But we manage. He helps me with mine, even going so far as to pretend to lick the scuffed brown leather of my right boot. Oh, how boys like to pretend they're into things that will in reality take them *years* to actualize.

We're soon just in our cut-off denim shorts, legs entangled. His energy excites me, urges me on. I decide it's time to claim my place on top and wrestle Eduardo underneath me. I grab hold of his nipples and clamp down, little fleshy knobs between my forefingers and thumbs. He groans. I sidle up over his chest and shove my crotch in his face. He bites the faded denim. "Suck it," I tell him, and he moans again.

I wonder how many cocks this twenty-two-year-old has sucked in his life. Even as he's unbuttoning my fly, I'm doing arithmetic. Even in a moment of such passion, I'm still up on the ceiling looking down. He's twenty-two. Born when I was ten. When Nixon was in office. He was *six* when I sucked my first cock. *Six.*

But he knows what to do. How *do* boys learn these things? How did I learn?

(His name was Gordon, one of my two best friends in high school. "You've done this before?" Gordon asked. *He* had, of course: with our other buddy Stick. "Sure," I lied. "Mmm, that's good," Gordon told me, vindicating my make-believe.)

I ease Eduardo up and kiss him. I taste my own cock in his mouth. "You're so nice," he murmurs into my ear. I bite his neck, my lips shielding my teeth like living condoms. He purrs in gratitude.

And now he's on top of me again, playing with my nipples while I stroke my dick and reach up to lick the head of his. He groans, "Aw, yeah," as I shoot—long stringy ejaculations of white that torpedo across the bed and make me proud. *See that, kid?* Go ahead and *try* to shoot that far. Just try.

He does. And almost succeeds. But I still win.

Then I'm exhausted. "Man," I say, falling back into the pillows.

He lies down next to me, on his side, his nose to my ear. This is the point where they always want to cuddle. Did I say the shoes were the most awkward part? *No:* this is.

"Are you one of those types who kicks a guy out after having sex?" Eduardo says, half-teasingly.

I look at the digital clock next to the bed, glowing green in the dust-colored darkness. It's 3:25 a.m. "If you want to stay, you can."

I'm distant. I'm a jerk. He picks up on it. "Do *you* want me to?" he asks in a little voice.

"You should know something," I say.

"Don't tell me. You have a boyfriend."

"Yes," I tell him.

"I knew it."

He sits up in bed. This, too, is part of the script.

Boys out on the street caterwaul, whooping about something. For a moment, I wonder if they're cute, cuter than Eduardo. In the distance, the soulful sound of a foghorn warns ships not to come too close to this place.

"I can't believe it," Eduardo says. "Why didn't you tell me before?"

"It wasn't relevant," I say. I know my lines.

"What do you mean, 'It wasn't relevant'?"

"I mean, it's okay," I say. "Lloyd does it too. It's okay."

Eduardo is shaking his head. "Well, not for me."

"So when *you're* in a relationship, be monogamous."

"You don't get it. I don't sleep with married men."

"Well," I laugh, "you just did." I reach over, putting my arm around him and sitting real close. "Listen, just because I have a boyfriend doesn't mean I can't get to know other people. That's the beauty of being gay. Not being fenced in by definitions, restrictions. I really enjoyed myself tonight. And I'd like to see you again."

"Why?"

Good question. Because you have the most beautiful nipples? Because you give good head? "Because I like you," I say.

"I'm not just looking for sex," he says, in that righteous voice boys use when they are attempting to stand firm for some principle in which they think they believe.

"So you were hoping we'd get *married*?" I ask, with emphasis on the incredulity.

It works. He sounds suitably embarrassed. "No, no," he says, looking away. "But I always hope that every new guy . . ."

"Every new guy?" I repeat.

"You know what I mean," he says, and of course, I do. Twenty-two-year-olds need to believe they're no different from what their parents expected them to be. They might be gay, but they're still in search of their parents' lives. Sex is something to be rationalized, even while they're all fucking like little queer bunnies. Sex, Javitz once told me, is the first thing we think of when we come out, and the last. It's hormones that first kick open the closet, and it's our eventual embrace of that primal drive—a drive disowned by the hetero hegemony—that allows us to finally slam the door behind us. It's the definitive awareness that we're different from our parents, indeed, from the rest of the world. But it'll take these boys at least until they're thirty to figure this out. It did for me.

So why do I bother? "Do you know how old I am?" I ask, breaking my own rule.

"Twenty-eight," he says, puzzled.

"No, I said 'around there.' I'm *thirty-two*." I don't add that come August I'll be thirty-three.

"No way," he says, and I imagine he's as shocked to learn he's just tricked with a thirty-two-year-old as he was with a married man.

"Yes way," I reply, somewhat regretful of my impulsive confession.

Eduardo smiles. "You look great for thirty-two," he says.

"Thanks. And you look great for twenty-two." I kiss him, hard and deep, on the mouth, to prove that I'm really not such a bad guy. In seconds, he's ready to go again, boyfriend or not. I could kick myself for reigniting his dick: once a night is usually as much as I can handle these days. Why do I try? Why do I persist? I'm asking myself as he starts nibbling on my sensitive nipples again. I can almost hear Javitz laughing in the other room.

Boston, January 1995

The snow is letting up. I wonder for a moment if it might actually be over, the storm.

"I hate the winter," I tell Javitz.

He shifts under the thin white sheets. His butt is sore from too much bed time. "That's because you're a summer baby," he says. "Like me."

Javitz's birthday is the day before mine: August 6 and August 7. He jokes that he'll admit to being older than I am: by a day.

"Girl," comes a voice, intruding into our stillness, "you haven't been a baby for a *long* time—summer or any other kind."

We look up. It's Javitz's friend Ernie, shivering as he steps through the doorway. "But *baby*—it's cold outside."

"What the *hell* are you doing here?" Javitz asks, his face alive for the first time all week.

They kiss. Ernie wiggles his fingers at me. "I was over at Fenway for a lecture on alternative treatments. Silly me. I thought they'd tell me something I didn't already know."

Ernie lives in Provincetown year-round. This makes him a special and rare breed, and he has proudly pasted a "Provincetown Year-Rounder" bumper sticker on his car. Trips into Boston for him are infrequent, especially in weather like this. I suspect there was more than just a lecture at Fenway that brought him here. Surely word had reached up the Cape that Javitz was back in Beth Israel.

"I may be going home tomorrow," Javitz tells him.

"So this isn't the big one, huh?" Ernie smirks.

Javitz sighs. "You know me. Always a pallbearer, never a corpse. How long are you in town?"

"Leaving tomorrow morning. Lots of stuff going on at the Collective. Oh, David, wait till you get back up there. You'll put those patronizing straight white women in their place." He rolls his eyes. Ernie's the only person I know who calls Javitz by his first name. He works as an outreach educator for the PWA Collective of Provincetown, handing out condoms at the dick dock and in the dunes. He does not suffer gladly condescending AIDS caregivers. "I don't need a mommy, thank you," he says. "One was quite enough." He's an artist, too, a painter, tall and lanky, with sand-colored hair and a face with freckles like a Jackson Pollock painting. He started out as a trick of Javitz's, three, maybe four, summers ago. Then he tested positive, got involved with the Collective. Now he and Javitz are inseparable during the summer. "See what can happen with tricks?" Javitz said to me. "Make a note of it."

Every Tuesday morning from June to August, Ernie comes by to pick Javitz up for their support group; on Wednesday nights they meet for the group's weekly dinner. "Want to come along?" Ernie has asked me a couple of times, but I've always declined.

"Well, the whole *town* is wondering if the three of you are coming back this year," Ernie says, pulling up a chair beside Javitz's bed and tossing me a glance. "What shall I report?"

"We need to start looking for a place," Javitz says.

"Pronto," Ernie agrees. "Girl, it's nearly *February!*"

"If the town's so *interested*," I suggest, "maybe they can pitch in and *find* a place for us."

"Preferably with a deck that has morning sun," Javitz says, winking.

Ernie smiles. "Faced with the possibility that Provincetown's most infamous threesome might not return, I'm sure they'd do just that."

Many have wondered about Javitz, Lloyd, and I. "What *do* the three of them *do* together in that house?" the Provincetown gadflies whisper. "Are the two younger ones his slaves? Or is he just their sugar daddy?"

They see us walking together down Commercial Street, shoulder to shoulder to shoulder, Javitz usually in the middle, the tallest of the three. "Didn't one of the younger ones date the older one for a while? Which one is which? Do you *know*?"

"The older one," a neighbor once told Ernie, unaware that he was Javitz's friend, "is merely trying to relive his own lost youth."

"The younger ones," said another, "are just waiting for the will to be read."

Another observation came from one of Lloyd's tricks, who woke up the morning after to find Javitz at the kitchen table. "I cannot for the life of me understand how a couple can live with a single," he said. "Doesn't it drive you *nuts*?" Whether he addressed the question to Lloyd or to Javitz, they were never quite sure.

"How to disentangle the myths of age?" Javitz sighed dramatically, sitting on our deck two summers ago, waving his cigarette.

I responded in kind: "How to explain to a world fixated on the paradigm of two the power of three?"

These are the discussions we have, late into the night. I laugh at our pomposity. We like the sound of our voices in the stillness of a purple night as we solve the problems of the world. I turn these conversations into essays for the queer and alternative press. That's how I make my living these days, as a freelance journalist. I roll the ideas around in my head, like dough in sugar and cinnamon, thinking them through in odd snatches of the day, at the grocery store, at the gym, between tricks or loads of laundry. Then I bring them up again with Javitz and Lloyd: "I was thinking . . ." I say, and we pontificate some more.

This is who we are. This is my family—audacious maybe, but constant, a fact that nourishes me. I will not allow what Lloyd said to me that Sunday morning last month to threaten the constancy we've created. I will not grant it the power to do so, no matter how much Javitz might say I'm denying the reality of the situation. I will not lose my family, not again. When my mother turned her back on me, I lost the family into which I was born. But it's what came after that matters: Javitz, Lloyd, and I, a new family, ill served by definition, constantly changing and accommodating itself. Three working-class boys—Javitz from the Bronx, Lloyd from a farm in Iowa, me from a dried-up little factory town in Connecticut—living beyond our means in a succession of summer houses in the rarefied resort of Provincetown, trusting always in the sustaining power of three.

The images are there, at the flick of a switch in my mind. Javitz on the back of a motorcycle, riding sidesaddle, being dropped off at seven a.m. by a trick on his way to work. "Who d'you think you are, worrying us all night?" Lloyd asks, only half-teasing. Javitz shakes his long black hair, the curly ringlets still wet from a shower at the biker's house. He adores the attention: "I've never ridden on the back of a motorcycle before," he gushes. "I felt like Nancy Sinatra in *The Wild Angels.*"

Javitz with a tray of raspberry croissants as we get up in the morning: Lloyd and me, Lloyd with a trick, me with Eduardo or Raphael or the kid I picked up at Spiritus whose name I failed to get. "Good morning," Javitz says, and the tricks stare in wonder. "Would you like a cup of coffee? Or do you *drink* coffee?" Only *I* get the dig.

"Who *is* that man?" the tricks ask later, as I kiss them goodbye and send them on their way. I just smile—for how can I tell them?

I feel caught in a sticky web that connects two separate worlds: the boom and the X generations, pre- and post-Stonewall, positive and negative, old and young. But what am I then, if not either? Javitz once said it was my role to bridge the gap, to connect with the children and tell them about what came before. This strange link that I provide, this tenuous grip on history: what good will it do when we too—those nebulous in-betweeners—are gone? Once I thought only Javitz's generation would disappear, but I was wrong. The boys I knew when I was a boy, the ones who first invited me onto the dance floor, back in those heady quixotic days when nobody believed it would last this long—they're disappearing too. Sometimes I think I see them, standing there among the children. I'll spot someone on the other side of the dance floor, and my breath will catch, thinking it's Gordon, or Stick, my high-school buddies, the ones I came out with, the kids with feathered-back hair and wide ties whose faces, even now, stare eternally in black and white from the glossy pages of our yearbooks. But I'm wrong: it's never them. I wonder if they're waiting for me to join them, if that's why I've seen them.

Yet that's not what I fear anymore, not really. I don't know if I have the virus. Last time I was tested I didn't—but that was five years ago. Neither Lloyd nor I plan on being retested. If Lloyd were to get sick, I imagine, that would be that, the end of the line for me. What was it that the Wicked Witch of the West said: "The last to go will see the first three go before her"? That's the horror of it all, right there: not that I too may die, but that I may go on living, by myself.

Ernie and Javitz laugh, bandying about names I don't know, names of the infected. I withdraw a little, watching the icy rain splatter against the window. The snow is turning into sleet. I wonder if Lloyd is home yet, if whatever crisis he was summoned to defuse is over, if yet another life has been saved because of my lover's quick actions. I think of Lloyd and grab hold of the thought, trying to keep it there, in my mind. I wonder what tonight might have been like if Javitz and I hadn't split up, if Lloyd had never come into my life, if I were still standing here tonight as Javitz's lover and not as Lloyd's. It is unbearable to comprehend: Lloyd is the last tether to the boat, the last rope that feels secure, and I will not admit that there are frays on that rope, right at the very top, no matter how much Javitz encourages me to talk about it. It's my fault, really, for sharing with him the conversation Lloyd and I had that Sunday morning not long ago, a conversation that now feels absurd and unreal, especially standing here in Javitz's hospital room listening to the rain.

"David—you are *bad*!"

Ernie and Javitz laugh outrageously at some ribald joke, the punchline of which escapes me. It's the first time Javitz has laughed like that in weeks, yet their laughter is alienating. I retreat farther into the windowsill, my nose nearly against the cold glass.

"Well, Jeff, it's been a pleasure, as ever," Ernie says suddenly, and I jump a little before I turn, face-to-face with his sincerity. "I've got to head back, before they close the roads." I shake his hand. He's a good man.

"Call Howard when you get back," Javitz instructs. "Tell him to find us something. *Anything.*" Howard's our real-estate agent, a buddy of Ernie's.

"Even a place with no morning sun?" Ernie asks.

"Oh," Javitz sighs, "I suppose we'd survive."

"You got it, girl." Ernie blows a kiss and then he's gone.

I turn to Javitz. "How you doing?"

"Tired."

I take his hand. He's quiet again, as he has often been with me of late. Laughter for Ernie, questions about dead tricks for me. I realize the nurse must think we're lovers.

He falls asleep within minutes. His breathing is so much easier than it's been for the last few nights, the infection in his lungs apparently beaten. Maybe tomorrow Lloyd and I *will* come to pick him up, and maybe next week we all *will* pile into the car and head up the Cape, searching for another house and another year, grateful but also fatigued by yet another chance, another summer, always wondering how many more, how many more. But this summer, none of us will be young.

Me least of all.

Provincetown, June 1994

Eduardo sleeps like an angel, a child actor in a Nativity play. My heart is breaking, as I knew it would. Tomorrow he'll be gone, and

I'll miss him terribly, as if he were the greatest love of my life. And maybe he is. Maybe all of them are. Raphael, from last summer, became an ideal only after he'd returned home to Montreal. Javitz remembers that while Raphael was still here in Provincetown, I'd twice not wanted to take his calls. But once he was gone, he became the boy who got away, the boy who stole my heart, the boy I never was.

And now Eduardo. Who *are* these children? I can't sleep. His sweet breathing is driving me crazy. I slip out of bed and pad through the quiet house. It's a hot dry stretch of late June, a respite from weeks of dripping humidity. I smell cigarette smoke from the deck overlooking the bay. Javitz is there, smoking, watching the inky waves lick the eroding beach. The moon is high, and the stars are out, scattered across a dark gray sky. The only sound is the foghorn from Long Point—the saddest sound I know: the call of the men who trudge on back to their guest houses alone, rejected even by the desperate outside Spiritus at two a.m.

"Hey," I whisper, respectful of the night and Javitz's space.

He turns, exhaling smoke. "All done?"

I smile. "He's asleep."

"A name?"

"Eduardo."

"I caught a glimpse as you came in. Beautiful."

I nod, sitting on a deck chair, propping my feet up on a small table. "And *young.*"

"How young?"

"Twenty-two."

Javitz sighs dramatically. "Are there such things as twenty-two-year-olds anymore?"

"One's sleeping in my bed right now. Go take a look." I close my eyes. "What did *you* do tonight?"

"Went to the dunes. Got fucked twice."

"Really?" My eyes are open now. "Is that why you're not sitting down?"

He laughs. "And neither of them was twenty-two," he tells me, hardening his lips. "When are you going to sleep with a *man?*"

"I *do*," I say, cattily. "His name is Lloyd."

"*Other* than your boyfriend," Javitz says archly.

"I *should* probably try," I admit. "All these kids want is love and marriage."

"This one too? Already?"

I nod.

"They've got it easy," Javitz says, exhaling smoke. "All they're looking for are boyfriends."

"They all think they're so far advanced—'Oh, I've been out since I was fourteen,' or 'I brought my boyfriend to my junior prom.' But they don't know anything about being gay. You know, I hate this age I'm at: stuck in the middle. A foot in both camps. You on one side, the kid in my bed on the other. Sometimes it feels as if I'm on a merry-go-round and it keeps going faster and faster and everything around me is getting all blurry and I can't make out what side I'm on anymore. It's like everything is spinning out of control, like at the end of *Strangers on a Train*."

"You were like him once."

"No I wasn't." I've thought about this. "I knew all of you guys. He doesn't." I laugh. "Who does he have to teach him how to be gay?"

"You?" I can't tell if he's being sarcastic. "Here's a test," he says. "Go in and ask him to explain the difference between Blanche Hudson and Blanche DuBois."

I laugh. "But that's just it. I can't expect him to know. Those old movies were yours to share with me. They aren't mine."

He sighs. "I imagine there *will* come a time when gay men know Judy Garland exclusively from *The Wizard of Oz*. Who do the queens do up here now in their acts? Madonna? Joan Rivers? *Oprah?* What a loss." He takes a long, melodramatic drag on his cigarette.

"I thought you were trying to quit," I say.

"I've decided I want to die of lung cancer," he answers, deadpan, and then guffaws, that hoarse, throaty laugh that sounds like a fork caught in the garbage disposal, a laugh I don't think I'll ever be able to forget, not even when Javitz has been dead for thirty years.

I'm smiling. "Wouldn't *that* get them?" I say. "Javitz died of *what*? Lung cancer?"

" 'AIDS Activist Succumbs to Cigarettes,' " Javitz laughs.

Now wouldn't *that* be something?

"What should I do?" I ask. "The kid's asleep in my bed. I can't sleep next to someone unless it's Lloyd."

"You need to decide what kind of a summer you want," Javitz says, suddenly serious.

"Yes, yes," I say, annoyed at the lecture.

"Youth isn't the only instant in time in which we don't know what the fuck we're doing," he says.

I know he means himself as well as me. This summer, next—the winter in between. What is it that we want from them? From each other? How much time do we have?

"It's so weird," I say to him. "Sometimes it feels as if I'm this survivor of a spaceship wreck on another planet. I manage to camouflage myself and fit in, but I know I'm just biding my time, because eventually they'll discover me—like Donald Sutherland did to Veronica Cartwright at the end of *Invasion of the Body Snatchers.*"

"Dawling," Javitz says, and when he wants to make a point, as he does now, his Bronx accent becomes thicker, "the merry-go-round metaphor worked, but barely. Now your symbolism is showing. You're a writah. You can do bettah than that."

I sneer, "Can I?" I've been having a miserable time writing ever since I got here last week. I've produced nothing.

"Yes," he says, serious now, "you *can.*"

"Aye, aye, sir," I say.

"And Lloyd will be here tomorrow," he advises. "Perhaps early."

"You know, I want to go in, wake Eduardo, and ask him if he's ever seen *All About Eve.*"

He arches an eyebrow. "And if he hasn't?"

"Kick him out." I smile.

"Why don't you try something easier? Like *The Wizard of Oz?*"

I stand up. "All right. I'll give him a break."

I leave Javitz to his cigarettes and lung cancer. It's almost five a.m. I'll be up in a few hours. Have breakfast with the kid. Send him on his way. Get down to writing. Wait for Lloyd. I know the routine.

Yet when I open the door, Eduardo is gone.

I feel as if I've been punched in the gut. The sheets are still warm and the scent of his semen haunts the room. I look around. There is nothing in the room but a bed, a dresser, a pair of dumbbells, my boots on the floor, and the cold dusty radiator against the wall.

And I have the nerve to ask what happened to the boy?

Hah. As if I didn't know.

LOVERS

Boston, January 1995

Queer word, *lover*.

Queer because it means something so radically different to queers than it does to straights. "She's my lover," a straight man says, and he's talking about an illicit affair. "She's my lover," my dyke friend Melissa says, and she's talking about Rose, the woman she's been with for eleven years. Straights use *lover* to mean sex; queers use *lover* to mean love.

My lover, Lloyd Duane Griffith, didn't come home last night.

"Jesus," I say, waking up hard with the realization. My cat stares down at me from my chest. He's a fat one, that Mr. Tompkins, nearly twenty pounds. He kneads my neck with his paws as he's done ever since he was a kitten. "Yes, baby," I assure him. "I'll feed you."

I throw aside the bulky afghan my mother crocheted for me when I was fourteen. The hardwood floor is cold on my feet. Outside the snow has started falling lightly again. Mr. Tompkins yowls to be fed. Where the hell is Lloyd?

It's 7:28 a.m. I hear the high-pitched whine of the garbage truck from out on the street, collecting the discarded scraps of a city's life. I inch up the thermostat. Old city brownstones like this—no matter how fashionably renovated—are always difficult to keep warm. Especially when one's lover has failed to come home.

"You have to be careful walking down Tremont Street late at night," Lloyd told a visitor from New York not long ago.

"I didn't realize crime was that big of a problem in the South End," the visitor said.

"It isn't. I'm talking about the *men*." And Lloyd grinned.

True, even in the depths of winter I've snared a trick or two on the corner of Clarendon and Tremont or outside the Metropolitan Gym. The South End is like a republic unto itself—we even have our own flags, those gaudy rainbow atrocities that wave from decks and doorways—and its citizens are known throughout the city for a fierce and lusty patriotism.

But Lloyd isn't like me. The South End can be a meat market, but that's never held him up before. When one is married to a psychologist in a crisis program, one becomes accustomed to falling asleep alone. Lloyd got beeped after dinner. That's why he wasn't able to go to the hospital to see Javitz with me. I fell asleep expecting him to crawl in beside me as usual, that comforting shuffle in the black of the night. "I'm home, Cat," he will whisper, a breath near my ear, his warmth settling into the bed like butter melting into a piece of toast. Then, even in the indigo haze of sleep, I mold my body into his, curling into what we call the breathing position: legs locked together, Lloyd's right arm around my chest. We fall asleep breathing in unison: up and down, up and down, up and down.

But not last night. I check the machine. Good. It's blinking. I press play. Lloyd's voice: "Sorry, Cat. It's 1:15 and I'm still here. Might not see you till morning. Love ya."

I breathe.

Lloyd, unlike me, has a real job. He spends his days in a crisis stabilization program, persuading flipped-out husbands to give up their knives and overwrought mothers not to hurl their babies out of tenth-floor windows. When he gets home, he's understandably strung out.

"Why did I choose this life?" he asked last night, as I prepared a typical casserole dinner: canned tuna in spring water, egg noodles, Campbell's cream of mushroom soup.

"Why?" I asked. "What happened today?"

"This kid," he said. "This wiry little white boy from South Boston attacked his sister with her Beautiful Chrissy doll. She had to get fifteen stitches."

"I didn't know they still made Beautiful Chrissys."

"His mother brought it to show us. She said he goes nuts like this all the time. The kid's only nine years old, but his mother wanted him arrested. 'Throw him in jail! I don't want him!' she screamed."

"How sad."

"No wonder the kid has problems. He's probably been abused himself. I'm trying to get him placed in a foster home."

Lloyd grimaced to see the tuna casserole I was scooping onto his plate.

"Well, I'm *sorry* it's not nouvelle cuisine." I sighed airily, pausing in mid-scoop. "It's the best I could do with what we had here in the house."

"It's fine," Lloyd said, taking a bite and grinning up at me. I plopped a helping onto my plate and replaced the casserole dish in the oven. It didn't look much more appetizing to me, but I'd never admit it.

"It's just that I'm so tired of always being the one who has to save everyone else," he said with his mouth full. "Is that what I was put on this earth for?"

That's when his beeper went off again. He groaned. "What karma am I working through?"

Lloyd is what they called in the eighties "new age." Of course, the term is passé now, but he still meditates and talks about karma and dharma. Lately it's all become more intense—a photo of a guru on the wall, a string of visits to psychics—but he's been into "alternative spiritualities" for as long as I've known him. "All wanderlust types are," Javitz said, shortly after meeting Lloyd for the first time.

"What do you mean, 'wanderlust'?" I asked. I didn't like the sound of that. True, Lloyd hadn't expected to settle down as quickly as we did. Ever since we've been together, he's periodically mused about moving out west. Or maybe to the desert, or to Amsterdam. It's always someplace. After Javitz got sick a couple of years ago, Lloyd didn't talk about moving so much anymore, but it's still there. "Honey," he said just the other night, "what would you think about living in India for a year?" I threw a pillow at him.

"Don't worry, darling," Javitz had promised, years ago. "You'll be good for each other. Remember what they used to say about Astaire and Rogers? He gave her class and she gave him sex. Well, you'll give him nest and he'll give you flight."

Opposites attract. He's fair, I'm dark. He prefers the White Party, me the Black. Or used to, anyway, when the party circuit page from *Genre* was torn out and highlighted in yellow, hung on our refrigerator door. Now we're too tired most of the time, too cranky after a week of work. Just a couple of years ago, we trekked on down for Hotlanta, made it to the Morning Party on Fire Island, and that's not counting all the parties in Provincetown. Then, we always had a surplus of energy, and not just from the chemicals. Then, we could stay up dancing until six in the morning and go out for breakfast still high and horny from X. We don't much talk much about the weariness that's settled in: it's just there. "There's a new party in Montreal," I told Lloyd not long ago. "The Wet and Wild. They give you water pistols at the door." We both just smiled; nothing more was said.

Yet our energies have always been different. Off I'd go with my ACT UP buddies to storm City Hall and Lloyd would stay home, shaking his head. "Send them love, not anger. Putting that kind of negative energy out into the world only makes things worse." It's not that he wasn't supportive, or even sympathetic to the cause, but he honestly believes the world can be changed from within. "Look inside your heart for the answers," he told me on our second date.

"But I haven't asked any questions," I said in response.

He smiled indulgently.

It has been six years. Once, I could not imagine being with one man for so long. Once, six years seemed an eternity. Now it seems no time at all. Once, I primped in front of the mirror before Lloyd got home, trimming my eyebrows and snipping errant nose hairs. Once, Lloyd and I loved each other the way I loved Eduardo last summer, all hot dicks and open mouths. Once, people predicted we wouldn't last another year when we opened the relationship. Once, it hadn't mattered what people thought: we knew they were wrong.

I pause on my way to feed the cat and look at myself in the hallway mirror. This is why I prefer tricks not spend the night: this face. Lloyd, of course, has grown accustomed to it. "Here," he'll say, handing me his tweezers, "you've got a nose hair." I'll never forget the day Javitz told us the truth about hair in the nose and the ears: "That's where it goes, you know. What you lose up top. Into the nose and the ears."

"The *ears*?" I'd gulped.

"And your back, too, I'm afraid," Javitz offered, slipping down his shirt to reveal a path of curly black follicles across his shoulders.

Every morning I step out of the shower and strain my neck

around to see my back in the mirror, waiting in dread for the first offender to sprout. I stand in front of the hallway mirror and stretch the skin on my forehead. Those damn circles under my eyes, the crow's feet. I've tried everything: moisturizer at night, vanishing cream, flesh-toned makeup in the morning. "Damn," I say to my face. My hair stands up like a shorter version of Elsa Lanchester's in *Bride of Frankenstein*, complete with the ever-expanding streak of gray.

This is how I must have looked that morning when Lloyd told me how different everything had become. I try not to think about that conversation, but sometimes I cannot escape it—like now, waking up without him, seeing my reflection in the mirror. That day, we lay in bed, the lazy warmth of a late Sunday morning tugging at us like a weight. When he spoke, when he told me how different it had become, I was suddenly self-conscious of my breath, as I had been the morning after the first night we'd slept together. I was certain also that my eyes were bloodshot, that more hair than usual littered my pillow, that a stray nose hair was destroying whatever might have been salvaged of my Sunday-morning face.

Mr. Tompkins yelps up at me like a puppy. Lloyd says he's ridiculous looking: way too fat, big clumsy double paws. But that only makes me love him more. He's grown impatient waiting for his breakfast. He's so fat he could probably live off his own weight for weeks, but he acts as if every meal might be his last. "Okay, okay," I assure him.

I shake dry cat food into his dishes. He devours it hungrily. "Slow down, baby," I say, "slow down." Mr. Tompkins has a heart murmur. That and his weight make it likely his life will be short. Prime candidate for a stroke, the vet said. Mr. Tompkins is a bully, always jumping from countertops onto poor unsuspecting Javitz whenever he walks into the room. He seems driven, as if he'll squeeze out every last bit of life while he still can. Every day I look at his angry little eyes, and I end up loving him more. "Shouldn't he lose some weight?" I asked the vet a month ago, who simply shook her head.

"Just let him *live*," she told me.

One day, I'm sure, I'll come home and Mr. Tompkins will have had a stroke. I wait for it to happen, think of it every time I leave the apartment. I imagine him lying there, unable to move, his back legs paralyzed. Summer is the worst: dumping him with our friends Melissa and Rose while we remove ourselves to Provincetown. What kind of parent am I? I think of Junebug, the cat I had as a boy, the cat I left behind, the cat they were going to feature in the newspaper because he was so old, but who was run over by my sister backing out of the driveway the day before the photographer came. His old spine was snapped in two, but it took the final guillotine of my father's shovel to end his long and honorable life.

That's when I hear the sound of Lloyd's key in the lock, and he comes inside with a man I've never seen.

"Jeff," Lloyd says, "this is Drake."

I'm taken by the surprise of an unfamiliar face so early in the morning. My instinct is to dodge him, slip back into the bathroom and flatten my hair, check for boogers. But it's too late for that. "Hi," I manage to say, and shake hands.

There's a lot in that "Hi." There's: So where were you? There's: Who is this man? There's also: Did you sleep with him? Is that why you didn't come home?

Lloyd reads some of it, if not all. "Drake works with me. He let me crash at his place." He adds, pointedly: "He lives just a block from the hospital."

"Oh," I say.

"He wanted to see our apartment because he's considering buying a condo in this building," Lloyd continues.

"Oh," I say again.

Drake is looking around the place awkwardly. He's older than us, mid-forties probably, classically Anglo-Saxon: Robert Redford with thick gray hair and fewer wrinkles. The kind who never lose their hair or their jawline. The kind that come from money, lots of it. Old money. Back to the *Mayflower* probably. I can tell this by the way he moves his chin, by the enunciation of his words, by the kind of coat he's wearing (avocado green with a brown corduroy collar). While his back is turned, I look at Lloyd and gesture at my Bride of Frankenstein bouffant. "Oh, stop," he whispers.

"A nice place," Drake is saying.

"It's a mess," I say.

"Oh, you should see *my* place." He laughs.

No, thanks, I think. I look at Lloyd and prepare to drive the dagger. "Javitz is feeling better," I tell him, accusation hovering just below my nonchalance. "He may come home today."

"Yeah, I talked with him." Lloyd levels his eyes at me. They say: Don't you dare accuse me of being negligent with Javitz. "I called him last night, but you had just left."

"So you woke him up." I'm trying to get that damn dagger in, but it won't puncture.

"I don't think he minded."

The edginess dissipates. We've held eye contact long enough, and neither has blinked. Meanwhile, Drake is looking back and forth between us.

"Well, I appreciate seeing the apartment," he says. "It's a great building. I don't know why you don't consider buying your place."

I look at Lloyd. I assume he has told Drake that our lease is up in May and that we were offered a chance to buy this apartment. If we don't buy, the owner is putting it on the market. We've made no decision, so I find it peculiar that Drake makes it all sound so finalized.

"It's that old down payment problem," I explain. "Maybe you've heard of it. Struggling writers don't have a lot of capital in their checking accounts." I smile, trying to sound less sarcastic. "But still, we'll see."

Drake smiles. "Of course. I understand."

That's bullshit—he's a richie if I ever saw one. My father used to say you can always tell a rich man by his shoes and his gloves. Drake's wearing those L. L. Bean duck boots, the ones with the green rubber toes. His gloves are soft butter leather, the kind that move with your fingers instead of turning them into robotic appendages.

"Well," he's saying, "I'll be heading home now to get some shut-eye." He puts his gloved hand out to me. I shake it, firmly.

"Thanks for the ride," Lloyd says.

"Hope you end up staying," Drake tells the both of us. "It'd be nice to have such attractive neighbors."

We all smile.

Lloyd shows him to the door. I retreat to the kitchen, listen as they mumble their good-byes. Then Lloyd returns, staring at the back of my head as I push things around in the refrigerator.

"What's up with *you*?" he asks.

"It's not even eight o'clock in the morning and you bring somebody here! Look at me!"

I turn around and glare up at him from the cold air of the refrigerator. I'm not a pretty sight, I'm sure, especially with my face so green.

"You look fine," Lloyd placates.

"So." I look back into the refrigerator. "Did you sleep with him?"

"Jeff . . ."

"Okay," I say, taking out the egg carton and closing the refrigerator door, "you did."

"And there's something wrong with that?"

I take a breath and relax. "No." Of course there isn't. Why am I acting as if I'm Erica Kane just discovering Tom Cudahy's affair with Brooke English? Lloyd and I can't cheat on each other, not when we've redefined all the rules. "No," I repeat. "There's nothing wrong with that."

But I look at him, trying to understand why it's different now, why suddenly it feels so hard, why I feel so tired. I think again of the conversation we had that Sunday morning as we watched the rain clouds through the skylight, but I push it away, as usual.

"So why'd you tell him we *weren't* buying the place? Have we decided on that?" I ask.

"Jeff, I can't come up with the down payment all by myself."

"I *know* that. I just didn't think we had decided *definitely*." I take out a silver metal bowl from the cabinet, the reflection of my face concave and distorted.

"We haven't. Just let it go, okay?"

"It's gone," I pretend.

Lloyd yawns.

"What?" I ask, all eyebrows. "Didn't you get *any* sleep?"

He looks at me. "No," he says deliberately, then turns around and heads into the bedroom.

"He's in love with you," I call after him in my best just-a-friendly-warning voice.

"Good night, Jeff." He closes the door.

"Just a friendly warning," I say, and crack five eggs into a bowl, not caring if half of the shells go in there with them.

Provincetown, June 1994

"I'll be at the breakwater," I tell Javitz. "Have Lloyd meet me there."

I make my way through town from our house on the East End. It's early morning, before nine. On Commercial Street only a few vendors have opened their doors. The Portuguese bakery is one of them, the wheaty aroma of fresh-baked loaves braiding with the thickness of hardening fudge from the candy store across the street. Few gay boys are out this early, only bleary-eyed sales clerks opening up the shutters on the T-shirt shops. The tanginess of the sea assaults them: they scrunch up their noses, unsure whether the smell is pleasant or foul. It is the odor of rotting seaweed, baby crabs and snails, the scent of a salty low tide.

I cut between two shops and pad across the brown-sugar beach toward the pier. The surf approaches tentatively. Waves lap the shore, offering the only sound beyond the call of the gulls that cut wide swaths in the sharp blueness above me. The sun slants across the bay, thousands of twinkling lights whose brilliance is lost as quickly as they appear. A couple of white-rumped sandpipers run ahead of me on the sand. Washed up here and there are tangles of weed: long twisting green trails, like the discarded boas of an army of drag queens.

There are days, like today, when I need the soul of Provincetown.

Not the heart. The heart beats loudly every afternoon from four to six at tea dance, a bass backbeat that can be heard all the way down Commercial Street. But this morning, waking up alone, I wanted to find something else. So I'm heading here, to the very tip.

I climb up onto the stones of the breakwater and find a suitable one, sitting down to face the rising sun. It's gonna be a scawchah, as the locals say. The humidity is creeping back, in the haze off Long Point, in the stickiness of the wood along the pier. Here, on the breakwater, it's cooler, with a breeze rolling in from the bay. A gull keeps circling in the blue above me, complaining perhaps that I have taken her spot. For a second I pretend I'm Tippi Hedren, about to get my forehead gashed. Then I close my eyes and doze a little, trying to forget about the trick who ditched me.

Of course, I didn't sleep last night except for fits. Once I woke up and wasn't sure if it was my trick or my lover in bed next to me, but it ended up being neither. Eduardo ditched me, I remembered, forcing myself back to sleep.

A couple of women pass me on their way out to Long Point. They're holding hands. "Good morning," they say, almost in unison. I smile back.

The breakwater is a catwalk of cut granite stones connecting the town to Long Point. Massive slabs of granite, sparkling silver in the sun, the breakwater keeps the sandy dunes from dissolving into the sea. At high tide, the surface of the water on one side is textured with blue swells; on the other, it is smooth and satiny, like a dark turquoise mirror. The stones are scarred with the marks of whatever machines broke them from the earth, then lifted them and relinquished them into place. Scars that prove man is stronger than stone, more enduring. No cement holds these rocks together, no glue. Just their sheer weight keeps them in place.

Some people use the breakers merely as a bridge to get out to the beaches on Long Point, where the sand is finer and the cruising less heavy than at Herring Cove. I, however, use them as a test of my stamina: from stone to stone I leap, always landing on my feet and never in the cracks between. Then, satisfied that I can still do it, I lie on a flat rock in the sun, like a seal, belly side up.

That's how I am now, waiting for Lloyd. He should be here soon. He promised he'd leave Boston by eight, so he'd be here by ten. So why am I thinking about *Eduardo*? Why does it bother me so much that he's gone?

I shouldn't be surprised. It's the same old script. "You *loved* Raphael," Javitz said last summer, and he was right. Many times I have fallen in love in the course of one sun-blistering afternoon. It lasted until barely the following day, when the rains came and washed away the humidity from the cracking clay of the Cape. Raphael was a sweet cocoa-skinned boy who spoke in the mellifluous tones of French Canada and who became transfixed by my tongue.

"Give it to me," he implored, and I thrust it into his mouth, into his ear, into his armpit. Then I'd laugh: laugh at his eager passion, and roll off of him and make him ask again.

"Jeff," Javitz said a day later, holding the phone out to me, "it's Raphael."

But now I did not take his call, for the crush of love inside my rib cage had eased. I told Javitz to tell him I'd left. Gone back to Boston. And Javitz, of course, lied for me.

Yet only a few days later, I yearned for Raphael as if I were Heathcliff and he Catherine, brooding about the house in a cloud of gray. Even now, the pinch of a Quebecois accent still pains me. I do not try to contact him. Such would not make the pain go away, only worsen it. For within a day of seeing him again, I'd send him home, and the ride would start anew.

But when Lloyd's here I don't have the desire, don't have that burning in my belly to lace up my boots and struggle into my tank top at eleven o'clock at night. When Lloyd's here, I have no urge to sweat on the dance floor, no ardor to see who will shoot the farthest in a cum contest.

Instead, we rent videos: Bette Davis or Tennessee Williams or *The Creature from the Black Lagoon*. We order in pizza and bake brownies, the fragrance of chocolate wafting out the windows. "Lloyd must be here," Javitz says, returning from dinner with Ernie, widening his nostrils to savor the aroma. Sometimes he will stumble over Lloyd and me asleep on the floor, bundled together in the breathing position, while Ava Gardner swings her hips at Richard Burton above us on the screen.

I once whispered to Javitz: "How much passion should be left after six years?"

"Define 'passion,' " is all he said in response.

But I couldn't. I just sat there, staring into that netherworld that exists between the time Lloyd leaves Provincetown for Boston and the time I pull on my tank top and stride out into the dark.

Javitz tried to reassure me. "Don't worry about passion," he said. "It has a way of showing up in the unlikeliest of places."

Like the time I threw my grandmother's ceramic German shepherd across the room, the one she'd given me the year she died, watching it shatter into a dozen pieces and Mr. Tompkins scurry into the other room. In my other hand was a notice that my car insurance was due. "How am I supposed to pay for *this*?" I screamed, sending the bill across the room after the dog. "What, do they think money just falls from the *sky*?"

I'd just left my job so I could write full-time. It was a gutsy move, especially for somebody who grew up working-class. I was taught some basic truths by my parents, among them: You don't leave jobs where you get steady paychecks and health insurance. All I could hear was my father's voice: "You're doing *what*? How you gonna pay your *bills*?" I hadn't budgeted for the car insurance, had completely forgotten it, in fact. I'd made sure that a freelance check was coming to cover my share of the rent, that a couple of book reviews would pay for my student loan that month, and that the minimum payment on my ridiculously high credit-card bills would be taken care of by a long political essay. But there was nothing earmarked for my car insurance, which caused the whole delicate house of cards to come tumbling down.

Lloyd stood helplessly as I twisted like a tornado. Then he shifted into crisis management, precisely what he did all day at the hospital. "Come on, Cat," he said, "settle down."

In the oven the salmon was burning. Now that I was working from home, I was trying to break away from casseroles and microwave pizzas. I wanted Lloyd to look forward to a nice meal, but now it was smoldering behind us. He eased me into a chair and rescued the fish, turning off the potatoes and bringing the water for the corn on the cob back to simmer. "I'll take care of things here," he said, sending me out for a walk through Copley Square to calm down.

The evening was salvaged. The salmon was not as rare as we liked, but Lloyd was happy. I regained my composure, even offered to clean up, thanking him for saving the day. He went to bed early. That's when I found, under my dinner plate, the sealed, stamped envelope for the insurance company and the detached slip with "Paid" written across it in Lloyd's handwriting. There was a Post-it note stuck to it, too, with the message: "Yes, in fact, sometimes money *has* been known to fall from the sky."

And over on the mantel, my grandmother's ceramic German shepherd had been painstakingly glued back together.

"Hey, Cat," I hear now, and I look up to see him.

Lloyd, shirtless, green-eyed and beautiful—same as he ever was.

"Hey, Dog," I answer.

We kiss each other: light, dry, puckered lips. I'm glad to see him: always am, even after just a few days of separation, that same old kick to the heart, the kind of kick my father used to give the furnace to get it going. "All it needed was a little kick," he'd say, and it's true for me too.

"Missed you, Cat," he says.

I don't know when our nicknames began, or how they came to be. It seems they've always been there. Javitz hates it when we call each other "Cat" and "Dog" in front of him. "Dawlings," he says, making a point, "what was cute the first time becomes annoying the fifth and positively nauseating the tenth or the eleventh."

Ah, what does he know? I touch my Dog's face. "I had a dream about you last night."

"Yeah? What was it about?"

"I can't remember much, but we were at my mother's house," I tell him. "I was sitting with my parents in the living room, and my mother was talking about getting new paneling. I was telling her that she should just rip the stuff down and go for the exposed brick."

"So where was I?"

"That's where it gets weird. You were in my old room, where we used to have a record player—it was plastic and bright orange, I remember—and you were standing over it, playing '(I Never Promised You a) Rose Garden' by Lynn Anderson."

He laughs, that happy little boy laugh that I love so much, the laugh he had when I first met him, when we both were young. "I had that forty-five," he says. "Used to play it all the time."

"Sister Mary Bridget used to play it for us in fourth grade," I remember. "She said there was an important message to be learned there."

"What?" Lloyd asks. " 'Lower your expectations'?"

" 'When you take you gotta give, so live and live or let go-wo-wo-wo-wo,' " I sing.

" 'I beg your pardon,' " he chimes in.

" 'I never promised you a rose garden,' " we warble together.

We laugh. He loves that I can still make him laugh, even after all this time. "You're such a funny Cat," he says. "So then what happened?"

"When?"

"In your dream."

"Oh. That was it. That's how it ended."

He laughs again. We sit quietly for a minute. "So," he says finally, "did you trick while I was gone?"

"Of course I did."

He grins. "How silly of me."

That's the way it is. I trick; Lloyd has meaningful encounters. At least, that's Javitz's take on the whole thing. Lloyd finds the soul; I find the dick. It's true that Lloyd doesn't have sex with other people as often as I do in Provincetown. When he does, it lasts a week—a week I'm in Boston, of course. At the end of the week, his trick heads back to New York or Philadelphia or wherever he came from. Then there's a series of postcards, an occasional phone call. Lloyd doesn't understand how I can move from one trick to another in the course of a weekend. He understands less the shock of love I feel after they leave. "Why not in the moment?" he asks, but he doesn't really want an answer, not really.

Lloyd tends to trick with older men—men five, ten, even fifteen years older than himself. Javitz thinks it's because it preserves his own image of himself: as *boy*. Lloyd says older men are more likely to be in touch with their inner spirits. Whatever. At least we don't end up very often competing for tricks.

He gets this far-off look in his eyes when I talk about my boys. He encourages me to talk about them, but he doesn't say much when I do. I like to imagine that maybe, deep down, there's a pinch of jealousy, the same tiny stab to the heart I feel when I play back a message and hear an unfamiliar male voice calling Lloyd "just to say hello."

"Jealousy is no indication of love," he has told me, and he's right: I even used it as the first sentence of an essay I wrote for a gay magazine last year. I argued that we needed to move beyond the constraints of jealousy, that jealousy is a heterosexist trap. I theorized that by opening our relationships, we queers were teaching the world how to rethink our lives. That's why Lloyd and I had done it, I implied: not because after two years of monogamy, our sex lives had settled into a predictable pattern and we were eager to see what else might be out there.

It's safe to hide behind a byline, where I can be such a pompous asshole. Because deep down inside, in my petty little jealous heart, I hate all of Lloyd's tricks. And how I wish he'd admit to hating mine. But he doesn't, of course, which makes me feel ridiculous for wanting him to do so, like a conventional hetero housewife, Lucy Ricardo without the laugh track.

Lloyd's asleep now, faceup in the sun, the earphones of his Walkman inserted, the tiny sound of R.E.M. managing to seep through the flimsy foam rubber. I look down at him: how young he looks when his eyes are closed. How perfectly content and happy. I think about how fast six years have passed.

I'm sweating, and I'm afraid that despite the sunblock I might be burning. Wrinkles, I tell myself: wrinkles. I can practically feel my skin creasing, shriveling up like newspaper caught by a new flame. I lay my hand on Lloyd's shoulder, pink and hot.

That's when I see Eduardo.

He's walking towards us, deep in conversation with another boy, a dark-haired child with no shirt and a short pleated miniskirt around his waist. Eduardo's wearing a white ribbed tank top, his brown skin made only more beautiful contrasted against the white.

They don't see me as they approach. I make quick calculations in my head: Do I strike up a conversation? Do I pretend to be asleep, lying here next to Lloyd? Do I introduce the two of them?

But choices are eliminated when Eduardo notices me.

"Hey," he says, unsure whether to approach.

Lloyd doesn't stir. He's still asleep, or appears to be.

"Hey," I respond.

Eduardo is two rocks away. His little boyfriend has fallen behind, but he's looking at me, as if he knows exactly who I am.

"Sorry about last night," Eduardo says.

I raise my eyebrows and feel the tightness of my forehead. I *am* burning. "You mean about leaving?" I ask.

He nods. "I just couldn't stay. . . . I felt funny, you know?"

For the first time he seems to notice Lloyd. He shrinks back.

"It's okay," I say. "He's asleep."

"Is that . . . ?"

"Yeah. That's Lloyd."

Eduardo smiles. "He's cute."

I hate that. I hate when a boy I've tricked with sees Lloyd and gets that look in his eyes. *Hey*, I want to say, he's mine. You're mine. Knock this off.

Besides, Lloyd doesn't like boys. He only likes *men*. Older men. Why do you think he's still with me?

"Listen," I say to Eduardo, "call me sometime. Okay?"

The boy looks at me. "Why?" he asks, the same question as last night.

I have no better answer today. "Well," I say, "if you don't want to . . ."

Eduardo holds my gaze. "Give me your number."

So I do, and we say nothing further to each other. He and his skirted friend continue their trek out to Long Point, surely in the midst of some deep intellectual conversation about the relative merits of tea dance versus after-tea, or else marveling over the peculiar characteristics of that particular generation of gay men who give out their numbers to young boys while their lovers sleep peacefully beside them in the sun.

Lovers who then sit up, look at them knowingly, and grin.

"So that was him, huh?" Lloyd asks.

I can't tell if my face is hot from being caught or if I'm finally sun-blistering, right here and now. "Yeah," I say. "I didn't know you were awake. I would've introduced you."

"Very cute," Lloyd says, looking after Eduardo. "Very *young*."

"Oh, don't talk to me about it," I josh. But I needn't worry.

He won't.

"Of *course* we should talk about our tricks," Lloyd had said, four years ago, right after we opened the relationship.

It was actually the day we adopted Mr. Tompkins. A child of our own. Lloyd really wanted one. He'd had a cat once before, in his last relationship, with a man named Marty. But Marty kept the cat when Lloyd up and left him one morning, even before Marty was awake. They'd been together little more than a year. I've never met Marty, seen only one picture, but he haunts me. We don't talk much about him, and neither do we talk about our tricks. But Lloyd thought we should give it a try. We discussed the idea on the ride over to the Humane Society, tossing it back and forth like the hot potato it was. We were still talking about it as we stepped inside the pound.

"Well," I said, "I'm not sure I want every *detail*. . . ."

"No, but we shouldn't be *afraid* of details, either."

A woman held out a kitten to us, so small he fit in the palm of her hand. It's hard to imagine Mr. Tompkins, all twenty pounds of him, ever being that tiny. But he was, and he mewled at us.

"Oh, Lloyd," I said, my heart breaking.

"That's him," Lloyd said. "That's the one we want." He looked at me. "That's Mr. Tompkins."

"Mr. who?"

"Mr. Tompkins. I don't know where the name came from. The universe just gave it to me. Trust me."

So I did. Always have. So I don't know why we don't talk about our tricks. I do know that on that day—the day Mr. Tompkins joined our family, hiding under the couch for hours, the last time either of us can recall him ever showing any fear—I know that on that day, Lloyd and I made mad, passionate love. First in the shower, then out on the deck, not caring if the whole South End could see. Then we made dinner, butternut squash and cornbread, because Lloyd had just gone vegetarian (except, of course, for those particular seafood dishes he couldn't resist, like salmon and lobster and my famous tuna casserole). I was gamely giving it a shot as well (I gave up after a week, missing my fried chicken too much). We were both famished, eating like bears, ending with an entire box of Little Debbies.

Then, spent, we climbed into bed and curled into the breathing position, our new little chunk of fur beside us on the pillow. Mr. Tompkins began kneading my neck with his soft baby paws as if he'd find a nipple there.

"I think he was taken away from his mother too soon," I said.

Lloyd smiled. "He thinks *you're* his mother."

"Well, he ain't gonna get no milk outta *me*," I say, laughing.

Lloyd just looked at me as if he knew better. "Don't be so sure," he said.

Boston, January 1995

The fight wasn't about Drake. It was about the laundry. And I'm still fuming about it as I get on the elevator at the hospital, where I've come to bring Javitz home.

"What floor?"

It's a cute guy asking, offering to push the button. I smile at him, noticing the curve of his nose. But there's nothing in his eyes back at me. He's straight, I tell myself. Or he just thinks I'm too old, as so many of the boys have since Eduardo.

Javitz called about an hour ago. He was very chipper, very up, no more talk about dead third-grade teachers. I was in the middle of laundry, and the phone woke Lloyd.

"Who was it?" he asked.

"Javitz," I answered. "I've got to go pick him up. We were right. They're sending him home."

"That's great," Lloyd said.

"Yeah, well, I have so much shit to do," I snarled. I wasn't resentful about picking Javitz up from the hospital. I was resentful that I had to do it when I had piles of laundry and Lloyd was asleep because he'd been *out having sex all night*.

"Do you want me to finish that?" he offered.

Wrong move. Gave me an opening.

"Don't bother. I just wish you'd pick up after yourself. We *do* have a place for dirty clothes. It's called a *hamper*."

"All right, Jeff. What's *really* going on here?" Lloyd is always doing this: nothing is about the here-and-now, nothing is about the mundane.

"It's about fucking *underwear*!" I screamed. "Fucking dirty *underwear* left all over the bathroom and every towel used up and getting moldy—*that's* what it's about!"

Of course, my hysterics only served to confirm his belief that it had nothing whatsoever to do with his boxers or the dearth of clean towels. In his view, it wasn't even about Drake; it was about my deep-seated rage against my parents—my mother for turning her back on me, my father for having the gall to die without ever telling me how proud he was of me. It might even go deeper than that: could it be karma from a previous life that I'm working through in this one?

"You need to get at the heart of your rage, Jeff." He stood there, shaking his head in smug self-affirmation. I wanted to throw the laundry basket at him.

It was not at all like the night we met.

"Hey," Lloyd said to me then, from somewhere behind a haze of dirty blue smoke.

We were at a cheesy club just outside Boston, one of those suburban wonderlands, where Millie Moon and her Pumpettes were trying very hard to be offensively funny. "I'm the Kmart queen," she sang in her stiletto heels, but half these queens were too: so what's the joke? I was there for only one reason: to trick. I was newly separated from Robert, the boyfriend who filled the gap between Javitz and Lloyd—very prettily, I might add, but the poor thing hadn't a thought in his Waspy head. Tonight, I expected the pickings to be easy. At least that had been my experience here before. Lloyd's approach seemed to justify my expectations.

"Hey," I said in return.

He was cute. A little shorter than I, dark blond hair, green eyes, a chiseled jaw, the requisite sideburns for that summer. He wore a white ribbed tank top and I noticed the cut of his body right away. When a potential trick is this cute, you don't look beyond him and make believe you're uninterested. That's a strategy that works eighty-five percent of the time, but not when they're this cute. Guys like this might think "Fuck you" and go on to someone else. I take many risks in my life—I use too much salt, I ride in cars without air bags, I suck without the use of condoms—but I draw the line here.

Rick Astley was the rage that year. Lloyd remembers that I did not look at him once the entire time we were on the dance floor. It drove him nuts. But I knew I had him then: there was no need to carry the attention to extremes. We spoke little: the script was a late-eighties minimalist experiment. New wave queer cinema, and in the very last scene we shake hands and go home alone.

How *very* eighties.

Yet it took me by complete surprise. "Maybe we can get together sometime," Lloyd said.

"What about right now?" I asked, a smile tricking my lips.

He smiled back. "Maybe some other time."

And I was snared.

That was the thing: I hadn't caught him, as I'd thought. He'd caught me.

The elevator doors open. I turn to the cute guy beside me. He stares straight ahead. His loss, I say to myself. I step out of the elevator and head down the corridor to Javitz's room.

Lloyd and I finally made love on our fourth date. It was a record for me to wait that long. I arrived on time, ringing his doorbell, a clutch of daisies in my hand. "Come on in," he called. "I'm upstairs."

I could hear water running. He was down on all fours, testing the water in the bathtub with his hand. Mounds of suds had accumulated. Candles were lit, suffusing the room in a flickering pink light. "What are you doing?" I asked.

He said not a word. He stood and kissed me, his lips like the flowers in my hand, sweet, soft, and delicate. He took the daisies, kissed each of them, then plucked off their heads and dropped them into the tub. Hey, I thought, those cost seven bucks. Then he unbuttoned my shirt, gently pulling it out from my pants. He unfastened my belt, unzipped my jeans. "What're you . . . ?" I asked again, laughing, but my voice sounded cold, incongruous to the scene. I tried to relax, but this was not part of any script that I knew.

"Undress me," he whispered.

I obeyed. I hadn't yet seen his body fully. I'd felt it through his shirt, and had been impressed. Now, paring him of his clothes, I felt a rush of blood into my face, my fingertips. My dick stiffened, lengthened. He was beautiful: every soft curve, every defined cut. Shorter than me by a couple of inches, he looked up at me from half-lidded eyes. I didn't move with the grace he had: I yanked and husked, rending every last stitch of clothing from him, even his underwear. Lloyd stood before me naked as a nymph, and I embraced him, biting down onto his neck.

We gingerly stepped into the hot oily water, scented with jasmine. I gritted my teeth as I suffered the sting of the heat on my butt and my nuts. I lost my erection, but it hardly mattered. We sat in the tub, facing each other, toes intertwined, daisy heads floating by like lotus blossoms. The water lapped against our chests with every subtle stirring we made. I felt its warmth pervade my body, soothing me. I closed my eyes. I could hear Lloyd's steady breathing. He began to stroke my calf.

Later, on his bed, our skin soft and moist, we made love. My lips discovered the places on his body that gave him particular pleasure—his neck, his balls—while his hands caressed me with a tenderness I'd never known before. It had been worth the wait. The fragrance of the scented bathwater clung to us and aroused a passion in me that I'd never experienced with Javitz, never encountered with any boyfriend or trick. I kissed Lloyd as hard as I could. When I entered him, there was such delirious pressure in my throat, as if I might cry or laugh, I wasn't sure. His legs encircled my shoulders and with every thrust I heard my own heart, high in my ears. We went on like this for a long time, and then we reversed positions and went on even longer. When we came, within minutes of each other, I didn't feel spent. I felt invigorated. Ready to go again.

We didn't sleep at all that night. We watched the sun come up, and I talked: talked a mile a minute, talked a blue streak, talked, talked, talked. "I'm such a Chatty Cathy tonight," I gushed. Usually it had been Javitz who talked: solving my problems, offering answers, giving advice. Maybe because solving problems was what Lloyd did for a living, and not what he wanted to do on a date, he simply listened. He listened to every word of it. I told him about my family: my brother, my sister, how my mother had turned her back on me when I told her I was queer. I told him about my dream to write a novel someday, to give up the job at the newspaper and really *write*. I told him about Javitz, and how hard it was to end that relationship, but I had to, really. "It was just time, you know?" I said. He nodded.

That night, Lloyd found my soul, touched it in a way it had never been touched. Six years later, we're still together. It hasn't always been easy. When we moved in with each other, just four months after we met, I thought we'd never survive our first laundry crisis. "I'll wash clothes if you take care of the garbage," I offered, and so it was agreed. But his pants came out of the dryer too wrinkled, an expensive blue shirt was ruined by a stray dot of bleach. "Then do it *yourself*!" I shrieked. "All right, I *will*!" he shouted back.

Yet we survived. We survived his going back to school. We survived his coming out to his folks back on the farm in Iowa. We survived my leaving my job, my career crisis, my father's death. We survived Javitz's bout with pneumonia. We survived him getting better and then getting sick again. We survived our own tests, sitting together on one chair, holding hands, waiting for the joint results. True, there were a few more ruined shirts in the course of six years, that damn jug of bleach never fully secure in my hands. But Lloyd said we could survive anything, so long as we trusted the universe, and each other.

So what had happened to change that? Why did it feel so hard now to trust?

"The drugs wore off," Javitz had said simply when I asked him what he thought.

"The drugs?"

"Come on, darling. That silly, ridiculous attraction that lasts a year, sometimes two. I call it the Bob and Rod Syndrome. Even with all their muscles, our pinup boys for gay marriage were still vulnerable to all those unleashed endorphins running through their bodies. But once the chemical flurry settles down, so, I'm afraid, do we."

Is that what happened with Javitz and me? I wondered, but didn't ask: we rarely discuss such things. But his words seemed to acknowledge that Lloyd and I were different than he and I had been—that the yin and yang that existed between Lloyd and me could possibly survive the end of the endorphins.

"You'll be good for each other," Javitz said. "You'll give him nest and he'll give you flight."

"Hey," I say, turning the corner now into his hospital room.

"Get me my pants," Javitz commands. He's stumbling around

the room in one of those johnnies they make you wear, a flimsy white apron that exposes the butt. "I just scared a nurse by winking at her with my asshole."

I barely smile. I hand him his jeans from the top of a cabinet. "You happy to be going home?"

What a stupid question. He looks at me, with that Javitz look. "No, I'm as glum as you. What'samattah?"

Damn him for always knowing. "Nothing," I say. "Let's just get you out of here."

"Not until you tell me what's wrong."

"Javitz, I'm here to take you home from the hospital after you have spent weeks languishing in your bed, obsessing on life and death. Let's take one thing at a time, shall we?"

He doesn't respond. He just stands there, hands on his hips, looking ridiculous in that johnny, and I know he won't budge from that silly pose until I tell him.

"Oh, Lloyd and I were bickering."

He sighs, as if relieved. As if so what else is new. He pulls up his jeans.

I'm annoyed that he's dismissive. "He didn't come home last night," I say, trying to make it more significant. I feel like a tattletale.

"Oh?" This seems to pique his interest.

"His name is Drake."

"*Ohh*," Javitz says, and he smiles. "Tell me more."

"I don't know much more," I say. "Except that he's in love with Lloyd."

Javitz is pulling on a shirt. I help him. He needs to sit down afterward, a little dizzy.

"You okay?" I ask, my hand on his shoulder.

"That's what happens when they keep you down for five days straight."

"You don't do anything straight," I remind him.

"Oh, right." He feels his shirt pocket for his cigarettes. "God, am I dying for one of these."

"Precisely," I tell him.

He gives me a face. "So tell me. How do you know he's in love with Lloyd?"

"His eyes." And I hate it, this power. Hate always knowing, always being right.

Javitz understands. "It's still bothering you, isn't it?"

"What?"

"That conversation. The one you'd like to forget you told me about."

And I *shouldn't* have told him, except that I tell Javitz everything. I had to talk to *someone* about it, even though it pained me to do so, to say the words, to repeat exactly what Lloyd had said that late Sunday morning several weeks ago.

"There's no more passion."

It struck me hard. As if this was it, the one conversation that was too primal to tell anyone, too frightening even to admit to ourselves. We were in bed, lethargic and lazy, or at least I was, until he said the words. We had been watching through the skylight as the sun seared the rain clouds. "It's going to be a nice day after all," I said, just before he landed the bomb.

"Jeff," he said. "There's no more passion."

I rejected his statement at first, because it came so soon after my father's death. I was in the *throes* of passion. Lloyd had been there, helped me through it. I loved him all the more for it. What was he *talking* about?

"Us," he said. "The passion between us."

"There's passion between us," I insisted. I touched his face. "Dog. Come on. Of *course* there's passion."

"Not like there was with Eduardo."

He had me there. If that was the kind of passion he said no longer existed, could I argue with him? But *define* "passion," I thought. Go ahead, I dared him silently, define it.

"Don't do this to me," I said, the only response I could muster. "Not now. Not so soon after my father . . ."

And so he dropped it. But I told Javitz about it, admitted to him that no, Lloyd and I hadn't had sex in months, that we didn't even *want* to have sex—at least, not with each other.

"Limerance," I told Javitz. "He said he missed the limerance."

Javitz had exhaled a thick cloud of acrid smoke into my face. I coughed viciously and cursed him. "Limerance," he said, ignoring me. "Go read a paperback with Fabio on the cover if you want limerance."

I didn't understand his bitterness. Now, as I stand in his hospital room ready to take him home, he can see that I don't want to discuss it anymore. "This is *your* day," I say, and he makes a face as if he knows that's a lie. Dear old accommodating Javitz. He deserves better than us.

"Let's go home," he says, taking my arm.

And so we do.

Provincetown, June 1994

We're out in a boat in the middle of the bay, and I'm frantically slobbering sunblock on my nose and forehead, feeling exposed and vulnerable to the sun and the wind.

But Lloyd's having a ball.

"Isn't this fun, Cat?" he shouts, gunning the motor and sending us lurching forward through the water in a sudden burst of speed and spray.

"Be careful," I admonish. "This isn't a speedboat."

Hardly. It's actually just a small shallop, rigged up with a motor, rented from the wharf for twenty bucks for three hours. I doubt we'll stay out here that long: Lloyd's original idea had been to dock at Long Point and spread out a picnic, but between us we had only four dollars after renting the boat, hardly enough to purchase suitable provisions for lunch. "Who cares?" Lloyd said, grinning. "Let's just go for a ride."

The idea had come to him as we lay dreamily on the breakwater. He suddenly sat up, looking over at me with the sun in his green eyes. "Let's rent a boat, like we used to," he said, taking my hand and pulling me along. My first inclination had been to decline: we hadn't prepared, we hadn't brought any water, we hadn't made any sandwiches or packed our bathing suits. But we also hadn't rented a boat in a long, long time—not since two summers ago, when Lloyd and Javitz and I had tried to learn to water-ski. The carefree spontaneity of those days suddenly rushed back at me in a nostalgic punch to the gut. I couldn't turn Lloyd's enthusiasm down.

"If we were going to rent a boat," I yell over to him now, "we should've planned to get some skis."

"I thought you never wanted to try that again." Lloyd laughs.

I did make that vow. I was under water more often than above, and suffered some major water burns after losing my grip and spiraling backward through the waves. Javitz and Lloyd did better, although they took their share of tumbles. Lloyd was determined to master the technique, but we never did try it again.

"Well," I admit, "maybe I'd just watch this time. But *you* could do it."

He shrugs. He slows down the motor, releasing his grip on the cord until it rattles to a stop. The boat eases into a steady drift. "I don't mind a quiet ride," he says.

"Really?" I laugh. "We seem to be taking a lot more of those than we used to."

Lloyd reaches over, touches my hand. "Let's do it," he whispers, getting close to my face. "Right out here."

"Lloyd!"

"Come on. Nobody will see."

"Somebody might. There are other boats out here."

He slides over to kiss my neck. He stands briefly to join me on the seat, and the boat rocks sharply to the left.

"Lloyd, this is too dangerous. This is just a little boat—"

He pulls back. We look at each other for several seconds, and then we smile. Lloyd turns his face up into the sun, and I notice how his ear lobes lift slightly, curling up as if drawn by the light. I had forgotten how they did that, how adorable he looks when he raises his face to the sky.

"I'm sorry, Lloyd," I tell him. "I know how you always want to be spontaneous."

"Don't be sorry," he says, reaching over the side of the boat and scooping up some seaweed in his hand. We've drifted into a garden of sea grass, growing up from the floor of the bay. He plucks a tiny yellow flower from the tip of a reed and hands it to me. "Let's go back," he says, and pulls the cord on the motor.

I hold the flower between my thumb and forefinger. It's like a miniature star in my hand, no bigger than a bead. Then the motor kicks into life, the boat shuddering in response. I grab ahold of my seat, dropping the flower. Lloyd lets out a whoop. We take off in a bolt of energy and forward motion. I laugh, too.

"I'm glad we rented the boat," I tell him as we walk back to the house. "I really am."

He puts his arm around me. "I know you are," he says. "You don't need to convince me."

"I'm not trying to convince you. Maybe next time we can go water skiing—"

"Oh, Cat, don't be so silly." He kisses me there on the front step of the house. I fall into his embrace. He kicks the door open behind him with the sole of his foot. We stumble inside.

Javitz isn't there. It's just as well, as Lloyd begins undressing me in the kitchen. I notice the redness of my skin right away. "Look at me, I'm burned."

My arm is as red as fingernail polish. Where my watch had been a white line now encircles my wrist. "You look like a candy cane," Lloyd says, grinning.

We kiss, falling down onto the bed.

"Be careful," I tell him. "I think it's a bad burn."

"Weren't you wearing sunblock?"

"Guess not strong enough."

We kiss again. Our door is closed but we hear Javitz return. He calls to us but we don't answer. He knows what we're doing. We hear him walk into the kitchen.

"Oh." I remember something. "Javitz wanted to get lobster for tonight." I look up at Lloyd while I take his dick in my hand.

"Sounds good." Now he's got mine.

I start to pull his. "Come on," I laugh. "Get hard."

I go down on him. He doesn't get very hard, so I stop, pulling him up on top of me. We kiss a little harder. I cover my hand with spit and start jerking myself off. The sheets are wrinkled and still a little sticky from the night before.

Lloyd starts playing with his own dick. We lie very close to each other, shoulder to shoulder. We breathe deeply, nearly in sync, spiraling our fists down on our dicks. For a few seconds the air in the room feels heavy with moisture, then we each pop, him first, then me. He beats me in distance; I manage to do little more than dribble, having come twice the night before.

Lloyd rubs my semen into my chest. "Careful," I implore. "That's my burn."

He stands up and reaches for his underwear to wipe off his hands.

"You two finished in there yet?"

It's Javitz at the door. Spooky how he always knows when we're done. As if he were outside the door, listening.

"Yup," Lloyd calls out. "Come on in."

I make a little sound and pull up the sheet to cover my nakedness. I don't know why; Javitz was once my lover. It's not as if he hasn't seen me nude. But, unlike Lloyd, I'm very particular about showing myself. On the dance floor is one thing; hanging out at home is another.

Javitz comes in. He sits down on the bed. "Lobsters okay?" he asks Lloyd.

"Sounds great. And I bought some corn."

"I was going to make veggie pie, but I guess that can wait," I tell Javitz.

He smirks. "Oh. Am I interrupting one of your nesting traditions?"

He knows that veggie pie carries significance. Comfort food. Mom food. Mom as in Jeff, in this case. When I make veggie pie, I go all out. Sometimes I even throw in those Pillsbury breadsticks that you twist and lay out on a cookie sheet. Both Javitz and Lloyd adore them.

"I'll get domestic tomorrow," I tell them.

"The flip side of Jeff," Javitz quips. "They wouldn't believe it at Spiritus."

Lloyd sits down beside Javitz and pulls him backwards. They fold together in their own version of the breathing position. Javitz nestles his head in the crook of Lloyd's shoulder. They're always doing this, these two. Here's Lloyd, naked, fresh from shooting his load, cuddling with another man who probably hasn't gotten off today and who most likely wouldn't mind doing so. Still, Javitz doesn't complain: he snakes his arm around Lloyd's waist and pulls him closer.

I sit with my back up against the wall, the sheet draped over my loins. Maybe it's my history with Javitz, but I don't participate in their love locks. Our skin is distant now; our touch remains rare.

"Look," I say. "Don't drop the lobsters in the pot while I'm in the room. I don't want to even hear them scratching in the refrigerator." Lloyd has to crack the tail and claws off and give them to me. "Get rid of the eyes," I say. "I don't want to see the eyes."

"Why are you so squeamish about *lobsters*, for God's sake?" Javitz asks. "They're the cockroaches of the ocean. You have no problem ripping the flesh off the rib cage of a chicken."

"I might if I had to see their eyes."

"Cat, you're meant to be a vegetarian," Lloyd says. "You should've stuck with it."

"Excuse me, but since when did lobsters become a vegetable?" I challenge.

He grins. "It's just that the meat is so *succulent*—"

"Oh, yeah, *baby*," Javitz says, simulating orgasm on top of Lloyd. "Suck you *lent*."

"Succulent if you don't mind that green stuff that oozes out," I say, cringing. "Just tell me when you're going to drop them in so I can go outside."

"If your tricks could only see you like this," Javitz laughs. "I don't remember you being such a femme."

"It's because *I'm* so butch," Lloyd laughs. Javitz rolls his eyes and tickles him. Lloyd shrivels up in hysteria.

"If you're so butch, how come I'm on top?" Javitz demands. Then he looks up at me. "You don't mind me topping your lover in front of you, do you?"

"Be my guest." I smirk, waving my hand.

Of course, Javitz would debate me on that point of privilege, the assumption that Lloyd was something I could offer with a grandiose gesture. "Why do lovers always assume first right of refusal?" he has argued, and we've all laughed, but he has a point. Why is it that Lloyd and I can roll around naked, yanking on our puds, but Javitz can only join in after we're through, a sheet discreetly placed across my lap? Despite our blurring of so many boundaries, we have never contemplated a three-way, no matter how feverishly the Province-town tongues have wagged in that direction. How I wish they could see this little scene. "Is *that* how they do it?" they'd gush. "The two of them down there, the one guy above, watching it all? Do they all sleep together in that one little bed?"

They're standing up now. My lovers. "Come on, Cat," Lloyd says, pulling on a pair of spandex bike shorts. "Get dressed and let's start dinner."

"You can husk the corn," Javitz instructs, "if we have to execute the lobsters."

"Fine. You always leave too much corn silk on them anyway," I tell him.

I wait until they're both gone before I get out of bed. I look at my skin now and conclude it's really not such a bad burn after all. It'll probably fade into a very nice tan. I lean against the radiator while I pull on my cutoffs. Of course, I'm thinking about Eduardo, whether he'll call me, what he's doing at this precise moment. I'm thinking about what makes a lover, what in the end sets someone apart in that special category, the category all queers aspire to fill, but where they too often come up short.

I can't think of anything insightful or profound. Nothing that I can write about later, nothing that I can share with Javitz and Lloyd in a late-night discussion out on the deck. So I just yank the sheets from the bed, finally ready to start over fresh.

Boston, January 1995

Javitz is taking a shower. Lloyd's cleaning up after dinner: takeout Chinese from Hong Lee's to celebrate the homecoming. Javitz is staying with us for a few days, just to get his strength back. Mr. Tompkins gave him his usual welcome when we came through the door, attacking his pointy cowboy boots as he walked into the living room. "Glad to know some things never change," Javitz said.

But it feels as if something *has*. I've got the oddest sensation something's *different*. "Do you feel it?" I asked Javitz, just a few moments before he lit up his cigarette and headed out to the deck, but he shook his head no, consumed by his habit.

Yet I did, and still do: cold and unsettling. It's like the time we were broken into, when the thief was so neat about it we didn't discover we'd been robbed for hours. Still, even in that time there had been a sense that things were *off* somehow, that they'd been moved and put back the way I'd left them. That's what lingered in the room: the very act of moving them. I sensed it. Sensed that my world had been invaded, then deftly covered over.

I open the drawer in the hallway table and check the little compartment in back. My father's ring is still there, right next to my grandmother's pieced-together ceramic dog and on top of the book from Eduardo. I relax, a little.

But then I notice a pair of gloves on top of the table. Soft brown leather, with white fur lining. Drake's gloves.

"Should I save any of the lo mein or throw it all away?"

Lloyd is looking over at me, poised to scrape the last of the Chinese food into the garbage. The stink chokes the room. Mr. Tompkins jumps up to sniff the garbage pail. Lloyd shoos him away.

"Lloyd," I ask, knowing fully the answer to my question, "do you know whose gloves these are?"

He doesn't blink. "Oh, they're Drake's. He must have left them here."

"They weren't there when I left," I say. "He had them on when we shook hands good-bye."

Lloyd stands up straight, the plate of lo mein still in his hand. "He came back while you were gone."

"He came *back*? In this weather? Why?"

"To see the deck. We hadn't shown him the deck."

Somehow I can see them, standing there in the kitchen, right where Lloyd is now. And they're kissing. I hate this power, hate always *knowing*. "So did you have sex with him again?"

He sighs. I know that if I ask, I need to prepare for the truth. Lloyd won't ever lie to me. "I just kissed him good-bye."

"Here?" I feel my anger surge, like a flame on a gas burner. So *that's* why the house had felt wrong. Drake had been *here*, in my space. Once, we had a rule: no tricking in our own house. But I broke the rule first, a couple years ago, with a guy I picked up at the gym. There wasn't anywhere else to go, so we came back here, for a quickie on the couch. Lloyd had made a face when I told him, but never said anything. I can't be a hypocrite now.

"I just went with the moment," Lloyd says. He decides to toss the lo mein into the garbage. "Look, Drake is a great guy. You'd like him if you gave him a chance."

That's exactly what I don't want to hear. "I suppose," I say, and my voice cracks a little, Norma Shearer in *The Divorcee*, "there's *passion* with Drake."

"Oh, Cat." He comes to me, pulls me to him. I'm tight, stiff. Then I relax, settling into his arms.

"Oh, Dog."

We hear Javitz finish his shower, the screech of hot water pipes abruptly shut off. "Aren't there any clean towels in this place?" he shouts.

I raise my eyebrows at Lloyd as if to say: See? He moves away to snatch one out of the dryer and bring it to Javitz. I feel nauseous from the smell of the food. I move out onto the deck. The snow has stopped, but it's raw and damp. I let the coldness cling to my skin.

"Cat?"

Lloyd has come outside.

"Cat, I don't like to see you hurting," he says, his breath white in front of his face. "I wish I knew what to say to you to make you feel better."

"You've said *quite* enough," I say, using meanness as armor.

He touches my shoulder. "Look what I bought for you," he says in his little-boy voice.

I grudgingly turn. In his palm, he holds a little green plastic cat, just as the woman at the Humane Society had once held Mr. Tompkins.

"They were selling them at Hong Lee's," he says.

I melt. This one will go with the others, the family on my dresser and bookcase. Lloyd buys them for me, has ever since the nicknames started. Green cats, red cats, orange cats, blue: it's like a Dr. Seuss rhyme, except there's no rhyme or reason to how I feel.

I take the cat. Lloyd and I kiss quickly, mending the pain for now, putting it where we can't see it, until it falls off the shelf again and we have to pick it up.

I watch him as he goes back inside. I hear him call to Javitz: "What're you *doing* in there? Rewriting Scripture?" I hear them laugh. I feel the love bounce back and forth between them like a rubber ball.

Lovers: those who love. Those who comfort and take care, those who hold each other, share each other's fears and dreams. It would apply to both of them, both Lloyd and Javitz. *My lovers.* Straights use *lover* to mean sex; queers use *lover* to mean love. So what if Lloyd and I haven't had sex in months? That's not what *lover* means, not to us. Javitz and I stopped having sex seven *years* ago—but he hasn't ceased being my lover, although we say he has and the world—with the possible exception of the Provincetown wags—believes that to be true.

If we were straight, Lloyd and I, we'd be married. Married in a church or by a justice of the peace, with blood tests and a certificate. Nobody would ever call us lovers. There'd be no Javitz, of course, just the two of us. We'd be husband and wife, for richer for poorer, in good times and in bad, till death do us part—and there's something comforting in the idea of that, something appealing as well as confining and deadening. As it is, Lloyd could walk out tomorrow if he wished. There's no joint checking account, no real estate, no piece of paper that insists he stay. True, we'd have to figure out who would take what, what in the course of six years was collected by him, what by me, who'd get Mr. Tompkins, of course. Then we'd settle into being *friends*—but would it be any different from what Javitz already is to the two of us? And how different would it be to what the two of us already are?

"There's no more passion," he had said.

Damn you, I think, looking down at my little green cat. How dare you? Yes, I want to love Lloyd with all the passion that's gotten stuck in my throat, the passion that collects behind my teeth, that threatens to break my ribs. I want to see how that passion ripens after six, sixteen, *sixty* years—an audacious dream in a world where time has become such a fragile commodity. True, I have fallen in love in the course of one afternoon, but I have also seen the rains come and wash that love away. There is love in those indiscriminate kisses, to be sure: but what of kisses that *do* discriminate, that grow drier and airier, that as often fall on the back of the neck as on the lips?

"Define *passion*," Javitz had dared.

When I finally go back inside, Javitz is on the couch, already asleep. Snoring like a dragon in his lair. I open the hall closet and pull down an extra blanket. I cover him, tucking it under his feet so that it won't slip off in the night. It's going to get cold. From the cabinet under the sink, I take out a jar of chocolate syrup, which Javitz always mixes with his milk in the morning. It's a little surprise for him, a little welcome-home. I leave it on the counter where he'll see it when he wakes up.

Then I tiptoe into bed beside Lloyd, who murmurs dreamily. I pull him gently into the breathing position and lean up on my elbow for a while, watching him sleep.

FRIENDS

Provincetown, July 1994

"There's no word for me," Javitz says, the foghorn across the bay making its mournful call.

"There soitenly isn't," I reply, Groucho Marx tapping an invisible cigar.

He gives me that Javitz face, all eyes and nose. "Well, what *am* I? Your *friend*?"

Good question. He's never much liked that word. He has a T-shirt that reads: "Fuck you. I have enough *friends*."

He doesn't expect to be called "lover," either, although that might be a more apt description to explain what he is to Lloyd and me. We hold power of attorney for Javitz. When the time comes, it will be up to us to determine when life support is shut off, when the morphine gets jacked up. And why? Because we're his *best friends* in the entire world. That's why he's given us this horrible honor.

"I know," Lloyd says suddenly, his eyes opening. He's getting a shoulder massage from Javitz, sitting out on the deck overlooking the bay. "You're a frendover."

"Friend of her?" Javitz grumbles. "Who's 'her'?"

"Frendover," Lloyd repeats. " 'Friend-lover,' combined."

I laugh. I'm leaning in the door frame, half in the kitchen. The sun is setting over the dunes to our right, a spill of primary colors.

"How about 'lovrend'?" I suggest. The water boils on the stove for the pasta. I go back inside, but leave the door open so I can hear Javitz's reaction.

It's just one of his long, long dramatic sighs.

"There's no way to describe me," he says, airily.

"Ain't that the truth," Lloyd mumbles, winking at me.

Javitz slaps the back of Lloyd's head, but he keeps up the massage. I break the brittle log of linguine in two, dropping the halves into the bubbling water.

Friend. What a concept. I have had many friends, friends who meant the world, who meant my life, meant their lives, our lives together. They have come in waves: grade school, high school, college. First job, grad school, the gay bars after first coming out. Each time, my friends became the most important people in my life. Each time, in the heat of the friendship, I expected that my friends would last forever. "To Jeff," Francine Niemerski wrote across my senior yearbook photo. "A friendship like ours will last an eternity. We'll never forget our weekend with Pooty Bear."

Fourteen years later I no longer remember what Pooty Bear was, or what that weekend was all about, and Francine's face is but a dim blur: a red-haired girl with a large nose. She went to St. Margaret's, the girls' school that was sister to the all-boy St. Francis Academy, which I attended. The two schools shared dances, school plays, and bus rides in the morning and afternoon. How well I remember those bus rides. They stunk of peanut butter and wax paper, carbon monoxide and the armpits of pubescent boys. Clare Aresco and Dave Wysocki would make out in the back, all hands and Clare's long auburn hair. I'd push my head into the hard green Naugahyde seat and turn my eyes to catch a glimpse of Dave's flushed face as he came up for air. Immediately, I'd get hard, quickly averting my eyes to stare straight ahead. But Gordon and Stick, my buddies, would keep twisting around to gawk.

"He's got a tit," Gordon would report.

"Her hand's in his pants," Stick would hiss through his teeth.

I'd sit without breathing, aware of the stirring in my crotch, wondering if those around me could tell, if they could see the prickly heat rising on the back of my neck. The idea that Dave Wysocki was gratifying his libido—something that had not yet occurred for me—was tantalizing. I felt no envy of Dave, only shared passion. Later, when I got home, I'd jerk off thinking about Dave's red face.

"You know why I hate getting old?" I say suddenly to Javitz.

He pauses in Lloyd's massage to look over at me. Lloyd taps the fingers on his shoulders, as if to say: "Keep going."

"Why?" Javitz asks wearily, as if there are no reasons he hasn't heard before.

"I hate it because I didn't have a chance to be young when I was young."

"Oh, that." Javitz resumes kneading Lloyd's sore shoulders. He says all the tension he gets on his job goes there. "What queer did?"

"They do now, some of them," Lloyd says, not opening his eyes.

"That's right," I agree. "Some of these kids up here are eighteen and nineteen. Younger even. They come up here with their gay *youth group*, for God's sake."

"Babies on parade," Javitz says, sighing.

"When I was eighteen, I couldn't *imagine* a place like Provincetown," I tell him. "I didn't get to be young until I was twenty-five."

"At least," Lloyd seconds.

"So are you trying to make up for lost time?" Javitz asks.

"Might be," I muse. The water has come to a rapid boil again; the pasta is nearly ready. I've made a ton of it. Chanel and Wendy and Melissa and Rose are coming by. It's Fourth of July weekend, and we're going to watch the fireworks from our deck.

"Really," I continue, draining the pasta, "I never got to make out the way Dave Wysocki did in high school. I mean, make out and *like* it."

"Translated," Lloyd says, "you didn't get to make out with *boys*."

"Exactly."

See, Lloyd understands. It was never that way with Javitz. "Not until I was well out of college did I start playing around," I say, and Lloyd nods in recognition.

Javitz scoffs. "Maybe that's what saved you."

I'm about to ask from what, then feel like a fool. Strange how it's always there, floating around, but sometimes you forget it, in the simplest way. In 1980, when Javitz was still getting buttfucked every Friday night at the St. Mark's Baths, I was being a good college freshman: coming back to the dorm after dinner to read Joyce and Fitzgerald, not getting drunk and plowing a girlfriend like the straight boys across the hall. Yet I was only biding my time: I knew about the party going on out there in that great big gay world. And I would join it, just as soon as I was able.

"You," I said, pointing to Gordon, "are *fucking lucky*."

Gordon grinned. It was Christmastime, freshman year. We were both between semesters, home for the holidays, me from the state university an hour away from the town where we both grew up, and Gordon from NYU, right there in New York, the Village, the gay mecca.

"I got a boyfriend," he told me. I couldn't imagine it: a *boyfriend*. "An older guy. I met him on Bleecker Street."

"Just like that?" I gushed. "Just walking down the street?"

"Yeah. He looked at me, I looked at him, and well, like they say . . ."

Gordon was *fucking lucky*. Gordon, the first boy I'd ever blown, in the back seat of his mother's car. Gordon, who—with our other buddy Stick—had been my boon companion, my colleague in crime as we survived four years at that all-boy Catholic high school. We'd skip gym class, smoking a few joints behind the janitor's office, talking about Joni Mitchell and Patty Hearst and Squeaky Fromme, our heroines. It wasn't until senior year that we all started fooling around with each other, our clandestine rendezvous suddenly made even more exciting. In college, I became envious of Gordon and his continued adventures, while mine had sunk into relative lethargy on my predictable, working-class campus. "Come visit me in New York," he urged, and I promised.

Of course I never did. We lost touch. He went on to become an actor, as he'd always dreamed of doing. I remember seeing him on *Guiding Light*, a handsome young intern under the benevolent eye of the good Dr. Ed Bauer. Then he disappeared from the role; someone else took it over, someone less attractive, someone who went on to become a star.

And Gordon came home to our little town, where he died.

Friends. Gordon and I had been inseparable. "I'm going to Gordon's" was a phrase my mother heard every day. "It's Gordon again," my brother would snarl, throwing the phone to me. Gordon had been the first to know about me, the first to teach me the words "queen" and "buttfuck." Then he had faded into merely a name, a face on a soap opera to impress my new friends. "I knew him," I'd tell them. "He was my very best friend in high school."

My sister called me in Boston. "Do you know who's home?" she asked. "Gordon Guthrie."

"Is he sick?" Why I should ask, I didn't have a clue. I hadn't heard from him. But, of course, he was.

"Jeff," he said, a week before he died, "I always knew you'd be here for me."

"No you didn't," I said to him. "You forgot all about me until you came home."

And that was okay. That was the way with friends. They come into your life, they listen to your hopes, your dreams, your fears. You make each other laugh, you piss each other off, you forgive each other, then laugh some more. You spend your time with them, you make plans with them, you think about them when they're not there: "Oh, Francine would *love* this," I'm sure I said once, many times probably, but what about I no longer know. Then friends go away, replaced by a new batch, who do all the same things.

I called Stick, the third stooge from those long-ago days. "No," he said. "I can't come see him." I was angry, but Gordon understood. "Poor old Stick," he said. "Still the same after all these years."

Gordon was just thirty when he died. Just a few weeks older than I. I'd known others who had died from the plague, but they'd all been in their forties and fifties. Gordon was my age. I watched as he shriveled into a little old man before my eyes, becoming smaller and smaller in a wheelchair that seemed way too big for him. Finally it seemed that's how he would die: he'd just keep getting smaller and smaller until he simply disappeared. When they cleaned his body after he was dead, I watched as they lifted his bedclothes. I glanced upon his penis, a withered gray thing, the first cock I'd ever sucked.

That's the image of Gordon that stays with me: a dead husk, his dick exposed like a rosebud torn from its stem, wilted under the sun. When Stick died, a little more than a year later, I visited him too, but Stick couldn't talk to me. Drugged with morphine, he could only buzz, as if an angry swarm of bees had gotten caught in his throat.

Of course, other friends have died, too: a couple of college chums, a grad-school professor, a host of boys from the gay bar where I first came out. But it's not just the plague: AIDS has just horribly exaggerated for queers what is, after all, the nature of friendship. They come, and then they go. Yet each time, we expect this will be it: this is the group we'll grow old with, Mary and Rhoda and Murray and Phyllis in the nursing home.

"They're here," Lloyd suddenly announces, bounding from his chair and throwing his arms around Chanel.

Our friends file in. "*Pasta?*" Melissa cries. "You know I don't like tomato sauce."

"Don't worry," I tell her. "It's pesto."

She pouts. "I thought you were my *friend*. You should know I don't like pesto either."

I shrug. "Okay. So you get some buttah and Romano cheese?" I do a good Jewish mama from the Bronx. Javitz has taught me well. Melissa smiles.

Later, as the fireworks snap, crackle, and fizz in the purple sky, a shower of reds and silvers and spiraling blues, we sit and eat our dinner on paper plates, balanced on our laps. Lloyd and me, Chanel and Wendy, Melissa and Rose, Javitz and his cigarette. Our little band, our little club: and how many clubs have I had? More important: how many more are still to come?

Boston, February 1995

"It feels so good to get up in the morning and put *clothes* on," Javitz says.

Lloyd cocks his head. "Never expected to hear *you* say that."

Javitz has been out of the hospital for a week now. We're at his place in Cambridge, right off Harvard Square, getting him settled in. Javitz is so happy to be back in his own space, playing his Billie Holiday and Nina Simone records. He's sorting through his mail as he sits on his ratty old couch with the foam showing around the edges. Lloyd is standing behind him, giving him a shoulder massage.

"I don't understand the blues," I say. "Here you are, supposedly feeling good about being home, moving out of your depression, and these women are whining, 'Ooooh, I'm so miserable . . . My life is horrible . . . I think I wanta die. . . .'"

Javitz arches that damn eyebrow. "You know, Jeff, it is really a shame the only records your mother ever played while you were growing up were Perry Como and Dean Martin."

Of course he's smoking. It's his house; we can't complain here. We call Javitz "Dragon" because of the cigarettes, although it's not as official as "Cat" or "Dog." Both Lloyd and I are virulent anti-smokers. It's funny how we've changed: there was a time, and not so long ago, when we never left for a club without passing around a joint. Now we hardly even go out to clubs, let alone smoke pot— at least, not together.

Up in Provincetown, where we share a space, Javitz never smokes in the house. We can't understand why he continues: it's making everything else about his health worse. That's what landed him in the hospital these last two times, we're convinced: all that shit in his lungs. Yet no amount of cajoling from us or his doctors has convinced him to even *try* to quit.

We've just come back from grocery shopping. I'm stocking his near-empty cupboard. Campbell's tomato soup. Six boxes of A&P– brand elbow pasta. Sardines. And of course his chocolate syrup for the morning.

They don't know I can hear their conversation from the other room. Javitz is talking to Lloyd in a hushed voice. "So," he says, "what's going on between you and this Drake?"

My ears perk. Lloyd is too quick with his answer. "We're friends. He's a great guy, a social worker at the hospital. We go to the same meditation group."

"So the two of you share *many* interests." I can hear Javitz's smirk even from in here.

I decide eavesdropping makes me too nervous. I walk in on them. "You'd like him, Javitz," I say. "He's around your age." That's a dig.

"Really?" Javitz looks at me hard, then back at Lloyd. "Is he single?"

Lloyd grins. "Is there relevancy in that question?"

"Maybe not to us," Javitz says, leaning back into the cushions of the couch, "but to the goddamn rest of the world . . ."

"Yes," Lloyd says, "he is."

There's a silence now that I don't like. Lloyd has come around to sit on the couch, resting his head on Javitz's shoulder. Javitz closes his eyes.

"Maybe we should talk about Provincetown," I say, surprising even myself with my suddenness.

Javitz opens his eyes. "Oh?"

Lloyd nods. "We should go up soon to check out the place that Ernie found."

"No," I say, and somehow that one syllable conveys the significance of what I am about to reveal. "I'm not sure I want to do it again."

Lloyd looks at me with suspicion. "Since when?" he asks.

"I just don't know if I want the whole *scene* again. Provincetown is very tiring. I'd rather go up to the mountains in Vermont or something."

Javitz looks at me intently. "Vermont," he says.

"Or something."

"There's no tea dance in Vermont," he informs me.

"I know," I say, snottily. "Precisely."

"Oh, Cat, you're being melodramatic," Lloyd says. He gets up and goes to the kitchen. I hear the air spit out of a twist-off bottle of Coke.

"Maybe I am," I say. "Point is, I don't want to do Provincetown again."

"That's final?" Javitz asks. "Last week you seemed up for it."

"Look. There are other housing issues to worry about. Do we try to buy the place we're in now, or look for someplace else?" I pause, gathering my argument. "Besides, I just can't afford it. I can't see coming up with two or three grand and just plopping it down for a summer place. . . ."

" 'Just plopping it down for a summer place . . .' " Javitz repeats.

Immediately I feel horrible, as if I've trivialized our last five summers together. "You know what I mean," I say, weakly.

"No," Javitz says. "I don't."

"I'm sorry," I say. "But if I can come up with that kind of money, why not use it for a down payment on our own place?"

"Because that still wouldn't be enough," Lloyd says, coming back into the room.

Javitz sighs. "I understand about the money."

And of course he does. He's just gone on *disability*, for God's sake. This past semester was his last as a teacher. It seemed to outsiders to be a rash decision, but he'd thought about it for a long time. He finally talked it through with us last summer, although by then he'd already made up his mind. In long, meandering walks visiting Ernie in Provincetown during the winter, he'd made the decision, quite on his own. That's also when he stopped the AZT. His loss of muscle tone, he's convinced, isn't due to HIV. It's from the antivirals they pushed at him for so long. He's undecided whether to even take the drugs prescribed for him since his last bout of pneumonia. "You were lucky," his doctor said. "You don't want to get PCP."

Yet stopping the drugs hasn't made much of a difference in his health, except perhaps making him more conscious of the present. Giving up his identity as a teacher was far more difficult, but he's determined to do other things while he still has the energy and the will. "I've never been to South America," he said simply, as if he'd give it all up and head for Peru. "I'm still on my feet. I don't want to be carried out of the classroom on a stretcher."

Yet landing in the hospital twice since his decision has taken some of the wind out of his sails, some of the bluster out of his words. "That's what I get," he said. "Apply for disability and become disabled."

So *of course* Javitz understands about the money. But it's not *him* backing out. It's me.

"Can't we just say we'll think about it for a few days?" Lloyd suggests.

Thank you, Dr. Griffith. Sometimes avoidance is the best defense. I look at Javitz. He seems to be considering something; his eyes are averted. "All right," I concede. And no one brings it up for the rest of the day.

Later, after Javitz has gone into his room for a nap and Lloyd has fallen asleep on the couch, I sit in front of the TV set watching a rerun of *Bewitched*. It's the episode where Sam conjures up a dodo bird and it gets loose all over town. It makes me feel even worse, so I turn it off before I see how it ends.

What kind of friend am I? I'm thinking. What is it that makes everything so *hard* these days? Why can't it be the way it was at the beginning of last summer, when I first met Eduardo, when the script still made sense, or at least still left us a little time?

Provincetown, July 1994

"I *like* older men," Eduardo says. "Always have. Always will."

He seems to have forgotten any dilemma he had about sleeping with a married man. He called me the Monday after I saw him on the breakwater. Lloyd had gone back to Boston, so I invited Eduardo over, and he's been here ever since.

"Then you're a lucky little shit," I say to him. "When you get to be an old man like me you'll be all set."

"I said 'older,' not 'old,'" he says, his face suddenly in mine. "You're *not* an old man."

We've spent yesterday and today together. Last night, we walked along the beach, barefoot in the surf, holding hands and talking for hours. "I have a confession to make," he said.

I looked at him.

"I was born here," he told me. "In Provincetown."

"Really? I never met someone who was actually *from* Provincetown."

Eduardo nodded. "Of course not. You gay tourists never do." He smiled. "My parents still live here. My father's a fisherman. Like his father, and his father before that."

"And you?"

"No thanks. There's no work here even if I wanted to stay. I moved to Boston a few years ago, after graduating high school. But I've come back this summer. Lack of money, you know what I mean?"

I did. "So are you really a houseboy?" I asked.

"Sure." He smiled. "I couldn't exactly live with my parents.

Would you want *your* parents watching your every move in the summer?"

I would not. I reached over and gave him a quick kiss behind the ear. Eduardo was charming, much more so than I had given him credit for. And bright, too. In the fall he'll be going back to school in Boston to study graphic design. He's out to his parents. They're accepting, even if they think exposure to all those drag queens on Commercial Street during his formative years may have had something to do with it. Mostly, though, they worry about AIDS. They've seen all the memorials announced in the local paper. Unlike many small-town families, they haven't been able to ignore the plague.

"I haven't lost any friends, not yet," Eduardo said. "But it scares the shit out of me. That's why I could never, *ever*, fuck without a condom. Maybe even two."

I laughed. "That's a smart boy," I said, the right line for this particular role.

"But a lot of my friends," he confided, "don't think like me."

"I know." Too many of the boys I have been with have eagerly spread their legs without any negotiation, without any conditions. I've nudged at their holes with the head of my dick and they've groaned, "Yeah, come *on*." But I've always declined, with horrible difficulty, wanting so badly to ram it up there, to ride their asses, to break their baby arrogance, their sense of youthful invulnerability. "How about that?" I'd tell them afterwards, in my fantasy. "And do you know what? *I have AIDS!!*"

Yet I've never done it. And so fucking is rare for me—especially since condoms repulse me. Their very smell, the very touch of latex. No matter how much those safe-sex educators have tried to eroticize them, condoms reduce my hardness to withering pulp.

But not Eduardo. "I *like* condoms," he said. "I *do*. Just the sound of the tear of cellophane makes me hard."

"Pavlov's bottom," I said, grinning.

"And the ones that taste like mint? They're *awesome*."

I leveled my eyes at him. "Sucking dick was not meant to be minty fresh."

"Oh, you jaded old queen," he laughed, lunging at me.

That's how Javitz had introduced himself to Eduardo the night before. "Don't mind me," he said, walking in while we were making out on the couch. "I'm just a jaded old queen."

They eyed each other with keen interest all night, although I'm sure neither would admit it. "You were at *Stonewall*?" Eduardo fawned, looking at the photos Javitz always stuck up on whatever refrigerator door he was currently using.

"No, dear," Javitz corrected, indulgently. "That's the March on Washington. From 1987. A while after Stonewall."

"Wow," Eduardo said. "Nineteen *eighty-seven*."

Javitz cocked an eyebrow at him. "Don't you *dare* tell me how old you were then."

"Fifteen."

Javitz exhaled monstrously, then stood up, lit a cigarette, and strolled out towards the deck. I laughed. "You keep quiet," he shouted back. "It's been a long time since *you* were fifteen, too."

"I don't believe in age," Eduardo offered.

Javitz turned around. "What a delightful child," he said, sitting down again. "Now tell me, Eduardo, what do you see in *him*?"

"Everything," the boy said, the moon in his eyes, and I melted.

Now he's trying to convince me I'm not an old man, bless his little heart. "I would never date somebody who's *old*," he's saying. We've just gotten back from the beach. My skin is nearly as brown as his. "Old is a state of mind. If you're old, you can't keep up with me." He snaps his fingers on both hands. "Who said Gen X are slackers?"

He grabs my crotch as I walk past him. I pull back. We've had sex a total of five times in two days. The last time, he wanted to fuck me. With two condoms, I'm sure. But I'm not yet ready to let Eduardo top me.

"Come on," Eduardo coos, getting real close and putting his lips on my neck.

It's happening again. Eduardo's sweet—sweet as the nectar that seems to exude from his pores. But that zesty sense of newness is gone, after just a couple of days. I don't know why I should be surprised.

"I need to crash," I say, gently moving my head and extricating myself from his grip.

He looks at me tightly. "How come whenever you want it, I give it? Doesn't it work the other way around?"

No, I want to say, it doesn't. But instead: "Eduardo, I'm just tired. All that sun."

He pouts. "Well, what are you doing later?"

"I really need to get some writing done."

"So you're not going out?"

"No. I don't think so. If I do, it'll be last-minute."

He makes a sound in his throat. If he were a comic-strip character, it would have been "harrumph." But he's not, of course: he's flesh and blood, with a heart and a soul, and for the slenderest of moments I pity him for having stumbled into my lair.

He's in my face again, but tenderly. "I really like you, Jeff. Really."

"What do your friends say about that?"

"Who cares what they say?"

That tells me exactly what I need to know. "They say I'm using you," I tell him.

"I told them we're becoming friends," Eduardo insists.

"Are we?"

"Sure." He looks at me with suddenly scared eyes. "Aren't we?"

"Of course we are."

"Friends who fuck." Eduardo laughs, as if this is something we've invented, something that's never happened before.

"They're called fuck buddies," I explain.

Eduardo seems to consider this. "No. I don't like that term. It's too—*seventies*."

"Seventies?"

"You know: all those baby-boomer gay men with the flannel shirts and handlebar mustaches, the Village People and all that. . . ." He smirks. "Surely *you* must remember."

I narrow my eyes. "I didn't graduate from high school until 1980."

I'm not surprised he's confused. Nobody much talks about my generation. Nobody thinks about those of us in our thirties anymore. A decade ago, they did. There was even a television show called *thirtysomething*. It made history by showing a gay male couple in bed together. I think that was the only episode I ever watched. Because see, back then, *a whole decade ago* when I was *twenty*some-thing, the show had no relevance for me. Of course, it held *great* relevance for that generation which precedes mine: those ubiquitous baby boomers. Being "thirtysomething" in the 1980s was the subject of major national discussion. Talk shows and books and movies all concerned themselves with the trials and tribulations of thirty. I tuned out: what, me worry?

"Ah, youth," Javitz would say, while he and his ex-hippie cohorts lamented that they had become the people they'd once said were too old to trust.

I knew them all, Javitz and his friends. Now Javitz is one of the few who are left. Many of the rest are sick, and those who aren't are well into their forties, edging fifty. There's been a lot said about their generation, about their contributions, their achievements. But you don't hear much about the thirtysomethings of the nineties. Part of the problem is that we're not easily defined. "You're just a young-ish baby boomer," Javitz told me. And technically, he's right: the baby boom wasn't officially over until 1963, a year after I was born. But ask someone born in the late 1950s or early to mid-1960s if they remember anything about Woodstock or the assassinations of Robert Kennedy or Martin Luther King, those essential creation myths of boomer culture. Without those events in your conscious-ness, Javitz insists, you're no boomer.

Others would lump us into the X population: the thirteenth gen-eration since the signing of the Declaration of Independence, a group of babies apparently born between 1961 and 1975. But ask a guy in his early thirties if he cared when Kurt Cobain offed himself, if he thinks rap is music. We might not be aging flower children, but we ain't no slackers either.

"While you were watching *The Partridge Family*, we were out fighting to save the world," Javitz has said, and he's right. The boomers may have fought at Stonewall, but we—their younger siblings—were the kids they were fighting for. We were the first generation of queer boys and girls who could pick up a newspaper and read about gays and lesbians fighting back, marching in the streets. I remember hearing about Harvey Milk being elected and then assassinated. "That fruit in San Francisco," my father called to my mother as he sat in front of the TV set. "They just got him."

I'd scour my thin, ill-spaced hometown newspaper for any mention of the G or H words. I knew the name of the enemy then, and it was so much simpler in those days: Anita Bryant. Dade County. Proposition 6. John Vern Briggs. It all seemed winnable somehow, back in those days before the plague, before the rise of the religious right. I couldn't wait to get out there, claim my space. In high school, my buddy Stick—always so much more *worldly* than Gordon or I—would tell us of his friends in New York, dancing and fucking until dawn. I couldn't wait to be old enough to join them. Of course, I never did. By the time I was old enough and comfortable enough with myself to go out and play, I couldn't anymore. "Sex equals death" and all that eighties bullshit. Maybe that saved me, Javitz has said. Maybe, but it still was a drag.

"I'll tell you something about the seventies," I say to Eduardo. "There was a sense of promise, a sense of hope. You never had that. Maybe that's why all you guys are slackers."

"I'm *not* a slacker," he reminds me.

And he's not. He's got his hopes, his dreams. Yet he didn't put *his* muscle into an ACT UP or a Queer Nation, the way my generation did.

Maybe that's because we knew Javitz and the fags and the dykes like him, those guys in the flannel shirts and handlebar mustaches, the women with the labrys signs dangling from around their necks. "Who do the children have to teach them how to be gay?" I'd asked Javitz.

"You?" he'd answered, and I couldn't tell if he was being sarcastic.

"I'm tired," I say, unsure for just a second to whom I'm responding. "I need to sleep. Maybe we can get together tomorrow."

Eduardo makes a face. *"Maybe?"*

"Look," I say, "we're not married."

I kiss him good-bye at the door and assure him that yes, I will call him, that yes, we are friends, and that no, I don't view him as just a fuck buddy. I close the door and tell myself that's the last I'll see of him. He'll hurt for a while, I'm sure, but he'll get over it. He's a boy. Boys are resilient. Push them down and they spring right back up at you, in your face, all sloppy lips and fervent plans, desperate dreams and raging libidos. He'll bounce back, I assure myself. He's a *boy*.

Boston, February 1995

We're heading out to the suburbs on this bright, blustery, wintry day, but first we have to find our car.

It's not always easy to remember where you last parked your car when you live in Boston. During the winter, we use our cars so rarely that they can get piled over with snow for weeks. Lloyd thinks he parked on Clarendon, but we haven't seen it yet, so of course he's getting paranoid that it's been towed. My cheeks are stinging from the cold wind and I'm trying not to get cranky, as it *is* Lloyd's birthday, after all, and going to the suburbs was what he wanted to do. Javitz finally spots the car over on Milford Street, so we hurry across the street to follow him.

The boys in the windows of Mildred's look warm, reading their newspapers and sipping their cappuccinos as giant-sized mattes of Joan Crawford loom over them. One boy even looks up and smiles. We call the cafe windows along Tremont Street "display cases," where both the customers and the merchandise can have their pick. But today I want nothing of their pretty little lives, for we're on our way to the Big Boy.

The closest Big Boy is out in the suburbs, and Lloyd insisted we celebrate his birthday there. He grew up with the Big Boy chain in Iowa. "Down-home white-trash cooking," he said, and I agreed. Sometimes, when Lloyd and I are feeling down, we sneak out to the Big Boy, ordering fried chicken dinners (me) and spaghetti with that thick red sauce (him), remembering when our mothers would take us to the Big Boy for being good. Our excursions always end with the heaping hot fudge cake, slobbered with fake whipped cream and topped with a maraschino cherry. The trendy restaurants in the

South End just don't have the same appeal when you're feeling blue.

Thankfully it hasn't snowed in a few days; the roads are clear and dry. We see the giant statue of the Big Boy as we turn into the parking lot. "Once somebody stole the Big Boy from out in front of the restaurant back in Iowa," Lloyd says. "The whole town was in an uproar. They finally found him, all scarred and cracked, out in the woods. Everybody felt so bad."

The same elfin fellow greets us here: tall and ceramic, with his big round rosy-cheeked white face and that shock of shiny black hair. Javitz had nothing like this in the Bronx. "Do you know what we would have *done* with that?" he asks as we make our way past the creature into the restaurant.

"Tell us," Lloyd dares.

Javitz just lets out a long exasperated breath of air.

Inside, they're all waiting for us. Chanel and her new girlfriend. Melissa and Rose. Tommy. And Drake. The last had been at Lloyd's request. "It's *your* birthday," I'd said, picking up the phone to call the man. I suppose I shouldn't be resentful. After all, Eduardo was at my birthday party last summer. Sometimes there's a twist of guilt in my gut, remembering how I nearly abandoned Lloyd for a summer with Eduardo. Should anything he says now surprise me?

I've arranged for there to be balloons. Blue, red, and green. I think the waitress expected a child's birthday: she's wearing mouse ears when she brings us our menus. When she returns, they're gone, and she looks at us queerly.

But of course.

"You remember Kathryn?" Chanel asks, sitting back so that her girlfriend's plain Waspy face can smile at us. We tell her sure (although we keep wanting to call her Wendy, Chanel's last girlfriend) and reach over the table to bestow the customary kisses.

We're a quirky little group: Chanel, a round-faced Filipina, and her very white girlfriend; Melissa, very femme in long blond curls and dangling earrings, and Rose, very butch in short black hair and tie; Tommy, chubby and nearly bald at thirty; and Javitz, of course, kissing all of them with sloppy wet lips, accepting their homage as the returning prophet who has yet again triumphed over the angel of death.

And yes, did I forget? Drake, off by himself a bit, steely-eyed and fixated on Lloyd.

"Javitz," Lloyd says, "this is Drake."

Javitz looks the man up and down with no attempt to conceal his inspection. "Hello, Drake," he says, in his best Hedy Lamarr voice. "You're *everything* I expected."

I watch as Drake blushes. He looks handsome, I admit to myself, with his red face and thick gray hair, thicker than either Lloyd's or mine, I note. I smile and say hello, settling down next to Tommy.

"Haven't seen you for a while," I say to my old friend.

Tommy smiles. We've had our issues, Tommy and I. Once, Tommy was my compatriot both in ACT UP and in the bars of Provincetown. He led the demos, bullhorn in hand—but on Commercial Street in July he was the one who tagged along behind, watching while the rest of us tricked. Every season his hair receded farther back on his head, much sooner than the same curse began inflicting the rest of us. Still, his eyes are more beautiful than any other man's I have ever seen: silvery blue like a Siberian husky's.

I've known him longer than I've known anyone else here but Javitz. I'm not sure why we're friends: he's edgy, moody. But like *I'm* anyone to call someone else moody. I guess it boils down to a shared history—of friends lost, battles won. We don't have a lot in common, especially since the activism has died down, except for our memories: taking over the T one day in 1990, chanting until our lungs were hoarse; visiting the bedside of yet another fallen comrade, grateful for the shoulder of the other after we left; sitting on the steps of Spiritus at four a.m., calling ourselves vampires—that is, until I found a suitable victim and left Tommy sitting there alone.

I wasn't always the kindest friend to Tommy, and I wish there was a way of undoing that. Tommy was the best friend to go tricking with, because he was always *there.* Javitz would head off to the dunes, other guys would try to compete with me, but not Tommy. "Go ahead," he'd urge, pushing me to talk with some cute guy across the bar. "If he turns you down, come back and we'll have another beer." Once, when I'd spiraled down into a K hole, it was Tommy who made sure I got outside, got some air, got home without getting into trouble. He was *devoted* to me. Looking back, I realize that now, and although we've distanced some in the last few years, I remember how delightful his devotion was, and how undeserving I was of it.

True, he'd get resentful now and then. Last spring, there was a guy he really liked—Douglas, I think his name was, or maybe Donald—who turned out to be interested in me. It wasn't the first time such a thing had happened. This Donald or Douglas kept asking Tommy for my phone number. Finally Tommy told me about the situation, all tight lips and furrowed forehead. I told him not to worry, that I wasn't interested—but then one night at the bar, this Donald or Douglas introduced himself to me, and he *was* pretty cute. So I went home with him. Tommy found out, and he was furious with me. For *three whole weeks* he wouldn't speak to me. Finally I apologized profusely, told him I was a real shit, and promised never to do it again. He grudgingly forgave me, even if he's kept his distance ever since.

"I've been seeing a guy," Tommy says now.

"Really? Who is he?"

"I'll bring him by," he says—and there's something in his voice—"so you can meet him."

Chanel throws a straw wrapper at me. "So are you all set on a place for Provincetown?"

I'm not sure which of the three of us will answer. Finally I realize they're leaving it up to me. "We're still negotiating," I say.

Javitz doesn't look at me. I know him well enough to know he's angry, but not *really* angry, more disappointed that I've threatened tradition. But I just can't bear the thought of it all again, not after last year.

Now the waitress is asking if she can take our orders.

We all laugh. "Any specials tonight?" Melissa giggles. They're indulging us by coming here. But they all have a little trash in their backgrounds; they understand. We order, and then we eat: fried chicken and onion cheeseburgers, heaps of french fries and cole slaw. We toast Lloyd with plastic mugs of root beer and Sprite. "May you live to be as old as Javitz," Chanel says. He behaves himself and refrains from a retort. He's busy impressing Drake with his knowledge of Jung.

Of course, there are gifts. Javitz gives Lloyd tit clamps. "Who am I supposed to use them on?" Lloyd asks, dangling them across the table, shocking the waitress as she cleans away our green plastic plates. Javitz takes them and holds them across Drake's chest. Drake blushes, again. Chanel gives Lloyd a T-shirt with her picture on it, jagged because she had to cut Wendy out of the photo when she dropped it off at the novelty shop. Tommy's gift is a postcard book filled with sexy men. "Not a baldy in the bunch," he chirps. From Melissa and Rose, Lloyd unwraps a "grass man": a round stocking head filled with grass seed. "Pour water on him and he'll grow hair," ever-practical Rose instructs. "Wish it'd work on me," Tommy quips. Everybody laughs.

From Drake there's something different: a crystal in a little white box lined with purple velvet. Everyone oohs. Drake blushes for a third time.

"Thanks," Lloyd says meaningfully, and they share a moment across the table.

"Okay, everybody, cake time!" I barge in, and the waitress brings over a huge hot fudge cake with vanilla ice cream. We sing, and after we're done, the whole restaurant applauds. Rose hands the waitress her camera and we all huddle close together, making silly faces into the bright pop of the flash. Lloyd turns to me with his little-boy look. "Oh, Cat," he says.

"You're catching up with me," I tell him.

"Not quite," he says.

Everyone's talking among themselves now: Javitz and Drake, Chanel and what's-her-name, Melissa and Rose and Tommy. I take Lloyd's hand under the table.

"I love you," I tell him.

He smiles. "I love you, too."

"Guess that's why we're lovers, huh?"

We're quiet for a minute, each thinking his own thoughts. Or maybe they're the same, I don't know. I'm thinking about friends, how they're different from lovers, how they're the same. I'm thinking about passion, of course, how to define it so that it's real, so that it works, for Lloyd and me most of all, but for the others sitting around this table, too. How long before we all drift apart, this little party just a vague memory, memorialized only by a goofy photo in Rose's photo album? "Who are those people?" someone will ask her, years from now. "Old friends," she'll say, but she'll be damned if she can remember every name.

Provincetown, July 1994

Of course, I never expected to write or take a nap.

Once Eduardo is gone, I shower and shave: my face *and* my chest. Haven't shaved my chest yet all season. Too much work these days, and the stubble the next day is infuriating. But tonight I go for it: I want the line from my throat down to my navel sharply defined, dividing my pectorals, delineating my abs. I pull the razor up against my skin, white foam amassing, sprinkled with tiny black hairs like chocolate shots on whipped cream. I nick myself between my pecs. *Damn.* A prime spot. I hope the blood doesn't congeal into a scab. I let the warm shower beat against my chafed torso, soothing my hide.

I worked out at the gym this afternoon in anticipation of this. Eduardo had watched from the sidelines, idly picking up free weights, oblivious to the stares of the thirtysomethings around him. Everybody seems to want what they think they don't have—youth and big muscles most of all. One man stared at himself in the mirror that covered the wall and pouted. "There's no gain, no gain," he grumbled. Yet he was a muscle queen of the first order: bigger tits than most women have, biceps for days. Why don't mirrors tell the truth?

I step out of the shower and towel myself dry. I'm satisfied—if no longer impressed—by the sculpture in the mirror. I run my hand down the smoothness of my torso. Javitz isn't home tonight; he'd give me hell if he were here. "I don't understand why everyone shaves their body," he says. "Everyone wants to look *eighteen.*"

Outside the air is thick and damp. I can taste the sea on my tongue. The fog is rolling in off the bay, so dense that when the headlights of cars hit it, I see my shadow moving across the vapor. I see lots of shadows, in fact: queers on parade. Commercial Street at eleven o'clock is a colorful bazaar. Men in leather, women in rubber, girls who look like boys, boys who look like girls, glamorous drag queens in full-length sequined gowns, boys in tiny lycra shorts. These nightly hordes replace the heterosexual throngs of the day-light hours, who push their strollers in and out of the souvenir shops and gawk at the queers. We joke that at 8:45 every night a siren goes off announcing: "Attention all heterosexuals. Province-town will be closing in fifteen minutes. Please bring your purchases to the register. Thank you for shopping in P'town. Now get the hell out."

Now I'm surrounded mostly by boys. The boys from Montreal wear light-colored blue jeans and tight white T-shirts, big black belts and boots. The boys from New York wear ripped black shorts and white tank tops, their heads always buzzed. The boys from Bos-ton wear cut-off denims and colorful form-fitting tops. This season it's rainbow stripes. I'm a hybrid: tonight I wear baggy blue jeans and a sleeveless flannel shirt, unbuttoned.

The bar is packed, as ever. I worry for a minute that I'll see Eduardo. Then I catch the eye of a boy across the room. He's dark, possibly Asian, a Keanu Reeves type. He seems to consider me, then averts his eyes. I feel a momentary twinge of rejection. I lose him in the crowd on the dance floor.

The smoke is heavy, as thick as the fog outside. I buy a beer and hold it, cold and wet in my hand. I will nurse this one bottle the entire night. Gone are the days when I'd consume five, six, seven, *eight* bottles in a night. It was such a silly phase, and I can understand why it's over, despite how it sets me apart from most of the boys here. How could I continue to do all that and still stay removed, up on the ceiling, always watching while participating at the same time?

Standing here, everything about me is heightened: my eyesight, as sharp as a falcon's, detecting the slightest stirring in a darkened corner; my sense of smell, recoiling from cheesy cologne amid the suffocating smoke; my sense of taste, so sweet in anticipation that my tongue caresses my lips; my hearing, tuning into the mock con-versations that persist around me. My breath comes in a steady, deliberate rhythm, and I am aware, very aware, of how I tighten my stomach muscles to give the illusion of defined abs.

Tonight I watch them all: strung out and high, out of control. I am not one of them, not one of these children who pop their pills, drink their drinks. I know no one here. Yet I remain in place, still trying to find that boy on the dance floor, the boy with the deep dark eyes, the Keanu clone. Where did he go?

"Hey," a voice says near my shoulder.

I turn. But it's not him. It's something nondescript, a tourist from one of the suburbs, most likely. He's probably my age, in a knit shirt and khaki shorts. I smile and move past him. I feel him watching me as I move away.

Keanu is across the room, deep in conversation with a muscle boy, a boy whose pecs and biceps have been pumped considerably larger than mine. Steroids, I console myself. He suddenly tweaks Keanu's nipple, and they kiss. I turn away and finish off my beer.

For the rest of the night, no one approaches me. I find pairs of eyes, but they move on, skipping past me, like stones on the surface of a pond. I buy a second beer, something I haven't done in a long time, feeling desperation rise from my shoulders like perspiration in a sauna. I look for the guy from the suburbs, the one in the knit shirt who dared to approach me. I fight twin demons: the condescension and self-doubt over why only such a one as he would approach me, and the desperation that sends me back to him. But it's a moot dilemma: he's gone. He either scored or was rejected, plodding now up Commercial Street to his empty room. The announcement of last call is made. I stay in the bar until the lights come on: a stupid move, given the wrinkles. I set my half-finished beer on the bar and push out into the damp night, falling into lockstep with the crowd as it moves towards Spiritus.

I know no one here. Five summers ago, there was a posse of houseboys and waiters who were my friends. *We* were the boys then, the boys who laughed and tricked and thought nothing about it. Now one of them is dead. Two of them closed their open relationship and never go out. The others I see from time to time, walking down Commercial Street. We nod to each other as we pass, but there are others on the steps in front of Spiritus now, others with more hair and fewer wrinkles and bigger, more youthful muscles. One member of my old group, who went from being a summer waiter to a year-round poet, gave a reading at the Fine Arts Work Center just the other night. I went, and he was covered with purple lesions. I asked him if he wanted to go out to the club, but he gently turned me down. Does anyone go out dancing with spots?

Now I feel foolish, even a little shameful, standing here on these steps in front of the pizza joint, thinking of my old friend. Who's to say he's so different from me? He's not: we dressed the same, we did the same boys, we danced the same dance.

I watch the crowd dwindle. "Desperation shows," Javitz has said, and he's right. It *smells*, too: sour and fetid, and the boys here on the steps keep their distance from me. There are no eyes here at all. Try as I might—and still I try, even at a quarter to two—I make no connection. I watch as the boys leave in little pairs. I watch as men in leather chaps yank their chains and pull their slaves back to their guest houses. I watch finally as the pizza makers from Spiritus haul out their garbage and shut off the light.

I trudge back towards home alone, trying to banish the sound of the foghorn.

At least I hadn't seen Eduardo. At least he hadn't seen me like this. But if I *had* seen him, I wouldn't be going back to an empty bed and a scrotum heavy with unshot sperm.

I spy a man heading down the alley towards the pier. The rhythm of Provincetown goes like this: if you don't score at tea dance, you can score at after-tea. If you don't score at after-tea, you can score after eleven at the bar. If you don't score then, there's always Spiritus, and if even that fails, you head on over to the dick dock.

I have never been to the dick dock. Until tonight, I have never fallen this far down the food chain. Javitz has been there, of course, bypassing the bar entirely, but where hasn't Javitz been? I consider it, decide against it, and walk past the alley. Then I change my mind and turn around.

It's hard to see through the haze. Here, on the lip of the bay, it's like steam—appropriate, perhaps, for the activity that stumbles within it. I can't even see the water; I can only hear the steady slap of the surf against the sand. The harsh overnight lights from the wharf only magnify the density of the fog. They do nothing to illuminate the movements of the men under the pulpy wooden pier. I can discern just vague silhouettes. A flash of red, a tattooed arm. Finally I make out, not a foot away, a cluster of bodies, like a circle jerk among boys in their clubhouse. But in the middle of the circle is a man on his knees, moving with difficulty on the wet sand, cocks surrounding him like the spears of conquistadors—every faggot's dream, and don't let anyone ever tell you it's not.

I feel a hand on my crotch. I turn, confronted by a face. It's not unattractive, but it's hard to categorize. Old, young, I don't know. Montreal, New York, Boston—who cares? For in moments he's on his knees and my dick is out of my jeans, and he's sucking as fast as he can. He's high on something, I'm sure. At one point he pulls off my dick and takes a hit of poppers. He offers them up to me, but I decline. He gets back into his work, and I turn my head, discovering the crowd we've attracted. The cocksucker from the circle has apparently been sated; now seven dicks point at this one. The men attached to these dicks have shuffled into a ring, closing in on the man in front of me, tempting him away. Some of them begin to paw at me with shaky, graceless hands. I feel fingers suddenly from behind, creeping up under my shirt and finding my nipples. The man in front of me on his knees looks up, the round whiteness of his eyes in the dark, and runs a hand over my chest. I'm glad I shaved. I imagine the slick smoothness he feels, and I tighten my stomach so he can feel my abs. My dick swells now, ready to shoot. I attempt to withdraw, but he holds me there, and I come despite myself, ejaculating down his throat, the way I once did, more than ten years ago, with Gordon in the front seat of his mother's car. I know the force with which I come, the force that sends my load across the room, and I imagine how that must have felt for him, taking it down his throat. Define "passion," Javitz had dared. This, then: how he *swallows*, every last bit of it. Another man from the circle shoots: "Ah, yeah," pumping out bullets of semen that land in globs on my chest. I stumble away, while the man on his knees moves on to the next.

It takes me a second to think, to quiet my heart in my ears. He *swallowed*. In ten years, that hasn't happened to me. I've always been so damned *good*, such a fucking role model, pulling out of the boys' mouths just before I came. That's how I was with Javitz, and Lloyd too: I have never tasted either's cum, and they have never tasted mine. Strange, isn't it, that this faceless man at the dick dock should have that part of me, and they don't? Maybe it's that generation thing again, that weirdness of being in between. Javitz laughs at me for my inexperience; Eduardo's friends simply disregard the warnings. But for me, for Lloyd: we came out at the same time as the virus did, and were immediately bombarded with those hellish "safe sex" pamphlets that told us: *Do it and die.*

I think about the man on his knees. It was *his* decision, I tell myself. And besides, I'm negative. Or was, anyway, last time I checked.

What worries me more, as I walk home in the sticky night air, is the cum drying on my chest, a flaky confection that resists my attempts to brush it away. I shaved my chest tonight; I nicked a spot. *I bled.*

When I get home, Javitz still isn't back. He and Ernie must be taking one of their long walks—or else he's gone to the dunes. I wish he were here so I could talk about what I'm thinking. Instead, I slip into bed and watch the mist seep into the room, like a vampire in one of its many forms.

Boston, February 1995

"He's *gaw-jiss,*" Javitz says when we get back home.

I roll my eyes. "He's not *gorgeous.*"

Lloyd doesn't say a word. Javitz, of course, is talking about Drake. The two of them had talked intently for the last hour of the birthday party.

"He's part of a safe sex program at the hospital," Javitz says, in awe. "He asked me to come and speak."

"Really?" Lloyd asks. "What did you say?"

"I said of course." He winks. "Providing dinner comes included."

"Go for it," Lloyd says, giving permission.

"Yeah, right, darling. So he can talk about *you?*"

I decide to change the subject. "They're good friends, aren't they?" I ask.

"Who?"

"Chanel and Rose and Melissa and Tommy. It was such a nice time."

"They're all your friends," Lloyd says to me. "They all came because of you."

This is one of Lloyd's issues. It pisses me off. It's true I knew them first. Chanel worked with me at the newspaper before I resigned. I met Melissa in a writers' workshop. Lloyd gets an attitude about this.

"Chanel adores you, and you know it," I snap at him. "So do Melissa and Rose. And as for Tommy . . ."

Tommy had a crush on Lloyd when we first started dating. He even had to stop seeing us for a while, in fact, the crush got so intense. Add Lloyd to the list of reasons for Tommy to resent me.

"I'll tell you something about Tommy," Javitz says. "He barely said a word to me. He can't handle it. My health."

This is *Javitz's* pet peeve. He thinks the only reason anyone wants to see him is because they think he's dying, and anyone who avoids him is doing it for the same reason.

"Tommy's just socially awkward," I say, immediately aware of my condescension. "I mean, he's . . . shy."

"You had it right the first time," Javitz snips.

I can sense we've started rolling. Happens every time.

"Melissa went on, *and on*, about that food," Lloyd sighs. " 'Too much salt. How can they get away with this much salt?' I wanted to throttle her."

I don't try to stop it. I actually jump in. "And did you get a load of Chanel's latest thing? All the personality of a wet piece of dust." I sit down on the couch and take Mr. Tompkins onto my lap. He nips at my hand but I pet him anyway. If I pet him from behind so he doesn't see my hand coming, sometimes I can even get him to purr.

"Wendy was *much* cuter," Lloyd agrees. "Chanel's losing her touch."

"Getting old," Javitz says.

"Poor Tommy, though, huh?" I say. "Just keeps putting on the poundage."

"He said he's seeing someone," Lloyd tells me.

I laugh. "He even said he'd bring him by. Guess he trusts me finally."

"Well, *he'll* never learn," Javitz says, eying me.

Mr. Tompkins manages to land a nasty bite on my wrist. My fault: he saw my hand coming. I let him go. Now he's frustrated, looking around for something else to bite. Javitz is too far away, so he decides on his tail, and spins around for a few seconds like a whirling dervish before collapsing in a heap. His little murmuring heart is surely high in his ears.

"Oh, you crazy thing," I say to him, bending over him to stroke him while he pants. "Take it easy. Your heart can't take it. One of these days you're going to overdo it."

"He'll outlast us all," Javitz says.

That's when I decide to end our cattiness. "Listen to us," I scold, "a bunch of stereotypical queens, backstabbing our friends just hours after partying with them."

Javitz sighs. "That's what friends are for."

"No. It's *not*." So why do we do it? It's just like my family. "Oh, *hiii*, Auntie Loretta," my sister gushes, embracing her beside the Christmas tree, hating the woman and her lofty airs. "Didn't think they'd *ever* leave," my father used to grumble behind his smile as he waved to my brother and his three unruly children, backing down the driveway in their station wagon.

"Well," Lloyd announces, "I'm going to bed." He has to get up early: he has a real job, even if we don't. "Thanks for the party. Try not to talk about me too much after I'm gone."

Javitz approaches. "Wait, Lloyd."

We both turn. Javitz seems uncomfortable.

"I need to say something, just to get it off my chest." He hesitates. "We can process it tomorrow if need be."

"What?" I ask. I hate prefaces like this. I get up and stand next to Lloyd.

"It's just that I've been . . . I've been thinking about what you said, Jeff, about not wanting to do Provincetown again."

I feel impatient, pressured, guilty. "I haven't made a final decision. You asked me to rethink it, so I am."

"I didn't ask you to rethink it," Javitz says. "But I've been doing some rethinking myself."

Lloyd and I are quiet.

"I've decided I'm going to *move* to Provincetown. For good."

"For good?" Lloyd asks.

"Yes. Ever since going on disability, I've tried to visualize my life. What it would be like. What I would do, how I would live. I can't see doing it here in Boston. For over a decade, this city has come to mean dying for me. So many of my friends, the people of my generation, are gone. It has been one long preoccupation with my own mortality, and that's not going to change, not in the near future. I'm still kicking, still living—yet here, all I think about is death, how many have gone before me, how many times I've been to Beth Israel, how many workshops I've put together at Fenway. I want to do something new, take another leap while I still can."

We're both silent.

"It's something I need to do," he says, "and I just hope you both understand."

We all stand there silently for several seconds, just looking at each other and not blinking. Then the clock chimes eleven over the wood stove.

"So," I say, looking past him out the window, where it's started to snow again, "what you're saying is—*you* don't want to do summer in Provincetown."

"Well, that would be one result of my moving there permanently. I think the place Ernie found can be rented year-round. I'd like to avoid a summer lease."

"So that would exclude us?" I detect the sharpness in my voice.

"No, it wouldn't exclude you." Javitz is talking in his steady, calm teacher voice. "But it doesn't necessarily *include* you, either."

Lloyd sighs. "You've obviously thought about all the implications. The winter in Provincetown, the isolation . . ."

"The support group, the community," he says in response.

"The access to services?" Lloyd challenges.

"There are excellent services in Provincetown. And a free shuttle to Boston."

The back of my throat begins to tighten. "You've already made your decision," I say. "You're not talking about this with us. You're telling us. Just like when you decided to leave teaching and go on disability."

Javitz looks uncomfortable, but doesn't say anything.

"Well," Lloyd says, the psychologist now, "maybe there's some need to discuss all this further, but the bottom line is that we support you, Javitz, in whatever you decide." He looks over at me.

I look from Lloyd to Javitz. I'm quiet for a moment. Then I say: "Of course."

"We'll talk tomorrow," Javitz promises, "and the next day, and the next, I'm sure."

We all agree. Lloyd goes to bed. Javitz and I watch CNN for a while, not saying much, talking a little about Bosnia, about how it's genocide all over again, another Holocaust. Javitz decides to go home then. We kiss good-bye and I walk him to the door. "We'll talk tomorrow," he promises, and I nod, convinced he's talked all this through with Ernie already, that our discussion is merely a courtesy.

I hit the dimmer switch. The light fades to a dull gold. I open the door to the bedroom.

"Lloyd?" I whisper.

But he's asleep. I don't feel like cuddling; not yet. I sit in a puddle of moonlight, a bright patch of blue a few inches from Lloyd's meditation table. Incense tickles my nose like the soft fur on the petals of wildflowers. Its fragrance comforts me, the way the scent of the lilies around my father's coffin consoled me at his wake. My family had all gathered then: aunts and uncles and cousins and in-laws, people I hadn't seen in years, people I don't expect to see ever again. Strange thing about family, how they come, how they go.

I close my eyes and picture myself all alone in the middle of a field, surrounded by daisies and black-eyed Susans. That's called meditation, I hear Lloyd say to me. Maybe it is. Maybe that's what I'm doing, sitting here, rocking myself in the dark. Maybe I'm meditating. I just know that if I'm going to be alone, this is where I want to be: in a field filled with flowers, under a warm summer sun, with no one around me, not a soul, not a single person who can ever leave me again.

FAMILY

"Yes, strange thing about family, how they come, how they go," Javitz agrees. We're sitting at the kitchen table. We've just cleared away our late-breakfast dishes and now we're drinking tea and reading the Sunday *Globe*. "My father left us when I was eight months old. But I've told you that."

Many times, in fact. "I just don't understand it," I tell him.

"What's to understand? He was tired of living over a delicatessen in the Bronx with four screaming children and a wife who was as cold as Long Point in February."

"No," I tell him, irritably. "I'm talking about *me*. My mother's phone call."

"Oh. Right. That *is* how this started, isn't it?" He takes a long sip of his tea.

I had slept until noon. I woke up with a stranger's cum dried on my chest. I showered in a frenzy, rubbing my skin with the loofah until it was raw and red, angry at myself for not washing the night before. Already the stubble on my torso was pushing its way against the surface of my skin, little purple dots speckled across my pecs. Tomorrow it will itch. I won't be able to shave it again for a few days unless I want to risk severe razor burn.

Javitz made breakfast: Bisquick waffles. "You can't fuck up with Bisquick," he says. It's something we share: memories of mothers cooking "from scratch" with Bisquick. His waffles always taste the same, crispy but dry. Sometimes he sprinkles a little cinnamon into the batter to perk them up, but not today.

"Oh," he had said, suddenly remembering. "Your mother called while you were in the shower. She wants you to come down for your birthday."

I'm shaking my head now in protest. "But my birthday's not till next month. Has she forgotten even that?"

"Darling, *call* her," Javitz says.

"I will. Later."

I hadn't heard from my mother in seven weeks, but who was counting? Like friends, family comes, family goes. But family are not friends, despite what we might say. "My friends are my family," Chanel insisted in an essay that won her an award from the Lesbian and Gay Press Association. "I have recreated what I lost—or rather, what was taken from me."

My mother, until her retirement, was a greeter at Kmart. You know those women: "Hel-*lo*, and welcome to Kmart. Have a flyer." They stand there in their blue smocks, and their voices are raspy with years of cigarette smoke. My mother is no exception. "Gawd," she'd say at the end of the work week, "I've got corns on my feet from standing all day, and the edges of my mouth are cracking from smiling."

She held that job for eleven years, until Kmart started cutting back, hurt by the giant Wal-Mart that went up across the street. They gave her an early retirement, and she still has the gilt-framed Employee of the Decade plaque they gave her hanging on the wall. She worked in housewares, too, but it's as the front-line greeter that she's still recognized on the street. "Hey," I've heard more than one kid say, "that's the lady from Kmart."

The one and only time she and my father ever met Lloyd she was still wearing her blue smock. I cringed a little, but I knew Lloyd would understand. His parents were farmers; the one and only time I ever met *them*, on a side trip to Iowa during our trip to Chicago three years ago, his father was actually wearing denim overalls and chewing on a sprig of wheat, just as I imagined him. I'm not sure how Lloyd imagined my parents. "This is Lloyd," I announced to them, and my mother looked up from the kitchen table, exhausted, then rose and greeted him just as she would her customers. "*Wel-come*," she said, raspy voice and cracking smile. Then she sat back down to take off her shoes.

My father never held a job as long. Shoe salesman, night watch-man, cab driver. "It's not his fault," my mother insisted, the most devoted wife on the planet. "He's a hard worker." Stores were for-ever going out of business, new employees constantly being laid off. The afternoon he first met Lloyd he had just been laid off yet again—either from Klein's Formal Wear or the cab company—and my mother was dog tired from working double shifts. "Just until you find something else," she told my father. "I can carry us for a while." But my father carried most of the conversation with Lloyd and me that day, as anxious as he was about work. My mother just sat there, massaging her feet.

"So what is it that *your* folks do, Lloyd?" my father asked.

"They're farmers."

"Ah." My father nodded. "Salt of the earth."

"You going home to see them for Christmas?" my mother finally asked.

"No," Lloyd said. "Jeff and I are planning to have some of our friends in for the holiday."

My mother raised her eyebrows, then lit a cigarette. That's just what she thought: her gay son had abandoned his family for a group of faceless, nameless *friends*.

But if friends become family, then they're no longer friends. They've become our new mothers, our chosen fathers, our replaced brothers, sisters, and cousins.

"Which am I?" Javitz asks now, bringing me back home.

"You're our maiden great-grandaunt Agatha, the one everyone suspected was a lesbian."

He doesn't seem pleased with the association. "Couldn't I at least be one of those funny uncles?"

"The kind that play tickle-tickle with the prepubescent nephews?" I leer.

"I *abhor* children, and you know that. How about tickle-tickle with their fathers?"

I stand, approaching the window and wishing the clouds away. It's the first overcast day we've had in weeks. I'm becoming greedy. "Maybe I'll call Eduardo," I say.

"No luck last night?" Javitz asks, with those eyes.

"Depends on what you'd consider luck."

"Do tell."

"I went to the dick dock."

I wait for his response. He's got the *Globe* up in front of his face. He lowers it slowly, dramatically. "The dick dock?"

"Yup."

He beams, like a proud father whose son has just said he was joining the firm.

"It was hot," I admit. "Never thought such a scene could be so hot."

In fact, I'd thought just the opposite. There's a rest stop on Route 3, the highway between Boston and Provincetown. I see the cars there every time I drive to or from the Cape. Once, our first summer here, a time when a little naïveté still lingered blissfully in my soul, I didn't understand why so many cars stopped at that particular place. I was always in a hurry, my windows down, my radio blaring, anxious to be in Provincetown in time for tea dance. I used to pride myself on not stopping the whole trip, not once between Boston and Provincetown, not even to take a leak. "You're young," Javitz said, sighing. "Your bladder holds."

Then, a year later, when I was rapidly becoming no longer as young, and my bladder no longer as impervious, I had to pee as I passed by the rest stop. I noticed four empty cars parked there. Someone was behind the fence: a man, older than I, gray hair, a beard. Why had he gone all the way back there to take a pee? I wondered. Surely these bushes here were privacy enough.

As I hauled out my dick and let my water flow, feeling the rush of relief settle all through my body, I spotted another man, and another, this time treading out of the bushes en route to their cars. Now, and only now, I began to suspect.

"Silly boy," Javitz chided me later, sitting on the deck of our house in Provincetown. "Every rest stop in the world is a gay cruising spot. If you weren't so focused on tea dances and which boots were popular this year, you might have discovered that a long time ago."

"You know all the secrets, don't you?" I asked, smiling.

"Most. Not all. I'm not through learning," he said. "You'll learn them, too, one at a time. If you're open to learning them."

Secrets, I thought. Gay life is filled with secrets. Well, I didn't want secrets. No sex in the bushes for me. I was out, loud, and proud, a Queer National, marching in the streets. How could anyone find sex on the side of the road hot? Sure, maybe after an action, when we'd be all hot and sweaty from chanting, a couple of us might grope each other on the sidewalk or in an alley. But we always went back to an apartment or hotel room: we always did it on *sheets*. "No offense," I said. "But those guys—well, they're . . ."

"What?" Javitz asked, arching an eyebrow. "Too old?"

"Well, there aren't many guys my age who do it."

"How do you know?"

"Oh, come on. The guys there are all—so—sleazy."

"Sometimes they are." Javitz smiled. "When you're lucky."

I laughed. "Whatever floats your boat. It's just not my thing." In the mirror, I checked my hair—how *thick* it was then—and headed off to the bar. Javitz could keep the rest stops, the dunes, the bath houses. It just wasn't my scene. I laced up my boots and headed out to find a trick—someone who would look, I realized then, exactly like me.

"So what did he look like?" Javitz asks now.

"Who?"

"The guy at the dick dock."

I smile. "There wasn't just one."

"This gets better and better." He grins like a madman. "How many were there?"

"A whole ring. It was hot." I sneer. "Of course, they were all servicing *me*." That was a bit of an exaggeration, but it made the story better.

Javitz sniffs. "And here I was hoping you'd learned a lesson."

"I *did*. Javitz, I was *rejected* last night."

"Doesn't sound that way to me."

"Not there. At the bar. Not one guy looked at me. At least, not one guy I'd go home with. That's why I went to the dick dock."

"Oh. I see. Lowered your standards."

"Well—"

"Fuck you, Jeff."

And he sounds as if he means it. He stands up, pours himself some more tea. He carries it into the living room and stands facing away from me.

"Hey," I say.

He doesn't respond for at least a full minute. Then, still facing away from me, he says: "You were *not* rejected if you ended up having hot sex at the dock." He turns around. "No matter how *old* they were. In my book, that is *not* a rejection."

"Okay, okay, mea culpa." I hate it when Javitz gets like this. "Look," I say, "there's something that I need to talk about. . . ."

"What?"

"Well, I shaved my chest before I went out." Javitz rolls his eyes over his teacup. "And I nicked myself. Then, later, one of the guys shot his load all over my chest and it dried there."

"And?"

"And so—well, I worry."

He sits down again, staring at me across the table. "About *what?*"

He's still angry. What the *hell* is his problem this morning? "About *transmission*," I say, articulating the word carefully, exasperated.

He matches my mood. "Oh, for God's sake, Jeff."

"That's direct semen-blood contact. I have a *right* to worry."

"Yes," he says, but he's not compassionate, not at all. "You have a right."

There's a knock at the door. Our anger pulls back, not wanting to face public disclosure. It's Ernie. "David?" he sings. "You home?"

Javitz gets up and opens the door. Ernie bounds in, full of energy, despite the dreary day and his dearth of T cells. "Hi, girls. Want to come watch drag-queen softball with me? They're going to play even if it rains! Can you imagine sequins in the mud?"

"No thanks," I say. "I've got plans." I do. I plan to call Eduardo.

"Let me put on my shoes," Javitz says.

"David, I checked on that application for you—"

Javitz shoots him a look. I notice it. Ernie looks apologetic, as if he'd just spilled the beans about something.

"What application?" I ask, trying to sound indifferent as I pick up the phone.

Javitz looks down at the floor. "Well, I wanted to tell you and Lloyd together, but didn't get a chance this weekend."

I wait, my finger poised over the first digit in Eduardo's number.

"After next semester, I'm going on disability."

"What?" I ask, hanging up the phone. "Just like that?"

"It's not a rash decision. I've given it a lot of thought."

I look over at Ernie. Yes, and I know who you gave it thought *with*. Not with us, your supposed very best friends in the whole world, but with *him*. Because he's got it, and we don't. Because of one stupid little micro-organism that's chewing its way through Ernie's cells, and not ours. I let out a long sigh and return to the phone. "Guess we can talk about this later," I say. Poor Ernie looks like an embarrassed newlywed watching his wife and her mother argue for the first time, not quite a stranger but not really part of the family either.

Ah, family. It's like Bisquick. No matter how you bake it, it always comes out the same.

Boston, February 1995

I'm pissed that we're here, because I wanted to write today. I've started a piece, something that feels fresh and alive and makes no sense at all, which gives me a rush, a big old hard-on. Don't ask me to explain what it's about: I don't know. It just started flowing the other morning, making my fingertips itch and my heart push blood past my ears. It was the morning after Javitz told us he was moving to Provincetown for good, in fact—a morning after a particularly restless night. I haven't shared it with anyone yet. I have to wait a week or so and see if I still like it. It often works out that I don't.

"Over here," Lloyd is saying. We've come to a psychic fair at the mall in Cambridge. Lloyd and his straight friend Naomi, a nurse at the hospital, have been to see one of the psychics here before. "Her name is Magda," Lloyd said. "She's *amazing*. Please come, Cat. We can ask her about the apartment, what we should do." Lloyd and Naomi are into this sort of thing. After all, they go to the same meditation group—along with Drake—and chant around a statue of the Hindu god Ganesh.

We make a hardy little band off to see the wizards. Javitz is here, pretending to be open-minded about this sort of thing. Naomi had jumped at the chance to see Magda again. I called Tommy and begged him to come. "For my sanity," I pleaded. "Everybody else is going to be acting wavy gravy." He consented.

Magda sits at a small cardboard table surrounded by tarot card readers and astrologers. The fair is a fundraiser for the pediatric AIDS ward at Mass General. ("Of course it's for the *babies*," Javitz snarled.) I catch a buzz of fortunetelling as we walk through the rows of tables. High-school girls with big blond hair ask about their boyfriends. Wiry old hippies with receding hairlines and ponytails ask whether O.J. will be found guilty. Magda is taking a break when we come upon her, eating her lunch, an egg salad sandwich and a pear. She's a fat dyed redhead with a small blue tattoo of a star on her chin. She recognizes Lloyd and Naomi, grins up at them. "My friends," she says grandly.

"Hello, Magda," Lloyd says, reverentially.

"Hello, mind doctor," she says. "And you, healing woman." She wipes her mouth with a red paper napkin and puts away her lunch. "Who are your followers?"

"This is my lover, Jeff O'Brien," Lloyd says. I smile. "And these are our friends, David Javitz and Tommy Lundquist."

She puts out her palms to us, fingers pointing down, like a carnival Buddha. "Welcome. I feel your energy, and it is good. Who will start?"

"We thought Javitz would," Lloyd says. "He's planning to make a significant change."

She gestures at the chair beside her. He sits, appraising her, eyebrows taking over his face. "I'm planning a move—"

"Tell me no more," she cuts him off. He reaches into his back pocket and withdraws his wallet, handing her a ten. "Not yet," she scolds, her eyes closed. "Money disturbs my energy."

That's the point where I roll my eyes and gesture to Tommy. We head down to the food court, where I get a fat-free raspberry frozen yogurt from Ben & Jerry's and Tommy a chocolate honey-dipped cruller from Dunkin' Donuts. He's been quiet all day, much as he had been at Lloyd's birthday party.

"So what's going on with you?" I ask him.

"Oh, stuff." He puts away the donut in just three bites.

The frozen yogurt has a bitter aftertaste, so I toss it into the trash bin. "Like what kind of stuff?"

"We're organizing a letter-writing campaign to Clinton," he says. "Asking him to come out against Amendment 2 in Colorado."

"I thought you'd given up on Clinton," I say.

"Yeah, well . . ." He looks around as if he's considering another donut. "Got to do something to keep the masses organized and active. AIDS sure doesn't excite them anymore."

Tommy has always been involved in some queer cause or another. Has been ever since I met him, at an ACT UP demo in front of the State House, back when I was still with Javitz. Tommy's always been fiercely passionate about queer politics. He was one of the founders of the Queer Nation chapter here. The first meeting was held at his house. Javitz and I went, and Tommy caused a stir by asking any straight supporters to leave. "Queer Nation hates straights," he announced, and he got booed.

He's not so fierce these days. "What's the matter?" I ask him, touching his sad cheeks. "I thought you said you were dating a new guy."

He looks at me as if I'm being stupid, as if I don't get it. And maybe I don't. But I thought that's what Tommy's always wanted: a boyfriend. He hasn't had all that many.

"Come with me to Chanel's after this psychic silliness is over," he says. "We can talk then."

I shrug. "All right." Somehow him calling this silliness bothers me. *I* can say it, because Lloyd's my lover. But Tommy can't. Lloyd *believes* in this, and I don't like people mocking him. Only I can do that.

Tommy decides a cinnamon cruller was calling him after all. He wanders off to buy it, while I sit here amid the potted plants, breathing the sweet stale air of the mall. I marvel at all the mini-dramas that pass in front of my eyes. A father scolding his son for being mean to another boy. A woman flirting with a man who seems not to care. A girl momentarily lost, terror in her wide blue eyes. Then her mother finds her, takes her hand, and the child trots alongside her like an obedient puppy. How I envy the pink flush of relief that spreads across her baby-fat cheeks.

"Let's go back," I say to Tommy. "I think I want a reading of my own." He just gives me a look.

We head back to the fair. "Ah, here they are," Magda says as Tommy and I return to her table.

"How'd it go?" I ask.

Javitz seems stunned. Lloyd and Naomi are beaming. "Incredible," Lloyd says. "She told Javitz some *amazing* things."

"She told *me* I was about to meet a man," Naomi grins. "And he *won't* be gay."

I laugh. "And what about you, Lloyd? What did she say about us and the apartment?"

He looks at Magda, then back at me. "I'll tell you later," he says, and I feel my stomach drop.

"Which of you boys wants to go next?" Magda asks.

"Count me out," Tommy laughs.

I look at Lloyd. "I'll go," I say.

I sit down. She passes her hands in front of my face, creasing her forehead. "You are a weaver," she says at last. "Do you sew?"

"No," I tell her.

She looks puzzled. She closes her eyes and waves her hands in front of me again. "Yes," she says at last. "You are weaving together a large piece of fabric that you will hang on your wall."

"I'm a *journalist*," I tell her.

"No," she insists. "You're a weaver."

"What about my home?" I ask her suddenly, gripped by a force that takes me by surprise. I lean forward in my chair. "What about my home and my family?"

She opens her eyes and looks at me. "Let the images come. Don't rush it."

I sit back in my chair.

"I'm sorry," she says. "I don't see anything."

"Nothing?"

She shakes her head. "I'm sorry. I guess I'm tired. Come back after lunch. I won't charge you."

"Guess you all tired her out," I say as we head outside.

Javitz walks as if in a daze. "She said I was moving to the water, to regain a sense of time and place," he says, lighting a cigarette as soon as we're outside. The air is cool but vibrant, a sunny day in the middle of this dreadful winter. "She said I was going to a place where I would find my soul, and in so doing, rediscover my life. Death, she said, would not dare approach me in such a place."

"Isn't that *amazing*?" Lloyd gushes.

Naomi closes her eyes and shivers.

"What's amazing?" I ask. "You *told* her you were moving. She only said what you wanted to hear."

"Maybe I wanted to hear that I was making a mistake," Javitz says. "That way I'd stay put, and not take the leap."

"Well, I guess this just confirms it then," I laugh, trying to sound light, but the nasty edge creeps through. "You're leaping."

"Yes," Javitz says. "Yes, I am."

"I'm so proud of you," Naomi coos.

"I'm hungry," Lloyd says. "Let's have lunch. Where should we go?"

"I told Chanel I'd meet her," Tommy says. "Jeff, are you . . . ?"

"Yeah," I say. "I'm going with Tommy. We'll be at Chanel's if you want to come by later."

They barely hear me. The three of them cluster by Lloyd's car deciding on a place to eat. Lloyd and Naomi are vegetarians, of course, so every place Javitz suggests is nixed by them.

"What about Denny's?" he asks. "They've got a nice salad bar and I can get veal parmigiana."

"*Veal?*" Lloyd scolds. "Don't you know that's the worst you can eat?"

Naomi makes a sad face. "A calf. A baby cow."

"Look," Javitz says, arm on hip. "Why don't the two of you just head over to that field across the street and *graze* for a while?" They all laugh.

I don't. Instead I'm thinking about my poor old aunt Agatha, whom my father and I found dead on her living-room couch when I was ten and she was ninety-six. She'd been dead for a week—at least. Her apartment smelled like the shed out in back of my grandparents' house, where they kept plums and pears and apples. Some of the fruit would start to rot, way down in the barrels, and when you opened that shed door, it was the sweetest, most loathsome smell you ever could imagine. That's how it smelled the day Dad forced open Aunt Agatha's door, and told me to wait in the hall.

But what kid ever minded his father when the corpse of a dead aunt beckoned from another room? She was tipped to her side on the couch, her mouth and eyes open and the television on. What had she been watching when she died? Bob Barker was on the tube when we came in that day, calling for the next contestant to come on down.

Aunt Agatha died alone. She had no children. Even her sister's children were dead, leaving only grandnieces and -nephews like my father to come in and check on her every once in a while. I try to imagine what that must have been like, day in and day out. Sitting there alone, never quite sure what day of the week it was because it no longer mattered. During the day, she had Art Linkletter and Dinah Shore and Bob Barker for company, but at night she was left only with the ticking of the clock and the clanking of the radiator.

"Not the way it's supposed to be," my mother had clucked, shedding no tears over the coffin of this ancient lady she barely knew. "You're supposed to have *family* around you when you're old."

That used to be the fear parents had for their homosexual children. "But who will you have to *grow old* with?" they'd cry, wringing their hands. But we took back that myth: "We create new families," Chanel wrote, "new families to replace the ones taken from us." Sure we do. But that doesn't mean we still won't end up like Aunt Agatha, or those old plums in my grandparents' shed: shut up alone, old fruits left to rot.

Provincetown, July 1994

I can make the ride from Provincetown to Boston in two hours. Sometimes less, depending on traffic. It's at least twice that to my parents' house in Connecticut, and getting into my car this morning I predict all of five.

"That's only because you'll dawdle," Javitz tells me.

"Bladder ain't so strong anymore," I tell him, and I wink.

True, on my way to Boston I'm usually anxious to get home. Some deadline to meet, some party to attend. I'm usually excited to pick up Mr. Tompkins from Melissa and Rose and share a little gossip while I'm there. But driving back to the town where I grew up elicits less of a hurry. Not that it's actually unpleasant at my parents' house. Sure, my mother says very little, and my father and brother sit all day in front of the TV, but Chanel's father has threatened to *kill* her if she ever comes home again. Tommy's parents always start weeping: "Our son, our son." It's as if he were laid out in a casket in front of them. It's not that way for me. I just pass in and out of the house like some inconspicuous ghost, my life on hold, suspended for the duration.

"I took my mother to tea dance once," Eduardo told me last night. He had cooked me dinner—salmon with a fine tomato sauce and a fresh Caesar salad with homemade croutons. It was really quite adorable: folded paper napkins and mismatched silverware by candlelight.

"And what was her reaction?"

"A little overwhelmed, but she liked my friends. She even danced with my friend Roxanne."

"A lesbian?"

Eduardo nodded. "Of course, Roxanne looks like a boy."

I shook my head. "What a difference a generation makes."

My mother has never said the word *gay* to me. She pointedly refuses to ask about Lloyd. My father tries, occasionally, although he stumbles on Lloyd's name. Ever since I came out, my mother has not once inquired about my life, not when Lloyd and I moved in together, not when I left my job, not when I told her that Javitz was in the hospital with pneumonia. She responds with silence on the phone when I tell her such things. She changes the subject to one of the cousins, who's having his or her tenth baby or getting married for the third time.

"So challenge her," Lloyd has urged. "Tell her it pisses you off."

"What's the point? She's not in my life anymore." I've just stopped telling her anything.

Once, I was jealous of my father, my brother, my sister—of anyone with whom I might have to share my mother's affection. One night, when I was very little, waking from a dream of flying monkeys and wicked witches, I shrieked for her, over and over. In the next bed, my brother, Kevin, scolded me to be quiet, to go back to sleep. I ignored him and continued to scream, but it was my father's voice I heard above me in the dark. "Jeffy, calm down," he said, but I only screamed louder. I didn't want *Daddy*. I kicked my feet and pushed at my father's hands.

And then, in the near-dark, I saw a little red glow moving towards me. I stopped crying, with only involuntary, leftover gurgles escaping my throat. My mother sat down next to me on my bed. She removed the cigarette from her lips, the cigarette she always lit as soon as she woke up, even in the middle of the night. I watched as the little red glow made an arc in the blackness. "I'm here, Jeffy," she said, her words taking shape in the dark. I felt the terror subside like mercury falling on a cold day. Within a few minutes I was back to sleep.

It takes four hours, not five, to get home. I pass Hartford, then head into the rolling hills of industrial Connecticut. It's hardly the image of the state from the movies: no pretty churches, no stately white homes. These are milltowns, built with old red brick and rusting iron. In the town where I grew up, the factories still stand: big old husks of brick and steel and journeymen's ghosts. I stop my car at the crest of a hill and gaze out over the ruined castles below. They have decayed ignobly for decades, many of them since before I was born. I once played among those ruins: a king—more often a queen—a knight, a mad monk, the Hunchback of Notre Dame. "Stay out of those places," my mother scolded, but what child ever paid his mother any mind when the iron claws of a rusting factory awaited his imagination?

My father, many years before, had worked in one of my castles: as a young man, as a young husband, before he finally moved on to better things, like selling shoes—before the factories themselves moved on, leaving the town behind. "This was once a thriving place," the old-timers in front of the post office would say, "till the factories shut down." As a boy I'd listen to them, not comprehending their loss, their melancholy.

For as a boy, what was there to be sorrowful for? For grand adventures in ruined palaces? For long and twisting walks along daisy-dotted railroad tracks, for discovering forgotten tunnels and the occasional overturned caboose?

They've boarded up the factories now. Even from way up here I can see the signs posted to keep out. Those who dare to enter are no longer boys or imagined queens, but rather hard-eyed addicts with the map of the world etched upon their faces—men who, like my father, may have once worked in these ruined places in days gone by. Today, children do not venture into the crumbling fortresses of my youth; the moat has gone dry and the drawbridge has rotted to pulp. The sadness is now—even to the children, I suspect—palpable.

The street on which I grew up is called Juniper Lane, but there never were any juniper trees. Maples, a few old oaks, a scattering of sick elms, but no junipers. The houses are all the same, built in batches in the late 1950s, starter homes on neatly subdivided half-acre lots. "We'll get a bigger house someday," my father always promised, but it was never to be. How did we manage all those years, three children, two adults, one bathroom, no dining room?

I pull into the driveway and sit a few seconds, breathing, before I open the door, lock it out of force of habit, then head up the cracking cement walk and step inside.

"Mother," I say, and she pulls me to her, the palms of her hands against my shoulders.

My father embraces me roundly. "Jeff, it's *good* to see you," he says.

Everyone's there: Kevin and his wife and children, my five-month-pregnant sister, Ann Marie, and her boyfriend. My mother returns to the kitchen. She's baking a ham. Good thing I gave up my experiment with vegetarianism. Once during that period I came by for dinner. My refusal to eat pork chops seemed to offend her far more than my predilection for sucking dick. "What—are you going to eat *lettuce* all your life?" she asked.

But before anyone else, I greet my old cat. He's sprawled on his back on the floral print couch we bought from Sears when I was in the tenth grade. He lifts his paws in the air to welcome me. "Aw, Junebug," I say, nuzzling my face on his stomach. I hear his old motor kick into gear, the rattling purr that was once as smooth as a hummingbird's song. He's twenty-four years old, an amazingly ancient age in cat years—like being thirty-one (almost thirty-two) in gay years. "My old friend," I whisper, feeling the tears well behind my eyes.

"They're coming to take his picture for the newspaper," Ann Marie tells me. "They said he's the oldest cat in town."

Junebug—named for the month Ann Marie and I found him, a shaky little kitten dropped out of a car by a heartless human—is the one I miss most from this place. My parents hadn't wanted him; Ann Marie and I had begged to keep him. All those nights, under the covers of my bed, reading Gordon Merrick novels, and all those days, hanging out with Stick, smoking pot, pulling on our puds—Junebug had been there, watching us with those yellow feline eyes, never judging, always understanding, always accepting. And now I was gone and he was still here: my old friend with my old family. "I miss you, Bug," I tell him, just before my sister-in-law, Danielle, pulls me away to kiss the air to the right of my face.

"Happy birthday, Jeff," she says, echoed by Ann Marie and the kids.

"I've still got three weeks to go," I say, but they know I won't come home then, that there are others (faceless, nameless others) with whom I will choose to spend my real birthday.

"Well, here's a cake anyway," my mother says, her voice quick and efficient, producing the cake from the refrigerator. It's a Duncan Hines yellow cake with canned chocolate frosting, topped with a kaleidoscope of M&M's.

"I put the candy on," my oldest niece tells me, her eager face so like her father's, like mine. I tousle her hair.

That's it for now. They all go back to what they were doing: watching TV, yelling at the kids, talking about people I do not know or no longer remember. No one asks me anything about Lloyd, about Javitz, about my work, about how I manage to pay my bills without having a "real" job. After my father registered his disapproval when I left the newspaper, he never said another word about it, except to thrust a twenty-dollar bill at me whenever I come home. My brother speaks the least of all, choosing instead to sit in the living room and watch whatever sport happens to be playing on ESPN. Ann Marie tries, best that she can. For someone who dropped out of school when she was sixteen, she's surprisingly accepting. "How's Lloyd?" she whispers. "Good," I tell her. "Thanks for asking."

Maybe it's because Ann Marie knows what it's like to have disappointed the family too. High-school dropout, arrested for selling coke, shacking up with a couple of boyfriends, at least one abortion that she told us about. Now she's pregnant, and she wants this baby, desperately. She'll be *thirty* next year; my baby sister, the one I walked to kindergarten on her first day, telling her not to cry, will be *thirty*. I realize I don't even know her boyfriend's last name.

Neither of us lived up to the shining example of Kevin, a high-school history teacher, a baseball coach, a Knight of Columbus like my father, married in a Catholic church, the father of three children, all born within wedlock, the first child arriving exactly ten months after her parents' marriage. But Lloyd and I have been together for as long as Kevin and Danielle—longer, I think, by a couple of months. I told that to my mother once, and she went silent on me, again.

"Hey, Ma," I say to her now, looking out the kitchen window into the backyard. "I thought you were going to plant your rock garden again this year."

She's stirring something at the stove, her back to me. "Not enough time. It takes a lot, buying all those bulbs, planting them, weeding."

"I miss your rock garden," I say.

She shrugs, still not turning around to look at me.

We're alone in the kitchen. The kids are outside with their mother and Ann Marie. My father and brother and Ann Marie's boyfriend are in the living room watching the game. Just as it's always been: the segregation of the sexes, with me in the middle. I sit down at the table, snitching a pickle. I hear the men shout all at once at the TV in the other room.

"Hey," my niece says, coming in from outside, her cheeks flushed from running. "It's Uncle Jeff's birthday and he's sitting all by himself at the table!"

I blush. My mother turns sharply at her. "It's Uncle Jeff's choice, honey. He likes to sit by himself."

My niece shrugs and heads for the bathroom. I finish my pickle, sitting there for a few minutes, letting the angry sounds of the men in the living room rush past me. Then I stand. I walk up behind my mother, who's still stirring with that goddamned spoon. Nothing in the *world* needs to be stirred that much. I put my hands on her shoulders and she jumps a little. I place my lips beside her ear. "No, Mother," I whisper. "I *don't* like to sit by myself."

My father spies us. He probably thinks he's just interrupted a tender scene of filial love. But he's hardly in the mood to care even if that were the case. The Yankees are losing, and he's furious. He grabs a pickle, bites it in half.

"It's five and oh," he snarls to my mother. "Don't you want to come watch the game?"

Once, my mother hated baseball. In the old days, when my father and Kevin would shout themselves hoarse at the television set, she and I would sit and talk about Aunt Loretta's most recent trip to Florida or Las Vegas, or else we'd be out weeding in her rock garden. But now, alone with my father, she's become his companion in the living room, cheering on those Yanks. My move to Boston was just one more sign of my treachery: "You'd better never become a Red Sox fan," my father has said. Nothing to worry about there.

Now my mother turns carefully, not wanting me in her face. I've moved off a bit, leaning up against the sink. "I'll join you in a minute," she tells my father. "And don't get so worked up. That vein is popping out on your forehead again."

She sets down her spoon, goes to him. As I've seen a hundred times before, she smooths out the vein on my father's temple, gently massaging his forehead until he closes his eyes and breathes. Ever since he had a minor heart attack twelve years ago, he's been told to watch his blood pressure. My mother has counted his cholesterol, broiled instead of fried his hamburgers, and smoothed out the veins that pop in his head. "There," she says gently, in a voice I remember from long ago, from the days when she would touch me with the same concern with which she touches my father now, the days when she would hold my head as I puked my guts into the toilet, retching with the flu, calming me, soothing me, comforting me.

My father smiles at her. Grateful. Their eyes hold like young lovers' in the spring, the way they must have first looked at each other some forty years ago. That, finally, is their legacy to me: their enduring love for one another, despite the disappointments of their children.

For all of my talk about recreating family, have I managed even this? My parents will be together until the day one of them dies, and it won't be because of obligation or responsibility. It will be because they have loved each other, loved each other with a constancy that seems reserved only for themselves, forsaking all others. Oh, sure they love us, they'd bend over in the proverbial backward stretch for any one of us. At least, they would have before. But the commitment is first and foremost to each other—and that's what I want, what I've *always* wanted, in my relationships. First with Javitz and then with Lloyd, I have wanted precisely what my parents have. But when the minimum expectation is this, have I merely set myself up for the inevitable disappointment? One hears a great deal about the effects of broken families on children, how psyches are damaged when parents do not love each other. Well, what about *us*—those kids cursed with parents who adore one another, who have made commitment seem so attainable, as easy as smoothing away a vein?

Boston, February 1995

"So smile for a while and let's be jolly, love shouldn't be so melancholy, come along and share the good times while we can—"

It's a dance version of "Rose Garden," and Chanel is dancing around her living room when Tommy and I enter. Kathryn, her girlfriend, sits on the couch looking embarrassed. Chanel lives on the second floor of an old Victorian in the heart of Jamaica Plain. From her bedroom window you can see the pond: all iced over now, with cold gray skeletons of trees laced around it.

"I can't believe how they're remaking all these old songs of my childhood," I announce.

"You relate everything to age," Chanel says, stopping in mid-boogie. "Don't you ever quit?"

Kathryn smiles up at me. "Hi, Lloyd."

"I'm Jeff," I tell her. She blushes furiously. I ought to call her Wendy and see what she does. Poor thing. It's hard to penetrate a group as the replacement lover in a couple that's split up. Chanel and Wendy were together for four years. Wendy wanted babies; Chanel wanted a dog and a career. Melissa and Rose sided with Wendy in the breakup. They tolerate Chanel at events like Lloyd's birthday party, but the whole affair has put a little seam down the fabric of our group.

"Don't worry," Chanel reassures Kathryn. "Everybody gets Lloyd and Jeff mixed up."

"You look so much alike," Kathryn offers.

"Oh, sure," I say. "All men look alike to dykes."

Chanel raises her hand in a mock threatening gesture. "Watch it," she says, then laughs. "Actually, Kath, they *used* to look a lot alike. But then Jeff started getting *old*."

Tommy isn't participating in any of this. He's gone into Chanel's kitchen and helped himself to an orange. He's peeling it over the sink now.

"Just you wait," I tell Chanel. "You're catching up pretty fast."

"Do you know I found a gray hair?" she asks suddenly, turning off the music.

"No," I say, feigning horror.

"Yes, I did. But I'm glad. I think gray hair looks sexy mixed in with black."

"Sure," I say. "On Lily Munster."

Chanel shakes her long straight hair. "Stop it. On Asian women, it looks *striking*."

Chanel was born in the Philippines, where—she grudgingly admits—her father worked for Marcos in some cushy government job. After the revolution, her family fled, and Chanel quickly became Americanized. "That's why my parents think I'm a lesbian," she says. A lesbian and an Aquino supporter, in fact—a one-two punch that prompted her father's ferocious threat that he'd kill her if she ever so much as stepped across the threshold onto the white marble of their home in McLean, Virginia.

"I get asked to serve on all sorts of committees because I'm a woman of color," Chanel has admitted, "and of course, I do. But it's not like I grew up *oppressed* or anything. In fact, we were the oppress*ors*." As a girl, she had a chauffeur, a maid, and a cook, and her family is still affluent. Her father found another cushy job under Reagan and Bush, although lately, Chanel suspects, with the coming of Clinton, he must be having a harder time of it. But then again, maybe not.

She's the fifth of six daughters: hence the name. "Chanel Number Five," she says to slow-witted friends. "Get it? Hel-*lo*?"

"Guys," Tommy says from the kitchen.

"What is it, honey?" Chanel asks. She and I have flopped down on the couch opposite Kathryn. She's just pulled out a photo album to show me pictures of the trip she and Kathryn took to Maine last month. I notice that all the photos of Wendy have been trashed or cut in half.

"I want to talk to you about something," Tommy says.

We both look over at him. There's a quality to his voice that compels our gaze. Kathryn seems to notice it, too, and she stands up, the awkward outsider. "I guess I'll go to the store," she says. "You said you're out of milk and eggs."

"You don't have to—" Chanel stops in mid-sentence, looking back over at Tommy. "Yeah, okay. And a pack of cigarettes, too."

Kathryn leaves. Tommy stays seated at the kitchen table, talking across the room at us. "So, I just wanted to tell you guys something."

"What?" Chanel asks. "Stop dragging this out. You've been a mope for days. Just tell us."

"It's—look, I don't want you freaking out. . . ."

"Tommy," I say. "We won't freak out."

He sighs, as if he's impatient, as if we were the ones hounding him, as if he hadn't been the one to bring this up. Finally he says, "I tested positive."

"Get out of here," Chanel says, breathy in disbelief.

"That's what I wanted to tell you."

I stand up. I hesitate a minute before walking into the kitchen, but I do, and I sit at the kitchen table across from Tommy. Chanel joins me a moment later.

He looks at us hard. "I haven't been fucked without a condom in eight years."

I feel a terrible coldness well up from my scrotum. I press my legs together fiercely to drive it away. "Then what made you get retested?" I ask. "Five years ago you were negative. Why did you get another test?"

"The guy I'm seeing," he says, looking at me, almost as if he's accusing me of something. "We went for the test together. It's a big issue for him."

"But if you've been safe, then how do you think . . . ?"

He shakes his head. "I don't know. Oral sex? I know we're supposed to believe it's safe, but . . ."

"I just read an article saying it's not," Chanel offers, as if that helps right now.

"That's the problem," I say. "Nobody knows anything for sure anymore. Not that they ever did, but we believed they did for a while."

"But I never swallowed," Tommy insists. "And no condoms ever broke while I was getting fucked. *You* tell *me* what it could have been. Did I brush my teeth too hard and irritate my gums? Did some precum get into my bloodstream that way? Did I get some blood on my tongue kissing a guy whose cheeks were nicked from shaving?"

"That's impossible," I say.

Tommy shakes his head. "At first I wanted to believe it was a false positive, but they checked again. *Twice.*"

"Shit," Chanel says. She stands up, goes back into the living room, begins flipping through the photograph album.

"Once, just once," Tommy says to me, eyes almost pleading as they stare into mine, "I fucked a guy without using a condom. A year ago. I think he's got AIDS. I've seen him. He's got that hollow look, starting to turn yellow." He closes his eyes and breathes in. "I didn't even come inside him. I just fucked him for a few minutes. I know it was stupid, but I thought the risk was his, not mine."

"Hey," I say, reaching across the table, taking his hand, but he pulls it back. "That's just it. Nobody *knows.*"

Least of all me. I think about last summer, about the night at the dick dock, my fear of infection through a nick on my chest. And then later, letting passion overtake me, with Eduardo—

"Here." Chanel has suddenly returned. She places the photo album down on the table between Tommy and me. It's open to a page of photos from the Hands Around the Capitol demonstration, several years ago. There we all are: Tommy and Chanel and Javitz and me, all in our leather jackets. In the top photo, our cheeks red and rosy, our mouths open as if in mid-chant, are Tommy and I. Tommy's carrying a sign: "The Government Has Blood on Its Hands."

"We fought back then," Chanel says. "We'll keep on fighting."

"Yeah, well," Tommy says, "we were all negative then. We were just working off our guilt at not being infected. I don't have to do that anymore."

I look over at him. For a blinding, stupid second I wonder if this isn't his ultimate activism: getting infected himself to keep up the passion for the fight. But the terror in his eyes is too real.

Back in the days when we marched through the streets, it was easier. It was a way to pilot our grief, our rage, our fear. In a strange and twisted way, it allowed us to be hopeful—and this in the days when Reagan and Bush sat in the Oval Office. It's different now: the government still has blood on its hands, but we no longer march in the streets. It's more than simple complacency lulled by the honeyed words of a deceitful president. It's a sense of holding on, of resisting no more, of finding a little cave and retreating there, hanging on for dear life with whatever is left of one's energy, one's family, and hoping to God to still be there when it's all over.

Last week, walking along Newbury Street, I ran into my former editor from the newspaper. He was with his wife. "Are you still involved in ACT UP?" he asked, trying to be friendly.

"There's not much of an ACT UP to be involved with anymore," I told him.

"That's too bad," he said, and his wife nodded in agreement. "They were an important force."

I hate liberals. I especially hate straight white liberals. If they really thought ACT UP was so important, why didn't they know it had faded from the scene? Why did he—in that pomposity that masquerades as professionalism—make life miserable for me when I worked for him? "You need to be impartial in your reporting," he'd scold. "We can't have you parading around with a radical street action group."

"Fuck you," I should have said to him then, and "Fuck you," I should have said to him that day on Newbury Street. But I rarely say "Fuck you" to anyone anymore. I'm proud that I left that job, proud that I can now write whatever I want, take any viewpoint I choose. But what good has it done, really? Everything I've written —all my angry diatribes, all my calls to action? Tommy just sero-converted.

"We thought we knew it all," he says bitterly, running his fore-finger over the photos in the album. He traces the outline of the U.S. Capitol. "Follow these guidelines. Hot, horny, and healthy. This is how it's done."

I look down at the photos. There's one of me, the quintessential activist clone: sideburns nearly to my jaw, three earrings, an "Earn Your Attitude" T-shirt, cut-off denim shorts, white socks rolled up over shiny black Doc Martens. How young I looked, how involved with everything going on around me.

Then I see a picture of Javitz. How much weight he's lost be-tween then and now. How full his face looks in this old photo, how round his cheeks.

Kathryn comes back inside. Nobody says a word. She puts the milk and the eggs in the refrigerator, then hands the cigarettes to Chanel, who immediately opens the pack and lights one. Then Kathryn reaches into the brown paper bag. It crinkles as she pulls out a chocolate-covered donut for Tommy.

"Had a feeling you might appreciate this," she says, and he smiles.

He does.

En Route to Provincetown, July 1994

I pulled over to pee. Really, that's why I stopped. Sure, I was curious, and still am, particularly about the man sitting in the car in front of me. But that's not why I pulled over at the rest stop. I really had to pee; my bladder was going to burst.

Okay, so it wouldn't have burst. I could've waited and gone at the McDonald's at the rotary before the Sagamore Bridge. But ever since I left my parents' house I've been in the queerest mood.

I reach into my pocket with some difficulty. There: I feel it. The perennial twenty dollars my father slips me whenever I leave. Why does he do it? To assuage his guilt? To make me feel like a child because I don't have a real job? I'm tight, tense: four hours at my parents' house is too long.

"Come see us again, soon," my father had said, shaking my hand as I left, the sweaty twenty slipping from his palm to mine.

"Dad, I don't want this—"

He raised his hand to silence me. "Just don't stay away so long."

My mother offered me her cheek.

"Thanks for dinner, Ma, and the cake."

She just smiled.

"Wait a minute, Jeffy," my father said, rushing back into the house. My mother lifted her eyebrows as if to signal she didn't know what he was after. When he returned he had something in his hand. "I almost forgot," he said.

It was his school ring. The one the nuns gave him when he finished eighth grade. It was the highest level of education he ever achieved. He held it out to me now in his open palm.

"Dad, why are you giving this to me?"

"Just because I want you to have it."

It's an ugly thing. I open the ashtray, where I dropped it after getting into the car. No one smokes in our car. I keep change for the tolls in the ashtray. My father's ring glares up at me in the dull orange light of the setting sun. An ugly thing. A big fake amethyst. The initials of his Catholic grammar school: SJB. St. John the Baptist. What will I ever do with such a thing?

The guy in the car in front of me steps on his brakes, sending out a flash of red. Yeah, yeah, I think, I know.

I fully intended to drive away after taking my leak—although I didn't. I'm still sitting here, and the guy in front is looking at me through his rearview mirror. I'm being crazy. I'm sure he's hardly my type. I can't see him very well, but I'm positive he's older than I am, by a decade at least. Except that doesn't seem to matter much right now. I'm suddenly hornier than I have been in a long time.

"Thanks, Dad," I had said, hugging him quickly. My mother said nothing.

I walked out to the backyard to kiss the nieces and nephews. Poor old Junebug had been shooed off the couch, and now he sat there on the back step looking forlorn. "Hey, Bug," I said, kissing the top of his old head, his mangy fur smelling dry and dusty. He looked up at me, with those old yellow eyes that had seen so much. "Pose pretty for the photographer, you hear?" I said. "I'd take you home with me, but I think Mr. Tompkins would make a meal out of you."

Ann Marie was watching the kids play. "I wish Mommy would plant her rock garden again," she said, gesturing toward the grassy mound where once marigolds and petunias and daffodils had bloomed.

"Yeah, but let's not hold our breaths."

We both loved that rock garden. All the different flowers, all blooming at different times, perfectly synchronized so there was always color among the slabs of granite and brownstone. I can still see my mother, kneeling in the dirt, planting her flowers, a kerchief on her head, a cigarette between her Passionate Ruby lipsticked lips.

The yard was different then. The old maples were just saplings, held up by fragile wooden posts and white ribbon. The back of the house hadn't been completely painted yet. Much of it remained bare wood. The half that was finished was painted primary blue, like my kindergarten crayons. A fluorescent-green rubber hose was coiled like a long, beneficent snake under the kitchen windows. Similar houses stood all along the street, their half-acre lots evenly drawn, dotted here and there by newly planted shrubs.

Once, Ann Marie and I played in our mother's rock garden. I'd drive my Matchbox cars through the soil, or make up elaborate scenes with my little plastic orange witch, a leftover Halloween decoration that had once been filled with candy corn. I loved that hollow witch more than any other toy, and she's lasted in my memory much longer than any expensive battery-operated gadget from Mattel or Kenner. I can remember her face, even today, big orange eyes and a long nose with a wart. My mother hadn't wanted me to keep it. "Oh, Jeffy," she said, "boys shouldn't play with *dolls*."

"This isn't a doll," I insisted, although secretly I knew it was. What was the difference between my witch and Ann Marie's Dawn dolls? Not much, except my witch was much more interesting. The day after *The Wizard of Oz* aired in its annual showing, my plastic witch became Margaret Hamilton. I imitated her cackle, taking her out to the rock garden and driving her around on the tops of my Matchboxes. I couldn't have been more than seven; Ann Marie, four.

I buried the witch in the soft soil of the rock garden, newly turned by my mother's hands. "She's going to rise from the dead now," I told Ann Marie, who sat cross-legged and wide-eyed in front of me.

"Like Jesus?"

"No," I said testily, "like Barnabas Collins." I pushed the dirt around trying to find the witch.

"Do you think the witch on *The Wizard of Oz* will rise from the dead?" Ann Marie asked.

"Yes, she already did," I said, asserting the wisdom of my older years. "She did, but they never showed it." I continued to feel around in the dirt, certain this was the spot where I'd buried her. "After Dorothy left, the winged monkeys molded her back together and then she captured the Lion and the Scarecrow and the—"

I stood up, terrified all of a sudden. "I can't find her!" I cried. "She's *gone*!"

"Gone where the goblins go," Ann Marie whispered in awe.

I never found her. It was as if she'd been snatched away from me by some angry macho god. "Boys shouldn't play with dolls," a booming voice said in my head, and some unseen spirit hand reached up through the soil to whisk her away. For several weeks I would go out there and kick the dirt around with my feet, hoping she'd poke out her little plastic orange head. But she never did. After a while, I gave up.

The man in front of me tosses a cigarette out of his window.

Probably some fat old troll, I think to myself—yet it's a hollow thought, as hollow as my witch, as if I don't mean what I think. I can't deny that I'd prefer him to be some hot young thing, wearing the right boots, suitably muscled. But something about sitting here makes such qualifications irrelevant, even ludicrous.

Another car pulls in behind me. I check my rearview mirror. The driver looks like a librarian: fortyish, with round glasses. Small, thin face. Nothing remarkable. Yet the thought that he's here, that he's here for the same reason I'm still sitting here, that he's as horny as I am, his dick mine for the taking, and mine his—I have to catch my breath, literally, by closing my mouth and looking away.

In the bars, on the dance floor, there's this elaborate ritual. It's hot and exciting in its own way. You ask the required questions: "What do you do?" "Where are you from?" "Come here a lot?" You buy each other drinks. You pretend you are not at all interested in sex, that you are just meeting casually, that there is no ulterior motive. Until that final question, which still ignores the truth: "Want to come back to my room?" When in reality, what you should be saying is: "I want to suck your dick" or "I want to fuck you up the ass."

Suddenly the honesty of this place—this rest stop on the side of the highway, and all places like it—hits me. I don't care what the man's name is in the car behind me. I don't want to have to buy him a beer. I don't care what he does, or if he comes here often. I don't even much care whether he works out, or has a great haircut, or if his underwear is Calvin Klein or Sears. I just want his sex. Here. Now.

I get out of my car.

Behind me, I hear a car door close. I don't look back. I walk briskly along the path, and the realization that it has been forged and matted down by thousands of feet belonging to men as horny as I am thrills me. How many loads have been shot here? That's what makes these woods so alive, so energized, I think—the decades

of cum that have fallen to the ground, revitalizing the earth, fertil-
izing the trees.

I turn, stopping by a cluster of bushes. The librarian continues
on past me, and I'm perplexed for a moment, until he turns and
looks over his shoulder, once, quick.

Now I'm the one who follows. He's dressed in loose-fitting beige
chinos and a white polo shirt. He wears blue-and-white running
shoes that don't match the rest of his outfit. But somehow he's the
picture of sex, and I want his lips around my cock.

Finally he stops, partially obscured behind a large bush. I stop
too, not a foot away from him.

This is it: the moment of truth. I'm going to do it. All of Javitz's
stories come back to me at once, of down-and-dirty sex in public
rest rooms and in the dunes. When the man's hand reaches out and
grips my crotch, I let out the kind of sigh I usually make only after
long, long foreplay, when I'm getting close to orgasm.

The librarian wastes no time. He gets down on his knees and
awkwardly begins unfastening my belt buckle. I have to help. Then
he pops open my jeans, and sticks his face into my open fly. I look
down at the top of his head: a bald spot like my father's. It's an odd
thought, and what's even odder is that it makes my dick get harder.
That's when the librarian pulls down my black boxers and fumbles
my erection into his mouth.

I lean back against a tree and look skyward into the lacy network
of limbs that crosshatch against the bright blue sky. The man's
mouth is warm and slippery. His hands inch up under my shirt to
feel my pecs. I instinctively flex and pull off my T-shirt. This is
hot—like the dick dock. Raw sex. No games, no script. I suddenly
have an image of myself: a young stud having his dick sucked, being
worshiped by an aging librarian, who wishes with all his life he was
as young and attractive as I am. For once, I'm the youngest one
around.

I'm not sure what to do with my hands, so I thrust them into
the pockets of my jeans. Wrong move: my fingers make contact with
that damn twenty. I think of my father again, and this time he's
standing over me, watching me touch the flat space on my G.I. Joe
where his genitals should have been.

"Jeffy," he says, "why did you take his uniform off?"

The horror of that moment returns to me now as this man sucks my dick. In that moment—I couldn't have been more than eight or nine—I felt my father's whole attitude toward me change. I felt humiliated, shamed, dirty. "I was just giving him a bath," I said weakly, looking up from the pail of water in my mother's rock garden. But my father simply looked down at me, as if he knew the truth. And that truth was plain: I took off his uniform because I liked the hardness of his sculpted chest, and I wanted to know what he had beneath his pants. Nothing, I discovered with no little amount of regret. His crotch was as smooth as his chest, and far less interesting.

"I don't care if it *is* a soldier," my mother had said, after a classmate had given me the G.I. Joe for my birthday. "I just don't think boys should be playing with *dolls*."

My father had defended the gift. "You don't want him growing up to be one of those antiwar protesters, do you?" he asked. This was 1970. The year of Kent State. My father was a Korean War vet. He thought a new war every generation was not only inevitable, but maybe not a bad thing. "Isn't it better that he make friends with soldiers now so he doesn't march against them later?"

Interesting logic, thinking back. But it all seemed moot that day in my mother's rock garden, when my father saw me touching my naked doll. "Why did you take his uniform off?" Such a simple, direct question, one that has never left me, never stopped haunting me.

I hear the sharp snap of a twig. I look up. Another man has just stepped into the clearing, probably the man who had been in the car in front of me. He looks like a lumberjack. He's got short black-and-gray hair, with a large mustache over thick, full lips. He fills out his jeans well, with strong, round thighs. I don't wear my jeans that tight—it's considered out of style these days—but suddenly I'm glad his generation still does. Big biceps—and I mean big, not the "defined" muscles on which Lloyd and I pride ourselves—emerge from his cut-off flannel sleeves. His brown eyes fix on mine.

The librarian stands up, checks out the new man, then goes back to his knees, hands reaching up to unbutton another pair of jeans. "No," the man says, still looking at me. The librarian, confused, stands up again. The lumberjack reaches over and places his large hand on my shoulder, pressing down. He wants *me* to suck him. Yes, I thought, falling to my knees. I'll be your boy. I'll suck your cock.

But he takes the top of my head in his hand and pushes me away from his basket, and instead into the flat beige crotch of the librarian. I start to recoil, but his hand is firm. And then, as a new flood of desire washes over me, I think: Yes, yes—this *is* what I want.

I pull down the zipper of the librarian's fly, and smell something clean. Like soap. His blue bikini underwear—tacky, I would have called it yesterday—is wet with precum. I take his dick into my mouth.

"That's a good boy," I hear above me. I know it's not the librarian talking. I pull off his dick and look up. The librarian's body tightens, his face contorts, and he draws in his breath—just before coming in thick, forceful spurts, all over my face and hair.

"Yeah," the lumberjack moans, now stroking his own tool, sticking straight out of his jeans. He shoots his load all over me, too, and then I come: rough, violent, eruptions, aware of the fact that the sticky jizz of two men now streaks my face, my hair, my shoulders, and my chest.

The librarian zips up quickly and leaves. The lumberjack winks at me. "Play safe," he says, then crunches away through the woods.

I wait until they're both gone. I wipe my face with the back of my hand and then use a leaf to clean it off. I pull my tank top back over my sticky body. I head back to my car, feeling drained, totally sapped. But giddy, too, giddy and alive. By the time I cross the Sagamore Bridge—what Lloyd calls "crossing over to the other side"—and start the trek up the Cape, I'm singing along to the radio, a retro seventies station: "Bad girls, toot toot, beep beep."

When I get back, Eduardo's there waiting for me.

"Hey, hot stuff," he says to me.

Aw, shit. What am I supposed to do now? I don't want sex again, not after that incredible experience in the woods. And certainly not with Eduardo. God, does he think we're *married*?

"Listen, I'm really tired—" I begin.

Then Javitz appears in the doorway. "Call your father," he says.

"What's wrong?" I ask.

"Just call him."

So I do, and he tells me that Junebug is dead. "Ann Marie ran him over as she backed out of the driveway," he says, his voice thick. "Poor old guy. Just couldn't run like he used to. Just couldn't get out of the way in time. Give your sister a call, Jeffy. She's a wreck."

I can't say anything for a moment. Then I ask: "Did—did he die instantly?"

"No," my father says. "Poor old guy. Twitched like the devil. I had to break his neck with a shovel."

"Oh . . ."

I don't want to cry, not with Eduardo standing here, but I can't help myself. The tears just come: hot and stinging. I hang up and go to my room. Eduardo follows.

"Please don't—" I start, but he embraces me and I just let go, crying into his arms over an old cat I left behind when I thought I'd grown up.

Boston, February 1995

"The guy I'm dating," Tommy says, "knows both of you."

He looks at me with eyes that I remember well. Eyes that have accused me in the past.

"What's his name?" Chanel asks.

"He's meeting me here," Tommy says. "You can see for yourself."

Javitz and Lloyd and Naomi arrive. "Surprise!" Lloyd calls out. They've brought ice cream and hot fudge.

Chanel nudges me. "So is Naomi still straight?"

"Of course," I tell her. "It's not a condition that goes away, like a case of the hives."

"I don't know about that. On *Ricki Lake* today—"

"Please." I scowl at her. "Besides, you're monogamous."

Chanel rolls her eyes. "I'm getting a little tired of serial monogamy. I think you and Lloyd have the better idea."

"Ah," I say, "are we getting weary of Kathryn already?"

Chanel puts her arm around me, ducks me into the hallway where we won't be overheard. "She's not Wendy," she tells me.

"Duh."

"No, I mean, she doesn't set my heart racing the way Wendy did."

"You've cut Wendy's picture out of every photograph you own. You told me the romance was over."

She pouts. "It is. She's already found a new girlfriend. And they're having a baby."

"I'm sorry," I tell her.

"Did I make a mistake leaving her?" Chanel asks. "Hell, what am I saying? She started it."

"You were *both* pretty impetuous." I think about Lloyd and Marty, the little I know. One morning, after an argument the previous night, Lloyd just left, convinced he'd seen Marty's true, petty side. I don't know what the argument was about; I prefer to not know details.

I think about Lloyd and me, about that conversation we had, the idea that the passion was gone, how easy it was for me to fall in love with Eduardo. "Maybe it's not too late," I tell Chanel. "Maybe you should talk to Wendy. Don't let her go if you still love her."

She shrugs. "She's having a baby with her new girlfriend. I have no right to disturb her new life."

"Maybe not," I say, "but she loved you. You loved her. That was very obvious. And I will never accept that love like that just goes away. Baby or not. New girlfriends or not."

"No," she says, definitively. "I won't contact her. It's over. Besides, I have my career. I'm finally doing some interesting work, writing some pieces I think are going to get me attention. I've decided to get an agent. I don't have time for personal emotional baggage."

"But without that—"

"Kathryn will suffice for the time being," she says. "Unless Naomi turns queer. Keep me posted."

I watch her move off towards Tommy. She goes up and strokes

his face, kisses his nose. I remember how angry she was at me last summer, just as she and Wendy were breaking up. The excuse for her anger was what happened with Eduardo—but it was really her own grief about losing the woman she loved for so long. How could she have let it happen? I cautioned her to go slow. "You *love* each other," I pleaded. "Don't give up so easily. Work it out. Find a way!"

I hear Tommy's laugh, a small, high-pitched sound, cut through the chatter. And how might *he* work it out now? What way might *he* find? My old friend. *The last one to go will see the others go before her.* I'm still numb from his news. Yet he seems liberated by his revelation, as if all he needed to do to feel better was tell us.

Lloyd is suddenly beside me. "You've got to go back to Magda. She said she wouldn't charge you."

"What did she tell you?" I ask. "Should we try to find a way to come up with a down payment and buy the apartment?"

He looks solemn. "It's not a good idea, Jeff."

"Did she say that?" I flash red with fury. "Are you going to base your decision on what some Gypsy in a mall tells you?"

"That's not what I'm basing my decision on."

"Then what are we going to do? We have to be out of there in a few months."

"Can we talk about this later?"

"Fine." I'm pissed, and he knows it.

Are our lives that disposable? *See you later, Wendy. Let's give up, Jeff.* If such things are not worth fighting for, then what is?

My eyes wander back to Tommy. What does *he* think now, about the value of his life? What would he fight for, even now? Once, we fought like lions: closing down the Brooklyn Bridge, staging die-ins in the middle of Commonwealth Avenue. What will we fight for now?

Lloyd takes my hand, trying to bridge the gap between us. "You should go back, Cat. Ask Magda about your novel. Bring her a page."

The earnestness of his eyes wins me back. "All right," I say. "Maybe I will." What is it about Lloyd that will not permit me to stay angry at him?

"So what was up with Tommy?" he asks.

Now it's my turn to be evasive. "Can we talk about it later?"

I imagine his reaction—and Javitz's—when I tell them about Tommy, who's now heating up the hot fudge in the microwave. You'd never know he just dropped a bombshell on us less than an hour ago. Everybody's laughing now, even Tommy, carrying on, the familiar banter of the group masking what lurks below the surface.

Javitz is gushing about the place Ernie has found for him in Provincetown. "I can move in anytime. Now I can put one of those bumper stickers on my car that says I'm a Provincetown year-rounder!" He grins idiotically, like those kids in fourth grade who were told they'd made the "ceiling club"—that elite clutch of egg-heads who would chalk up straight A's for a week. Big deal to the ceiling club, I always used to say. Big deal to year-rounders, I say now.

"Do you know the psychic said she saw *boats* when she visualized my new house?" Javitz continues. "I never even told her it was near the water. She just *knew*!" How quickly the skeptics are converted.

Naomi pulls me aside. "You have such a wonderful family," she says.

"You mean this motley crew?"

"Yes." She smiles. She's only an occasional participant in our little gatherings, a canny observer because of her outsider, hetero status. "You're very fortunate. I've tried telling that to Lloyd."

"What do you mean, 'tried'?"

"Well, with everything he's going through . . ." she says, trailing off. Which immediately sets off a paranoia button in me. What has he confided to her? What has he told her about us—about me? What do the three of them—she and Lloyd and *Drake*—talk about to and from their meditation group? Does Naomi know more than I do about what's going on between Lloyd and Drake? Does she encourage it, or discourage it? "I've *tried* telling that to Lloyd," she said. Does that mean he refuses to listen?

Javitz holds court in the kitchen, teasing Kathryn about being so shy, telling Tommy to wipe the hot fudge off his chin. Lloyd and Chanel have moved off into the living room to gossip, as they usually do, not interested in playing Javitz's games. The dividing lines are not by gender here, as they are in my parents' house, but rather by personality—yet the lines divide, nonetheless. No one mentions Melissa and Rose, but their absence is felt, a physical thing.

Family. That's what they are, after all. Friends, lovers, yes—but *family*. With all of the tricky nuances and idiosyncrasies that breed within families, the little secrets and doubts and fears and resentments.

And the hopes and dreams and love.

Then there's a knock at the door. Tommy rushes to answer it. Chanel has put the music back on. She and Lloyd are dancing around the room. *So smile for a while and let's be jolly—*

Tommy embraces the man at the door. I look over to see who it is.

Love shouldn't be so melancholy—

"Everybody," Tommy says.

Come along and share the good times while we can—

"Say hello to Eduardo."

And of course, he looks over at me.

CLASS

Provincetown, July 1994

Our deck this summer has afternoon sun, something to which we've all resigned ourselves. "Our last deck," I tell visitors, "faced the east. Not only could we see the bay, but having coffee first thing in the morning with the sun full on our faces . . ."

I don't need to finish. They understand.

Here in Provincetown, decks matter. The strategic placement of the deck—whether it takes morning or afternoon sun, whether it looks out over the placid bay or the cacophony of Commercial Street—directly affects a house's summer rental price. "But where's the deck?" we always ask, first thing.

Sitting here now, moving my chair to follow the arc of the sun despite the sunblock plastered all over my face, I'm thinking about decks, and views of the bay, and summers in Provincetown. Each season we've sought a better place than the one we had the year before. We've become more precise, more particular about what makes for good summer space. Except, of course, for the concession regarding the deck, this year's house is the best yet. It has two bathrooms, and somehow we've managed to snare *three* precious parking spaces—among the rarest of rare commodities in this town. Such things make up for a lack of morning sun: we shall, as Lloyd says, survive.

And sitting here, baking in the midday rays, the cellular phone on a table near my elbow, I laugh. How the hell did you ever wind up here, kid? I think to myself.

"What's so funny?" Eduardo asks.

He's stretched out on a towel a couple of feet away from my chair. His long thin body reflects the sun: he glistens as if he's been bronzed.

"Just being here," I tell him. "Every once in a while it just hits me."

"What does?"

Of course he can't understand. He grew up here. This is home. To him, this isn't some rarefied queer resort town, where decks and parking spaces matter, where they become things to flaunt in front of one's neighbors from Boston. This is where he went to high school, where he fought with his parents, where he dreamed of things to come.

"I just never grew up thinking this would be my life," I try to explain.

He can understand that much at least. He never imagined this life for himself either, hanging out with the queers on their decks. "We're the same person, at the core," I explained to him. "Working-class boys who find themselves in the midst of a distinctly middle-class gay culture."

He'd never thought about such things before. "I always assumed my family *was* middle-class," he said to me.

"We always do," I smiled. "Nobody ever likes to think of themselves as being on either end. Nobody's ever rich, nobody's ever poor. Everybody's in the middle. I had a boyfriend once, in between Javitz and Lloyd, whose family had a butler. He thought *he* was middle-class. Did you have a butler?"

"Not quite."

"Even Chanel tries it sometimes. She'll tell me about her father's financial troubles in Manila. But it's not just money that matters."

"Then what does?"

"Experience. Position. Assumptions."

Eduardo nods, as if he gets it. "How'd you ever get to be such a know-it-all?" he joshes. I just throw a towel at him.

He's been with me for three days now, ever since I fell into his arms and cried over Junebug. There was something in his embrace that was much more solid than I had expected. He held me all through the night, caressing my face when I'd wake up from strange, disorienting dreams, remembering as I awoke the death of an old cat, hearing in my mind the snap of his neck, the shovel against bone and asphalt. In the morning, I looked at Eduardo with no small degree of embarrassment. "Sorry I acted like such a child," I said.

But he just reached across the bed and took my hand in his. "I had a cat when I was a kid, too."

Later, walking out on the breakwater, watching the sun set over the dunes, I said to him, "It must have been interesting, growing up gay in a gay town."

"It was hell," Eduardo said plainly.

It was hell not because his parents were necessarily homophobic, but because the gays were viewed as the rich out-of-towners, coming in to take away their village.

"It's not so much that you all are gay," Eduardo said to me, "but because they think *you* think you're better than them."

The twist on the conventional gay-straight dichotomy was not lost on me, nor was the significance of Eduardo's reference to me as "you all"—as if I were part of something he was not. Here was a man with whom I had been making wild, intense love for nearly a month now, and yet he saw us as different, as part of two worlds, separated by a chasm as large as the one he no doubt felt between himself and his parents.

How to explain I too felt that way? That sometimes I had this unnerving notion that my life here, on this deck, in this sun, was a charade?

Eduardo's father is a fisherman, although there aren't many fish left, and the state has been threatening to close down the waters to commercial fishing. It's a situation similar to my own family: it's Eduardo's mother who brings home the more steady paycheck. She makes sandwiches and rings up groceries at Costa's Deli on Shank Painter Road, far enough away from the hordes of summer that most of the clientele are Portuguese natives. At the end of the day, Eduardo tells me, his mother comes home complaining about her feet. So I *can* say: "I understand."

He wasn't sure I did, but at least he knew I was trying.

Because my parents aren't all that different from his. "What's that, the style now?" my mother asked, the second summer Lloyd, Javitz, and I rented a place in Provincetown. "Going back to the same place every year for your vacation?" It was a rare comment on my life, and no matter that it was slightly belligerent, I decided to seize the opportunity.

"It's not really a vacation, Ma," I explained. "It's a place we go to get away."

"Get away from what?" she asked.

For my parents, vacations mean a break, but not necessarily a rest. For them, vacations were an opportunity to do the things they didn't have a chance to do the rest of the year—like cleaning out the attic or painting the garage. So it was difficult for my mother to fathom the allure of Provincetown. "What do you *do* when you go up there?" she asked. "There's only so many times you can go on a whale watch."

Eduardo doesn't see the allure either. "I can't wait to go back to Boston," he says, sitting up on his towel and resting his chin on the arm of my deck chair. "Once I'm in school, I'm never coming back here."

I kiss the top of his head. "I'm glad you'll be in Boston this fall."

He looks up at me, as if he doesn't trust me when I say things like that. I'm not sure I trust myself, either, but Eduardo has lasted longer than any of the others.

"Hey," I tell him, "your dick looks great in that bathing suit."

Even in the sun I can tell he's blushing. He's wearing a cock ring—his first ever, and I taught him how to put it on. "You need to leave it on all day, to get used to it," I told him. It's forcing his dick up and out. I reach down and grab it through the Lycra.

"Jeff, stop—" he says.

Javitz waltzes out with a pitcher of iced tea. "French maid at your service," he chirps.

"You are *so* sweet," Eduardo says, accepting a glass gratefully, then quickly sitting up to shield his stiffening prick.

"If you'd only find out," Javitz says.

"You don't like boys," I remind him.

Eduardo frowns. "Stop calling me a boy."

"That's true," I admit. "He's wearing his first cock ring."

"Jeff!" he scolds.

Of course Javitz makes him stand up and model. Eduardo is glaring at me, but I can tell he loves the attention.

"He's right, you know," Javitz says. "You need to wear it, leave it on for as long as you can, so you can get used to it."

Eduardo sits back down, pulls a magazine over his crotch. "It does keep you pretty horny," he admits.

"Oh, let me tell you," Javitz says. "I used to wear one when I was teaching. If those students only knew that my dick was hard the whole time I was teaching them about Alexander the Great. Once I tried to get through the day with a butt plug stuck up me. I must concede that only lasted until after lunch."

Eduardo is shaking his head, giggling. "You guys are too much."

"What about that older generation, huh?" I tease. "Just look at the things we can teach you."

He smiles. "I must say that I never knew sex could be so funny."

Earlier today, we had both laughed our way through his cock ring initiation. He has a great cock, incongruously big and thick for such a thin body. And with the cock ring wrapped around his shaft and his balls it looked even bigger—except we were too busy giggling to really pay much attention.

"Ow, ow," he whimpered. "You snagged a hair."

"Eduardo, you're going to have to accept the fact that a few hairs are going to get pulled in the course of things."

"Careful," he urged.

I snapped the final clasp into place. "There." I burst out laughing.

"What?" he asked, hurt.

"Nothing. It's beautiful. I just can't picture you yet as a leather man. But your dick looks great." I kissed the head. Then I sucked him for a while, just to get him going. "Now keep it on all day," I instructed, pulling on his bathing suit. "More of that later."

Now he's saying to Javitz: "I *would* like to have dinner with you. Just the two of us."

"Well!" I say.

"Don't worry, darling," Javitz says, eying me, "I'm sure the topic of discussion won't be the fall of the Roman Empire."

No, I imagine it will be me: Eduardo will want to know just how deeply he should get involved with me. He'll ask how secure I am in my relationship with Lloyd. It's happened before. *Raphael* took Javitz to lunch, too, but by that time I'd grown weary of him, so his questions were pointless. Eduardo, however, is different. I want him in my life, somehow. So I'm glad he's connecting with Javitz.

"I'm sure my ears will be ringing," I say.

Eduardo looks over at me. "Don't you be so cocky, buckaroo."

He calls me this, as if I were the young whippersnapper, not him.

"What are you going to do with him?" Javitz asks, as Eduardo goes inside to use the bathroom.

"What do you mean?"

"I mean, he's falling in love with you."

I look at him. "And you, Javitz, would be the first to say that's a wonderful thing, that we should be able to have many lovers in our lives, define relationships as we see fit." I pause. "Lloyd's tricks fall in love with *him*. That's never been a problem."

"Except when they try to call him at home," Javitz says, pointedly. "Let's see, who has a fit about *that*?"

"Well, maybe I'm learning a lesson," I say, closing my eyes and facing the sun again. "Maybe I'm putting all my pontificating about a brave new queer world to the test."

"Maybe," Javitz says. "Just be careful you don't get hurt."

"Me?" I ask. "I'm not the one at risk here."

He gives me a pained look, as if I'm his most ignorant student, the one he'd like to pass but who just can't seem to get a grade higher than a 55. Then Eduardo calls from the kitchen: "Javitz, how about this Thursday?"

Javitz is still looking at me. "Go ahead," I tell him. "Make a date with him. He's the one who needs watching over. Maybe I've changed, maybe I haven't. But it's good you'll be there for him, in either case."

"Thanks for the assignment," he sneers at me, standing up to walk inside. "Thursday sounds great," he calls out to Eduardo.

My ears are already ringing.

Boston, February 1995

"Hi," I say.

Tommy stands between us. "Hi," Eduardo says in return. We don't shake hands.

Tommy is smiling. "When I mentioned your name a couple of weeks ago, Eddie told me he knew you from last summer."

Eddie?

"Imagine my surprise," Tommy says.

I look at him but can't find my focus. I fumble for an opening, for something to say. "How's school going?" I ask finally. My heart is in my ears and my mouth has gone very dry.

"Very well," Eduardo—*Eddie*—says. "I just got an internship at a newspaper doing layout and production this summer."

"That's great," I say, or at least I think I say it.

Tommy puts an arm around Eduardo's waist. "We should get together sometime, the four of us, you and Lloyd and Eddie and I."

I try to find something—anything—in Eduardo's eyes. But there's nothing: no sadness, no hurt, no recrimination, no anger. It's as if I hadn't mattered at all, as if I'd been no more than—a trick.

Then Lloyd is there to say hello, and Eduardo smiles. "Hello, Lloyd. It's good to see you again." Chanel takes him by the arm and introduces him to Kathryn ("Wendy and I broke up," I hear her whisper). And then he approaches Javitz, who alone gets a hug.

"You okay, Cat?" Lloyd asks.

"Sure," I say. "I'm just a little surprised. I mean—*Tommy?*"

"Don't be mean," Lloyd says.

How much does Tommy know? Did Eduardo—Eddie—really only say he "knew me" from last summer? Did he not tell Tommy that we had been lovers? Does Tommy not know how his darling Eddie broke my heart, made me love him against all tradition? Does he not know about the sex—that night, that night of passion when I fucked Eduardo, fucked him without—

"Oh, Jesus," I say to myself.

What had been the result of Eduardo's HIV test? Tommy had said the guy he was seeing wanted the test. That must mean Eduardo was tested, too—could he be positive? My boy, my sweet, sweet boy. And what had he told Tommy about us? Tommy's accusing eyes and voice come back to me now. Did he think I—?

"Cat, let's get going," Lloyd is saying. "I've got to drop Naomi off and then I need to do some paperwork that I brought home."

"Yeah, sure," I say, but I don't take my eyes off Eduardo. He's deep in conversation with Javitz. I hear Javitz ask, "You happy?" but I block out Eduardo's reply.

Tommy notices us getting ready to leave. "Going so soon?" he asks. "Why, this little party has just begun."

Suddenly all the compassion I'd felt for him earlier evaporates like a witch under water. He dances over to kiss us good-bye. When he gets to me he says, with an attempt at genuineness that I find repellent: "You all right, Jeff? You look pale."

"Fuck you, Tommy."

He seems taken aback. "What? What's the matter?"

I just glare at him, then turn to the rest of the group. "See you all later."

There's a chorus of good-byes, from Chanel and Kathryn and Javitz. And from Eduardo, too, a friendly "Bye, Jeff," as if I never mattered at all.

We don't say much in the car on the way back. It's a gray sky overhead now, the clouds moving in. "Looks like snow," Naomi observes. She's in the front seat with Lloyd; I'm stretched out in back. I close my eyes and see Eduardo, and it's raining, and we're standing under an awning, caught in the midst of the storm, our umbrellas turned inside out, and then we kiss, just as the lightning flashes and a new curtain of water rushes down the street. I open my eyes and I'm not in the car anymore. I'm out on Long Point, and it's September, the end of the season, and I'm watching Eduardo run away from me, back across the breakwater towards town. His untucked flannel shirt flaps in the wind and his hair—his thick, beautiful hair—blows back, revealing the sharp, pained contours of his face. It's the last image I'd have of him, until he walked through that door today.

"Jeff," Lloyd says.

"Yeah."

"You going to get out of the car?"

I sit up. "Where's Naomi?"

"I already dropped her off."

We're parked on Dartmouth Street. It's started to snow lightly. "Guess I must have fallen asleep," I say.

We trudge up the sidewalk, without words. Actually, I should be surprised that I haven't run into Eduardo before this. He lives in Somerville—what the boys of the South End dismissively call "Slummerville"—but Boston gay boys, wherever they are, have a way of crossing paths with alarming frequency. The truth is, I haven't been going out much this winter, have hardly tricked at all. Javitz was sick, plus there's been this stuff with Lloyd. Still, it was inevitable that I'd see Eduardo eventually. I should just be glad it's over with.

But Tommy? *We should get together sometime, the four of us, you and Lloyd and Eddie and I.*

Fuck *you*, Tommy.

What could Eduardo—Eddie—possibly see in Tommy? Oh, Jeff, I scold myself, stop being such a shithead. Tommy has beautiful eyes and a good heart. Eduardo sees the same things I've always seen in Tommy: his loyalty, his reliability, his devotion.

My anger evaporates. It's not as if I didn't deserve the comeuppance. Tommy must have anticipated it gleefully. Who can blame him, in a way? Might I have done something similar? Right now all I can think about is the terror and the rage that must be overpowering him. We were once compatriots, comrades in arms, and I suppose that bond can never be broken. How long ago it seems now. I feel for him, feel for his pain, his disillusionment.

And what if Eduardo is positive too? *It scares the shit out of me. That's why I could never, ever, fuck without a condom. Maybe two.* That poor, frightened child. I want to hold him, protect him. Could he possibly think it was me who infected him? It couldn't be—even though I always say I have no idea whether I'm infected or not. But I can't be positive; I won't entertain the thought.

But what stings the most out of everything is the complete lack of emotion I saw in Eduardo's eyes. These are the eyes that when last I saw them flashed red with anger and tears. Had I been that simple to get over, that easy to forget? Had it not been painful for him to see me again? Had he not wanted to touch me, caress my face, the way I had wanted to touch him? Surely he could see the anguish in *my* eyes.

Stop playing Susan Hayward, I tell myself. But I can't push Eduardo's friendly, full-of-nothing eyes out of my head, that untroubled "Bye, Jeff" from my ears.

At least, not until I see Drake standing on our front step, ringing our bell.

"Hey," Lloyd calls.

Drake gives us a big wave. Great. Just what I need.

"Hi, guys," Drake says, warmly shaking my hand. He appears excited, agitated.

"What's up?" Lloyd asks.

"I just had to come over." He's beaming. His face is flushed, red from excitement as much as the cold air. "I did it, Lloyd. I did it."

"You *did*?" Lloyd gushes.

"I *did*!" He lets out a whoop, as Lloyd lunges at him, embracing him roundly. Drake picks him up and swings him through the air.

"Excuse me?" I ask.

"Congratulations!" Lloyd laughs when Drake sets him down. "That's so great!"

"Thanks," Drake says, and for a moment it seems as if he might cry. "It *is* great. It's a great day. I have been thanking the universe all the way over here."

I smile, make a little wave as if to say: Remember me?

"Oh, Cat, sorry," Lloyd says. "Drake just quit his job."

I don't get it, and they can tell.

"I've hated it, really hated it," Drake explains. "Lloyd has been so wonderful"—and he looks at Lloyd now with profound gratitude and surely more than that—"encouraging me to break free from the hospital. It's a big change. I'm walking away from a lot of money. But as we've learned at our meditation group, the universe takes care of those who leap into the dark."

"Well, then," I say, with a little shrug. "Congratulations."

"Thanks, Jeff," he says, and he hugs me. *Ick.*

"I'm so proud of you," Lloyd says. "And envious, too."

"You'll take your leap, Lloyd. I'm sure of it."

I point towards the house. "I'm getting cold. How about we go inside and I'll make some tea?"

They exchange a look. "Thanks, Jeff," Drake says, "but I was just stopping by to give Lloyd—to give both of you—the news. I thought I'd go on over to Naomi's now and tell her, too."

"She'll be so happy for you," Lloyd says.

I smile, leaving them to one final hug and whoop through the air. I unlock the door, step inside, pull off my boots, turn up the heat, and sit down next to Mr. Tompkins on the couch. "May I *please* pet you?" I ask. I try, and he lets me for a few seconds, then turns to nip at my hand. I push him off the couch. "There," I say. "That's what you get for always being so nasty."

"What did you mean, you're envious?" I ask Lloyd when he comes inside.

"I'm envious of anyone being that free," he says, kicking off his boots in the hallway, shaking snow onto the hardwood floor.

I walk over and snatch up his boots, placing them beside mine. "I keep a newspaper next to the door for a *reason*," I scold.

But Lloyd's still talking, not listening to me. "I'd love to be able to walk out of that crisis program and never come back."

"How's Drake going to live?" I ask.

"Maybe he'll start a private practice. Maybe he'll travel and wash dishes in diners."

"Don't you see, Lloyd? The only reason he's able to do this is because he's from the upper fucking middle class. I mean, come *on*. Like *we* could ever do that."

"But you *did*," Lloyd reminds me.

"But not just like *that*," I protest. "I had to plan, and organize, and save."

"How do you know he hasn't?"

"Oh, come on. He doesn't have the kind of debt we have. He must have a nice little family trust fund somewhere, doesn't he?"

Lloyd doesn't answer. He's found Mr. Tompkins, and now they're rocking in the wooden rocking chair next to the wood-burning stove. There's no biting, none at all.

"Drake's a richie, isn't he?" I ask, getting in close. "The kind of guy we've never had much patience for." I place my hand on Lloyd's chair, preventing it from moving. "*Isn't* he?"

Lloyd looks up at me. "Let my chair go. I want to rock."

"I knew he was a richie the moment I met him. He's one of those rich Wasps with last names for first names. Drake. *Please*. Hasn't that always been a rule of ours? How we could never trust someone who had a last name for a first name? Carter? Forsythe? *Drake?*"

"Javitz?" Lloyd says sharply, looking up at me.

"That doesn't count," I snap. "Javitz's first name is *David*."

Lloyd turns his face away. I let the chair go and he starts rocking again. I watch him for a few seconds, but he just buries his face in Mr. Tompkins's long gray fur. I turn and walk to the door. I pull my boots back on, wrap my coat around me. Back down the steps and out to the street I go. I don't know where I'm heading, and I don't much care at the moment. The tears come, freezing on my eyelashes, but it matters little: all I can see is sand anyway, long windswept dunes of sand.

Provincetown, August 1994

"I've never realized how beautiful the dunes really are," Eduardo says, and I stroke his hair as he sits between my legs, his head resting against my chest.

We're on the north side of town, where few tourists venture, facing the beach at Race Point, sitting in a warm soft valley of sand, staring out over the rolling dunes. The sun bleaches them white as far as the eye can see, long graceful curves of sand, sediment that once was the stuff of mighty rocks, ground to fine powder by eons of waves. The sky over us is a sharp, cutting blue, unbroken by clouds. A few yards from us a strange, twisted tree grows out of the sand, its branches like gnarled arms reaching out to embrace us.

"I used to come here as a kid," Eduardo says, as if he were all grown up now, "but I never appreciated how beautiful it was, especially contrasted against the blue ocean." He reaches up to kiss me. "Not until you showed me."

"Well, at least you can say I taught you something." I smile.

"A lot more than that."

We kiss again. I've got that silly, spacey feeling, that absurd high I last felt sitting in the jasmine-scented bathtub with Lloyd half a million years ago. I had forgotten its giddy bliss, its preposterous delight. I rub my nose against Eduardo's and he laughs.

"I have something for you," he says. He sits up, reaches over to his backpack, and fumbles around inside. He produces a small white box. "Happy birthday, buckaroo," he says.

"Hey," I say. "The party's not till tonight."

"I know. I wanted to give you something when we were alone."

I carefully remove the lid from the box. It's a necklace, a small four-pointed star on a fine old gold chain.

"I found it in an antique store. I just love the shape." He gets real close. "I've never told you, but the first night we met, the night I slipped out—do you remember that?"

Could I ever forget? I tell him yes, I remember.

"That night, on my walk home, I saw a star just like that in the sky."

I caress the star between my fingers. "How could you tell it was like this?"

"It was amazing. It was so big. At first I thought it was a UFO. It had four points, just like that, really bright."

I smirk. "Maybe it was a Coast Guard helicopter."

"It was a *star*." He frowns. "You're *so* unromantic."

"That's not true." I kiss his ear, running my tongue over its ridges and then down his neck, the way that drives him crazy. There's a hollow spot behind his ear that I love. I press my tongue there, sending him into a paroxysm of passion. I see his fingers clench in a futile attempt to grip sand. We do it right there in the dunes. A passing ship might spy us; a ranger might stumble over us; we don't care. We kiss long and deep, turning our faces wet with saliva. We roll over each other, pulling off shirts and shorts as we do so, sand up my crack and in my pubic hair. I suck the flesh of his soft neck into my mouth. He gasps weakly, "No . . . marks," but it's too late, I'm sure of that. I go down on him, sucking his dick with as much fervor as I sucked his neck. He shoots, surprising me, and I taste his salty cum before pulling off and watching him erupt over his hard flat belly.

"Sorry," he says. "I couldn't hold back."

I just smile, wiping my lips.

The sun sinks lower in the sky. "Wish we had time to watch the sunset," Eduardo says.

I wrap my arms around his small waist. "Did you know that Provincetown is the only place on the East Coast where the sun sets over the ocean?"

"No way."

"Yes," I tell him. Javitz has told me this a dozen times. He seems to love the idea, brags about it, as if that explains his fascination with the place. "It's because of the way the Cape curls back into itself."

"I never knew that," Eduardo says. "And I grew up here."

I shrug. "Hang around me long enough, kid, and you'll pick up all sorts of stuff."

We get dressed, gather our stuff to head back. "Hey," I say suddenly. "Where's my necklace?"

We search. It's nowhere. I kick the sand furiously. It's like my little plastic witch: *gone*, gone where the goblins go, as if the earth just swallowed it up, snatched it away. As if I wasn't supposed to have it, yet again. "Boys shouldn't have necklaces," I can hear my mother say. "Boys shouldn't love more than one person at a time." I'm desperate to find it, cursing my carelessness. Sand flies in our faces as I dig, a dog after a bone.

"Jeff," Eduardo says, "take it easy."

"But you *gave* it to me. I don't want to leave here without it."

Eduardo smiles. "I can just see this in one of your short stories, how some poor soul lost a precious keepsake in the sand."

"No way. It's *such* a cliché. I'd *never* use it." I look up at him. "How come you're not upset?"

"Because I'm touched by how upset *you* are."

I continue to dig.

"Jeff," Eduardo says, embracing me, stilling my hands. "Did you ever see the movie *Harold and Maude*?"

"Of course I have. Ruth Gordon, Bud Cort."

"Whoever. But there's that scene, when he gives her a ring, and she throws it into the water."

"So she'd always know where it is," I finish.

"Right."

"Even when I don't know where *you* are?" I ask, touching his face.

"I'm not going anywhere," he promises.

We trudge back through the sand to the house.

He continues to surprise me, Eduardo does. Last night, he took me to meet his parents, although he debated the wisdom of doing so. Not because of their reaction to me: their acceptance of his queerness had been lukewarm but real. It was *my* reaction he worried about, something I understood fully. The boyfriend who filled the gap between Javitz and Lloyd had been upper-middle-class. Robert Chase Chandler. The Fourth. Later, when I told Lloyd about him, he said to me: "Never trust anyone with a last name for a first or middle name. Or with numerals as a suffix." I never did trust Robert. His family had three homes: the big house in Newton, a New York apartment, and a country house on a lake in New Hampshire. I couldn't imagine Robert ever seeing my parents' home, their faux oakwood paneling, their lack of a dining room, the way they ate every meal in the kitchen.

The house where Eduardo grew up was a small, one-floor ranch, not unlike my own parents' home. In the short driveway a child's bicycle—belonging to Eduardo's eleven-year-old sister—was trimmed with long green and red tassels. Along the edge of the house were planted pink and blue plastic roses, presided over by the Virgin Mary in a clam shell. Last night, as we approached the house, I remembered passing through the neighborhood a couple of summers ago. I was with a friend, one of the "fabulous" boys from Boston, the kind who had the big loft apartments in the South End and the lofty airs to match. He commented how many of the homes here in the Portuguese section displayed artificial flowers. *"That's* unfortunate," he sniffed, pointing to the rows of blue roses. "Plastic. Can they not afford *seeds*?"

"You're the first guy I've ever felt comfortable bringing home to my parents," Eduardo said, moments before we went inside.

"I'm honored," I tell him.

It's a queer thing being gay and working class. Sometimes I wonder what I might have been like had I not been gay. If I had been my brother, for example. My brother and I attended the same state university, but only I ventured into a world my parents had never known. And the truth is, had I not been a gay kid, I never would have been invited into that world. A visiting gay lecturer took me to dinner, and later introduced me to well-known activists and writers when I visited him in Boston. Every June, I'd head down to New York for the gay pride celebrations. I met people; I read books; I listened to speeches.

Had I not been gay, I wonder, would I have been like my brother, happy to be a Knight of Columbus chugging beer on a Friday night, playing basketball with the guys, taking his kids to spaghetti suppers at the local Italian eatery and his wife to the annual Spring Fling thrown by the Junior Women's Club? There's a beauty in that, of course, a simple but nonetheless profound beauty. Had I not been gay, that could well have been me, and I might not have been unhappy.

"It's nice to meet you, Jeff," Eduardo's mother said, shaking my hand. His father was behind her. He was a tall man, thin like Eduardo, but with a deeply lined, cracked face and big, rough hands. He shook my hand as well. Eduardo's younger sisters all watched me with curious brown eyes.

"Will you stay for dinner?" his mother asked. "It's just frozen fried chicken."

"I love frozen fried chicken," I said. Always have, ever since my mother would serve those Swanson's TV dinners and Ann Marie and I would eat them off TV tables watching reruns of *Gilligan's Island*.

Eduardo's parents warmed to me when they saw how I devoured that chicken. We talked about student loans and car payments and the problems with health insurance and cash advances on our credit cards. We had both used such advances to pay bills in the past: paying off debt by accumulating more. I'd used cash advances a couple of times as my share of the deposit on our summer places.

"*That's* how you afford it?" his father asked me.

"That and friends," I said. "We have a rather unique arrangement. Each of us puts in as much as we can, and somehow, we always manage to end up with enough to rent a place every summer."

"But somebody ends up paying more," Eduardo's father said.

"Yes. And it's not me, I'm afraid. I'm always on the lower end."

"Seems to me everybody should pay equal," he insisted.

"This way it allows those of us who don't have as much to share some of the privileges," I offered. "We all contribute to the summer in different ways. In the end, I think things balance out."

He seemed to consider this. "Pass me that chicken, will you?" He took another drumstick. "So what does your father do, Jeff?"

"He's retired now. He did a lot of things. Sold shoes, worked as a night watchman."

"Hey," Eduardo's father said, brightening, "I was a night watchman for a couple years over at the Coast Guard."

"Does your mother work?" Eduardo's mother asked from the other end of the table.

I turned. "She's retired, too, but for eleven years she worked at Kmart."

"Wish we had one of those around here. All we've got is the Bradlees down in Orleans." She smiled at me. I could tell she liked the fact that my mother worked. "Want some more chicken?"

"Don't mind if I do," I said.

After dinner she brought out a Duncan Hines chocolate cake with sugar frosting and M&M's on top—just the way my mother always made for me—and it was better than anything I'd ever tasted from the trendy French bakery all the gay boys patronized on Commercial Street.

"It's all in how you beat the eggs," his mother confided to me with a wink.

After we left, Eduardo said, "I can't believe how much they liked you."

"They're good people."

Eduardo stopped in his tracks, as if what I said had stunned him. "You don't know how much I appreciate you saying that."

"They are. They remind me a lot of my parents—if my parents were younger and cool."

He laughed. "If anyone had ever told me I'd have brought a guy home to meet my family, I would've said they were crazy. If they'd said the guy would end up thinking my parents were cool, then I'd have known they were *really* nuts. But listening to you talk to my dad, watching you eat my mom's cake—you made me like them more tonight than I have in a long time." He kissed me quickly. "Thank you for that."

"Do they know about us?" I asked.

"I told them you had a lover." He shrugged. "Let them draw their own conclusions."

"You going to be okay with Lloyd at my birthday party tomorrow night?" I asked.

"Sure," he said, as cocky as only boys can be. "Is he going to be okay with me?"

An interesting question. And suddenly I realize I haven't seen Lloyd in nearly two weeks, that we may have spoken only once in that time on the phone. "You seeing Eduardo?" he'd asked that one time. "Sure," I'd said, not thinking any more about it. Could he be staying away because of Eduardo? No, not Lloyd—such things didn't bother him.

Yet I feel a trifle guilty nonetheless, as if I'm betraying Lloyd somehow. How silly. How can we betray each other when we've opened up all the rules? He falls for *his* tricks all the time: those warm, funny cards he gets in the mail, the laughter from an unexpected phone call. But still, I can't quite shake the feeling that all this is somehow—different.

Now, on our way back from the dunes, I look at Eduardo as if I'm not sure who he is. "How come you never ask me about Lloyd?" I ask him suddenly. "About our relationship?"

"What's there to ask?"

"I don't know. What we're like as a couple, if I think we'll be together forever . . ."

"You will be." He smiles. "What *else* should I think?"

Now we're approaching the house, and I can tell Eduardo is looking to see if Lloyd's car is there yet. "Don't worry," I say. "He's not here yet."

"I'm not jealous of Lloyd," Eduardo says, turning to me suddenly. "It's the others."

"What others?"

"I know you go out sometimes without me."

"You mean, to trick?"

He nods.

"I haven't, not in a while."

"Could you tell me you never would again? That from now on, it would just be me—and Lloyd, of course?"

I shake my head. "I—I don't think I could tell you that, honestly."

"If you had," he says, smirking, "I would have known you were lying."

He turns to go inside. "Wait a minute," I say. "Would you *want* that? Are you *asking* me to do that?"

"No," he says deliberately, "I would never ask you to do that."

Javitz's words. He's been talking to Javitz. They had their lunch—a long, rambling walk along the pier as Javitz described it. Neither would reveal what they talked about, but I can hear Javitz's voice as plain as the sun setting up there in the sky: "You can never *ask* him to stop. That's the surest way to lose him."

I watch Eduardo as he goes inside the house. The screen door bangs behind him. I give him a few minutes to connect with Javitz, to tell him about our trip. Javitz will take care of him, I tell myself. Javitz will see to it that he doesn't get hurt.

I turn and face the setting sun. Damn the cliché. All I can think about is my lost star, somewhere out there in the sand.

Boston, February 1995

I'm packing, taking down the ornaments of our lives, the accumulations of six years, the little bric-a-brac that suddenly trigger a rush of memories and cause me to stop, sit down, and remember. The slightly moldy Indian corn from the drive through western Massa-

chusetts three Halloweens ago, the time we picked our own pumpkins and Lloyd tripped and smashed his on the sidewalk when we
got home. I felt so bad I gave him mine. The napkin holders I
bought for our first Thanksgiving here, shaped like little turkeys,
when Javitz made that horrible tasteless "Jewish soup" and we all
went crazy with the salt shakers. A Christmas angel, a gift from
Rose, that's topped our tree for the last five years. A program book
from a Boston Pops concert, the one where Chanel fell asleep and
snored through the overture.

"I've cleaned out the storage area," Lloyd says, coming in
through the back door.

"It's like I'm wrapping up little bits of our lives," I muse, folding
newspaper over a sculpture of a cat and a dog, made for us by an
artist friend who's since died.

"You need help?"

"Just in figuring out when and where we're going to unwrap
them."

We've been checking the paper every day looking for another
apartment. Nothing's jumped out at us yet. We go back and forth
on this subject, getting nowhere. Lloyd suddenly announced last
week he was tired of living in the South End; perhaps we should
move out to JP near Chanel? "I'm sick of living in a ghetto," Lloyd
said, and I raised my eyebrows at him. This was the first I'd heard
of it. Drake's words, probably.

"Might as well start packing, regardless of where we end up," I
said a couple days ago. "It'll make it easier to move at the last
minute."

So that's what we've been doing. Packing up all the little knickknacks, all the little decorations that serve as links between our past
and present, that connect our lives, that ground us in this place.
"Let's get rid of as much as we can," Lloyd said, and I agreed: six
years is a long time to accumulate stuff. But what could I throw
away? The Indian corn, maybe. But not Rose's tattered angel. Not
the photo magnets we brought home from our trip to St. Croix four
years ago, showing a long white beach and deep blue water. Not the
hundreds of little cats Lloyd has given me over the years, red cats,
green cats, yellow cats, blue. Not the little notes and cards ("To my
Cat—Love, your Dog") that have all gone into one drawer each

time I've found them hidden under my pillow or taped to the bathroom mirror. There are so many now that the drawer won't properly close. I search for one in particular. I find it: "Yes, in fact," it reads, "sometimes money *has* been known to fall from the sky." I stare at that note for a long time.

"I don't think I adapt well to change," I say.

"That's just hitting you?"

"I loved our life here."

Lloyd makes a sad smile. "All things to their season."

"I'm sure our next place will be just as wonderful," I say, but there's a part of me that doesn't believe a word of it, that I'm just talking to make myself feel better. "Yet this place will always be special."

"Of course it will."

I open the drawer in the little table near the door. My father's ring sits inside, the one he'd been awarded upon graduation from eighth grade, the one he gave me the last time I saw him, just a few months before he died. I never wear it: it's gaudy, with a big fake amethyst in the front. I keep it here, where no one can ever find it, where no one can ever take it from me.

Beside it is the ceramic German shepherd that was my grandmother's. I run my finger over the lines of glue that hold it together, right across the poor dog's snout. "Hey," I call to Lloyd. "Remember this?"

He smiles.

Finally, underneath, one last treasure: a thin green book. *The Giving Tree*. I'm afraid to open it, to see the inscription written on the title page.

I close the drawer.

"I'd like to have one last dinner party here," I announce. "Invite all our friends."

Lloyd makes a face. "It's too much work, Jeff. Let's wait till we're in a new place. Let's wait till we have some new friends and invite them too."

"What's wrong with our old friends?"

"Nothing."

"You're always talking about making new friends. What's wrong with the friends we've got?"

"Don't you want to expand our circle? Don't you want to see who else is out there? Wouldn't it be nice if we found a gay male couple to be friendly with? We've got dykes and single guys. Ever wonder why that is?"

"No."

"I'd like to find some friends who take chances, who take leaps—"

"Like *Drake*?"

He gets a defensive look on his face. "Yes," he says. "Like Drake." He pauses. "Like Javitz, too."

"I *like* our dyke friends," I say.

"So do I. That's not the issue." He comes to me, touches my face. "But think how it is for me. The way it's always been. When we met, I'd just broken up with Marty. I had no friends. I moved right into your world. All of our friends today came through you." He laughs. "Everyone at my birthday party was there because of you. Only Drake was there for me."

I get angry. "What about me? *I* was there because of you. Don't *I* count?"

"Of course you do," he says, backing down, avoiding an argument. "I didn't mean to imply that."

"I'm sick of packing," I say, tossing a plate into the pile of crumpled newspapers. "I'm going to start dinner."

"What are we having?"

I look at him and attempt a smile. "I thought I'd make you a vegetable pie."

There's not much that I can cook well. Casseroles come out always tasting the same, whether they're tuna or potato or garbanzo bean. And there's only so much you can do with pasta. But I make a mean veggie pie—a tumble of fresh vegetables (okay, sometimes they're frozen) in a cream sauce (Campbell's cream of potato soup) baked in a flaky (albeit store-bought) crust. For the past six years, that's been my delicacy. Whenever I tell Lloyd on the phone that's what we're having for dinner, he replies that he can't wait to get home—and that always makes me happier than he could ever possibly know.

"Jeff," Lloyd says.

"Yeah?"

"I need to be up-front with you about something."

"What?" I hate that tone. I hate always knowing when something's coming. He's going to tell me that he can't have dinner with me, that Drake's taking him to dinner, that Drake will be here shortly, that Drake is the man for him, that he's leaving me and I'll never see him again—

"I think I've OD'd on your veggie pies."

I look at him for a few moments as if I don't understand him. And I don't, not really. I haven't since that awful morning he told me there was no more passion. It's as if there had been a pod growing in the basement of this house, a pod that produced a new Lloyd, one who looks just like him, talks like him, but isn't him, not at all. The old Lloyd *loved* my vegetable pies, just as the old Eduardo loved *me*—just as the old Javitz would never leave me, not in a million years.

"Please don't be offended, Cat," he says, coming at me, hands wagging, unsure as to whether he should laugh or cry or embrace me or go away. "It's just that—well, you make them so often . . ."

"I thought it was a treat for you."

"It's very sweet, honey. Go ahead. Make the pie. You know how I love them."

I don't know who this man is standing in front of me. "So what *else* have you been keeping from me?" I ask.

He sighs. "Don't get melodramatic. We're only talking about a pie here."

"You know, I think I need to go for a walk."

"Okay. A walk's good. How about if *I* fix dinner? That'd be a nice change, huh? I mean, for you. So you don't have to cook."

But I'm already out the door.

I ignore the boys in the display cases along Tremont Street. I remember a time, and not so long ago, when I'd walk down this stretch and look for eyes. And I'd find them, too. Once, and not so long ago, a pair of eyes actually came outside of Mildred's and introduced themselves. That no longer happens—at least, not to me.

I find myself on the T. I change at Downtown Crossing, shouldering my way through the Saturday crowd. I settle into a seat on the red line, one of those spiffy new cars with the automatic voice announcing every stop. Except today it's stuck: "Central Square," it says over and over, and one old Eastern European woman looks terribly confused. I get off at Harvard, pushing my way through the throng of tourists and students who clog the street, just as the sun sinks below the horizon, bathing Harvard Square in long purple shadows across white snow. I trudge a block north, knock quickly on Javitz's door, and let myself in.

He's packing, too, of course.

"Hello, darling."

I sit on the floor where his old ratty couch once rested, where once a scared twenty-two-year-old lingered, new to Boston, staring around this room at all the books, listening to Javitz talk about activism, about the movement, about social justice and personal revolution. Now the shelves stand empty, covered with dust.

"When's the moving date again?" I ask.

"Next Saturday." He rests against a large cardboard box marked "Books." That's what all of these boxes are. That's the accumulation of Javitz's life, not the silly little knickknacks I've been packing. "So why is it you keep forgetting which day I'm moving?"

"I just forget which day of the weekend, that's all."

"Do you want this?" he asks. He holds a book out to me. *Love Goddesses of the Silver Screen.*

"*I* gave that to you," I say, hurt, taking it from him. I open to the first page. Inscribed there in my handwriting: "To Javitz from Lana Turner, Hanukkah, 1991."

"Guess I can't give away a personal autograph from Lana Turner," he says, taking the book back.

"Her daughter's a lesbian," I say.

"Yes, I know. She killed Johnny Stompanato."

"Can you ever imagine finding that much rage?"

"Yes," Javitz says, struggling to close the folds of one of the boxes. "Absolutely. Didn't we all feel it when we used to march through the streets?"

"Not rage like that."

"You're talking about fury. Blind fury. Poor little Cheryl lashed out in a furious attempt to save what was precious to her. She saw Stompanato beating her mother. It was completely understandable. That's why no jury could ever have convicted her."

"I can't imagine acting on that kind of anger."

"If you did, I think you'd level several blocks of your neighborhood." He comes over to me, cups my chin in his hands, as he used to do when we were lovers, when I was just twenty-two and eager to find my way in the world. "Do you want to talk about Eduardo?"

"No." I won't look at him. I'm quiet for a moment. "What did he say about me?"

"Nothing."

I laugh, bitterly. "That's what I thought."

Javitz strokes my cheek. It makes me uncomfortable. "Why don't you at least tell me how angry you are with *me*?"

"I'm not angry with you."

"Hah."

I pull away. "Okay, so maybe I am. But it's because I *care* about you. What if you get sick again? We won't be there."

"You talk as if Provincetown were on the West Coast."

"It's not the same. We couldn't be there as quickly."

"If I get very sick, I'll be brought here to Boston. This is where my primary doctors are."

"It's not the same."

He sits down on a box. "No," he says. "It's not the same."

"And I just don't understand why you have to leave so *soon*. The place Ernie found isn't going anywhere. You've paid your deposit, and your lease here doesn't run out till *May*."

"It makes more sense to try and get out of this lease, since I'm already paying money in Provincetown—"

"Yeah, yeah," I say. I've heard all the rationalizations. "It just feels as if you can't wait to get out of here."

"Part of me can't."

I swing around at him. "*That's* the part I don't understand."

The phone rings, cutting through the scene like the cry of a bird.

Javitz answers. It's Ernie. There's a rush of laughter, hitting me. Then Javitz gets serious. "*What* did she do?" he barks into the phone. It's something about a case manager at the Collective. One of those straight white HIV-negative women they all can't stand so much. Javitz will have his hands full when he moves. They already want him to serve on the board to stir things up, get rid of the deadwood, bring more life into their activism. He will, of course. That's what Javitz does best.

He raises his finger to me as if to say "One minute" and I nod, smiling a little. But when his back is turned I slip out the door, out into the deep cold night. I consider heading down to Jamaica Plain to see Chanel, or over to Dorchester where Melissa and Rose live, but I don't think I want to see any of them right now. Tommy's out of the question, of course—might he and Eduardo, even now, be locked in a lover's clinch?—and I certainly don't feel like tricking. So I just sit on a bench in Harvard Square until my cheeks get so hard I can no longer stand it. Then I stand up, head for the T, and go home.

Provincetown, August 1994

"Happy birthday, dear Jeff-and-Javitz," they all sing, squeezing in both our names, "happy birthday tooooooo youuuuuuuuuu."

Everybody claps and we both bend over, blowing out the *eighty-one* candles on the cake, the sum of both our ages. The cake looks as if it's a torch, but we manage to get them all.

"How old are you now?" Rose continues singing.

"I'm a day older than him," Javitz says, nodding at me.

"Funny," I say, "you don't *look* twenty-eight."

"Neither do *you*, darling."

"Thanks for reminding me."

Lloyd gives me a big kiss. I sense Eduardo on the other side of the room watching. Rose snaps a picture of the two of us, then Melissa pulls Javitz and me together with her in between. "Take a picture of me with the two birthday boys," she instructs her girl-friend. Then she whispers in my ear: "Are you sleeping with that child?"

"Yes," I tell her through my grin as Rose snaps yet another photo.

"Be careful," Melissa says, smiling too. "He's in love with you. I can tell."

So? I want to ask. Why is that something I need to be careful of? Why isn't that seen as a good thing?

Chanel and Wendy are here, too, but Tommy didn't come. I think he's still mad at me over that guy last spring. What was his name again? Daniel? Dave? Hell, what was I *supposed* to do? Tell the guy, "Sorry, I can't sleep with you, but my *friend* is interested"? (I can hear Javitz telling me, quite plainly, "Yes.")

Chanel's in charge of the music. "I brought both Joan Baez *and* Donna Summer," she assures us. "I promise to play an equal balance of the sixties and the seventies."

Javitz has his arm around Eduardo. "What about something for the boy here? He'll want something contemporary." He pauses. "Although, for the life of me, I'm not sure I know what *is* contemporary these days. Tell me, Eduardo. What's your musical taste?"

"I like older music," Eduardo says. "Like early Madonna, the Material Girl period."

A beat. Then Javitz says, "Oh. That far back, huh?" And he rolls those Javitz eyes.

"I *love* the decorations," Melissa smiles, pulling me aside. Red, pink, and purple crepe paper, twirled together, hangs in arcs from the ceiling. "*Very* classy." She winks.

"Hey," Lloyd says, mock offended. "I didn't have much time."

Classy. The very first out gay men I ever met, back in the early 1980s—the Material Girl period, in fact—used that word. I was still an undergraduate, and they were two wealthy white men who lived in a great apartment, held great jobs (architect and lawyer), and had great taste. "Oh, he has no *class*," they sighed when I expressed my attraction to a local salesclerk with a mustache and a 1979 Pontiac Firebird. I quickly observed that to be gay meant one had to "have class"—in other words, to reject anything in one's background that was less than absolutely, positively fabulous, and to pretend we all grew up upper-middle-class.

I look around at our little family. None of them here is very "classy." Melissa in her long carrot-shaped earrings, an aggressive femme from Brooklyn. Rose, a car mechanic, born and raised in the industrial valley of central Massachusetts. Wendy, a parson's daughter from the South. Only Chanel came from money, but her dark skin, her slanted eyes, her accent—just a pinch left, but still there —will always set her apart, stand her out as something *other*. She'd never be "classy" the way that architect and lawyer defined the term. She'd never be invited to their fabulous apartment, no matter how much money her father made.

When I dated Robert—that tall, blue-eyed, square-jawed blond Wasp who had the most amazing set of pecs I've ever seen but no soul lurking beneath them—I had none of these friends. Oh, I knew them: I worked with Chanel, I was in a writing course with Melissa. But we weren't *family* then. Robert and I spent our weekends with two or three other gay white male couples, all of them solidly middle- and upper-class. Two of them had gone to prep school with Robert; another graduated with him from Princeton. They were friendly, and bright, but I was always in the kitchen when they were in the living room, always reading a newspaper or watching television while they laughed their laughs, talked their talk.

Lloyd sometimes grumbles now that our little family only exists because of some connection through me. But he's wrong, really. It's because of *him* that our family lives: because of him and me together, as a couple, drawing them around us. I had no family when I was with Robert. When I finally had had enough, telling him and his pecs to go get lost, I made no attempt to keep up with the others. I ran into one of them a year later. "I'm sorry we haven't been in touch," he said to me. But I wasn't: that's just the way it is. Friends come, friends go.

But I don't want these friends to go. Lloyd and Javitz and Chanel and Melissa and Rose—and Eduardo, too: finally, *finally*, can't we find our own? Can't we pull this one and that one in from the rain and say, "Stay here. Stay here and let's be together when we all get old"?

That's when Lloyd gets beeped.

"Shit," he says, coming back from the phone. "I've got to go back to Boston. One of my patients was threatening to jump off the Charlestown Bridge. They've got him now at the hospital."

"Lloyd," I cry. "It's my *birth*day."

"I'm sorry, Cat. Really I am. But you're coming back this weekend, aren't you? We'll celebrate then. I'll take you out. Give you a break from cooking."

I feel like Lucy being patronized by Ricky, who can't stay for dinner because he has to go sing at the club. "I could go back with you now," I offer in a small voice.

"Stay here with our friends." He smiles, a little twinge of something at the corners of his mouth. "And Eduardo."

Oh, yes. Eduardo. I look across the room and there he is. But I don't want him—I want *Lloyd*, I want to make love to Lloyd tonight so desperately, even though that's becoming so rare these days, little more than jerk-off sessions while we talk about lobster and corn on the cob. I want the breathing position, and I want Lloyd's heartbeat in the still of the night. Can this strange, unexpected distance be because of Eduardo? I realize I haven't missed Lloyd at all in the past two weeks, two weeks wrapped up in the passionate embrace of my new lover, and I feel guilty about that. Tonight, however, I *do* miss Lloyd—miss him already, and he hasn't even left. "Don't go," I say in a small voice, but he doesn't hear me. He's already kissing Javitz good-bye, apologizing for darting off. It's Javitz's birthday, too, and Javitz is, as usual, more understanding than I am.

"See ya, everybody," Lloyd calls out.

There's a flutter of good-byes, like the Munchkins to Dorothy as she starts off down the Yellow Brick Road. Eduardo walks over to Lloyd and stops him.

"I'm sorry you have to go," he says. "I was looking forward to getting a chance to hang out with you."

Lloyd appears touched. "Well," he says, a little awkwardly, "maybe some other time."

"I hope so."

Javitz eases into me. "Well, wasn't *that* sweet?" he whispers.

It certainly was. A surge of feeling rises in my chest for Eduardo. I'm not sure what it is, but it's something. He continues to surprise me, that boy.

"Are you very disappointed that Lloyd had to leave?" Eduardo asks, coming up behind me timidly after we've all waved good-bye.

"Yes," I tell him.

"You don't like it when things don't go your way, the way you planned."

I look at him. "Who does?"

"But you take it personally." He's not making a judgment. He says it as a matter of discovery, as something he thinks he's realizing for the first time. Who *is* this child? What makes him an expert on me all of a sudden?

Still, I concede a little. "I don't deal well with rejection," I admit.

He smirks. "I don't suppose you've had much experience with that."

Javitz overhears us. "Please. Don't encourage his ego."

"Well, it's true," I say. "I've never been dumped. I've always done the dumping."

"You mean in relationships?" Eduardo asks, and suddenly I feel horrible, like a complete asshole, an uncaring, unthinking idiot. Javitz just smiles.

"Yes, in relationships," he says to Eduardo. "Jeff has never been the dumpee."

The party breaks apart shortly after that. Melissa and Rose are heading back to Dorchester, Chanel and Wendy are staying at a guest house. They've been fighting. They barely spoke to each other all night, popping in CDs without so much as making eye contact. I can't figure out what's eating them, but Melissa thinks it's because Wendy really wants a baby and Chanel says she isn't ready. "Wouldn't that be *lovely*, though?" Melissa said to me. "Our little family would all become aunts and uncles."

Javitz heads off to the dunes. "My birthday gift to myself," he purrs.

That leaves just Eduardo and me.

"Well," I say, "want to spend the night?"

He laughs. "Maybe I should just get used to it."

"Get used to what?"

"Oh, that whenever Lloyd's not around, I can come by. I mean, if Lloyd hadn't gotten beeped, you'd be sleeping with him tonight. I'd have to go on back to my guest house, sleep by myself."

"Or you could have gone out and tricked."

He sighs. "This is all very new to me, you know."

"Me, too," I admit. "No one's ever lasted the way you have."

I stretch out on the bed. Eduardo joins me, laying his head on my chest. "It's just that you always hold the upper hand, Jeff. That makes me uncomfortable."

"Look," I say, getting a little impatient, "can't you just see it as an opportunity? That whenever we have an opportunity, we'll be together? It might be that some night I'll want to be with *you* and *you'll* have other plans—a date or something. I'll just have to accept that."

He looks at me as if I'm being absurd. "Everything's got to be equal," he says.

"Fine. Then it is." I put my arms around him, my lips finding that spot behind his ear.

"Wait," he says, pushing me away.

"Eduardo, what *is* it?" I'm impatient; I can't help it. "Why does this have to be so difficult?"

"I can't help my feelings. They may be irrational, but they're my feelings."

"I can't help *my* feelings either," I say. But what am I feeling? I look over at him, at his big brown eyes, that shock of hair tumbling into his face. How alive I feel next to him, how vital. How—and I laugh to think it—*young*. My dick is heavy whenever I'm with him, my laugh quick in my throat.

"You've been incredible, buckaroo," he says, touching each of my eyes with his forefinger. "When I'm with you, I feel so good— so good about myself, about being gay, about everything ahead of me. But sometimes—"

"Sometimes it's not enough," I finish.

"Yes," he says, and the sadness in his voice is thick. "Sometimes it's not enough."

This is what I fear. This is that nameless gremlin that lives deep down inside my gut. *They will leave me. They will all leave me, because it's not enough. Because I'm not enough.* "Please don't go," I whisper, and I hear the shakiness of my words. Immediately I take a deep breath and change my tone, a veneer of strength rather than an admission of fear. "All right," I say, confident again, the way Eduardo wants me to be. I pull myself up, look away from him. "Go if you must. We can end it right here. I can't give you any more than I already am. If that's not enough, I understand."

But I wouldn't understand—no, not at all. Can he not see how I really feel? *I love you, Eduardo*—would it be so hard for me to say? Lying here beside him I feel adrift and confused. I thought we could rewrite the rules so we all could be together, define our own very special places in each other's lives. But why then is it so hard? Why does it feel as if I must choose between the two of them, and why do I feel that ultimately there will be no choice for me to make?

There's silence. "You can't go," I finally say, a cocky grin masking my fear. "It's my *birthday*."

It works. "Oh, Jeff," he says, lunging at me, kissing me so hard I think my teeth might crack. I wrap my arms around him, squeezing him, grabbing my right forearm with my left hand. He feels so thin in my arms, so slight. I can feel his heart beating between us. I taste the sweat of his skin, the staleness of his breath. Clothes are shed quickly and feverishly. We resume our tangle, our kissing, our breathing heavy in each other's face. "Eduardo," I say, pushing the word out with my tongue, using that tongue to lick his neck, his ears, driving him wild, making him pull at the sheets, utter oaths to God. My mouth is on his belly, his dick, his balls. I push my hand under his ass and take hold of it. His eyes peer up at me through his legs, now in the air, around my neck. "I want you so fucking bad," I tell him, and that's true: I want him more than he can ever possibly understand, I want all the blood inside him, all the thoughts in his head. He just cries, rolls his eyes back and cries. I feel as if I might cry too, but I don't: I hold it in, hold it back, the fear, the rage, the pain, the lust, the love.

I enter him knowing full well that I have not broken contact to find a condom in the drawer. I enter him feeling nothing but passion, and he says, "Yes, yes." I fuck him harder than I ever remember fucking anybody, and finally I do cry, because I can't believe how incredible this is. Fuck them all, fuck condoms, fuck all those hot healthy horny bastards, fuck safe sex, fuck AIDS, fuck Eduardo, fuck myself, fuck getting older, fuck the rules, fuck family, fuck love, fuck, fuck, fuck.

Then I come, pulling out as fast as I can, suddenly sick and ashamed of what I have done. I shoot onto his stomach, but I know my first explosion shot up inside him: the eruption of my love for him, shot up into the living, breathing, pulsing warmth of his body, shot with all the fury and the passion that has been bottled up for too long inside me, the most beautiful, most exhilarating orgasm I have ever had.

SEX

Boston, March 1995

What I can't seem to get off my mind this morning is that day with Eduardo last summer, the day it rained and we got caught on Commercial Street, taking refuge under an awning as the thunder clapped overhead, as the rain came washing down the street like a great torrential flood, and we kissed there in plain view of everyone, and never before or since did everything seem so perfect.

There have been too many gray, overcast days of late. I had become convinced spring would never come, that I was trapped in a twilight zone of eternal winter where time was frozen and change impossible. But no such luck: the days have ticked by, the boxes of bric-a-brac have grown, Lloyd and I continue to search without success for another place to live. This morning he went off on a spiritual retreat with Drake, a weekend at an ashram in upstate New York. "Maybe I'll come home with some answers," he whispered as he bent over the bed to kiss me good-bye.

I had only one thought: The Fens will be hopping.

My computer remains covered. There will be no writing today. Whatever it was that had aroused my passion just days ago is gone, evaporated like the snow on the sidewalks under a surprising March sun. I pull on a white sweatshirt and jeans with holes in the knees, exposing long thermal underwear. Then I slip into my old black leather jacket, faded remnants of old crack-and-peel slogans still on the sleeves.

The Fens are the Fenway Victory Gardens off of Boylston Street. For years they've been a cruising area. I'd heard the stories, read the reports of police crackdowns and gay bashings in the area. But here straight people also walk hand-in-hand among the roses in June. Fathers push strollers and yuppie women in Nike sneakers jog along the paths on their lunch hours. It's down by the river, where the reeds grow tallest and clump together, that gay men suck each other's dicks. A couple of years ago, the reeds were hacked down by police to stop such activity. At the time, I thought it was a sensible thing to do.

Now the reeds have partially grown back, and I'm glad for it. The first man I see is off the path, over near the river. The reeds in the still-icy water are bent and broken from months of snow. They look like the skeletons of flamingos whose feet had gotten stuck in the mud last fall. It is not a pretty place, not yet. Soon, the green will return to the grass, the leaves to the trees. Thousands of wildflowers will bloom: daisies and buttercups and bushy pink clover, shaking their little heads in the spring breeze at all the sordid activity around them. Now, under the first sun of the season, there are no other witnesses to what we do here.

The man nods at me. I think: Perhaps. He reminds me of the librarian. Slight of build, slight of hair, timid, startled to see me. I think again of the scene at the rest stop last year, when the tables were turned on me, when I played bottom to such a one as him. I shudder, for just the briefest of moments, discarding the thought. It is too intense, too frightening. To fall to my knees before this man is a terrifying thought. If I did, I fear, I would never stand up again. *He* would walk away sated, a sweet, sickening look of satisfaction on his unassuming face, but I'd remain where I was, unable to rise, my ankles caught by my desire and pinned to the ground. They'd find me much later as they would those flamingos: nothing but thin dry bones.

I move past him, farther down the path, towards a ring of trees. Here I feel safer, and the man I see in the shadows appeals to me. He is big, handsome, broad-shouldered. That his gut falls over his belt does not disturb me: here, in this place, perception is different. Anonymous sex is not, as Javitz likes to pretend, egalitarian. The very fat and the very old, the ugly and the sick still lurk on the sidelines, rarely allowed to participate and only occasionally permitted even to watch. Such a one as I remains prized: more than one scene have I broken up, the sound of zippers in my ears as I pass by, the scuffle of feet in the dust following me as I continue down the path.

But a paunch here is irrelevant. At tea dance, it would render the man unsuitable—no, more than that: invisible. At least, that is how he would be treated, although we would see him quite well enough and comment about him later, as if to say: "How dare he come here? How dare he offend us in this way?"

"That's the whole part of gay life that I can't stand," Eduardo's voice is saying, even as the man's thick, stinking cock is in my mouth. "You got to act a certain way, look a certain way."

"Oh, come on, like *you* don't play that game, with your boots and your vests without any shirt."

When was that? Why, even now, even here, do my thoughts wander back to Eduardo, of a long walk along the beach, ice cream cones melting over our hands in a hot midday sun?

"I don't," Eduardo insisted. "I'm not big and buff like you're supposed to be."

"You're twenty-two. You don't need to be."

"Puts a lot of pressure on us. I hate the whole tricking scene."

I laughed at him. "You sure could've fooled me the night you picked me up."

"You picked *me* up," he said.

"As I recall quite distinctly, *you* approached *me*," I pointed out.

He pouted, as if I'd never understand. "Why are gay men so addicted to sex?" he suddenly asked, and of course, I lectured him, telling him that sex was wonderful, beautiful, a rare gift—and that we as queers had one up on straights because we could embrace that gift, revere it. We'd already rejected part of the paradigm in fucking our own gender; why not go all the way and rewrite the rules of sex? "Sex makes us different. Not just *who* we have sex with, but *how*." Was it me who said that to Eduardo, or Javitz who said it to me?

"But why is being different always *good*?" Eduardo asked me, his face pained with an expression I didn't fully understand then and can only surmise about now. "What's so great about being *different*?"

I gag. The man is getting a little rough, pushing my head into his crotch, impaling my face on his dick. I struggle to break free, but he holds me there. I push at his thighs, finally wresting enough control to stumble backwards. His dick pops out of my mouth and wobbles in front of my face. There's another man now beside us, a fat, bald man whose stubby pink dick stands at attention. He pushes in toward me, but I turn my cheek to him. I cannot bring myself to touch him. I return to the first dick and resume my task.

He's gentler now, and he comes rather quickly, big gobs of white that streak the scuffed black leather of my jacket. He reaches down and tousles my hair, as if I were a good boy, or a good dog. I stand up and our eyes connect for the slenderest of seconds. These are the moments that continue to surprise me: the unexpected humanity of these places. Just when I've reduced this man to nothing more than a fat, smelly cock, he winks at me, and in that flash of eyeball I see a mother's devoted son, a grieving lover, a frightened father perhaps. He moves away brusquely, buttoning up his fly. I watch him as he goes, and wonder for a moment if I'll ever see him again.

In these places, few words are ever exchanged; sometimes not even a glance. But with each body comes another encounter, a deep, primal interplay of flesh. In those moments when a man comes, when he looks into my eyes with all the gratitude of a child, or when I come, feeling the warmth of a hand suddenly on my neck and the purr of appreciation in my ears, in those moments I love these men with all the passion with which I have ever loved anyone. I am lost in a deep and awful bliss, caught in a cycle of giving and receiving, discovering a generosity in myself and others I'd never known before.

Except, of course, for the fat man who stood on the sidelines watching, who zips up now and moves back along the path.

My heart aches for the man I have just sucked. The love comes fleetingly here; that does not make it any less profound, any less real. But in my mind I imagine him returning home: to his lover, perhaps, a gentle, understanding man for whom the fires of early passion have long since smoldered, but whose warm embrace is constant and enduring.

I consider leaving. I've gotten what I came here for: a hot memory, to hold in reserve, for some rainy weekend when Lloyd is gone, as he is so much of the time these days. I'll lie back on the bed and spit into my hand, stare up at the ceiling, and remember. No: I'll reconstruct. I'll view the scene as if I'm up there in the trees, looking down, watching myself and these two other men—yes, even the fat man will be part of my reverie. Mostly what I will recall is the flash of the man's eyes as he left, when our souls connected for that most tender of moments.

"I don't want to be fifty and prowling around rest stops," Eduardo said once when driving past the rest stop on our way to Boston.

"Don't be judgmental," I cautioned him.

"Okay. I accept your premise that sex is good, that we queers can define how we practice it without the rules set up by society." He leaned across the front seat to kiss my ear. "But I don't want to be an old queen jerking off alone in my bedroom to thoughts of little boys."

That image hangs around me like a pesky fly, and I actually swat at it a few times, until I realize it really *is* a fly, or some sort of insect anyway, roused by the unexpected warmth. I must have disturbed its nest as I trudged through the weeds.

Off to my right two men are fucking. I make my way to them cautiously. If they spot someone approaching, they sometimes break, bounding off like deer into the woods. These two don't. In fact, the one being fucked, bent over with his hands on his knees, gestures for me to join them. I decide not to. All at once I'm tired, aware of how my day is just slipping away, aware that tomorrow the gray skies could return, that more snow could still fall. Spring has a way of teasing you, and I'm not in the mood suddenly to be teased.

I hear the fucker come behind me: I imagine he has not pulled out, that no condom blocks the way of his infected sperm. Right now, as the sun beats warm upon my face, thousands of tiny microscopic viruses eagerly swim up the ass of the man who gestured to me. I do not linger long on the thought. "If a man asks me to fuck him up the ass without a condom," Javitz had said last summer, "I will." I was shocked then, disillusioned even.

I'm not anymore.

Provincetown, August 1994

"How could you do that?" Chanel rails at me. "He's just a kid!"

"It just happened," I explain. "I don't feel good about it."

I look over at Javitz, who's sitting across from me at the kitchen table. He says nothing. He just lights up a cigarette, breaking the rule about smoking in the house. Already the day drips with humidity. I'm shirtless. My back sticks to the chair.

"Things like that just don't *happen*," Chanel insists, scolding me as if I've personally offended her. Maybe I have. There was a guy who used to work with us at the newspaper. I didn't know him well. Teddy was his name. He was Chanel's best gay male friend before me. He's dead now.

She stands up. I wish she'd keep her voice down. Eduardo's still asleep. When I got up, after a night of dreams between sticky, sweaty sheets, I'd found her here, sitting across the table from Javitz. She and Wendy had had a fight, a major one, after they left the birthday party last night. Chanel had come here, refusing to share a bed at the guest house with her lover.

"She's completely selfish," Chanel had been protesting when I stumbled out to the table.

"Who?" I asked.

"Wendy." Chanel's eyes were bleary, from lack of sleep and—possibly, could it be?—from crying. I'd never known Chanel to cry, didn't think her the type. "She's a fucking selfish bitch."

"Whoa," I said, sitting down.

"She wants a baby," she explained to me, as she must have already explained to Javitz. Of course, I already knew that, but pretended not to.

"But you don't," I said.

"I'm not ruling out anything," Chanel said. "But she said she has to know *now*. Like today. Says she's waited long enough. If I don't decide, she's leaving me."

Javitz gave one of his long, long sighs. Chanel had come to him when the relationship was new, for his approval. He'd met Wendy, liked her, and that was that. Now, he was presiding over the end as well.

"Darling," he said to Chanel, "don't make any rash decisions just because she's being rash. And that includes saying no as much as it includes saying yes."

"She wants an answer," Chanel said.

"She also wants you," Javitz told her.

"I'm going to tell her no. I can play this game too."

I reached across the table and put my hand on hers. "Chanel, you can't just walk away from this. It's been four years. You've invested a lot in this relationship. Stick around for the dividends."

Javitz flipped me an eye. "Well put," he offered.

"Thank you," I said.

But inside, all I could think of was the boy in my bed, the boy I'd betrayed.

"He trusted you!" Chanel says now, pacing the room. "Hell, he *loved* you. I could see it in his eyes. How could you do it?"

"Give me a fucking break," I plead, standing up now myself. "I'm not the first one to have unsafe sex. It happens."

"Yeah. And people die because of it!"

"All right, stop," Javitz says finally, stubbing out his cigarette in the ashtray. "Stop it, both of you. Calm down." He looks up at Chanel, then at me. "Back to your places."

We retake our seats.

"What you did wasn't smart," Javitz says to me. Then to Chanel: "What he did wasn't wrong."

"What do you mean, it wasn't *wrong*?" She's pissed, whether at me or at Wendy or both I don't know. But she's pissed, and that's getting me pissed as well.

"It wasn't wrong. There was no malice involved. Can we remember for a moment that we are human? That we all make choices, and that we sometimes do things we might regret?" Javitz looks as I imagine he must look in his classroom, after he delivers a long soliloquy on the rights of man and is asked by a student if any of that will be on the final exam. He's tired of teaching us. Are we forever to be apprentices?

"All I know is," Chanel says, "he fucked that boy—"

"I'm not a boy."

It's Eduardo. Oh, shit. He stands there in the doorway of the bedroom and I imagine he must hate me as much as I hate myself. Not because I came inside him: he was good about that, saying it was an accident, we'd talk about it later. No, if anything, Eduardo would hate me for revealing what had occurred, for speaking without him here, treating him exactly as the child to which Chanel referred. More than anything else, that is what Eduardo resents.

He approaches the table. "*Two* people had sex last night. *Two* people fucked. Get it right."

I watch him in silence. I might even go so far as to say in awe. He commands the room, this tall, thin boy-man, this angry, tight-jawed twenty-two-year-old whose hair stands like a daisy field on his head, whose skin bears the wrinkles of sleep. He is the picture of dignity. I need say no words in his defense.

"*He* did not fuck me," he tells the table. "I *let* him fuck me." He looks down at me. "I let him *make love* to me."

"That's right," I say, and my voice, already small, cracks just a bit.

Chanel simmers in her chair. "But aren't you afraid, Eduardo? I mean, Jeff—"

"—isn't exactly a virgin," Eduardo finishes. He sits down. "Any coffee?" he asks. Javitz pours him a cup. "Believe me," he says after he's had a sip, "I'm *well* aware of Jeff's sexual history."

"I'm sorry, Eduardo. Sorry about talking about this without you."

He makes a wry face. "If I'm to be a part of this little group, I guess I have to accept a certain amount of loss of privacy."

"We do tend to operate a bit like the *Oprah* show," Javitz concedes. "Discussing unsafe sexual behavior and the dissolution of relationships around the breakfast table."

"It's pretty weird, huh?" I say.

Chanel reaches over and places her hand on top of Eduardo's. "It's just our way. Nothing leaves the room."

Eduardo laughs. "Oh, go ahead and tell the world. I don't care."

"Are you all right?" Javitz asks.

He shrugs. "I don't know. What does 'all right' mean?"

"Ah. *That* is the question," Javitz says. He turns to Chanel. "The problem is, my dear, no one knows what *anything* is anymore."

"I've got to get back to Wendy and give her my decision," Chanel says, standing up. "This is too much right now."

"Can we talk later?" I ask.

She shrugs. "I don't know where I'll be later." She kisses Javitz, who cautions her to go slow. She turns to Eduardo. "Take care," she says, as if she'll never see him again, as if he'll be dead by tonight. She doesn't say a word to me.

"I'm going to take a shower," Eduardo says. He looks at me. I can't tell what he's feeling.

When I hear the water, I turn to Javitz and tell him it *was* wrong.

"Define *wrong*," he says.

"Oh, shut up!" I've had it. I spin on him. "Shut up, please! You know what *wrong* means! We can't redefine *that*! Sure, he let me fuck him. Sure, he shares part of the responsibility in this. Forget even that I'm older, more experienced. Forget that I've seen people die, that I've lived through all this with you, and he hasn't. Forget all that. I was still wrong in what I did!"

"Why?"

He's so preternaturally calm it almost scares me, as if there's something he knows that I don't that he's going to spring at me, like a snake in a jar. But I persist.

"It's just wrong," I say, and I remember my terror, not long ago, when the man at the dick dock shot his load on my newly shaven chest. I remember Javitz's bitterness when I told him that story. I didn't comprehend it then, even less now. I sit down hard on the couch, banging my shin against the coffee table. "Fuck," I say, and think for a moment I'm going to cry.

"There's an article in this issue of the Collective's newsletter," Javitz says. "It discusses the theory that HIV is merely a cofactor in causing AIDS. That there has to be some other causal agent as well, that the routes of transmission as we have known them for the last decade are simply not enough to explain every case of AIDS."

"Yeah, yeah, I know all that. And some people say HIV has nothing to do with AIDS at all, that you can buttfuck to your heart's content and it's perfectly safe. And they're all as loony as the loons on Golden Pond."

He smiles. "Perhaps." He comes to me, sits beside me on the couch. He is not angry now, not bitter. "The point is, we just don't know enough to draw any conclusions about anything. There are certain precautions we should take—using condoms is one of them—but we've got to stop blaming ourselves for everything we do. We are human, after all. We are not saints."

I look him straight in the face. "You laughed at me when I was scared about being infected through a nick on my chest. But you're right, Javitz. We *don't* know enough about *anything*. Maybe sucking *isn't* safe. Maybe all those guys who are infected who think they got it through buttfucking really got it from sucking dick, through little tiny tears left by their toothbrushes on their gums. I mean, come *on*—how can we know for sure where the virus entered?"

"The odds are—"

"Fuck the odds. You just said it. Buttfucking without condoms cannot explain every case of AIDS. Neither can blood transfusions or needles. If even *one* guy got it through sucking dick—whether there's one or none or sixteen cofactors—if *he* got it, so could any of us." I look at Javitz and silence him before he can come back at me. "What if you're getting head—not even giving it, but getting it—and the guy sticks his tongue up your piss slit so hard it hurts? You know there's a tear there. There's got to be. And if the guy giving you head has got HIV in his saliva—and all the cofactors that are needed—well what then?"

"You get AIDS, I guess."

"Don't patronize me."

"I'm not. But saliva has not been shown to transmit HIV."

"Well, cum up the butt has. You can't have it both ways, Javitz. If we don't know nothin', we don't know nothin'. Maybe your big sloppy kisses have indeed infected us all."

I touch a sore point there. Once, a fellow activist, someone who was supposedly enlightened about safe-sex dogma, had recoiled from Javitz's lips. It had stung him. "Anyone who won't kiss me is no friend of mine," he'd insisted.

Javitz stares at me long and hard. "If a man asks me to fuck him without a condom, I will," he says quietly.

I feel something twist inside me. "You'd tell him you had AIDS, wouldn't you?"

"Why?" He smiles malevolently. "What did you say to Eduardo before you stuck your dick up his ass? Isn't the canon 'We should assume everyone is infected'?"

I'm stunned. "You're saying it's his responsibility, and not yours."

"That's exactly what I'm saying."

"So we've come to this now," I say. I want to get out of there, I want to go away from Javitz, not think of him in this way.

"Yes," he says, lighting a cigarette and not caring if he puffs up the room. "We've come to this."

Boston, March 1995

I'm clipping a recipe for tuna soufflé from the newspaper. Javitz is here. We've spent the day together, just lying around, drinking coffee, eating graham crackers, reading the Sunday *Globe*, talking about whether Dole will be the Republican nominee next year and if we can support Clinton again.

"We don't have much of a choice, do we?" I venture.

"Darling, we *always* have choices."

We're waiting for Lloyd to get back from his spiritual retreat. He's late, and Javitz hasn't seen him in two weeks.

"Wonder what could be keeping him," I say, checking the cabinets to see if we have enough egg noodles for the soufflé.

"Maybe he and Drake rented one of those by-the-hour motel rooms," Javitz says.

"Fuck you."

"I've decided against doing that safe-sex workshop, by the way, even if it does mean missing a dinner with Drake."

I check the date on a can of tuna. "More's the pity," I say.

"Darling, come on. You don't think Lloyd is going to leave you for *Drake*, do you?"

"Of course not." I place the tuna on the counter, sit down at the table across from Javitz. "But come on. *Something's* up with him. I mean, you guys haven't seen each other in almost two weeks."

Javitz tightens his lips. "I tried, but he was always too tired. Even for one of our late-night walks through Copley Square."

"He's going off the deep end, Javitz. I'm worried about him. These psychics and gurus—"

"He needs to do whatever sustains him."

I shake my head. "*We* used to sustain him, Javitz. You and I. And he us. The three of us. What's happened all of a sudden?"

Javitz grins. "I got sick and you met Eduardo."

"Oh, come on."

"Darling, you're being incredibly oblivious if you can't see how your affair with Eduardo affected Lloyd."

"He falls in love with his tricks."

"Not like that."

I squirm. "But Eduardo is gone. My place is *here*, with Lloyd. Now we're boxing everything up and we don't know where we're going and *you're* bolting out of here—"

" 'Bolting out of here'?" He grins wider. "Why don't we talk about that? I don't think we finished that conversation the other night."

I'm quiet for several seconds. "I can't imagine what Boston will be like without you," I say finally.

He reaches across the table and places his hand over mine.

"Take away one," I say, "and it's no longer three. Three has worked so well for us. The back-and-forth. The give-and-take."

"The yin and yang," he says, smirking.

"Whatever. But everything's become so hazy, so ambiguous—"

"I wish I could tell you I could see the future, but I can't." He stands up, props open a window, lights a cigarette, and aims the smoke outside. "Do you mind?"

"No," I say, "go ahead."

"I've known all along that Lloyd had wings on his back. I told you a long time ago that you'd be the one to build the nest, that he'd be the one who wanted to keep flying up to the clouds."

"I've never clipped his wings," I insist. "He goes off to these spiritual weekends, gets together with old tricks. We've *both* had enormous freedom in meeting other people."

"But Lloyd is looking for passion." He exhales and continues looking out the window. "Tell me about his relationship with Marty."

"I don't know much. I guess he was pretty surprised when Lloyd left. He was somewhat controlling, from what I gather. Tried too hard."

"Sound at all familiar?"

I ignore him. "But there are always two sides to every story. Maybe Lloyd just got it into his head one day that it was time to go find another path. I imagine poor Marty was devastated when he woke up to find Lloyd gone."

"Darling, I told you once that you'd give him nest and he'd give you flight. You've done an admirable job nesting. But what flights have you accepted?"

I scoff. "What am I supposed to do—move to *India* for a year?"

"Maybe."

I give up. I begin banging around the kitchen, hunting for the soufflé dish.

"Jeff, when I was in the hospital this last time, do you know how many times Lloyd came to see me?"

"No, but I'm sure you do."

"Just twice. And I was in for nearly three weeks."

"He was always getting beeped."

Javitz smiles, deadening his cigarette in the soil of a potted Swedish ivy. "Don't you remember how distraught he was the first time I went in, right before Thanksgiving?"

I did. Lloyd was a wreck. "I can't imagine life without Javitz," he said then. "I can't even *think* about it."

Javitz sits back down at the table. "You're not the only one pissed off at me for moving."

"I'm *not* pissed off at you," I say, exasperated.

He just laughs. "Oh, I suspect the three of us are going to have some very long talks along the breakwater this spring." He stands all at once, reaching for his coat.

"Aren't you going to wait for Lloyd? Don't you want to stay for dinner? I'm going to make this tuna soufflé—"

"Thanks, but I think I'll pass." He gives me a wry smile. "No offense there, Betty Crocker. It's just that I have a sense Lloyd is going to come back filled with white light—and there just might be some sparks." He kisses me on the forehead. "Have him call me. Tell him I miss him."

He walks through the living room toward the door. Mr. Tompkins bounds off the couch and grips him by the ankle, biting down. "See?" I call out, laughing. "*He* doesn't want you to leave."

"If there were lunatic asylums for cats, this one would be admitted for life."

Then he's gone. I prepare the soufflé, set it in the oven. I'm getting pissed and worried at the same time that Lloyd is so late, but then the sound of his key in the lock reassures me, as always. "I'm home, Cat," he calls.

The usual dry, light kiss on the back of my neck. "Did it go well?" I ask.

"Oh, honey, let me *tell* you—" He pauses. "Is that dinner you're making?"

"Don't worry. It's not veggie pie."

"Honey, I *love* your veggie pies. Please let that go."

"It's a tuna soufflé. I found a recipe for it in the food section of the *Globe*."

"Sounds great," he says.

"You just missed Javitz."

"Oh, that's too bad. But Cat, let me *tell* you . . ."

He informs me that the retreat was a silent meditation followed by a meeting with the guru of the ashram, an old, old man with long white hair and a long, long Indian name. Lloyd has his picture hanging in our bedroom over our bed, the way I once hung a crucifix as a boy. The guru apparently found much to gush over in Lloyd. Big fag, I'm sure—although Lloyd would insist that the guru is so realized that he's transcended any definition of sexual orientation.

"He told me that he could see my aura, that it was brighter than anything else in the room," Lloyd is continuing. "He put his hands on my shoulders and, honey, I could feel his energy in all my chakra points, especially here." He points to his third eye. He's taught me that the space between our eyebrows is a secret eye. If I didn't pluck the hair from that spot regularly, I'd have one big long eyebrow. I'm not sure what that would do to my third eye.

"We were allowed one question to the guru. I asked him how to find my path." Lloyd looks over at me. "He told me I would only find my path by myself."

"What does that mean?"

"That no one could show me, I guess. That I had to find out on my own."

"Find out after dinner, okay?" I place the soufflé on the table. "It's ready."

"You're being trivial about this," Lloyd protests.

"I'm sorry. I don't mean to be. But all this talk about your path. About taking leaps. My God, Lloyd, our whole lives are changing. We don't know where we're going to live. Javitz is moving away from us. Can we deal with this first and then worry about leaping and third eyes and how brightly our auras are shining?"

The soufflé smells horrible. It seems to cower on the plate below us, collapsed into itself like a deflated inner tube.

"Jeff, I can't separate what's going on with us from what's going on inside me."

"Fine. Can we eat?"

We're silent as I cut a piece of the soufflé and shovel it onto Lloyd's plate. It breaks apart. A hunk of tuna falls to the floor.

"I should just give up trying anything new," I complain.

"It's fine," he says, but he's testy.

It tastes terrible. I'm wondering to myself if I left out an ingredient when Lloyd asks the same thing.

"No," I snarl defensively, but suddenly I don't remember adding any milk. I *must* have. "Don't eat it if you don't like it," I tell him. "Here. Have some peas." He eats these from the bowl with his spoon. He picks at the soufflé. I force myself to finish my entire piece.

"So, are you angry with Javitz?" I ask, breaking the silence.

"Why would I be angry at Javitz?"

"For leaving us."

"Cat, he's not leaving us."

"What do you call his waltzing off to Provincetown?"

"He's hardly waltzing off." He frowns. "Have you shared these feelings with *him*?"

"That's not the point. I don't want to burden him right now. But you act as if it doesn't even affect you that he's leaving, and I know it does!"

He puts his spoon down. A couple of peas roll off the table. "Of *course* it affects me. I think about it all the time. Don't you get it, Jeff? Can't you *ever* see through your own shit and see what's going on for someone else?"

He stands up, pushing his chair back, scraping the linoleum. He's angry. Lloyd doesn't often get angry like this. But when he does . . .

"You know, you have been walking around here for weeks moping about leaving this apartment like it's the worst fate anyone's ever faced! And you know why? Because your routine has been tampered with. Your little schedule—getting up, writing, doing your interviews, going grocery shopping, shooting the shit with Melissa or Chanel in the middle of the day—"

I stand up, too—ready, *itching*, for the fight. "—*and* cooking and cleaning and washing your clothes and making sure dinner's on the table for you when you get home, even if it is just slop like this. . . ." Oh, God, even *I* can tell I'm playing a very bad Harriet Craig—or a psycho June Cleaver, I think with some horror—but somehow I just can't stop the tears.

But they calm Lloyd, as they usually do. "The point is, Cat, that's *your* routine. It's not mine." He leads me to the couch and we sit close together, his arm around my shoulder. "Look. Three years ago, you changed your life. I was so proud of you. You left the newspaper. You took a major leap, and it's worked for you. You define your life now as you see fit. You structure your days as you decide. Well, I want that, too. I want to find a way to get out of my job, do something else. . . ."

"Then why don't you?"

"It's not that easy. It's not just about changing my job, getting out of the stress of the crisis program. It's about looking at my whole life, and making some decisions based on how I live my life as a whole."

My tears dry on my face. I feel my testicles tighten into a cold little ball.

"What are you talking about?" I ask.

"You asked me if Javitz's leaving has affected me. Of course it has. But not in the way it's affected you. I think about him taking that leap, that chance, and I say, Why not me? Javitz has chosen to make his way, to find his path, according to his own needs. His own karma. That's all we can do, any of us. Ultimately."

I look at him. "You want to break up."

"No, no, you don't get it. I don't know what my path is. Maybe we're meant to be together for the rest of our lives, passion or not. But the only way I can discover that is on my own."

"There's passion between us," I say through tight lips.

Lloyd strokes my face. "Look, Jeff, I know your heart is aching for Eduardo. That's the kind of passion I'm talking about." He turns my face so that I am forced to look at him. "I need to be on my own to sort all this through. I can't be caught up in your karma, or Javitz's either for that matter. Not that I don't love you both. Not that I don't care, not that I don't want to be involved. But it's all become too complicated, too intense." He pauses. "I don't think we should live together for a while. We can put most of our stuff in storage. I can live at Naomi's. She has an extra room. And Melissa has a room in her basement where you could—"

"I'm *not* living in a basement room in *Dorchester*."

"Whatever. We can find you a place—"

"You don't have to *find* me a place. I'm perfectly capable of finding my own place." I stand up harshly. I'm rolling now. I can feel the rage swirling around inside my rib cage and surging upward, like heartburn after I've eaten too much broccoli or garbanzo beans. It forces its way up my throat and burns my tongue as it spews out of my mouth. "In *fact*, Lloyd, I know *exactly* where my place is. Right *here*! Right here with you, with Mr. Tompkins, with Javitz. Watching videos, and baking brownies, and making each other laugh. Holding each other as we fall asleep, waking up in the middle of the night and feeling the other one beside us. Right here, in this *fucking* apartment, right *here*, the three of us—you, me, and Javitz —because there's nothing wrong with the way things are *right now*!"

"Jeff," Lloyd says, his serenity an eerie contrast with my histri-onics, "I don't think even you believe everything is right between us."

I'm silent. I move over towards the window, finger the stub of Javitz's cigarette in the potted plant. Down below on the sidewalk two boys bundled up in red parkas pass by, holding hands. Lloyd comes up behind me.

"What are you thinking?" he asks.

"About my aunt Agatha."

"Who?"

"That, and the sustaining power of three." I turn around to face him. "It was supposed to last."

He seems speechless, so I continue, regaining my composure. "Oh, Lloyd, I can't claim to know the answers. I'm not even sure I understand the question. But I do know that we're both struggling, both trying to find our way in a world that no longer makes sense, where everything seems so unfamiliar and strange. We're heading into uncharted waters. And Javitz getting sick this winter—and then his move—have just driven home the fact that he won't always be around to help us navigate. I keep hitting my head against the wall as I struggle to find my way out of the maze—but *you*, Lloyd, you keep thinking you've *found* it—that this psychic or that guru will show you the way. And when you end up still unsure, still dissatis-fied, you blame yourself, that *you've* failed to find the true path. Might it be that it's right in front of your eyes?"

Lloyd's quiet for another moment; then he looks up at the ceil-ing and takes a long breath. I notice the curve of his earlobes, how they seem to lift upward, that adorable little quality that breaks my heart. "Oh, Jeff," he says, "maybe I am always searching. Maybe all my journeys *do* lead me around in circles. But at least I'm moving. At least I'm not settling, holding desperately to the status quo."

"Is that what you think I'm doing?"

"Actually, no," he says. "Oh, Cat, I want this to work out for us. I really do. But I don't think even you believe the path we're on is where we're supposed to be."

I look at him.

"If you did, if you *really* did, Eduardo would never have become so important to you." He reaches over, strokes my hair, runs a finger along the line of chin. "What attracted me to you at the very beginning was how stable you were, how nurturing you were. You grounded me, gave me a sense of place, a sense of home. But don't you see, Jeff? It's not that we don't have sex anymore—or that we've given up going to the Morning Party or trying to learn to water-ski. None of that matters, not really. I *love* our nights together, baking brownies and watching videos and sitting out on the deck with Javitz like three pompous old stooges. I *love* all that. But—"

"But *what*, Lloyd?"

"It's just different, that's all. It's not what I thought it'd be."

And he's right. Even now, in my terror, I have to admit that he's right. It *is* different, far different than I ever imagined it. Now the very qualities that had initially attracted us to each other—Lloyd's spontaneity, my nurturance—are what push us apart. My nest threatens to entrap Lloyd's wings; his need for flight leaves me terrified that I'll be left behind. Is that why I long for Eduardo? Or might it be for the reason Lloyd suggests, that I too crave to find what else is out there, what else might lie ahead on my own particular path? Whatever it is, I cannot deny the difference of which Lloyd speaks, cannot deny that I fall asleep with thoughts of Eduardo uppermost in my mind, despite the steady reassurance of Lloyd's breathing beside me.

"The difference frightens me," Lloyd admits. "Frightens me very much."

I want to comfort him. I want to reach over and caress his face the way he caressed mine. I see the pain and the fear in his eyes. He is a good, *good* man, I realize, as if for the first time. How much he loves me, and how well he knows me. But I cannot bring myself to touch him. To do so would not change the way he feels, would not persuade him to stay by my side, to never again talk about leaving. I curl my hands into fists to keep them from reaching out to him.

He seems to feel the rejection. He moves away, and whatever moment there might have been between us is over. "Lloyd," I say, sounding hard, "if you want me to apologize about my affair with Eduardo—"

"No," he says. "I don't want you to apologize."

"Well, then, I'm not sure what else to say." I pause. "Except that Mr. Tompkins stays with *me*."

"I would want him to," he says without emotion.

He moves silently into the kitchen and begins clearing away the dinner plates. I sit there on the couch while he stacks all the dishes in the dishwasher and turns it on. I sit there long after it's finished running, the steam seeping out the edges of the door. I sit there long after Lloyd has gone to bed, without saying good night to me. I sit there, in fact, until I wake up the next morning, sun streaming in through the skylights, Mr. Tompkins pawing at my chest, wanting food, wanting nurturance. Around me the afghan from the bed is draped: Lloyd must have covered me during the night so I wouldn't get cold.

Provincetown, August 1994

Javitz is talking about baskets and buns, how people don't seem to talk about them much these days. "Nobody says 'nice basket' anymore," Javitz grumbles. "All they talk about are pecs and biceps."

What's gotten him riled up is Mitch, a bartender at tea dance. "Look, he wasn't worth this much aggravation," I tell him.

"It's not him," Javitz insists, but he has rarely been so transparent.

Here's what happened: Javitz, Eduardo, and I went to tea dance this afternoon. There's this bartender, Mitch—six foot, big shoulders, big pecs, big arms, blond, blue eyes, naturally smooth, great smile, incredible butt. He's also HIV-positive. He gave an interview to one of the local gay papers about it. "I just want the world to know," he said, "that PWAs can be as buff and attractive as anyone else."

He and Javitz met at the Collective. "Come on by tea dance," Mitch had told him. "I'll give you a drink on the house."

So we went. Javitz wore his hot pink shirt ("I look my best in hot pink") and super-short white cutoffs. Now, Javitz doesn't normally go to tea dance. There aren't many with legs as thin as his who dare venture through the gates. But Mitch was there, behind the bar. He beamed when he saw Javitz approach.

"I thought you wouldn't come," Mitch said, grinning.

Javitz smiled coyly, actually batting his eyelashes a couple of times. Eduardo and I looked at each other. Javitz as coquette was not a sight we thought we would ever see. "I'd never decline a handsome man's invitation," he cooed, and I could've sworn there was trace of a southern accent.

"Oh, *please*," I muttered under my breath.

"Well, I'm really glad you came," Mitch said.

Javitz grinned over at me. That grin spoke for itself. It said: "See? You're not the only one who can get cute ones." It said: "See? I can still play the game."

The truly sad part was, Javitz has always disdained the game. But the moment he thought he could *play*—well, that's why I'll always despise Mitch.

He handed Javitz a rum and Coke, on the house. "I really wanted you to come because I respect you so much," he confided. "I respect you for how up-front you are, how you speak your mind and change people's opinions about PWAs." He dropped a big arm around Javitz's shoulders. "I thought maybe you could help me out."

"Help you out?"

"Yeah. See that guy over there?" Mitch pointed with his chin.

Javitz stopped grinning. "Yes?"

"The one with the abs? Isn't he gorgeous? Name's Albert. We call him Abs Al around here." His voice turned serious. "But he's scared, David. About the HIV shit. I thought maybe you could talk to him. I'd really like to ask him out, and you're so good at making people feel comfortable . . ."

I wanted to toss my beer in the asshole's face. But Javitz just resumed smiling. He looked back and forth between Abs Al and Mitch. "I'm surprised, Mitch," he said at last. "I would have thought your shining example would have been enough to convince him that not all PWAs were sickly, spindly creatures like me."

Mitch, big dumb brute that he is, didn't get the sarcasm. "No, I haven't been able to convince him." He tightened his arm around Javitz's shoulder. "Hey, we should get you in a workout program. Build up those pecs. I don't think it's ever too late."

"What is so goddamn wonderful about *pecs?*" Javitz asks now, hours after the experience. "Why have we become obsessed with a part of the male anatomy that serves absolutely no function?"

"Breast envy?" I suggest, trying to lighten things up.

"Today we accentuate those areas that are sensuous, but not sexual," Javitz continues, oblivious to my humor. He's on a roll. The sun has just set, and we're out on the deck, one of our usual sessions debating the state of the world, except that Eduardo occupies the chair where Lloyd usually sits. "All you hear about these days, all you *see* practically, are pecs, biceps, triceps, and washboard stomachs."

"There was a sign at the gym that read, 'No Pecs, No Sex,' " Eduardo offers.

"Can you *imagine?*" Javitz says. "No pecs, no sex. You can *play* with somebody's pecs, but in my book that's not sex. At least baskets and buns deliver. Nipples do *not* deliver. They're *supposed* to be foreplay."

"Well, it's very difficult for me, and it was even more difficult for me when I was a couple years younger," Eduardo says.

"Is that possible?" Javitz asks archly.

"You watch it, mister," Eduardo says, shooting him a look. "No, I mean it. When I was sixteen, seventeen, just coming out to myself, walking down Commercial Street, seeing all those guys with their shirts off parading out of tea dance, I thought, This is how I've got to look if I'm going to be considered attractive."

"Well, don't you worry, Brad Pitt," I tell him. "I like you just the way you are."

Eduardo makes a face at me. He's said he could look like Brad Pitt if he worked at it. "He's thin like me," he insisted. "I could be him."

"Yeah, and I could be Jean-Claude van Damme," I teased.

"Point is, all this focus on how we look has inhibited our activity," Javitz is expounding. I turn my attention back to him. He's really wound up. Mitch has touched a very raw nerve. When Javitz gets this way, he reacts with his best defense: his mind. "The image has become *so* idealized, so unattainable, that we actually stop playing the game. We think we can't compete. We think we're out of our leagues." He gives me that nose-and-eyes look. "Even *you*, Jeffrey. Don't pretend it's not so."

"I admit these past few years have increasingly been a challenge," I say, smiling.

"The image is *so* young and *so* white and *so* buff and so—*clean*—for want of a better word," Javitz says. "That very cleanliness seems to imply there are certain limits with what one might do with that body. *Please*—Mitch is a fucking antiseptic android. So clean, so safe, that it doesn't allow us to explore the limits of our fantasies."

"I don't follow," Eduardo says.

"In other words," I suggest, "you wouldn't consider putting Mitch in a sling."

"I wouldn't consider putting anyone in a sling."

Javitz points his cigarette at him. "Exactly. You have not been encouraged to push your limits."

"Oh, I don't know about that," Eduardo says, looking at me.

"Of course," Javitz goes on, standing now, tossing back his long hair, sweeping across the deck with the moon behind him, the steady rushing sound of the waves on the sand seeming to keep time with his steps, "it all comes back to one thing: fear of sex in the age of AIDS."

I knew we'd get back to that. My head still hurts from this morning, when Chanel had practically accused me of attempted murder, or at the very least, risk of injury to a minor. But when I watched Eduardo's sinewy body move across the room, I wondered what risks we had *really* taken. My mind was still soft and tired from the talk with Javitz. Eduardo and I haven't really had a chance to talk by ourselves yet. We've avoided the topic all day. Was Javitz deliberately bringing us back to this point?

"It's a redirection of energy," Javitz continues. "Instead of sucking and fucking, we're pumping. It's having your body exposed, and acknowledged, but in a safe way. In the sixties and seventies, there wasn't this kind of flaunting, this 'look but don't touch but make sure you look and look again' attitude. Sure, we took our shirts off in bars, but not on the dance floor merely for display. We took off our shirts—and more importantly our *pants*—in the back room for sex."

"Back rooms scare me," Eduardo says.

Javitz has concluded his pontification. He's tired himself out. He merely sighs standing over Eduardo. "They should, darling," he says. "They should."

With that, he leaves us alone. He'll go into his room now, lick his wounds by himself. What a world, I think to myself. This whole scene. Strange what your dick can lead you to do.

Eduardo and I don't say anything for a while. We just sit here, looking up at the sky, listening to the surf and the occasional high-pitched call of a piping plover. Finally I ask:

"Do you want to get tested?"

He turns to look over at me. He reaches across the space between our chairs and takes my hand. "No," he says. "Why, so I can take poison if I turn out to be positive?"

He's listened to me more than I've realized. "I'd go with you, get tested myself, if that's what you wanted."

"What good would it do us to know?"

"Okay." I sigh. "Eduardo, I never meant to do anything that might harm you. I—I care about you too much."

"I know that."

"I'm sorry."

"Jeff, there's no need—"

"Yes, there is. I mean it. I don't want to hurt you." I get off my chair, squat down in front of him, his hand still in mine. It's as if I'm proposing marriage or something. "I don't mean just about this. I don't want to hurt you in any way."

He seems touched. "Then don't get caught up in the scene," he says earnestly. "The whole tricking scene, the whole body image, cruising, bar scene." He grips my hand tightly.

"Are you asking me not to trick?"

He looks at me. The earnestness is gone, and he relaxes his grip on my hand. "No. I could never ask you to do that."

Go ahead, I want to say. *Ask me.* In this moment, I would promise him anything. But I say nothing in response.

Eduardo stands then. "I think I want to sleep alone tonight," he says.

"Okay," I say, but I feel confused, abandoned. I think about playing with him, pouting like I usually do to get my way. But I don't.

He gives me a quick kiss on the cheek.

"Want to do something tomorrow?" I ask.

"I don't know, Jeff. Maybe I need a couple days on my own."

"What's the matter?"

"Nothing. I just need some time."

"Talk to me—"

"Please, Jeff. It's been a long day, a long couple of weeks. And you always holding the upper hand, telling me when I can come over, when I can't. I just need some time to think, to be by myself." He kisses me again on the cheek. "Okay?"

I shrug. "Whatever."

So I watch him go, off down the beach, disappearing into the haze and the dark purple night, a small, slight figure leaving behind only a trail of footprints to mark where he's been. Eventually these too are claimed by the unrelenting tide, and I'm left with nothing but the stars and the sky and the sound of the surf.

Boston, March 1995

It's the night before Javitz leaves us. He's all packed, the boxes of books are piled high. The movers will be here promptly at eight tomorrow morning. We asked him if he wanted a party, some sort of testimonial. After all, he's been an activist here for a long time, been involved in some key fights. He's a fucking *icon*, for God's sake, or so the newspapers have claimed. A lot of people would want to wish him well. But no, he insisted. "It'd only turn into a wake." No doubt he's right.

It was supposed to be just the three of us tonight, a small pizza-

on-cardboard-boxes kind of celebration. But I hardly feel very celebratory. Lloyd got beeped, of course, and isn't here. Sometimes I
wonder what would happen if I took the battery out of that damn
thing without him knowing. Who might die? Who might hack their
husband or wife into a million little pieces? Who would care?

"Well." I lift a paper cup of champagne. "Happy leaping."

Javitz smiles. "I felt a touch of the melancholy this morning. I
want you to know that. It isn't all joy leaving Boston. There are
many things I'll miss."

"Like what?" I ask.

"All-night convenience stores. Fresh produce in January. Live
theater. You."

I smirk. "You talk as if Provincetown were on the West Coast."

"Come with me."

"What?"

"You heard me."

He's being cryptic. I try to figure out his riddle. "I don't understand."

He takes another slice of pizza. His side has pepperoni, meatballs,
and pineapple. I'll never understand his eating habits. He takes a
bite, wipes his mouth with a paper napkin, and says, "Where else
are you going to go?"

I watch him swallow. "Are you serious?"

"Lloyd's going to stay with Naomi. Darling, you just need somewhere temporary to stay. Why not Provincetown? I've got a second
bedroom, remember. It was supposed to be our summer house."

I can't think. "You mean, leave Boston?"

"Look at it as going to Provincetown for the summer one more
time. I know you didn't want to do that scene all over again. So
don't. Come and finish the novel."

"Do you *want* me to go with you? I mean, is that it? Are you
concerned about being alone?"

" 'Want' is the correct word. Yes, I *want* you to come. No, I
don't *need* you to come."

"Are you just feeling sorry for me? Because if that's the
case—"

"Fuck you, Jeff." Javitz stands up. He accidentally knocks over
the pizza box. I catch it before it falls facedown on the hard-

wood floor, burning my hands slightly as I grip the greasy underside.

Javitz lights a cigarette. He exhales with a flourish. "Can you never look beyond yourself? Are you so trapped by your own perception of the world you can't imagine there are other ways of seeing things?" He takes another deep drag.

"I think I have an open mind about things. *You're* the one who thinks he's always right."

"Where's *that* coming from?" He exhales smoke and I cough.

"Can you please? I know this is your house but these are my lungs." I stand up now. I've lost my appetite.

We both pace around the room a bit, our footsteps echoing along darkened, empty corridors. I rest my head finally against the old couch, tipped on its side. I smell Javitz on its cushions: the smoke, of course, but coffee too, hazelnut coffee and cream, and bacon, and Bisquick waffles, from hundreds of breakfasts prepared in this place, many for me. I remember sitting on that couch my first day here, so very long ago, in another time, another world. The couch smelled of Javitz then, too, this exact fragrance. It will smell like this even after he is dead, and the couch sits in the back of some thrift shop, marked "$100 or Best Offer."

"I'm sorry," I say.

"I would hope so, Jeff." He's not letting this go. "This has all been about you. My whole decision to leave. That's all you've seen, how it would affect you. That's okay, if you had expressed that to me. If you had told me why you were angry with me."

"I did. I told you."

"No you didn't. You said you were angry because you were afraid if I got sick, I wouldn't have you to take care of me. The reality is, you're angry with me because you're afraid I'm not going to take care of *you* anymore."

I look at him for several seconds. "That's not true," I lie. "I don't need anyone to take care of me."

"Oh, please, don't be so transparent, Jeff. You're made of better stuff than that. If you're going to try noble, give me Bette Davis at the end of *Dark Victory*. Or Crawford in *Mildred Pierce*. You're not even up to the standard of Luise Rainer."

I'm insulted. "Now it's my turn to say 'fuck you.'"

"Go right ahead. I wish you had a lot earlier. Gotten it off your chest. Then maybe these last few weeks wouldn't have been all you, you, *you*."

"That's not fair," I protest.

"Don't talk to me about fair," he says. I'd forgotten: Javitz won't use that word. Nothing's fair in life, he says. Fair has nothing to do with anything. "Talk to me about why you're angry with me."

I walk over to the window, look down on Harvard Square. Tomorrow Javitz won't live here anymore. I turn back to face him. "All right," I admit. "I *am* angry at you. Angry because you're walking out on me. On our family. There was magic, *real* magic between us. Now you're just walking away from that. And not just by moving to Provincetown. Once it was *us*, Javitz. The three of us. We made a family, whole and complete. But now I feel I'm no longer in your club, not in your league. You've turned your back on me because I'm not positive—or don't know if I am, anyway."

He makes a face. For once, I can't read him. I don't know if it's anger, surprise, or hurt. He starts to say something, then reconsiders. I'm not sure if I should go on, if I've already said too much, and you can't take back words once they're out of your mouth. But the silence unnerves me. I continue.

"Ernie," I say. "It's been him each time you've made a life decision over the past year. It used to be me. Me and Lloyd."

Javitz sits down on a cardboard box.

"Now you're leaving, packing up and going. You're moving totally into that world now. A world that doesn't include me."

"I just asked you to come with me."

"But why?"

"Oh, Jeff." He reaches for another cigarette, then reconsiders that, too. "I'm not going to sit here and deny that I need the company, the community, of other positives. Yes, I've gone to Ernie. That's because I feel I have too often closed myself out in the past from what I really need by populating my family exclusively with negatives—or, excuse me, with people who *believe* they're negative. And yes, I'm moving into a much different world now. But if you think that world excludes you, then that's your issue, not mine. Seems to me I remember you turning down a couple of invitations to join us for dinner at the Collective. How much distance have you created yourself?"

He stands up and begins to approach me, but stops midway across the floor. "Think about it. When was the last time I had a date? Not a quickie on the side of the road or in the dunes. I mean, a *date*."

I don't remember.

"*Four years*, Jeff." He holds his hands out to me, almost imploringly. "Talk to me about how *I* feel. Why I'm leaving Boston. Why I'm *really* leaving Boston. You've never asked."

"I thought I had," I say, but inwardly, I know I haven't. It was much too frightening a question to pose, and even now, I hope he doesn't answer it.

Too late. He tells me. "I'm leaving Boston because of you."

If he was hoping to startle me, he must be disappointed. "Maybe I already suspected that was the case," I tell him.

"Oh, really now. Why don't you expound on that?"

"It must be hard for you. I mean, Lloyd and I have been having problems these last few months. Perhaps that reminds you of us— you and I, when our relationship ended, all over again. Perhaps you see me struggling to make it work with Lloyd, and perhaps you feel I didn't do that with you. Perhaps the thought of our three-way friendship ending or changing unsettles you, because it brings up your feelings for me all over again."

He stares at me unblinking.

"I know we never processed the whole ending. I know you were hurt. And I'm sorry about that."

I take a step forward, prepared to embrace him. That's when he makes a sound, a sound I first take to be a laugh, but of course it can't be. I look at him through the gathering dusk. Is he crying? I'm not sure I can handle Javitz crying.

"Oh God, Jeff," he says, and then I realize he *is* laughing. He's laughing as if despite himself. His face is contorted in an expression of mirth and derision.

He's laughing at me.

"Is that why you think I want you to come with me to Provincetown?" he gasps.

He can tell by my face that I'm hurt. He stops laughing. But he still appears hard, brittle, distant. "You really *are* something, you know that?" he says. "You really are."

"I was trying to be sincere."

"Jeff, I love you. Profoundly. Always have, always will. But I am not *in* love with you. Does it hurt too much if I tell you I never was? Oh, you meant the world to me. You let me teach you. You let me see the world through your young and eager eyes. You gave me youth. You gave me a sense of myself I had forgotten. Oh, yes, I loved you. Very, very much. But when our relationship ended, it was right. The sweet joy of it all was finding Lloyd, and creating our family, finding a new way to be with both of you in our lives together."

I'm not sure I understand any of this. "Then what do you mean you're leaving because of me? It doesn't make sense. You're leaving that family we created."

"Precisely, Jeff." Now he *does* approach me, and he takes me in his arms. For once, I do not retreat, do not grow stiff. His touch feels as it did a decade ago, soft and warm and reassuring. I sink my face into his cashmere sweater, taking comfort in the warmth and the fragrance of smoke I find there. "That's why I need to go," he says, stroking my hair. "I need to find the next chapter of my life. One that most likely is going to be my last, and so extra care must be taken in its execution."

"But why does it have to be another chapter? Why not just let this one keep going?"

"Because we have to move with the times. Darling, I'm not the man I was two summers ago. Do you remember the time I came home on the back of that motorcycle? How glorious that was. Riding through town as the sun broke over the horizon, the wind in my hair. We'd fucked all night, not a moment of sleep. How utterly magnificent. But I couldn't keep up that pace last summer. It's age, it's AIDS, it's everything—why, I doubt if *you* could jerk off on the dance floor of an underwear party again."

"Could too," I say, muffled, my lips in his sweater.

He smiles. I can hear it in his voice. "Maybe you could at that. But do you know what? I don't think you *want* to anymore. I know *I* want something else. I'm not quite sure what yet. I know it's not about tricking, or even sex in the dunes. It's certainly not about activism anymore. It's certainly not about fights at the State House or going to jail. I'm not sure what this next chapter is, but I *am* sure of one thing."

"What's that?"

"I want it to include you."

"Families come, families go," I say.

"Not my family."

I start to cry. "Please don't ever laugh at me like that again."

"I'm sorry. I promise."

"Does your next chapter include Lloyd?" I ask, pulling out from him to look up into his eyes.

I see pain there. I'm not the only one who fears losing Lloyd.

"I hope so, darling. I truly hope so."

"Why can't we all be together? Why does everything have to change?"

"Who knows?" He gently frees me from his embrace. I'm not sure I wanted it to break quite yet, but that's okay. Javitz has resumed walking, lighting a cigarette but this time opening a window and aiming his smoke into the night. "Maybe it's because of Adam and Eve. Original sin and all that. Maybe it's all the karma built up from all our previous lives. Maybe it's American capitalism, teaching us never to be satisfied, to always want more."

He holds aloft a paper cup of champagne. "Maybe it's just the way things are," he says.

"To change," I propose.

He smiles.

"To change."

We both drink.

"Now," he says, "if you plan on helping me move, be here at eight o'clock tomorrow morning." He pauses. "That goes double for Lloyd."

Provincetown, August 1994

Provincetown storms in the summer are fast, furious, and very loud—much the same as Provincetown boys in the summer. This storm has caught us by complete surprise. We have no umbrellas, no caps on our heads. It tears down the street like a sports car out of control, veering this way and that, crashing into street posts and knocking over trash cans. We had not heeded the distant roll of thunder we heard when we left the house, that dull echo of things to come. The sky was slate gray, but we assumed we could make it back before the rain. The air was heavy, thick with unpopped moisture.

We were in the video store when the first resounding clap of thunder made Eduardo's eyes light up. "Did I ever tell you thunderstorms turn me on?" he asked.

"Ah," I said, grinning ear to ear, "now the fantasies start tumbling out."

So it doesn't surprise me that we've started to kiss standing here under an awning in the center of Commercial Street. Boys can kiss here; it's not like any other town in the world. Passersby will smile indulgently at the sight of two boys kissing. And in the midst of a rainstorm, it somehow takes on an even greater poignancy, a heightened appreciation for the passion between men.

"Are we attracting attention?" Eduardo lifts his upper lip from mine for just a moment.

"I think so," I mumble.

"Good," he says, and gets back into his work.

The rain whips under the awning, getting our lower legs wet. We yelp a bit, but don't stop kissing.

"I can't wait to fuck," Eduardo says. I can feel his hard dick pressing into my thigh. "God, Jeff, I never thought I could love sex this much."

Me either, I realize—except I *did* love sex this much with Lloyd once, a hundred sweet years ago.

This week is the last chance for Eduardo and me to be together. Next week he's off to school, settling into a new apartment in Boston. Oh, we'll see each other there, but I know he's scared that I'm going to disappear out of his life. Tonight, Javitz is out with Ernie; we'll have the house to ourselves. I figured we'd make dinner, rent a video, maybe even bake brownies. He's never seen *Whatever Happened to Baby Jane?* so that's the one we settled on. "Every gay man *must* see this movie," I told him. "You're not officially queer until you've seen it."

"Just don't do your Bette Davis imitation," he insisted.

I popped my eyes and clipped my words. "Whatevah you want, Ed-wah-do."

"Oh, *God* . . ."

Eduardo hates it when I launch into my Bette Davis routine. Lloyd thinks it's because I represent "father energy" to Eduardo, so it's a little disillusioning for him to see me acting queeny. "But that's homophobic," I told him. "He's *twenty-two*," Lloyd countered.

I've managed to spend the entire month of August here in Provincetown. Lloyd hasn't been with me very often. This weekend he's at a conference in New York. But he's taking all next week off, a long-delayed vacation. "Think you'll have any time for me?" he asked, half-teasingly. He knows how much time I've been spending with Eduardo.

When we got to the video store, *Baby Jane* had already been checked out. "Can we get *When Harry Met Sally* instead?" Eduardo asked.

"No!" I barked. "I'm tired of all that heterosexual pablum Hollywood forces down my throat." I decided on an impromptu queer-culture lesson. "You know, it didn't used to be that way. When Marlene Dietrich made love to Cary Grant, it wasn't hetero—it was *universal*. But Billy Crystal and what's-her-name—" I looked over at Eduardo. He was grinning. "You just said that to get me going, didn't you?"

He knows how to do that. I kissed him hard right there in the video store.

So we rented *Rebecca* instead. "Oh, you'll love this movie," I promised, but Eduardo wasn't so sure. "It's Hitchcock's only really romantic film. Trust me."

Now the rain stops. The sun comes out. "Damn," Eduardo says, pulling his lips from mine.

"Let's go home, watch our movie," I say. We step out into the wet street.

"Old movies aren't very realistic," he tells me.

"Yeah, so?" I ask him. "Why is it that such a premium is placed on reality these days? Why do we judge a film based on how *real* it seems? Why has that become a criterion? How about how emotional it is? How compelling? How *beautiful*?"

"I don't feel those things unless I can feel something's real."

"That's the problem with you younger gay men these days. Everything's got to be palpable."

"I don't know that word. Did you use it just to make me feel ignorant?"

"No. It means obvious. Easy to grasp. Touchable. *Real*."

"Yeah. My kind of movie."

I sigh. "Maybe we *should've* rented *When Harry Met Sally*."

"It was a great movie."

"Please. Hetero propaganda."

"You know? I think you are the first person I ever met who I can honestly call heterophobic."

I'm in his face. "When there is no longer any such thing as homophobia, I'll worry about any slights to straights."

He just shakes his head at me.

I smirk. "You protest, but deep down you really like that about me. How queer-centered I am."

He just laughs. "Oh, Jeff. You want to live your whole life in a gay ghetto. You live in Provincetown in the summer, the South End the rest of the year. You write for mostly gay publications. All your friends are gay. Well, not me. When I move back to Boston this fall, I'm moving in with my straight friend Sandy in Somerville."

"You're just going to the other extreme. You won't associate with anything gay—" I remember something I'd read the other day. "There's a new gay magazine starting in New York. They're looking for a designer. But you probably wouldn't apply, would you?"

"I don't want to limit how I identify myself, how I market myself. That's *your* way, Jeff."

"You Gen Xers, you think you know—" I stop. There, on his bike, swerving to avoid the puddles in the street, is Raphael. My sweet little Québecois from last summer. His head is buzzed this year, but it's him all right. The pouting lips, the cute upturned nose, the milk-chocolate skin, the jet black eyes.

"What? Who is it?" Eduardo asks.

"My love from last summer," I moon. Raphael is only a few yards away. He recognizes me. He slows to a stop.

"Alo, Zhef," he says, softening the *J* of my name. His eyes look into me.

"Raphael," I say. "How are you?" My heart thuds. I'm afraid he notices.

"I am fine. Are you here for anothair summair?"

"Yes. Yet another." I laugh. "Oh. Raphael. This is Eduardo."

"Hello," Eduardo says.

Raphael smiles at him. "Alo, Eduardo." Their eyes lock for several seconds, and then they both laugh awkwardly, as if some unspoken communication had just passed between them. For a second, I'm jealous. Hey, knock that off. He's mine. You're mine. Whatever.

"Well, I must get go-wing," Raphael says. "Tell me. How is Zha-veetz?"

"He's fine," I tell him.

"Give him my regards," Raphael calls, pedaling off. "Good-bye, Eduardo. It was very nice to meet you. Enjoy what is left of all thees. *Bon soir*, Zhef."

Then he's gone. I sigh like a lovesick puppy. "*That*," I say to Eduardo, "was *Raphael*." I say his name as he might: soft and long and full of air.

"What did he mean, 'Enjoy what is left of all this'?"

"The summer, I guess." We resume walking. "Ah, yes. Such pretty memories. He was so sweet, such a fun few days." I pause. "At least I know he's gotten on with his life."

"Fuck you, Jeff," Eduardo says. I just grin.

Back at the house, Eduardo's quiet. I notice a thin wrapped gift sitting on the table. "Who's this for?" I ask.

"Why don't you open it and see?"

I look at him blankly. "Why did you give me a gift?"

"I don't know," he says, a little distant. "The end of the summer. Maybe because you lost what I gave you for your birthday."

I think about that star out there sometimes. I think about it under the sand, waiting for me. Every once in a while I get the urge to go and dig for it, spend the entire day sifting through the sand.

"Open your gift," Eduardo urges.

So I do. It's a book. *The Giving Tree* by Shel Silverstein. I remember reading this as a kid, a classic children's book. "Once there was a tree," it begins, "and she loved a little boy." Every day the boy goes to swing on the tree's branches and jump in its leaves. But then the boy grows up and tells the tree he's too old to play with her anymore. He wants to build a house, not climb trees. So the tree gives him her branches, and of course, the tree is happy. That old tree spent her whole life always giving something to the boy and is even glad to be chopped down so he can build a boat and fetch his love from across the sea. Finally, when the boy has become an old man, the tree—now just a lonely only stump—has one last gift to give. "Well, boy," the tree says, "come and rest."

" 'And the tree was happy,' " I finish reading, out loud.

"Read the inscription."

He's written: "Only great passions can bring us to great things. I love you. Eduardo."

"Where did you get that?" I ask. "That quote?" Might I have said it to him? Javitz?

"It came from me." He smiles. "*That's* where I got it."

I don't know what to say. I look up at him and I want to say the right thing, but I'm not sure what that is. I know what I *want* to say—but I'm not sure I dare. Finally he spares me the choice and speaks instead.

"Please tell me I'll never be just an anecdote like Raphael. Promise me you'll never point me out on the street and say, 'There goes Eduardo, my love from last summer. So sweet, such fun times.' "

"Oh, Eduardo," I say, pulling him to me.

I kiss him. He's stiff for a moment, then relaxes. I can say no words, articulate nothing of how I feel. All I can do is this: kiss him and touch him, make love to him right here on the kitchen floor.

But he stops me. "No," he says. "Not yet."

He leads me into the living room by the hand. "We're going to make dinner, and we're going to watch a movie, and *then* we're going to make love."

"All right," I say, enjoying his assertiveness.

We make spaghetti with a thick tomato-basil-cream sauce. We uncork a bottle of wine. We watch the film huddled together in a black and silver glow. The dreamy, haunting opening: "Last night I dreamed I went to Manderly again," and the long sweeping shot up the road to the charred ruins of the great old house.

Of course Eduardo clucks over the obviously fake cliff from which Olivier is about to jump. And he says it's completely unrealistic that a man of Olivier's station would pursue a simple paid companion like Joan Fontaine. But at the moment it seems that they will never see each other again, just as Joan's nasty employer prepares to whisk her away without being able to say good-bye to Olivier, we're both caught up in the magic. I look over at Eduardo: his eyes shine with moisture. Of course, they *do* find each other, and Olivier proposes marriage, and all is right with the fairy tale.

Except—and I seize the remote and rewind the tape, playing the scene again.

"What are you doing?" Eduardo asks.

Olivier and Fontaine move backwards in grainy, jerky movements. Then I hit play.

"I was crying all morning thinking I'd never see you again," Fontaine says, all doe-eyed and dewy.

"Bless you for that," Olivier says, touching her cheek. "I'll remind you of that someday." His adoring eyes never leave her face. "You won't believe me. Pity you have to grow up."

Turns out, Eduardo adores the movie. His hands grip mine during the climactic fire scene as Judith Anderson looms large among the flames. I've seen it a dozen times. I prefer watching Eduardo, his eyes big and wondrous, and I marvel at how truly beautiful he is. Not beautiful like the boys at tea dance, all big and buff and glossy, but beautiful in a way that's all his own: real and sincere.

How safe, how completely at home I feel with him. I never thought it could happen, not with anyone other than Lloyd. I hear Javitz's voice inside my head: "Then tell him, darling. Tell him how you feel."

When the movie is over, he turns to me and says, "Thank you." I assume now we'll make love. We do, but we don't have sex. We fall asleep in each other's arms right there on the floor, while the video rewinds above us. When Javitz comes home, he has to turn off the TV and step over us to go to bed.

BEAUTY

Boston, April 1995

I'm finishing an article on the rise of gay conservatives that will run in a national gay magazine. They're paying me close to two grand, so I've been putting a lot of work into it. When I got the assignment, I thought it would be difficult. I mean, come on. I'm this old-time Queer National who once threw red paint all over Pat Buchanan's primary headquarters in New Hampshire. I own a total of two neckties and not one blue blazer with gold buttons. But I've been having fun.

The first Log Cabinite I interviewed was very cute. So was the next one. And the one after that. They're all so well put-together: great haircuts, sharp clothes, gym bodies to die for. With one guy, I even exchanged numbers. So what am I going to do? Trick with a *Republican*? I wish Javitz were around so I could process that one. But how do I know I already haven't? The South End is *crawling* with them. This is their fucking *birthplace*, for God's sake, what with so many gay boys creaming over Governor Bill Weld just because he smiles pretty and says nice things to them.

I type: "We have reached a point in our history where identity has taken on many permutations, where old notions of who and what we are have become irrelevant, anachronistic." I sit back and stare at the words on my computer screen. What the fuck does that mean? It sounds like one of those grand pronouncements Javitz would make out on the deck, late at night. I imagine myself saying such a thing to my Republican trick. He'd look at me strangely, I'm sure. What I'd be saying, of course, was that it was okay for us to fuck.

Eduardo once said to me, "Do you always talk the way you write?"

"What do you mean?" I asked.

"I mean that you're always using these big socio-cultural explanations for everything."

I shrugged. "I'm a journalist. I like to put things in perspective."

But now, staring at my computer screen, surrounded by boxes crammed with the remnants of my life with Lloyd, having thought of Eduardo yet again, it feels as if there is no perspective, none at all. I hit the delete key, determined to start over. But nothing comes to me, so I turn the damn thing off.

Why is it that I can figure out the root causes for the rise of gay conservatism, even coming up with a rationale for sleeping with Republicans, but cannot do a damn thing to explain—let alone *fix* —what's happening in my own life? I decide not to try to think of an answer for a change. Instead, I just pull on my sneakers and go outside for a walk.

It's a beautiful day. Spring has finally arrived. I can smell the sweet aroma of thawing earth, the crispness of new buds on trees. It will rain this month—it always does in Boston in April—rain so much it will feel like a biblical plague. But today is dry and warm. The sun even manages to break through the gray haze of the sky every now and then. As I walk, my shadow plays with my feet, sometimes there, sometimes not.

There's Lloyd, across Tremont, in front of the video store. He's on his Rollerblades, having hauled them out of the box I'd packed, overcome suddenly with the need to skate. He's even wearing shorts it's so warm, and his calves strain sexily as he pushes down the street. He lifts a hand to wave to me. I just raise my chin in greeting.

I've been sleeping on the couch since he told me he wants this temporary separation. Maybe I'm acting out, but it just seems too incongruous to slip into the breathing position when he's feeling this way. It's as if I don't know him anymore. Last night, he came home with his head completely shaved, and he's growing a goatee. I thought he looked hideous. "It's a way to deal with thinning hair," he said, shrugging his shoulders when he saw my lack of appreciation.

Now, on his Rollerblades, I admit, he does look rather hot, in that sharp, buzzed, rough kind of way. Javitz will adore it, I'm sure—but Javitz isn't here anymore to comment on it. This is the first weekend of the post-Javitz era. Last weekend, we moved him up to Provincetown, renting a truck and cramming our cars with boxes of books. On the way up, I rode with Javitz; on the way back, trapped with Lloyd for two hours, I slept in the backseat. Or pretended to, anyway.

Our little family. A year ago, there were no splits—none that were obvious, anyway. Wendy and Chanel still seemed happy, before all that talk about babies came up. Melissa and Rose still ate dinner with them every Wednesday night, and all of us celebrated birthdays together without any strain. And Javitz and Lloyd and I —well, who could have imagined a day like today, each of us alone, none of us together?

I'm on my way to see Tommy. I woke up yesterday morning and realized what a shit I'd been the last few weeks, consumed by my own turmoil and completely forgetting my promise to be there for him. Eduardo or not, I reasoned, Tommy was my friend. And he'd just seroconverted. So I called and left a message on Tommy's machine that I'd stop by this afternoon. He never responded, but I figured I'd try anyway.

Tommy lives about twelve blocks away, so far that he's practically in Roxbury. It's a tiny, cluttered studio apartment, four flights up, in a largely African-American neighborhood. This is hardly the bourgeois gay ghetto in which Lloyd and I have found ourselves, but Tommy seems to like living here. So many ACT UP meetings were held here, dozens of sweaty, angry activists crammed shoulder to shoulder in Tommy's little space, he standing on top of his kitchen table to address the flock.

I ring his buzzer.

"Yeah?" his voice crackles over the intercom.

"Tommy? It's Jeff."

He doesn't say anything. It's as if I can see right through the wires and up to his room. Eduardo's there. They're fucking. I want to turn and beat it off the step.

But then he buzzes me in, and I ride the rickety, closet-sized elevator to his floor. He's waiting for me in his doorframe. He looks anxious, sleep-deprived. "Hey," I say.

"Jeff, look, I'm on my way to my parents'. I should have been out of here an hour ago."

"Oh, okay. Well, I just wanted to stop by. I won't keep you."

"Come in for a second," he says. I step inside his apartment.

Inwardly I sigh in relief: there's no Eduardo, and the place is too small for him to hide. I can smell soap and deodorant from the bathroom, where warm, steamy air still hovers from a recent shower.

"Today's the day," Tommy tells me.

"The day?"

"When I tell my parents."

"Oh shit," I say. I look at him. His face is clean-shaven; what's left of his hair is combed down neatly, nothing like the tangled mat he usually sports. He hasn't slept in days, I imagine, worrying about his parents' reaction. They've always been hysterical types. Lutheran evangelicals out in Worcester. They're going to go nuts.

"Can I do anything?" I offer.

He shakes his head. "I just want to get it over with." He glances around. "Look, I don't have anything to offer you—"

"No, that's all right. You've got to go. I just wanted to stop by because—well, because I haven't, and I said I would."

He's quiet, avoiding my eyes. "Thanks, Jeff. I'm really all right."

"Are you?"

He sighs. "I've turned over a new leaf. No sweets. All healthy foods. I'm getting into an exercise program. Eddie and I are going to the Y—" He stops, as if he shouldn't finish.

"That's great," I say. "Do you want to join my gym? I can get you a discount—"

"No, thanks, Jeff," he declines. Of course not. Work out with me in the room? What an absurd suggestion.

"Look, Tommy. I just wanted you to know that I was sorry for saying 'fuck you' last month at Chanel's. It was stupid. And I should've come by to see you sooner."

"It's okay, Jeff."

"No, it's not. I let my own awkwardness—about Eduardo—" I look over at him. Maybe he doesn't know. Maybe he doesn't even know Eduardo and I had a relationship. But he says nothing. He just lets me continue. "The point is," I say, taking in a long breath, "I care about you, and want to be here for you. I've been so wrapped up in my own shit—Javitz leaving, Lloyd and I up in the air—I haven't given other people much thought. And that's been pretty selfish of me."

"Don't worry about it, Jeff." He gives me a weak smile. "I've got to go."

"Sure."

We both move out into the hallway. He turns and locks the door behind him. On the elevator, I ask him if he's going to try an antiviral. He says he doesn't know. He's heard Javitz's diatribes against them. "But there's something that may be out soon," he says. "Protease something. I'm looking into it."

I'd never heard of it. I wish him luck. We step off the elevator, and there's Eduardo.

"Hey," he says, his eyes moving fast back and forth between both of us.

"Hey," Tommy and I both say in response, almost in unison, the awkwardness now cranked up a hundredfold.

"I thought you'd be in Worcester by now," Eduardo says.

"I'm late. I'm leaving now."

"I saw your car on the street. I wondered what was up."

They look at each other sharply. It's a look that isolates me, cuts me off, makes me feel horribly outside. No matter that in Eduardo's voice I hear the same old accusation with which he once addressed me, discovering that I'd gone out to the bar when I said I was staying home to write. No matter that in his voice there's that same old pitch of censure, as if Tommy had been lying about planning to visit his parents. What stings me is the reminder that there exists between them enough connection for such a confrontation.

"Jeff came by for a minute," Tommy's saying. "I've got to get on the road."

"All right," Eduardo says. "I'll see you tonight?"

"Sure."

"Good luck," he says. Tommy smiles wanly.

The three of us head outside onto the sidewalk. Tommy hurries ahead, down towards his car—a rusty blue Volkswagen bug—parked at the end of the block. I turn to Eduardo and raise my eyebrows.

"So," I say. "Hello."

"Hi," he says, not looking at me, watching Tommy get into the car. He tries to start it several times. It rattles and chokes, finally turns over. Then he's gone, in a grinding of old gears.

"So," I say again. "What brings you into the South End?"

"I wanted to go to the bookstore," he says.

"No bookstores in Somerville?"

"I wanted the gay bookstore."

"Oh," I say, smiling. "Welcome to the ghetto."

We walk a few steps before either of us says a word.

"Can we walk together?" I ask. "At least, until the bookstore?"

"Sure, why not?"

We're quiet again. He seems so comfortable, so completely at ease. As if he were just walking with an old friend of his lover's, somebody he doesn't know very well, somebody whose cock he'd never sucked.

"Eduardo?"

He looks over at me. "Yeah?"

"How are you?"

"I'm good. How are you?"

"I mean—about the *test*, Eduardo. If Tommy had it . . ."

He looks away.

"Don't you think I have a right . . . ?" I ask.

"I'm negative," he says.

"Well, that's good news at least."

We walk for a while.

"I feel bad I haven't been in touch with Tommy," I say. "But Javitz just moved away. That's been a big thing for me these last couple of weeks. I didn't realize how hard it would be for me. And Lloyd and I—well, we're going through some rough times."

"I'm sorry to hear that."

"Are you?"

Eduardo stops walking. "Why wouldn't I be?"

"I don't know." We start walking again. "I guess I just feel a little funny, you know, meeting up with you again. . . ."

"Why?" Eduardo asks, light and easy, as if he really had not a clue.

"Well, given last summer and all."

He smiles. "Such fun times. What's the big deal?"

I stop walking and look over at him. "Guess I'm the one who's become the anecdote."

Finally, his face shifts, the mask cracks. There's a flash of the old anger, just for a second, and despite its hostility, I love seeing it again—because it's familiar, it's real. Not like the friendly vacancy that was there before.

"Jeff, just let it rest," he says, his face returning to calm. "It's better for everybody that way."

We're standing on the edge of Union Park. A couple of lesbians stroll by us arm in arm. "No, it isn't," I say. "Eduardo, how can you just act as if we meant nothing to each other? Why did you never return any of the calls I left for you? Why didn't you respond to my letter?"

"I needed to get on with my life," he says calmly.

I'm not calm. I can tell my voice is loud. One of the women turns around and glances over her lover's shoulder at me. "I thought I *meant* something to you," I'm saying. "I never *heard* from you again after you left. We went from passion to nothing."

"Feelings change," he says simply.

"I don't believe that. Maybe *we* change—"

"Jeff, I went back to school!" Now his voice comes alive, just enough to show a little of the fire that so aroused me months before. "I was finding my way. My life got crazy, school and work and friends. . . ."

"So you just wrote me out?"

"Jeff, if you recall, our last day together in Provincetown was not all that pleasant."

"Yes, but I never thought you'd just turn around and leave me. Walk out of my life. I thought we could work something out. I was coming back to Boston. I thought we'd be together here. I thought we could continue our relationship."

He smirks. "What—did you think we'd get *married?*"

My words back at me again. Funny how one's own words can wound far more sharply than anything someone else might say on his own.

"You made me care about you," I say, my voice thick.

Eduardo's silent.

"And I still do. I have not forgotten one moment we spent together. I think of you every day, Eduardo. And I don't care if I sound like Joan Fontaine or anybody else. I *do* think about you, and I do miss you, and I wish we could find some way to be together."

"I'm seeing Tommy," he says, looking away from me.

"I'm well aware of that. But can we be friends at least? I haven't been having a very easy time of things lately. . . ."

His eyes dart back to me, and now the anger is there full force. "Of *course*. I should have known. Same as it ever was. I'm supposed to come back into your life now that you need me. It's still on your terms. You're unhappy, so you want me to make you happy. Sorry, Jeff, things are on *my* terms now." He sets his jaw. "I hope you and Lloyd work things out. I've got to go."

"Eduardo—"

"No, really. I've got to go."

He walks away, his hair caught by a light breeze, his jaw set just as it was the last time he walked away from me. I'm not angry with him for walking. Part of me understands. Part of me even admires him for doing so. That fire, that spunk, that vitality, that *life*. That's what I loved him for.

And how beautiful he looks, how radiantly young and beautiful. But me—all I feel is tired, tremendously tired, just as spring breaks out in the sky overhead.

Provincetown, September 1994

We're not sure what kind of accent he has, but it's beautiful, whatever it is.

"It's Greek," Javitz says finally.

"Are you sure?" Lloyd asks.

Javitz raises that damn eyebrow. "You are talking to a man who has PLATO-7 as a license plate."

I turn to Chanel. "Who *is* he?"

She shrugs. "Never seen him before."

"It's *your* party," I say. "Find out!"

Chanel has rented a condo here in Provincetown for the Labor

Day weekend. We're out on the deck overlooking the dunes. Originally, the plan had been for her and Wendy to rent the place. But Chanel and Wendy are history now. Two weeks ago, Chanel packed her bags and moved out, despite Wendy's tears and pleas for a second chance. "I can wait on the baby," Wendy had cried, but Chanel was done with it. "It'll just come up again in another month or so," she said simply, and walked out.

"You can't just *leave* her," I argued, but Chanel and I had only just patched things up between ourselves after the unpleasantness across the breakfast table last month. I couldn't push too hard. But I *did* try. "You *love* each other," I told her. "How can you just walk away?"

"We've become different people," she said, and that was that. Chanel can become very hard when she wants to. To other people, but also to herself. She would not permit herself to feel any pain or regret upon leaving. Now, she's throwing a big Labor Day party, inviting in everyone she knows and some she doesn't. She's had one too many bottles of beer, smoked just a bit too much pot. She'd like us to think that Wendy is the furthest thing from her mind.

"I think he's a friend of my friend Mary Alice," Chanel says about the beautiful boy with the accent, but then she giggles. "I'm not sure why I think that. Want me to ask him?"

"No," I say quickly. In her state, she's bound to say anything. I've never allowed anyone to play matchmaker for me. If I like a guy, I'll approach him. Or make him approach me.

Except I can't seem to do anything with this one. At first I think it's because Lloyd and Eduardo are both here. It just wouldn't be cool for me to start hitting on somebody else when *both* of them came to the party with me. But I think it's more than that. He is beyond beautiful; he is sublime. I would go so far as to say he is the most beautiful man I have ever seen, but I know it would sound like so much hyperbole if I articulated it. Lloyd would say, "Oh, come on, Cat," and Javitz would roll his eyes and say, "This week," and Eduardo would just store it away in his head to dwell upon and feel terrible about later.

But he is. The most beautiful man. He's not that much taller than I am, but his body is one of those born to perfection. This is not a man who has spent much time in the gym. Every curve, every line of his body is precise and graceful. His shoulders are broad, his torso a classic V, but without the bulk and rigidity that afflicts body builders. To his arms there is an easy flow of muscle and sinew, biceps gently appearing as he bends his elbow to raise his beer to his lips. His hair is so black it almost glistens with blue highlights in the sun. His eyes are dark brown, his skin a vibrant olive. Skin as fine as silk, as naturally smooth as a baby's ass.

"He's dark enough to be Greek," I observe.

"Now the question is," Eduardo says, big grin, "is he Greek active or Greek passive?"

He's ribbing us. Such terms are "too seventies" for him. "*Whatever* role he wants to play," I say, "would be fine with me."

"Why don't you go up and say hello?" Lloyd offers. "Don't let me stop you."

Eduardo reaches his neck up to see over the crowd, checking out the man. "He's cute, but he's not all *that* cute."

Javitz sighs. "Remember what I told you at lunch," he says to Eduardo, who backs down and frowns.

"What?" I ask. "What did you tell him at lunch?"

"Never you mind."

"I don't know what you've done to him, Eduardo," Lloyd says, grinning. "I've never seen Jeff so hesitant to approach his prey before."

Eduardo feigns disinterest. "He can do whatever he wants."

"I know," Lloyd says. "How about if you and I take off and leave him to his Greek god?"

"Sounds good to me," Eduardo says.

Would they really? The thought of Lloyd and Eduardo tricking is a curious one. It either would be a complete turn-on or would absolutely unravel me. Regardless, I'm not in the mood to find out. "I'm not interested in tricking today," I snap.

Chanel takes a hit off her bong and passes it around. Javitz takes it, and so does Lloyd. Eduardo seems to consider, then shakes his head. "Maybe you should have some, Jeff," he says. "Maybe it'd give you the courage to approach Apollo over there."

"More like Adonis," I say, sighing ridiculously.

"Hey." Lloyd nudges me. "He's coming over."

My mouth goes dry. I want to raise my beer to my mouth but I know my hand would shake if I did so. The man positions himself not a yard from me, in direct eye contact, leaning against a table. Javitz and Lloyd each grin and walk away. Eduardo looks at me and then starts to follow them.

"Hey," I whisper. "Where you going?"

"I don't want to be in your way."

"Excuse me," the man says, beside me.

I turn to him. I don't say a word. I don't know if Eduardo is still there or not.

"Do you have a light?" the Greek god asks.

His voice is like seasoned honey. His eyes, his face, everything, moves in a rhythm I've never encountered before. I have not felt this way since seventh grade, since Richie Rostocki came up to me and asked me if I wanted to be his partner in the relay races. *Me? You want me?*

"No," I say.

My voice is heavy. I say nothing else. We stand there, not speaking. I do not look at him. Finally he turns to another man, a man who *does* have a light, and they begin to speak closely, cheeks pressed together to hear above the music.

I walk over to the deck railing and join the others. They, of course, have witnessed the entire exchange. "What has come over you?" Lloyd asks.

"I—I don't know. I couldn't move. I couldn't do anything."

"Finally met your match, huh?" Eduardo asks, and there's that nasty edge to his voice again.

Javitz is looking at me, befuddled. "I've never seen you this way. In more than a decade, I've never seen you this way."

"I don't remember ever *being* this way," I say, almost as if coming out of a trance. "It's just that he's *so* beautiful. . . ."

"No, it's not him, darling," Javitz says.

"His name is Philip," Chanel says, coming up behind us. "I think that's what Mary Alice said. He *is* Greek. He's going to school in Boston. He's studying graphic design."

"Really?" Eduardo says, perking up. "Maybe *I* should go talk to him."

"Looks like he's already found someone," Lloyd says. "Looks like they're leaving."

I feel a churning in the pit of my stomach, as if I've lost the winning lottery ticket and tonight's drawing was for $20 million. "He came *over*. He asked me for a *light*. Did that mean he was interested?"

Javitz blinks. "I thought *you* were the expert on tricking."

"I guess not anymore. I mean, he was *so*—"

"Oh, cut it out," Eduardo says.

Lloyd laughs. "Bet you didn't know Jeff had all these human frailties, did ya?"

"Everyone's a little insecure," Eduardo says.

Except maybe for that Greek god, I think, but I don't say it.

"You're right, Eduardo," Javitz says. "Everyone here, all those boys you see in the bars and on the steps of Spiritus, are scared as shit. Especially the ones with pecs the size of grapefruits." Javitz lights up, inhaling deeply. "They look in the mirror and nothing's good enough. No matter *how* big they get." He blows the smoke out of his mouth long and lazy, like a jaded dragon.

"Javitz, are you talking about Mitch again?" Lloyd asks.

"*Whooo?*" His face bears down on Lloyd. They laugh.

Finally, I do, too.

But Eduardo is stone-faced. "What's the matter with you?" I ask.

"Are you sufficiently recovered now?" he comes back at me.

I get it. He's pissed. I'm only supposed to have eyes for him. And Lloyd, of course. He doesn't dare suggest I shouldn't have eyes for Lloyd. But that's it, he reasons. I've already got two. What do I need more for? Get your hand out of the cookie jar, Jeffy. You've already had two.

It's beginning to bug me. I just look away from him. He knows I get it; he knows I'm pissed. That, of course, just gets him more pissed. Maybe it's good that the summer is ending, that Eduardo will be back in school soon, that we won't have all this time to spend together.

He and Lloyd have gotten along very well this weekend. Except every now and then Lloyd looks up at me with his intense green eyes, looks at me as if trying to find something in my face that he had forgotten. Might it be that he's looking for whatever it is that Eduardo sees there? Or are those eyes of his merely looking to connect? I try to smile when I see his eyes, try to return their gaze.

But I cannot discern what kind of look this is, which makes me uneasy. I've always known the look in Lloyd's eyes.

"Actually, maybe his name wasn't Philip," Chanel says now. "Maybe it was Peter. Or Paul. Do any of those sound Greek to you?"

We ignore her. She's in her own, zoned-out world. Lloyd and Eduardo are talking in the corner. Ernie bounds in, big smiles, hugs and kisses. He and Javitz slip off to the kitchen. I'm left with Chanel, who's trying to remember just what Mary Alice told her about the departed Greek god.

"It doesn't matter," I tell her.

She looks up at me with glassy eyes. "Jeff, I'm truly sorry about last month."

"Don't worry about it. It's a touchy subject. I can understand why people get upset. I was upset myself."

"No, I shouldn't have taken my shit out on you." She sways back and forth a little. I know this self-analysis can only be a result of the pot. "I've always done that. Ever since I was a little girl and something would get me angry and I'd blame someone else."

"Like the maid?" I josh. I love teasing her about her privileged upbringing.

"You know, the thought of not having you in my life . . ." She chokes up. "Last night I had a dream Javitz died. I woke up crying so hard. I don't want to lose you guys."

I smile. "We're not going anywhere."

She rests her head on my shoulder. "I miss Wendy," she whispers.

"Chanel, I told you—"

She looks up at me. "Yes. Yes, you did." Some of the glaze seems to have left her eyes. "But I didn't tell you the rest of my dream."

"What was that?"

"That Javitz died, and you and Lloyd broke up. I don't know which part I was crying harder about." She smirks. "So pay attention to your own advice, buster."

"What? What are you talking about?"

"Eduardo is a darling. I love him. But I'm sensing a little distance between you and Lloyd."

"You sense wrong," I assure her.

"Really? Because I don't want you and Lloyd—I mean, our little group couldn't take another breakup."

I stroke her hair. "Look, I'm not about to let my relationship with Lloyd slip away. Relationships are fragile, precious, delicate. If you toss 'em around, leave 'em lying about—they're bound to shatter. You've got to hold them tightly, not let them drop."

"If you hold something too tight, it breaks," she says.

"Problem was, you stopped holding Wendy at all. You *love* her, Chanel. Don't just walk away."

She sighs. "It's too late, Jeff. What's done is done."

"It's never too late."

The pot returns to hang in a haze behind her eyes. "Why are you so afraid?" she asks all at once.

"I'm not afraid. Afraid of what?"

She shrugs. "Let's just keep talking, Jeff. Let's not fight, ever again. Let's just keep being there for each other, because it's going to get harder for us now."

It's the pot and the booze talking. "Of *course* we'll be there for each other," I assure her. "That's what family is for."

"And that man? That Greek god? Don't let him get in the way."

I smile. She's high. She doesn't know what she's saying.

"Don't worry, Chanel. I'm all done with him."

I might have added: Whether I like it or not.

Boston, April 1995

"Cat, I wish you'd decide one way or another, so I know where to reach you," Lloyd says. "But maybe that's just it. Maybe you don't *want* me to reach you."

We haven't spoken much in the last few days. Now he's leaving. He's all packed, ready to go. Naomi will soon be here with her van. Melissa and Rose, too, will arrive with their truck to cart off the bulk of our stuff to storage. We have to be out by Sunday, which is tomorrow. Lloyd's leaving a day early, so he can be settled into Naomi's by Sunday night and thus be able to get up for work refreshed on Monday morning. What he wants to know now is where I'm going to be, where I'll be living after tomorrow, when I can no longer stay here.

"Of course I want you to reach me."

"Wouldn't have known that from the last couple of days."

I look around at the apartment. It's empty now, hollow and cold. It doesn't look like the same place at all. Over there, in front of the window, is where the couch once stood, a cozy little corner with a big brass lamp and a magazine rack, jammed with issues of *Time* and the *Advocate* and *Men's Fitness*. It's not very cozy now, just a hard, bare stretch of floor. To the right is the spot where we always had our Christmas tree, with its big gaudy red lights and Rose's tattered angel on top. Over there, near the closet door, Lloyd once fucked me against the wall, right after a heavy breakfast of pancakes and syrup. I had to lie down for the rest of the day. Here, near the entry to the kitchen, we popped the cork on a bottle of champagne when Lloyd finally finished his dissertation; you can still see the black mark on the ceiling where the cork ricocheted. Over there, on the kitchen floor, next to the oven where I baked hundreds of veggie pies, Lloyd consoled me when I finally collapsed, finally cried over my father's death, a day after the funeral.

"How can we just leave here?" I whisper. "How can we just walk out that door—without a plan, without a goal, after so many years together?"

"Cat, this isn't permanent. I just need some time."

"Are you making me a guarantee?"

He frowns. "There are no guarantees in life."

"So let's rewrite the rules. Let's *make* some guarantees."

He seems exasperated. "You're asking me to do something I can't."

"Bullshit. You just don't want to."

"Let's not argue again, okay?"

Poor Mr. Tompkins. All morning he sat angry and confused in the middle of the room, sniffing around the piles of cardboard boxes looming over him. He could sense something momentous was about to happen. Then, big brute that he is, he padded out of the room with hard, deliberate steps. Now he's sulking in the bedroom closet, little green eyes glowing in the dark.

I'm cross-legged on the floor, taping one last box, when Lloyd bends down and hands me a cat. A purple one with pink dots.

"One more cat for the road," he says.

"Oh, Dog." And I melt again, goddamnit, standing up and falling into him. "Oh, Dog."

"I wish we had been there for each other these last few days." He's crying. It startles me. "I wish we could have had some kind of ritual, leaving this house."

"It's not too late," I say. "It's never too late." I step back to look at him. His face hasn't changed, not one iota, since that first night I saw him. Oh, sure, the wrinkles, and that damned shaved head and goatee, but his eyes are as green as the Emerald City, same as they ever were. He looks like a child, standing here in front of me crying. And I feel like a shit, giving him the cold shoulder these last several days.

"I've got some sage," he says. "We could burn it. We could walk through the rooms and remember our happiest moments in each of them and leave behind some of that energy for the people who follow us. And take some of it with us in our hearts."

I think it's a splendid idea. I really do. There are no more tears. Instead, we burn sage and laugh, remembering the time Javitz stepped on the Easter egg we'd hidden in his slipper, the time Melissa got drunk and sang "Whatever Lola Wants" on top of our kitchen table, the time Lloyd fucked me against the wall after all those pancakes. "It was like pumping cement!" he cries, and we laugh and laugh until we fall on the floor.

"Here we thought we'd find you both moping around like gloomy Gerts," says Rose, as we look up to discover her in the doorway.

Melissa's behind her. "Are they crying? Are they fighting?" she chirps.

"Looks like they were gettin' ready to boink," Rose concludes, stepping over us to pick up the first of the boxes.

"I can't do heavy lifting," Melissa says. "The nails, you know."

It takes us about an hour. Naomi arrives, and Lloyd's clothes and meditation supplies are directed into her van. Everything else goes into Rose's truck to be carted over to the storage bin. It's sweaty work, but Melissa has brought over some frozen lemonade. She makes a pitcher of it with the last few ice cubes from our freezer. "See?" she says. "I'm good for something."

Then Rose heads off to the storage bin, Lloyd and Naomi following. "Don't worry, Cat," he says. "We'll take it from here."

I kiss him good-bye.

"I'll be with Javitz," I tell him. "In Provincetown."

He hugs me. "Tell Mr. Tompkins I'll see him soon," he says. "I don't dare go in that closet. He'd probably bite my hand off."

I smile.

Then he's gone.

"I've been dreading this moment," I say to Melissa. As expected, my voice echoes in the empty apartment.

"That's why I'm still here."

"Oh, baloney. You just didn't want to unload the stuff at the storage bin."

"Maybe that, too."

We both laugh. We sit down on the floor. She refills my glass with lemonade.

"Tell me something," I say. "How long have you and Rose been together?"

"Eleven years."

I knew that. I just wanted to hear her say it. I want to believe it's possible. I want to close my eyes and imagine them together— just together, not necessarily doing anything, just being *together*. Not laughing or cooking or having fun or fighting or anything at all. Just together: Rose in front of the TV eating a bag of pretzels, Melissa writing poetry at the kitchen table, idly scratching her back with the eraser on her pencil. Neither would have any use, in that second, for the other; but they'd be there together, just the same.

"How long were your parents together?" I ask.

"Thirty years."

"Really?"

"Then they got divorced."

"After *thirty years*?"

"Yup. My mother found out Dad had been having an affair with their marriage counselor."

"No."

"Yes."

"Man or woman?"

"Woman, silly."

"Hope she at least reported her to the ethics commission." I laugh. "Fuckin' heteros. The things they do."

Mr. Tompkins suddenly appears from around the doorframe, poking his fat little face into the room. Melissa gestures for him, but all he'll show us is his snout, which I'd swear is pursed together in a mad little sulk.

"Me," I say, "I was cursed with a mother and father who really loved each other. They made a commitment some forty years ago, and by God they stuck to it. I'm sure there were times they didn't know what the fuck *path* they were on, or if it was the right one. But they figured it out *together*. They still got up in the morning and had breakfast together. They still watched TV together at night and shared the same bed. And when they got old, and their kids had moved away and disappointed them, they still had each other. They never let each other down. Right up until the day my father died."

Melissa gets up and walks gingerly toward the doorframe to the bedroom. "Come here, baby," she says, but Mr. Tompkins bolts away. She turns back to me. "How do you know your parents never disappointed each other? Parents aren't going to admit something like that to their kids—not if they're good parents, anyway, and they want to keep up a united front. How do you know your mother didn't stop putting out for your dad after the last kid was born, and he was bitter about it ever since? How do you know your mother didn't want a bigger, better house, and blamed your father for never making enough money?"

"I just know. In fact, my mother *did* want a bigger house, and I don't imagine she put out for my father as much as he once would have liked. But there was no bitterness. No resentment. They *loved* each other. They had a *commitment*."

"Blind allegiance to a commitment made forty years before is not something to admire," she says, kneeling beside me.

"It's not blind allegiance. It's called *love*."

She hugs me. "Oh, Jeff. For all your tricking, for all your queer theories, for all your boys, you're the most romantic guy I know." She kisses my forehead. "And I love you for it."

"I just don't want to lose my family."

"You won't."

"Oh no? What if I stay in Provincetown longer than a few months? What if Lloyd and I split up? You've already cut Chanel out of your life."

"Jeff, that's different."

"No, it's not. Look, my brother has barely spoken to me since the Christmas Eve I decided not to go to my mother's house and instead spent it here with Javitz and Lloyd. 'Families should be together on Christmas,' my brother insisted. Well, precisely. That's why I was staying with Javitz and Lloyd. My brother sits there on Christmas Eve with a beer in his hand, griping about my cousins, yelling at his kids, arguing with my sister, not speaking to whatever boyfriend she's brought that year. His wife gets drunk and silly and stupid, and then they all go to midnight mass. Do I want that life? No fucking way. But every year, it's still that same wife and those same kids and the same house and the same 'Angels We Have Heard on High' at midnight mass. And there's something to be said about all that."

There's a knock. We both jump. There, in the open doorway, is Drake—of all people—poking his head tentatively into the apartment.

"Hello?" he calls.

"Hi," I say, not bothering to stand up. Melissa does, approaching him and gesturing for him to come inside. He does, and he's carrying a bouquet of daffodils, their stems wrapped in aluminum foil.

"I just wanted to give you guys a little going-away gift," he says awkwardly.

"Lloyd's already left." I still don't stand up.

"Well," he says, smiling like an idiot, "these are for you too." He thrusts them at me.

I'm forced to stand and accept them. "Thank you," I tell him. "Unfortunately, all the vases are packed up—"

"That's okay. I wrapped them in a wet paper towel and then put the foil around them. That should keep them until you get to— wherever you're going."

Our eyes hold for several seconds. "Well, gee, thanks an awful lot, Drake."

"Oh, sure." He shrugs. "Sorry I wasn't here to help move. I had a job interview."

"So you're not hittin' the road now that you've taken your leap, huh?"

"No," he says. "I've decided to stay in the area."

Our eyes hold again. "Well," I say. "Thanks again."

"Sure." He smiles at Melissa, then turns to leave. "Oh, say hey to Lloyd for me," he says over his shoulder. "Tell him I'm sorry I missed him."

I just smile.

After he's gone, I look at Melissa. "Take these for me. Please."

She understands. She relieves me of the daffodils. We feel a warmth suddenly on our feet. Mr. Tompkins has dared to enter. He looks around the room, as if unsure where he is. "Oh, baby," I say to him. "Where did everything go, huh?"

We take advantage of the moment to stuff him into his traveling box, all twenty pounds of him squirming against our hands, trying to bite. Melissa's taking him for the time being; Javitz's new landlord in Provincetown strictly forbids pets. Anyway, I'll be back here in a few months. Poor Mr. Tompkins. He thinks he's going to the vet. Once he's inside, two fluorescent eyes peer out through the grating, radiating outrage at my betrayal. "It'll be okay, little one," I soothe.

Yet on what basis do I offer reassurance? I have no guarantee that this will all come back, that we will all be reunited under the same roof. I think of Junebug, who trusted me, too, once—but I push the thought away.

Melissa and I hug each other good-bye. "Thanks for taking him," I say. "And for talking."

"You'll be okay?" she asks.

No, of course I won't be okay. But I tell her yes, I'll be fine, and I watch her go, trudging along with the heavy cat box, the daffodils stuck ungainly under her arm. With Mr. Tompkins gone, that's the last of it, right out the door. This cold, barren flat is no longer my home; it is little more than shelter for the night, with just a mattress left in the bedroom.

The sun sets, and I watch the shadows lengthen across the hardwood floors. Finally I settle down on the mattress, but it's not easy falling asleep. All of the sounds are gone, all of the electrical hums and ticking of clocks, all of the little whispers Lloyd would make in his sleep. Even the street seems strangely quiet tonight. I long for a siren, anything. But no sounds, none at all.

Provincetown, September 1994

The weekend after Labor Day is Eduardo's last.

It's also his birthday. He shows up bright-eyed and eager. I've promised to take him out to dinner, as much a good-bye to summer as a birthday celebration. There's been something heavy in his voice for the last week, as if each word were an effort, self-conscious and labored. A couple of times he's fallen quiet; once, he turned surly for no apparent reason at all. When I ask him what's bugging him, he just looks at me as if I'm horrible for even asking. Maybe I am.

But today is his birthday, and tonight his mood is happy. That is, until I tell him I have no gift for him.

"What I thought was, we could pick it out together. Whatever you want. We'll go to a store. Here or in Boston. Whatever you want."

The truth was, I hadn't known what to get him. I didn't want to get him something too romantic. Given how he'd been lately, that would send the wrong message. He'd read it as saying I wanted to be with him forever, or that I'd never trick again, that it would just be he and I—and Lloyd. But neither did I want to give him something trivial. After all, his gifts to me have been very thoughtful— and he *has* mattered to me, a great deal.

Matters, I mean. Present tense.

Since meeting him, I've tricked only sporadically. One night, there was a boy from New York—Craig, I think his name was. Craig or Greg. I'd actually been more interested in his friend, a hunky

Chinese boy with big biceps, but he hadn't returned the attention. I was getting better at dealing with that. There were a couple of blow jobs at the rest stop, of course, and a kind of half-trick with a guy named Jeff I met at Spiritus one night. It was the first time I'd ever tricked with someone with the same name as I. Strange how rarely that happens to people. Maybe that's why the trick kind of fizzled out halfway through, and I told him I was tired and wanted to go home.

Or maybe it was for other reasons I don't yet fully understand.

"Really," I tell Eduardo now, "we can pick out something nice." I touch his face. He smiles to smooth over his disappointment.

He's in love with me. Yes, that should be a good thing. "Of *course* you love him," Javitz has said, and he's right. But how fast we fall from our pantheon of theory to ground-level reality. No, it's *not* a good thing. Not for anybody. I haven't had sex with Lloyd in a month, because all my passion's used up with Eduardo. Meanwhile, what Eduardo wants is love, commitment, and marriage, but he's had to settle for love with an already married man. I have never told him fully how I feel: if I did, what would that do to the apple cart?

"I want what you and Lloyd have," Eduardo said to me the other night. "I want that sense of being together, of being able to plan next month, next year, five years from now."

"You'll find it," I reassured him.

He made a sound in disbelief. "Do you know how lucky you are? How few people actually *do* find it?"

"Open your eyes, expand your heart," I chided. "It's not just Lloyd. I also have you. And Javitz."

"But I want what you and *Lloyd* have," he insisted. "Not what you and Javitz have."

"Or you and I?"

That's the crux. What *is* it that we have? What makes what Lloyd and I have—or at least *appear* to have—the prize? Ever since the summer began weaning itself away from us, I've felt Eduardo's struggle. I can see the pain in his eyes every time I look at him. Poor kid. What to make of me, of us? What to expect when the summer is over, when we go back to Boston, me resuming my life, him starting anew? What then?

"I can't promise him the world," I said to Javitz. "But I think that's all he'll settle for."

"He's young, Jeff. He *should* only settle for the world." He smirked. "But then again, maybe the two of you aren't so far apart as it seems. After all, that's what you demand, too."

But I can do only so much. "Maybe we can pick one day a week when we're back in Boston that will be our day," I suggested to Eduardo. "I'll come to Somerville or you'll come to the South End."

He laughed. "Except that will change. 'Oh, Lloyd's coming home early.' 'Oh, I can only stay an hour because I have to pick Lloyd up with the car.'"

"So we pick another date then."

He threw the pillow at me.

"Really," I'm telling him now, trying to banish the disappointment from his eyes and furious at myself for not buying a gift, "we'll go down Newbury Street and you can pick out anything you want. A sweater? You want something to wear? Or maybe jewelry." I smile, as if I've hit on the magic solution. "Jewelry. I could buy you a necklace like the one you got me."

"That was one of a kind."

"It certainly was." I try to kiss him, but he pulls away. "Oh, come on. Why does this have to be so difficult?"

He's about to respond, but Javitz has come into the room. "Can you believe it? One more week and then another summer hits the history books."

"It went fast, didn't it?" Eduardo says.

They exchange a look. "They always do," Javitz says.

"Do you remember the lunch we had together?" Eduardo asks him. "Do you remember sitting out on the wharf eating fried clams?"

Javitz smiles. "Oh, yes, how well I remember."

What did they talk about that day? Me, I'm sure. What did Eduardo say then? What did Javitz tell him? Has it all come to pass?

"You told me that day you'd show me a picture of what you looked like at my age," Eduardo says. "You never have."

Javitz's lips purse, twist, as if he's reluctant but tickled as well, delighted that Eduardo still remembers. "All right." He disappears into his room.

"I've never seen a picture of him at that age either," I say. "And I've known him a *long* time."

Just how long is made manifest when Javitz produces his wallet and flips through the photos encased in plastic. Me a decade ago, about which Eduardo makes no comment, despite my full head of hair and unshadowed eyes. Me and Lloyd, our first summer here, with gads of necklaces and our sideburns that grew to points in the middle of our cheeks. Me and Lloyd and Javitz, snapped by a neighbor of his in Cambridge, posing near the steps of the T station in Harvard Square. Then, finally, in the back, a small black-and-white photo, professionally done, probably one of twenty.

"Oh my *God*," Eduardo says.

I peer over his shoulder to get a good look. It appears nothing like Javitz. The boy in this photograph is young, full of bloom, expecting to live forever. I see it in his eyes: deep and dark, already taking it all in. From such a boy as this has come such wisdom, wisdom around which I've structured my life. And here he is as just a child, an eager, wide-eyed kid, staring into the photographer's lens blithely unaware of the eyes that would stare back at him some thirty years later, eyes of men who love him, revere him, men he loves in return.

And he's beautiful. My *God*, he is beautiful. As beautiful, maybe, as the man from Greece. The photograph was taken in the mid-sixties, before boys began to grow their hair long. I've seen pictures of Javitz from that later era, his kinky Jewish locks grown out and teased into a curly white boy's Afro. All the better to weave daisies through. But this photo is a snapshot of the end of another time: a time when Javitz was still David, still an awkward, short-haired working-class kid from the Bronx, before he rebelled against his family and moved to the Village and began his long career rewriting rules. When the other boys grew up and cut their hair, Javitz kept his, and it's still thicker than mine. "Thank God I've never gotten KS," he has said. "Then I'd have to take chemo and lose all my hair."

"Did you really look like this once?" Eduardo asks, having taken the wallet from him and studying it close to his face.

"Yes, once." He smiles. "And that's all that's necessary, really."

"To look like that just once?" I ask him.

"That's all that's necessary," he repeats, looking at me.

"You were so—*cute*," Eduardo says, handing back the wallet.

" 'Were'?"

"Well, now you're—striking."

Javitz laughs. "You see, Jeff? You have nothing to fear. You don't age. You become striking."

Eduardo gets up. "Well, *you* at least had some raw material with which to work," he tells Javitz.

"Hey," I protest, "why are you being mean to me?"

"Sorry," he says.

I make a face at him. "Javitz, tell him to be nice."

"Eduardo, be nice."

"Tell *him*," Eduardo says.

"Jeff, be nice."

That's when Javitz gives Eduardo his birthday gift: a small wooden sculpture of an owl. "It's Minerva, the goddess of wisdom," he says.

Eduardo adores it. "Thank you so much," he gushes, hugging him. "Thank you for everything this summer."

"Thank *you*, darling." Javitz kisses his neck. "Now I'm off to the dunes."

"You know, at the beginning of the summer, I had all sorts of ideas about the kinds of men who had sex in the dunes."

Javitz laughs. "They're all true, darling. They're all true." He winks, then he's gone.

Eduardo sits down holding the owl, turning it over and over in his hands.

"I'm sorry I didn't have anything for you," I say.

He looks up at me. "We'll pick out something really nice. A sweater. Or how about a piece of jewelry?" My words back at me.

"Hey, listen, I didn't know what to get. If I had gotten you that owl, you would've said, 'Why? Do I need more wisdom?' It wouldn't have been romantic enough. But if I'd *gotten* you a romantic gift, you would have taken *that* all wrong too."

"How so?"

"You know. You would've thought—"

"I'm going home."

"Oh, for God's sake, Eduardo."

"Good night, Jeff."

"We had dinner plans. I was going to take you to dinner."

"Some other time."

"But you're leaving tomorrow. Will I see you?"

"I don't know."

"Oh, for crying out loud, Eduardo. Do you know how hard it is to be your friend?"

He looks at me. Just stands there looking at me. As if I'm the one who's being outrageous. *"What?"* I ask, unnerved.

He finally stops looking at me and goes. Slams the door, in fact. Slams it so hard that I think the glass might break, shattering all over the floor into a thousand glittering pieces.

But it doesn't. It holds firm. It shudders a bit, but in the end it doesn't break. And for that, at least, I'm grateful.

Boston, April 1994

Why I'm still hanging around, I'm not sure. I've left the keys for the landlord on the counter. I've hauled the mattress out to the sidewalk. I've done one final sweeping. Now get the hell out of here, Jeff, I tell myself. Why are you dragging this out?

Carefully piled beside the door are my essentials: a suitcase of clothes, a toiletry case, a box of books, my computer and my printer. My article on gay conservatives is due in two weeks. I need to get up to Provincetown, settle in, and begin.

I look down at my little pile. "That's it, right there. That's what it all boils down to."

And yet even that seems far too much, way too heavy to lug through life. I'm so tired, so completely drained. I don't even feel sad anymore, or frightened. Just tired.

There's a knock. It makes a hard echo through the emptiness of the apartment. Who could be knocking now? Drake, with another batch of flowers? If it's a salesman or some kid selling Girl Scout cookies, I'm just going to step aside and say, "Look. I'm out of here."

But it's Tommy.

"Hey," I say. "How are you? I was going to call you next week—"

"To say good-bye?"

"Tommy, I'm just going to Provincetown for a couple of months. Then I'll be back." I stand aside and he brushes past me into the apartment. "I just didn't get a chance to tell you the other day where I was going." I laugh, awkwardly. "Can't exactly ask you to sit down. Everything's gone."

"I can only stay a minute, but I wanted to talk with you."

"Sure."

He stands in the middle of what was once our living room, where the couch once sat, where Tommy himself once sat, confessing his feelings for Lloyd. He thought it best that we not see each other for a couple of months. He needed to deal with his envy for me, he explained. "Do you ever realize how *fortunate* you are, Jeff?" Tommy asked me all those years ago.

"So," I say now, "how'd it go with your parents?"

"Okay." He's not looking at me. He's looking around the apartment, as if he were trying to remember what was where, trying to piece it all together in his head.

"Did they freak—?"

He turns to face me. "I heard you went for a walk with Eddie."

"What?"

"A walk. After I left. You asked him to go for a walk with you."

"I just—I mean, we were both headed the same way. . . ."

"Jeff, I know about last summer."

"Well," I say. "I would hope so."

"What does that mean?"

"Just that I hope Eduardo was up-front about our relationship."

Tommy's face is hard. "You didn't have a relationship."

"I'm afraid I disagree."

"You didn't seem to think so at the time."

I'm getting angry. "What's he been telling you?"

"Never mind. He's told me enough. He's told me how you fucked him without a condom."

Sudden anger tightens my lips. "Look, don't put your shit on me. I want to try and support you through this, Tommy, but my emotions are a little raw themselves."

He walks off toward the kitchen, his footsteps echoing across the bare hardwood floors.

"I also know that Eduardo turned out negative," I call after him. "So you can't—"

He turns back to me. "I can do anything I want."

We look at each other. "Why did you come here, Tommy?"

He narrows his eyes at me. "When Eddie told me that you went for that walk, I knew I had to come over. I knew I had to see you before you left to tell you that I won't stand for it. You've always gotten everything you want, Jeff. Well, not this time."

I laugh. Everything I want! "You don't know anything, Tommy."

"I know that you cared more about scoring with a guy than any sense of friendship for me. How many guys—?"

"I'm sorry. I know there have been times when I was a shit. I'm sorry. I've apologized to you before, and I'll do so again if you want. But can't we move on?"

He looks at me, and the depth of his hatred is clear. It hits me: he's *never* liked me. He's been waiting for this very moment the entire time we've known each other. He's probably even rehearsed it in his therapy, or at least in front of his mirror. He's hated me through it all—through the rallies, through the marches, through the bar-hopping, on the steps of Spiritus, here on this couch telling me he had feelings for Lloyd.

"Tommy," I say. "Why did you stick around? If I was so rotten, why did you stay my friend?"

"Because I wanted to be like you. I wanted to have the guys you got. I wanted a home like you had, a lover like you had, a body like you had."

His use of the past tense doesn't go unnoticed. But it's not what I respond to. "Tommy," I tell him, "did you ever think *I* might have envied *you*?"

He laughs.

"I *did*. You were the one people followed. You were the leader.

You were the one who had the political insights, the courage—"

"Cut the crap, Jeff. I won't let you take Eddie from me. Not this time."

It's on the tip of my tongue to say, "*You* took Eduardo from me and *turned* him into Eddie," but I don't. Because it's not true. Because I can't believe that Eduardo doesn't still have *something* in his heart for me, no matter how much hostility he feels.

It's as if Tommy can read my mind. "Did you think Eddie could never love me because I'm not good-looking enough? Not one of the beautiful boys?"

"No, no, not at all—and, Tommy, you're not—"

"Bullshit. That's why you approached him. Oh, it should be easy to get him back, you must have thought. He's just with *Tommy*."

"That's not true. I didn't think that. I know Eduardo cares about you." My voice goes husky. "And I guess I just have to accept that."

He's quiet. His face seems to brighten. "You *were* in love with him, weren't you?"

I face the truth. "More than he knows. More than I knew."

We're both quiet now. Tommy has had his victory. His little visit has gone even better than he planned. Not only did he assert himself, but he discovered how weak I really was. "Satisfied?" I ask finally.

"I feel sorry for you, Jeff," he says, walking toward the door.

"I'm sure that gives you a great deal of pleasure."

He ignores me. "But I feel worse for Lloyd. Here he is, all guilt-ridden about leaving you, while you sit here pining over someone else. Doesn't seem fair, does it?"

For a long time after he leaves I just stand there. His words hang in the air, as the humidity does on the Cape in those horrible days in the middle of August. The room feels stuffy and warm. I think for a moment of the little ritual of sage Lloyd and I performed, and wonder if Tommy's energy ruined all that. Or if the sage is powerful enough to repel whatever he left behind.

The phone rings, startling me. It rings from nowhere, from everywhere, bouncing off the bare walls and skipping across the floor. There's one phone still hooked up, a big old black model that came with the place and for nearly six years has sat under a layer of dust beneath our bed. I rehooked it last night, setting it on the kitchen counter, in case Lloyd called to see how I was. He didn't. It rings sharply now, almost cutting me with its sound, and it takes me several seconds to think clearly enough to turn my feet around and answer it.

"Lloyd?" I say.

"Jeffy? It's Mom."

"Mom?"

"Thought you should know. It's your brother."

"Kevin?"

"We're all a wreck here. He's done something very foolish."

"Kevin?"

"He's gone and left Danielle. And the kids. Jesus Christ." Her voice rasps a bit. I can tell she's pulled away from the phone to take a drag off her cigarette. "Can't believe I'm even saying this. He's left her for a younger woman. *Twenty-four years old*, for God's sake!"

"Kevin??"

"We're just broken up about this. Poor Danielle's here crying her eyes out. Nobody even knows where he is. It's like he just cracked up or something. Left a note for Danielle to find yesterday after she and the kids got back from the mall. Jesus, this girl he took off with used to baby-sit for the kids! I can't *imagine* what got into him."

Neither can I. Kevin—the perfect son, always in control. "Mom, can I call you back?" I ask. "I'm moving today and need to get going."

"Oh. That's right. Well, good luck. We'll keep you posted."

"Mom, are you okay?"

"Yeah." She sighs. "Just don't *you* go do anything foolish now, too, you hear?"

"Okay, Mom."

I hang up the phone. I even disconnect it. I walk over to my pile and carry my things one by one to the car. When I'm all finished, I come back inside and switch off the light. I don't even turn around for one last look before I close the door and lock it behind me forever.

It's time to get the hell on the road.

Provincetown, September 1994

He came back because he loves me. Sitting here on the breakwater, the steady whipping wind a sure sign of the encroaching fall, I watch Eduardo's eyes as they move across the waves, up to the brilliant blue of the sky, avoiding my gaze with a self-conscious fear.

"I'm glad you came down this weekend," I say at last.

"I had to get the rest of my stuff."

That's his rationale, but he came because of me. I know that. He left last Monday, started school on Tuesday. We saw each other briefly the morning after our fight. It was stiff but cordial. "Good luck," I told him. "Call me."

He didn't need to. I called him. That night, late, as he settled into his new apartment in Somerville with his straight friend Sandy. The phone woke him, and he was thrilled I called.

"I was missing you," he admitted.

"And me you," I told him.

We were like two high-school sweethearts sneaking a phone call in the middle of the night, our hearts aching for one another with the kind of ardor peculiar to teenagers, desperate and sweet and oh so horribly real. "I'm coming back on Saturday," he told me then. "Maybe we can get together."

So we have. One last time under the Provincetown sun.

"We'll see each other in Boston," I tell him now.

He just smiles, as if I'm handing him a line. Maybe I am. It's hard to tell sometimes when it concerns Eduardo. Sometimes I don't know if I'm protecting his feelings or my own.

We walked across the breakers to Long Point. It's something we'd wanted to do all summer but never did. Eduardo used to come out here with his father to catch littlenecks. "Baskets and baskets we'd haul back," he remembered, but today he doesn't want to talk about his father or sea creatures. He has only one thing on his mind.

"Jeff, I came back because I wanted to talk with you."

"So talk."

The wind whips his hair. Across the bay the whitewashed, weather-worn shops huddle as if for a storm. The clock tower on top of the town hall stands apart, dwarfed only by the majestic Pilgrim Memorial impaling the cloudless sky.

"I just don't know where we're going," he says.

"What do you mean, 'where we're going'?"

This seems to anger him all over again, as if my very question bespeaks my offense.

"You just don't get it, Jeff."

"What don't I get?" I take his hand. It's cold, hard. "Eduardo, I'm *trying* to understand. I just can't go on with you getting angry at me all the time."

"Then don't."

"Eduardo, next week we close up this place. Then I'm back in Boston. We'll be together."

"When Lloyd's away."

I look at him, exasperated. "You wish I wasn't with Lloyd."

"That's not true."

"Then I don't understand all the rage toward me buried in there." I tap his chest.

He pulls away, standing up, taking a few steps away from me. He stands on a rock looking out over the marshy side of the breakwater, where the Cape thins to its slenderest stretch, a fragile whiff of sand holding firm against the fury of the Atlantic.

"Maybe I do have a lot of rage for you," he concedes. "Maybe I do."

"Eduardo, if this isn't enough for you—" I say, coming up behind him. But I know this isn't the response he wants. He wants me to be angry, as angry as he is—angry that we're being separated, that our summer is over.

"It *isn't* enough, Jeff. Maybe being second should be okay. Maybe in how you see the world second is as good as first and sometimes even better. You go ahead and define 'second' all you want to, Jeff, but just you try it sometime. *Try* being second."

"Then end the relationship, Eduardo," I tell him. "If it's so unsatisfactory, end it. I'll just have to accept that."

"Is that all you have to say?" He turns and looks at me. His big brown eyes reflect the sun. "You'd have to accept it?"

"What more do you *want* me to say?"

That's it, I realize, even as I articulate the words. That little question just pushed him over. I *know* what more he wants me to say. And I *could* say it, too—I could tell him everything he wants to hear. It's been bottled up inside me for so long, but I can't let it out. I can't say it. Why doesn't he understand that?

He's crying now, long, soundless tears that fall down his angular face. I'm struck again by how beautiful he is. The quivering of his jaw breaks my heart. I reach over to console him, to take him into my arms, but he pushes me away forcefully. Defiantly.

I start to say something, something that might get us over this, bring him back, start the ride all over again—but he turns. Turns and runs, just as the wind swirls in rage unleashed. His hair catches in the gale, flying out from his head, his untucked flannel shirt flapping as he runs. I do not follow. I stand and watch him go as the sun sinks over the water, the only place on the East Coast where the sun sets over the ocean. His face is pained, his jaw set in resistance. He bounds across the breakwater with surprising ease. Of course. He's been doing it since he was a boy.

I do not start back until the sky is dark and the stars are out. I look for it, and of course it's there: the big, bright, beautiful four-pointed star, the one Eduardo saw the first night we met, the star in the shape of the necklace lost forever in the sand.

He was right, I say to myself. That's no helicopter.

It's a *star*.

AGE

Provincetown, April 1995

My first full day in Provincetown, a freak April snowstorm hits. I've never seen snow on Commercial Street before. It's quite the sight. Javitz, Ernie, and I are making our way through town, faces averted from the furious rush of wind and snow. The steps of Spiritus are blanketed in white, the pizza shop closed tight for the winter. Summer seems far, far away. Shingles hawking bikes and ice cream swing dispiritedly in the wind. We pass by the entrance to tea dance, where a warped, hand-lettered cardboard sign covers the locked fence door: "See You Memorial Day."

We're the only ones, so far, on the street. "Get me back to civilization!" I cry.

"Girl," Ernie scolds, "civilization is *vastly* overrated."

"All I'm looking for is a cup of coffee," I whine. "Isn't there *anything* open?"

"We'll have coffee at Cafe Express," Javitz promises, "but first we've got to walk out onto the beach."

"The *beach*?"

"It's *glorious* in snowstorms," he says. His eyes are wild, his hair caught by the wind, his cheeks red and full of life. I groan.

Finally, there's somebody in the road ahead of us. "Hey, Ernie —hey, David," a man calls over, bundled in a scarf and earmuffs. "Great weather this time of year, huh?"

They all laugh. Next we pass two women sitting on the post office steps. "Hi, guys," they say, waving mittened hands.

"Hey, Bets—hey, Sue," Ernie says, waving back. "Don't forget dinner at my house tomorrow night. David's cooking."

"I *am*?" Javitz asks.

"You are," Ernie says.

I smile at their camaraderie. Javitz is so clearly happy with his move, I can't resent it any longer. And I feel less excluded, being here, traipsing through the snow with them.

"Jeff, don't worry," Ernie assures me. "Just as soon as you get used to the off-season rhythm, it'll be Memorial Day and everything will start up again."

"I gather you year-rounders *prefer* the off-season rhythm," I say, winking at Javitz.

"That's what I moved here for," Javitz says. "Remember, Ernie? Remember that weekend last fall when I came up here?"

"Girl, how could I forget?"

"It was then that I really made up my mind." He pauses, looking at me. "Made up my mind to *consider* moving here, I mean."

I frown. "Yeah, yeah, just tell the story."

"We took a long walk across the breakwater, bundled up in scarves and coats. I never imagined how glorious the wind could be on the breakwater in the fall. Afterward we stopped for dinner and we didn't have to wait for a table. The owner came over and sat with us awhile. Then we drove out to Herring Cove and watched the waves crash against the shore. So calm, so peaceful. Big skies, no people."

We're at the beach now, too, the strip of sand behind Commercial Street along the harbor, just past MacMillan Wharf. It's high tide: the waves are big and white. The snow swirls in gusts. The sea holds such power in the winter, much more so than in the summer. It is fierce and fighting, not warm and seductive. We stand there and watch it crash against the cold sand.

"*This* is why I moved here," Javitz says softly. "These waves."

"You said it, girl," Ernie agrees.

This morning, when I awoke, I missed Boston feverishly. What was I going to do with my time here? I missed the movies at the Brattle, the free outdoor concerts in Copley Square, the Thai and Indian and Ethiopian restaurants. The night before, the vegetables at the Provincetown A&P had depressed me terribly: withered and dry, the remnants of last week's shipment. Provincetown during the summer had meant fun and dancing and partying and tricking. Provincetown in the snow made me feel lost and alone, abandoned and adrift.

But now, standing here watching the waves, I'm feeling a little differently. "I think I understand," I tell Javitz. "A little better, anyway."

Ernie puts his arm around me. "It takes some getting used to, Jeff, but you'll get it. I really think you will. Hey, you've got it easy. It's April. Think about those of us who were here in December, and January, and *February*. Not everyone makes it."

"What happens to those who don't?" I ask.

Ernie just laughs. Javitz raises an eyebrow. "Living in Provincetown year-round," he says, "is what separates the men from the boys."

We all smile. It's time for coffee. We push through the wind back to Cafe Express. In the summer, it's impossible to get a table here. Now, we share the place with only a couple of men in their late fifties, both smoking. Javitz lights up as well. Everyone smokes in Provincetown in the winter. I don't even raise an issue of it. A cloud of blue-gray smoke hangs over the whole cafe.

The waiter brings over our coffees. He's handsome: dark and bearded, my age or a little older. Funny how I haven't seen many boys since I arrived here. I find myself holding the eyes of the waiter. It's a little unnerving, cruising somebody possibly older than I am. Unnerving, but exciting, too. Haven't done that since—well, Javitz.

I pull my eyes away from him and sip my coffee. "I don't want to fit in *too* well," I announce. "I'm only here for a little while."

Ernie winks. "Girl, you're gonna love it so much you're *never* gonna leave."

Javitz eyes me. "Would that be so horrible?"

"You're forgetting something," I tell him.

"What's that?"

"Lloyd."

Javitz leers. "Oh, no, darling. I'd never forget Lloyd."

"Excuse me if I seem to be speaking out of turn, Jeff," Ernie says, "but it seems to me that boyfriend of yours just can't seem to make up his mind what he wants."

"You're right, Ernie," I agree. "And I guess I'm just a little too impatient."

"Patience is a virtue, so they say," Javitz observes airily.

I laugh. "I've forgotten how to be patient because it no longer seems as if I have anything to anticipate."

Ernie sits back in his chair. "Did I hear right, Lady Jane? *You* have nothing to anticipate?"

"It's just that my future right now seems so unclear."

"*Girl*," Ernie says, leaning forward, "do you understand who you're talking to? What the hell do *I* have to anticipate?"

"Hey, listen. I don't know what *my* future is any more than you do. I could be—"

"What?" Ernie says, cutting me off. He seems honestly indignant now. "Run over by a bus? Hit by a Mack truck? Struck by a meteor?" He sniffs in overplayed disgust. "You negatives or think-you're-negatives are always coming up with some godawful apocalyptic scenario to prove life is just as tenuous for you. And maybe it is. Maybe tomorrow you'll trip over your own two feet coming down the stairs and break your fucking neck and die. Boy, wouldn't I feel bad *then*. But damn it, Jeff, you can still plan for tomorrow even while you're moping around over your boyfriend. You can still *daydream*. That's the difference. I no longer have the luxury of indulging in daydreams."

Quiet descends on the table as swiftly and as chillingly as the snow outside. Javitz just lets out a long sigh. Finally I say, "You're right, Ernie. I was being an asshole."

"Aw, no you weren't," he says, shaking his head, a little embarrassed by his outburst. "I just get a little testy every now and then. You have every right to get uptight about your life. Nobody's got it easy."

"I think," Javitz weighs in, "the key word here is 'empathy.' "

"Ernie has a point," I say. "Unless something catastrophic happens, I assume I'll be here five years from now, with Lloyd or without him. You two can't say that with as much certainty."

"But to be empathic is to understand we all experience many different kinds of deaths, all the time." Javitz smiles. "Darling, it was very refreshing to hear you refer to my potential death so calmly and rationally. You've never done that before."

"Sure I have."

"No, you haven't. When I was in the hospital last December and was obsessed with dying, you never once entertained the thought." He pauses. "At least, you never articulated the thought."

"But I knew you weren't going to die."

"Not then. But I will."

We're at the edge, the border I know is there and won't cross.

Why does he do this? "I *know* you will," I acknowledge irritably. "I just said that."

I cannot imagine a world without Javitz. It is even harder to imagine than a world without Lloyd. Neither can I imagine a world in which Javitz is not sick. It's as if I expect that Javitz will just go on living with the virus for the rest of both our lives. He'll get sick, as he always has, and we'll go to the hospital, and he'll get better, as he always has, and then we'll be in Provincetown again, sitting here around this table, drinking coffee. How absurd, because my intelligent mind knows he'll die long before I do, that there will come a time when Javitz is no longer in my life. But to visualize such a reality is impossible.

"I'm just glad you're here, Jeff," he says, reaching over, taking my hand in his. "I'm glad you were here so I could show you the waves in winter the way Ernie once showed them to me."

"See what Lloyd's missing?" I quip.

"Oh, don't get me going," Javitz warns. But it's too late. He lights a cigarette, inhales deeply, and then blows the smoke over his shoulder. "Let me tell you about Lloyd. And you know I love him. More than the sun above and the waves of the sea. You know that."

"Oh, I have a feeling this is going to be good," Ernie says.

"And I understand his need to go searching for his path," Javitz goes on. "In fact, I applaud him for doing so. I admit up-front what I am about to say is completely selfish."

"Go on," I urge.

"He said one thing to me when you both helped me move that weekend. He turned to me just before you left and whispered in my ear. 'Don't worry,' he said. 'No matter how far apart we are, when you need me, I'll be there.' "

"How sweet."

Javitz stubs out his cigarette. "Was it? *When I need him.* When will *that* be, in his mind? When I'm too sick to get out of bed? When I'm down to sixty pounds and can't get up even to shit? Oh, I'm very reassured that Dr. Lloyd Griffith will be here to change my bedpan. But that's not when I need him. I need him *now*. When we can have *fun*. When I'm still living. I don't need him when I'm dying. I can hire a nurse."

"You miss him as much as I do," I tell him.

He smiles over at me. "I meant it when I said I was glad you were here, Jeff, so I could show you the waves."

"It's all so fucking confusing," I say. "I can't understand what happened to us."

"Well," he says, eyes over the brim of his coffee cup, "at least you can't go on anymore about how straights have it easier. How's your sister-in-law doing?"

I sigh. "I'm not sure. I talked to my mother last night. They found my brother, you know."

"Where?"

"In a motel just outside of town. That's where he's living. It's a big scandal. I mean, he's the history teacher at the high school!"

"Heteros," Ernie sniffs. "Have they no shame?"

"It's wild. Kevin was the only one of us who always played by the rules. Who lived the life Mom and Dad wanted. Now look. My mother actually *thanked* me last night."

"For what?"

"For not causing her stress. Said I was the only one of her kids she didn't have to worry about."

We all enjoy a big laugh over that. Outside the snow whoops and howls, rattling the windows. I wonder if I'll make it to Memorial Day. Will I still be here then? Maybe Lloyd will have called; maybe we'll have some new place to call home. Or maybe I'm here through the summer again, and the fall, too, and the winter beyond that. "Think about those of us who were here in December, and January, and February," Ernie had said. "Not everyone makes it."

Of course not: that's what separates the men from the boys.

Boston, October 1994

The day began as a celebration with Lloyd, but this is where I find myself now: behind a clump of bushes in a ravine, my heart beating wildly in my ears, a filthy twenty-dollar bill smoldering in my pocket, and the flashing lights of a police car reddening my eyes.

"Great, just great," I mutter under my breath.

The man standing beside me—my "john"—just grins through uneven brown teeth.

"Just great," I say again.

It's a police clampdown. I'd heard Javitz tell of such things. "If you're ever questioned, just say you were in the woods peeing," he instructed. "It's a lesser offense. And never come out of the woods with someone else."

"Go on," I tell the brown-toothed man, nodding for him to walk ahead of me through the bushes. "Go *on*."

He shushes me, still grinning, as if this were all some silly joke.

And maybe it is. What else could it be? The whole thing is absurd. Why I came out in the first place, looking for it, traveling all the way down the Mass Pike to find this rest stop Javitz told me about. Why I decided to take this man's money. Hey, a hustler worth his salt wouldn't have taken any cash before services rendered. Am I supposed to give it back now that the cops interrupted the blow job?

It's almost too pathetic. This was supposed to be a celebration weekend for Lloyd and me—our first weekend back in Boston together since closing the summer house in Provincetown. I knew all along about Lloyd's plans to go to the ashram in New York tomorrow. That was fine. I just didn't expect him to change his plans and go this afternoon, so he could be there in time for their sunrise meditation service. Maybe if I hadn't been in such a bad mood all day he wouldn't have gone. Maybe I started it. After all, I did call Eduardo this morning, just as I have for the past two weeks, and once again his straight friend Sandy told me he wasn't home. Lloyd asked why I persevered. "It's obvious he wants to get on with his life," he observed.

So I wasn't all that celebratory. "What do you want to do?" Lloyd asked. "Should we get a movie? Do you want to invite Javitz for dinner?"

"Whatever you want to do," I answered.

"This is supposed to be *our* day, Cat. What do *you* want to do?"

"I really don't care, Lloyd. Anything is fine."

Of course, that's when Naomi called, and told him about the sunrise service, and asked him what he thought about leaving today to get there in time. He held the phone to his chest and asked me what I thought. "Do whatever you want," I said impassively. He just looked at me for several seconds, then lifted the receiver to his ear again and told Naomi he'd go.

"Go *on*," I tell the man in front of me again.

He just winks at me. Oh, I get it now. Once the red lights stop flashing, he wants to resume his position on his knees. Hey, he has a right, I suppose. He paid for it. This is America, for God's sake.

His hand, in fact, is suddenly on my crotch again. When I first spotted the light, I'd pulled away and zipped up. The old man had just grinned, licking his lips.

"Don't worry, pretty boy," he whispers now, his first words this evening. "They'll be gone soon."

I miss Lloyd horribly. It started as soon as he left, as soon as the door closed behind him. What a shit I was. Eduardo was gone, out of my life. All he'd been was a summer fling. Why was I holding on so?

Sometimes I wish we had another gay male couple to talk with about all this stuff. "What's normal?" I'd ask. "What can we expect?" But all the couples we knew—Sal and Donnie, Mike and Theo, Hector and Kitt—are dead. Our friends tended to be older —Javitz's friends. Now Javitz is the only one left, and the rest are women. There's so much I could ask. "Define 'passion,'" I'd request of one of them, any of them, if they were alive. "Tell me what I need to know."

"You're going to be the first generation of out gay men to age in any real numbers," Javitz observed not long ago. "Not that you thirtysomethings aren't dying even now, along with the rest of us. But proportionately, there will be larger numbers of you reaching old age than any other generation since Stonewall. More of you are out, and fewer of you will die young."

"Great," I said. "Going boldly where no man has gone before."

"It's not easy navigating uncharted waters," Javitz admitted. "Especially when we've created a standard where eventually we all have to fail. *People get old.* It's not just gay men, you know. *Nobody's* dealt with this well, at least not here in the West. Two summers in Provincetown, then it's over. I'm not sure adulation of the elders is a better system, but at least it's something we could grow into, rather than out of."

Adulation of the elders. I met a boy at Mildred's this afternoon. I had gone there to sulk after Lloyd left. I was consumed by this gap between us, this ever-expanding gulf that I couldn't seem to fathom. Of course, I was looking—*hoping*—for a distraction, and I found it. His name was Claude. A dark boy, the way I prefer them, with the twist of a Québecois accent, my downfall. He smiled first; that at least is some small consolation. I moved over two seats to sit beside him. "You have pretty eyes," I told him. Whether he did or didn't is irrelevant now. It's a good line. Or at least it used to be.

"Thanks," he said. "What's your name?"

We exchanged vitals. He had just moved to Boston from Montreal. He was looking for work. "What do *you* do?" he asked.

"I'm a writer," I told him.

He didn't seem impressed. This child followed no script with which I was familiar. He did not even ask what it was that I wrote. Fact is, I haven't been writing much at all lately. Even the freelancing has been a bit scarce. Money's been tight; Lloyd had to pay both halves of the rent this month. But I'm expecting a big check in a few weeks, for a piece on gay artists in Provincetown. It's running in the *Globe*'s Sunday magazine. I thought about telling Claude this fact, but decided against it.

"So why Boston?" I asked.

"I'm dating a guy who lives here in the South End," he told me.

"Oh," I said, crestfallen. His eyes seemed genuinely lovely at that point, lovelier than any I'd seen in weeks. "Who is he? Maybe I know him?"

"Yeah, maybe," he said, brightening. "He's an older guy."

Now what connection was there between those two statements? I arched my eyebrows, but he seemed oblivious to his remark. He told me the older man's name. It meant nothing to me.

"And how old *is* he?" I asked.

"Thirty-two."

That's why I'm here. Poor pathetic Jeff. Reduced to selling himself to prove his own worth. Because some twenty-year-old didn't want to suck his dick, Jeff goes out and finds a sixty-year-old to do it instead. The money was merely icing: the man's eagerness was proof enough that I'm still a valuable commodity.

He had been sitting in his van in the parking lot. I was walking into the woods, and stopped to survey the scene. It was late afternoon; there should have been more cars. But this man was it, and he must have assumed only by flashing some green would he have a chance with me. Or—I could hear Javitz scolding—maybe it was simply a fetish of his. Maybe he would've paid a fat, balding seventy-year-old for the same thing.

I nodded at him and turned into the woods. I heard the slam of the van door behind me. He was panting by the time he found me, and he wiggled his tongue at me like a snake. He repulsed me, but that didn't matter. He dropped to his knees and began fumbling at my crotch. I said "Hey" and held out my hand. He didn't object. He just reached into his pocket and slapped the wrinkled, sweaty bill in my palm. It felt repulsive to the touch, and I shoved it into my jeans. It seemed to burn a hole there, singeing my thigh.

Now I'm scared shitless that I'll be arrested, hauled out from behind these bushes with this greasy, brown-toothed man, charged with impersonating a kid. But the lights are suddenly gone and we're swallowed up in darkness. "See?" the man rasps. "I told you."

He gets back to work. I'm soft as putty and just as malleable. It takes a while for him to get me up and hard again, but he's diligent. One thing you can say about these old men out in the woods: they know how to suck cock.

But so did Eduardo, after I'd taught him. "I never knew how sexual I really was," he once said. I miss him suddenly so much it hurts, and I think about him with another man, any man, and it kills me. I try to push it out of my mind, try to shoot my load down this man's throat, give him his twenty dollars' worth. But I can't, finally—even here I can't. I feel myself go soft in his mouth and he gums me, yanking my dick, stretching it obscenely. I finally pull out and zip up.

"Here," I say, thrusting the twenty back at him.

He looks surprised. He just backs away, into the bushes. I don't know what to do with it, this dead butterfly in my hands. I drop it onto the ground, then realize he'd never find it, not here in the dark.

So I take it. Money's been tight, I tell myself. It'll at least buy a quart of milk and cat food.

Provincetown, April 1995

The snow melted, right on schedule. The sun is even pushing its way through the clouds, and there's a tentative warmth to the air. The streets are still mostly barren, but the buds on the trees survived. Some of them are even beginning to blossom, bright green on limbs still cold with the gray of winter.

Ernie's right about the rhythm of the off-season. It's very comforting, very enveloping. So unlike the rhythm I knew from summer. This rhythm has nothing to do with tea dances or dick docks. This is the tranquility of a small town, a fishing village, an artists' colony, a community just waking up from the cold. This is the tip of the hat the old man in front of Zeke's Art Gallery gives me every morning. This is the hot coffee and gossip at Cafe Express. This is the quiet discovery of new places: a secluded stretch of beach, the hodgepodge of surprising gardens in the east end. They bloom now into sudden and colorful life, crocuses and early jonquils dotting a patch of brown earth as I round a corner onto Washington Street. A pot of miniature daffodils sits proudly in the sun on the ledge of a second-floor porch. An old Portuguese woman dressed all in black sweeping her sidewalk bids me a fond good morning.

The narrow streets of the east end, with their white houses angled together in close and unusual kinship, are almost like a maze, and yet I do not care if I wander too far inside. Some passages are so tight I need to jump onto a stoop to let a car pass me. I think of the winding avenues of Mykonos in the Aegean Sea. The analogy is a bit farfetched, but I can't help the association. Javitz, Lloyd, and I spent a week in Mykonos four winters ago, and we got ridiculously lost in that labyrinth of whitewashed corridors. I feel some of the same giddy disorientation now, having stumbled into a part of town I'd never taken the time to explore before.

I asked Javitz to come with me this morning, but he was too tired. "Come on," I urged. "We'll just keep walking. Let's walk as far as we can go."

The thought seemed almost to stagger him. He's been suffering from fatigue of late, a fact that worries me a little. He tries to hide it, but I can see it, there in his eyes when we're talking, a redness, a vacancy that vanishes as quickly as it appears.

"No," he said. "You go, darling. Discover the town yourself. Make it your own."

It was good advice. I need that grounding. I need to feel this is *my* town, too, that *I* have a place here—beyond Javitz, beyond Lloyd, beyond the boys of summer. Javitz's house is, after all, *his*. Unlike our summer places, which were furnished with the mismatched, discarded pieces of other people's lives, this is Javitz's *home*. His things surround us: his couch, his photographs, his books—the ones I remember seeing on his shelves in Cambridge my very first night there. I've suddenly dropped down into the middle of his life, and I've got to carve out my own little space somewhere in the midst of that.

Had this been one of our summer places, I could have been very comfortable indeed. It's the nicest house yet: a three-story condo, with a yard and a fireplace and two bathrooms and a deck—with morning sun, of course. From the top floor, Javitz's bedroom, one can actually see the ocean as well, between a valley in the dunes. The first night after the snowstorm we watched the sun set from up there.

"Do you know Provincetown is the one place on the East Coast where you can watch the sun set over the ocean?" Javitz asked. His voice was sincere in its love for the place. In that moment, he really didn't remember he'd told me that fact a dozen times.

I've crossed Commercial Street now and pad onto the beach. The harbor is much calmer since the storm, retreating bashfully into low tide. I follow the twisting high-water trail of blue sea grass. Along the way I greet a few who pass by: a woman with her dog, anxiously bounding ahead of her; a father with two little girls, fascinated by the sea birds scampering about on the sand; a teenaged boy, probably a local, sullen and withdrawn.

I walk for what must be at least half an hour. I must be nearing the border of North Truro by now: ahead of me, the little cottages of that seaside community decorate the horizon. I stand and breathe in the fragrance of the ocean. So clean, so alive, so real.

"Excuse me?"

The voice is distant, caught by a swoop of wind.

"Excuse me? *You* there."

I turn. About ten yards away sits a man at an easel. From this distance I can't tell much about him, except that he appears to be quite old. He's gesturing to me.

"Do you see that piece of driftwood over there? Would you bring it in closer, please?"

I look to my right. There's a crooked arm of black wood in the sand. The painter is motioning for me to bring it towards him.

I obey. It's slimy and rather heavy. "Where do you want it?" I ask.

"Right about . . . there." He points with his chin.

I let it drop. It makes a dull thud in the sand.

"Thank you," the painter says, his eyes moving back to his easel. I can see him better now. He's very tanned, with old, leathery skin, almost completely bald, except for some longish white hair around the sides. His white beard is close-cropped and neatly trimmed, which surprises me, given his unruly eyebrows, which look like little rows of unclipped wheat.

There's something about him that keeps me standing there. Might he be famous? Lots of well-known painters live down here in the east end. This is the heart of Provincetown's artistry: this is where Eugene O'Neill and John Dos Passos lived and wrote. Tennessee Williams rented a shack not far from here. I watch the man study his canvas intently. He lifts his paintbrush and glances over at the fallen driftwood. Then he raises his eyes to me.

"Yes?" he asks.

"Oh, I'm sorry. I was just—watching you paint."

He grins. "Why don't you just stand there a few minutes? Maybe that's what this needs. A man standing in the distance."

I'm honored. "Sure," I say, shifting my weight into a comfortable standing position, flattening out my hair before I have a chance to even realize I'm doing it. "Hey, will this be exhibited somewhere?"

"Oh, I've long stopped painting for exhibition. I just give my work away now."

There's several seconds of silence as he looks quickly at me, then back at the canvas. His eyebrow whiskers rise and fall in his appraisal of me. I'm not sure if I should say anything, if that might disturb his flow. But then he talks to me.

"You a tourist?"

"No. Not really."

"A townie then?"

"Well, not really."

His eyes peer around the canvas at me. "So what *are* you?"

"I don't know," I say, smiling. "That's the problem."

He chuckles. That's the right word, too: chuckles. His whole body moves when he laughs. He runs his cracked brown hand over his short beard and levels his eyes at me. "You're here because you have nowhere else to be," he says. "You have no idea how long you'll stay, but you can't imagine it'll be very long."

"Right on the money. How'd you know?"

"It's everybody's story when they first come to town."

"Was it yours?"

"Sure was. But that was a long, long time ago."

"How long?"

"I arrived here from New York in 1967."

"Wow," I say. Even Javitz was just a kid then. "I imagine the town has changed a lot, huh?"

"Guess it has. Don't really think about it much. There weren't so many tourists back then, I suppose. It was gay, but not gay the way it is today."

"What do you mean?"

"It was the counterculture. Hippies and free lovers. Not professional gay boys with lots of money to throw around."

"Were you one of them?" I ask. "The hippies and free lovers, I mean."

He chuckles again. "Oh, no, not me. I was already too old, even then. I was already at the age where they said you were too old to trust." He looks over at me. "I was about your age."

That stings, but just a little. "How old do you think I am?" I challenge.

He studies me for a moment. "Thirty-three," he says.

I smile despite myself. "Right on the money, yet again."

"And thirty-four this year, I imagine."

"This summer," I say. "Guess I can't get away with it anymore."

"Get away with what?"

"Well, summer in Provincetown can be pretty tough."

He makes an impatient sound with his tongue, as if I'm being a fool. "People are far too concerned about aging these days," he said, slightly irritated. "Gay people especially."

"Well, gay culture is pretty youth-oriented."

"Don't you believe it. That's your own fairy tale, concocted in your own head for your own reasons. If you choose to believe such things, there's nothing I can do to change your mind."

"Well, I guess if you don't play the game, you don't have to follow the rules."

"There was a man once a long time ago who came up here to live. Name of Henry Beston. Wrote a book about this place, what it's really like, what it's really about. You should read it. I can quote you some of it. Some of his words float around in my head every day: 'The world today is sick to its thin blood for lack of elemental things, for fire before the hands, for water welling from the earth, for air, for the dear earth itself underfoot.' "

He looks over at me. "*That's* what you need be thinking about, not how old you're getting."

I like this man. "Might I ask how old *you* are?" I venture.

"I'm sixty-*one*." He seems proud of it, sitting up straight in his chair. "And I haven't left this old town but once since I came here."

"In almost thirty years you only left here *once*?" It's a thought that seems incomprehensible.

"Just once. Had to then, couldn't avoid it. It was my lover. He got sick, and they had to take him up to Boston."

"I'm sorry. Did he . . . ?"

"He's dead." He paints a little more before continuing. "And not from the plague, either. Whenever I tell anyone my lover died they always assume it was AIDS. But we're too old for that. We're a generation ahead of the game. There's not too many of us around, but we're there." He squints at the painting. "Nope, Chester died from a plain and simple, good old-fashioned heart attack. He was fifty-three."

"Awfully young," I tell him.

"Suppose so."

"How long were you two together?"

"Thirty-one years."

"Really?"

"Yup. He was twenty-two, I was twenty-four when we met. We served in Korea together. There was no one before him, and no one ever since."

"Why, that's—" I'm a little choked up. "That's wonderful that you were together so long."

"What's the matter?" he asks, picking up on my emotion, pausing in mid-stroke. "Oh, never mind. I get it. You're here because of lover problems."

I smile. "We're in the midst of figuring out how to be together."

"There's only one way to be together," he tells me.

"What's that?"

"Be together."

I laugh. "But it's not that easy."

"No, it's not. It's not supposed to be." He stands, stretches, sets his paintbrush down on the easel and moves back to study his work. "How long has it been?"

"Six, almost seven, years."

"Ah. The old seven-year itch. It's true, you know. Seven's a hard number to come upon. Not sure why. Just is." He picks up his brush and makes a few strokes, then sets it back down. "It's the time when you pretty much stop doing the bedroom bingo with each other."

I laugh. "The bedroom bingo?"

"Sure," he says, sitting back down. "Come on. Don't tell me you guys are still groping each other under the sheets?"

"Well, not exactly."

"Well, you're not supposed to be. That's just the way it is." He moves in close toward his canvas, removing his face from my line of vision. I'm about to respond when he continues speaking, pulling back while keeping his eyes glued to whatever it was he was studying in his painting. "You know what the trouble is?" he asks. "We never prepare ourselves for difference. Therefore, when it arrives, like an unwelcome visitor some early Sunday morning, we assume it's bad. Now, if we enter relationships prepared to greet difference when it comes . . ."

I smile. "Do you speak from experience?"

"Hardly. Chester and I fought like the Bickersons." He looks over at me quickly. "Ah, but you don't remember them. A radio couple."

He's right. "So how'd you get through it?" I ask.

"Oh, we just weathered the storm. You learn to do that living out here on the beach."

"I used to believe that if you loved each other, you could make it," I tell him.

"Well, why'd you stop believing it?"

"Because everything seems so *hard.*"

"Look, with good intentions you can still miss each other. You aim in the right direction and pray real hard, but sometimes you still miss." He's back to painting, intent on something. "Just don't expect to be jumping each other's bones the way you did when you were twenty-six and had just met each other."

"But it shouldn't be that way. You should still be able to—"

He waves his hand as if to silence me. "Sure you should. And it should be summer all year round too, so we can always have lots of sun and warm water and boys in shorts. But without the winter, you know what we'd miss?"

I do know. "All this," I tell him.

"Precisely." He smiles over at me. "There's something transcendent that happens, you know, in the winter. You just wait and see." He looks again at his canvas. "Okay, thanks. I'm done with you."

I'm startled by his sudden dismissal, hesitant to leave. I turn, but then stop, looking over at him. "May I ask you a question?"

"Sure."

"How do you stand it, being alone? You said there's never been anyone since your lover died. You haven't left Provincetown in all that time. How do you *stand* it, being alone?"

He pauses, taking in a long breath and then slowly letting it out. He scratches his bald pate with the dry end of his paintbrush. "I never really thought about it. I just do." He sets down his brush. "Course, I'm not really alone. Chester, he's out there in the waves, and in the wind, and in the cry of the gulls. I don't really feel alone, to be quite honest with you." He smiles to himself. "Well, maybe sometimes I do. Sometimes I still miss him something fierce. But you just do it. You listen to the waves and the wind and you just do it. It's part of that transcendent thing I was talking to you about."

He gestures for me to come over and look at the painting. I do, eagerly. It's nothing much, just a muddy watercolor of blues and grays and a dark vertical line that I assume to be me. "It's wonderful," I tell him, and I mean it. "Just *beautiful.*"

He gives it to me. At first I refuse, but he insists, and so I ask him to sign it for me. I can't make out his name. "Doesn't matter," he says. "It's yours, not mine anymore."

All the way back home, carrying my painting ahead of me as it dries in the new spring air, I'm giddy. I can't wait to show it to Javitz, find a place where I can hang it on the wall, my own little corner of the house.

He's just gotten up when I get there. He sits on the couch looking like an old man or a little boy, or a combination of both. His hair's a mess, his eyes bleary. "You okay?" I ask.

"I'm just so tired," he says. "How was your walk?"

That's when the phone rings. Both of us jump as if a gunshot had just exploded behind us. Javitz stands slowly, his long limbs unfolding and lengthening. He walks over to answer the phone. His face betrays little. He laughs. "Yes, darling," he says at last. "He's here."

He hands me the phone. "It's Lloyd."

We exchange a look. "Hello?" I say into the receiver.

"Hi, Cat. I've got news."

"Oh? Good news?"

"I hope you'll see it that way."

I feel my stomach tighten. I hate ominous phrases like that.

"I'm moving back into our apartment," he says.

"What?"

"Cat, Drake bought it. You know how he was looking? Well, *he* was the buyer. He didn't want to say anything until the deal was final."

"*Drake* bought our apartment?"

I see Javitz's eyebrows rise from across the room.

"Yeah. And he said I can live there. We can take our stuff out of storage. We won't have to pay that huge monthly fee. And it's been way too cramped for me at Naomi's—"

"Wait a minute. *You're* moving back? You didn't say 'we.' "

There's silence on the other end of the phone.

"Well," Lloyd says finally, "Drake plans to live there, too."

I stop listening to him. What he says is lost on me. Maybe it's something to make me feel better, an attempt to reassure me. I don't know. I place the receiver down on the table and look over at Javitz. "Drake plans to live there, too," I repeat calmly.

I glance over at my painting, leaning against the wall. The blues seem to have dried into the same color as the grays. I walk out of the house. I have a vague impression that Javitz has picked up the phone and is talking to Lloyd behind me, but I can't be sure.

Besides, at that moment, all that concerns me is getting outside, getting into that new spring air, filling my lungs until they explode in my chest.

Boston, October 1994

It's Halloween, and I'm handing out candy to the trick-or-treaters. There aren't many. Back when I was a kid on Juniper Lane, there were hundreds of kids, it seemed. The street was mobbed with them, little green Hulks and orange pumpkins and the occasional giant ketchup bottle. Here in the South End, there aren't many children. A Puerto Rican family on the next block has a couple of kids still young enough to dress up as cowboys or Power Rangers. There's a lesbian couple with a baby and a six-year-old boy around the corner, and on our street itself a gay man has custody of his twin daughters, who last year dressed like Raggedy Ann and Andy. "They fought over who could be Andy," their father shrugged to me as I commented on the uniqueness of their costumes. "Drag kings in the making, I guess."

I wonder if they'll be back this year. Last year, of course, Lloyd and I had passed out the candy together, a tradition he's chosen to break this year. "Why don't you come with me, Cat?" he asked. "I think you'd like it."

"No," I said. "I want to see the costumes."

Occasionally there will be a clutch of twentysomething gay boys out for a lark, ringing doorbells dressed like Carol Channing or Lucy Ricardo. But so far no one has rung the doorbell all night, not a Carol or a Lucy or a witch or a pumpkin.

"Next to Christmas, Halloween is my favorite holiday," I tell Mr. Tompkins. "Such a wonderful way of letting a child *imagine*."

There's a bowl of bite-sized Three Musketeers bars sitting on the hall table nearest the door. I think I hear someone on the front step, but I guess I'm wrong after the bell fails to ring.

Lloyd has gone to a Halloween celebration held by some real witches, authentic practitioners of wicca. "It's important that it be held tonight, Cat," he explained. "Halloween is an important holiday in wicca. I'm sorry I have to break tradition. You could come if you want."

But again I refused. So he left, meeting Naomi and some of the other folks from his meditation group. Last week they all did a past-life regression. "You were my brother in a previous life," Lloyd told me when he got home.

"Was I gay?" I asked.

"I don't know," he said, a little impatient with me. "That wasn't important."

"Then I wasn't gay. It would've been important if I was."

Javitz was here. He listened intently to Lloyd describe falling into the trance, seeing the images of his past life surface on the black pond of his mind. Lloyd has always been a little wavy gravy, ever since I first met him, a lapsed Catholic like me who found the sudden lack of ritual and spiritual mystery in his life empty and unfulfilling. But now he and his friend Naomi seek out psychics and hands-on healers, meditate and hang crystals in their windows, chant "Om" as they walk home from the T.

"I don't understand his struggle, his search," I said to Javitz. "I've tried to talk to him about it, but he seems so restless. . . ."

"It's not that much different from your own, darling. You just have different ways of approaching it."

"My own? I'm not searching for anything," I counter. "What am *I* searching for?"

Javitz sighed. "Even the man with all the answers isn't going to try to answer *that* one."

Now it's Halloween and Lloyd's gone off to commune with witches. I asked him one last time to stick around, and he asked me one last time to come, but both of us turned the other down.

"Why don't you call Chanel?" Lloyd suggested. "She's probably just sitting home with nothing to do."

"Hardly. Ever since the breakup, she's been out every night. She's had sex with more women since leaving Wendy than she had in the entire time before her."

"What about Tommy? We haven't seen him in a while."

"Oh, I think he's still mad at me about that guy. What was his name?"

"Douglas."

"Oh, yeah. How'd you remember?"

Lloyd just looked at me.

"Why, Lloyd! Were you jealous?"

He made a face, then he was out the door.

Finally the doorbell rings. It's Freddy Krueger, and he flashes his hand of knives at me. "Trick or treat," he hisses. Behind him his mother waits impatiently.

I drop in a 3 Musketeers. "Happy Halloween!" I call out, delighted that someone has shown up.

Then the twin girls arrive, dressed as Red Sox players. "I tell you, I'm not doing a thing and they're turning into dykes right before my eyes," their father laughs.

"Happy Halloween!" I call after them.

I turn to Mr. Tompkins. "See what your father is missing?"

The doorbell rings again. It's a hunchbacked little old man with big green eyes and a scar across his forehead who looks as if he isn't wearing a mask.

"Trick or treat," he rasps.

I drop a 3 Musketeers into his outstretched paper bag and recoil immediately. "Great costume," I manage to say.

"Can you guess my name?" he asks.

"Rumplestiltskin?" I offer.

He just laughs.

I close the door. I turn, alerted by a noise. It sounded like a cough, but I can't be sure. "Lloyd?"

I hear it again. It's a deep, throaty sound. I peer around the corner into the kitchen. There, in the middle of the floor, stands Mr. Tompkins, and his body is contorting, shuddering, as if—

"It's a hair ball," I say out loud, trying to convince myself. "You got a hair ball, little one?"

He spasms. Dear God, this is no hair ball. It's a *stroke*. It's a fucking stroke. I've known it all along. I've waited for this moment, dreaded it—

"Hold on, baby. Hold *on*. I'm calling the doctor."

The doorbell rings. Damn the trick-or-treaters. I search frantically for the vet's number, rifling through the stack of papers we keep stuck behind the microwave. They scatter to the floor in confusion. Mr. Tompkins pays them no mind; his eyes are waxy and fixated, his whole body shivering with each new spasm. "Hold on, baby, *please* hold on."

The doorbell rings again, twice.

But what could the vet do even if I got to her in time? Don't think that way, Jeff, I scold myself. I find the number. I grab the cordless phone from the wall and pound in the digits. "Answering service," comes a tinny voice.

"Where's Dr. Hanley?"

"The office is closed, sir. Is this an emergency?"

"It most certainly is. My cat—he's having a stroke." I watch him. His body stiffens, his back legs shaking.

"I can page the doctor, sir."

"Yes, yes! Page her!"

I give her my number and hang up. I stand there, not knowing what to do. "Oh, God, Lloyd, why did you have to go *tonight*?" I cry. I squat on the floor next to Mr. Tompkins. I'm watching him die, I think to myself. I'm watching him die.

His little eyes suddenly turn up at me. "Baby . . . ?"

Then he upchucks a hair ball the size of a large turd and sits down peacefully on his hind legs.

"Hey," I say. The hair ball sits between us, long, slimy, and furry. Mr. Tompkins stands, sniffs it, then walks nonchalantly over to his dish and begins to eat.

"It *was* a hair ball," I whisper, almost in awe. "You're *okay*."

I reach down and hug him, pressing my cheek to his back. He reaches over and tries to nip at my ear. "You're *okay*," I say again.

The phone rings. It's the vet. "He's *okay*," I tell her, a little embarrassed. "Sorry to have disturbed you."

There are no more trick-or-treaters. It's just as well. I climb into bed and fall asleep, Mr. Tompkins at my side, breathing easily. I have a strange and twisting dream. I'm in some kind of long dark tunnel, and I can't see a thing. Somebody's following me. I turn and it's the hunchback who rang my doorbell. "Guess my name," he calls out from the dark. "Guess my name."

I begin to run. I run as far as I can, until I can run no farther. I'm winded, gasping for breath. I can't believe how out of shape I am. I used to be able to run and run and run in my dreams. I turn the corner into a room and I crouch down. I think the hunchback runs past the doorway but I can't be sure. There are other people hiding in the room as well: I can see the whites of their eyes. I reach out to touch one of them in the dark, to feel warm human flesh, to connect with another person. But I flail around aimlessly in the dark.

That's what I'm doing in my sleep, reaching out for Lloyd as I have so many times since we began sharing a bed and I'd wake up from nightmares. "Sometimes I think all I'd require of a lover is that he sleep with me," Javitz has said. "No sex. No chores. No obligations other than to be there for me in the middle of the night."

My hand slaps cold sheets: Lloyd isn't home yet. I curse the witches in my mind. But then I connect—he *is* there. I've found him. He sleeps deeply beside me, and the relief I feel shudders through my chest. I pull close to him and assume the breathing position. His arms wrap around me in his sleep. In moments, the nightmare is forgotten, and all is right in the world.

Provincetown, April 1995

"Where is he?" I hear Lloyd asking from downstairs.

"He's very angry," I hear Javitz say, and to my surprise: "I'm not sure I blame him."

"He didn't let me finish," Lloyd protests.

I appear at the top of the stairs. "What else is there to say?"

"Please, Cat, talk to me."

I relent. Slowly I descend the stairs, conscious of my effect. "Please, no melodrama," Javitz had begged after I'd returned home. He told me Lloyd was on his way here. "Just don't go crazy on him. That'll push him right away."

I had just gotten back from my walk along the beach. I found myself on the spot far out near Race Point where Eduardo and I had made love on my birthday last year. I sat down in the sand and shivered in the cold breeze, watching the dunes break apart gently in the wind, sand blowing into the sky, stinging my eyes.

And of course I began to search. My fingers pressed into the sand at my sides, and although I never took my eyes away from the sky, I moved my hands through the cold, damp sand, hoping, praying they might catch on a chain, and I'd pull from the earth an antique star, a four-pointed star that I would wear forever under my shirt, close to my heart.

But at the moment, I've given up on miracles. All I know is that Drake—Drake Anderson Knowles, a richie from way back—is living in *my* apartment with *my* lover, and I'm out here by myself. And I'm pissed.

"He's taken my *place*," I say to Lloyd after Javitz has left us alone. "It couldn't be more perfect. The furniture comes back; *you* come back. The only thing missing is *me*."

"Jeff, calm down."

"I won't calm down! Fuck you! It's all very pretty. All very neat. How did you ever think of it? I just can't believe you went to all the trouble of packing up all our stuff and hauling it to the storage bin when you knew all along that as soon as I was gone, you'd go and bring it right back."

"You think I *planned* this?"

"No," I say. I don't, not really. "But it feels that way."

He tries to touch me but I shrug him off.

"Jeff, I won't do it. It was a stupid, stupid idea."

I cross my arms and turn away from him. "That you would even *consider*—"

"It just seemed to make sense, Jeff. I'm sorry. I didn't think how it would affect you. I've been so caught up in my own shit. I'm sorry."

I'm still facing away from him. I don't want to give up being angry, not yet.

"Jeff, it's not like I don't miss you. I do, horribly."

"Then let's find an apartment together."

He sighs. He drops his arms to his sides and looks away. "Oh, Jeff. I'm just not ready to move back in together. We need time."

I turn to face him. "How much more time do we need?"

"I don't know."

"Is this about Drake? Did you want to move in with him because you thought you could be lovers?"

"No. I don't think Drake and I—"

"Well, I'm sure he does."

Lloyd sits down on the couch, exhausted. "I don't know what he thinks."

"Are you just trying to get back at me because of Eduardo?"

Lloyd seems to say a mantra in his head before answering. "Jeff, you're spinning out of control."

"And by the way," I ask, reveling in how nasty I can be, "whatever happened to Drake's going off to find his path, traveling across the country?"

Lloyd hesitates. "He got another job at the hospital."

"I thought he hated the hospital."

Lloyd swallows. "It's a better job. He couldn't turn it down."

I sneer. "Paid too much money, huh?"

He doesn't respond.

"So how do we leave this? How am I supposed to plan for the summer, the fall? When will you be ready?"

"Jeff, I think—I think we ought to just stay living apart for a while. Not plan to find another place."

Not plan to find another place. The gravity of those words threatens to pull me down, but I fight them. "What are you saying?"

He tries to hug me, but again I push off his arms. "I'm saying," he says, "I think we ought not to live together until I can figure out my shit."

"You want to break up, then."

"You can call it whatever you want."

I take a deep breath. My eyes find my painting, still leaning against the wall, and I focus on the dark figure that's supposed to be me amid the blues and the grays.

"It's just that it's gotten too comfortable," Lloyd says. "I want to see if we can find a way to make it less comfortable, less *settling.*"

" 'Too comfortable'? What the *hell* is wrong with comfort? I *like* being comfortable. It's a *good* thing, Lloyd."

"Too much of anything is never a good thing." He sighs. "Look, it's not as if this just *happened.* It's not as if this hasn't been building up. *You* had a hand in this outcome, too."

I make a face as if he's crazy.

"Ever since last summer, you've been different, Jeff. I know you'll never love me again in the way you loved Eduardo."

I stare at him. "Fuck you, Lloyd," I say huskily. "Fuck you a million times and then fuck you again."

"Don't talk to me that way," he says, getting indignant.

I snap. "Don't *you* huff up your chest at *me!* Don't *you* talk about Eduardo when you have *Drake* living with you in *our* apartment! Did it ever occur to you that maybe I'm not *supposed* to love you in the way I loved Eduardo? Did it ever occur to you that maybe we're *exactly* where we're supposed to be, that maybe what we feel for each other is not what it was six years ago but has actually become something even better, and brighter, and more—well, *transcendent*?"

"Oh, Cat, I want to say the right thing, I want to do right by you. . . ."

"Don't bother. I don't *need* anyone to take care of me. Not you, not Javitz. I can do it myself." I look at him squarely. "And I'll start right now. Get the hell out of here, Lloyd."

He knows I'll throw a major fit if he refuses. He understands me well enough to know that in moments I might just throw something across the room. I've done it before. And this time, he won't be around to glue it back together again.

He pulls on his coat. He yells up the stairs: "Javitz, I'm going for a walk. I'll be back."

Javitz is downstairs as soon as he hears the front door close. He doesn't say anything, just stands there looking at me. Poor guy: he feels miserable, I can tell, and here I am, yet again in the throes of a personal crisis. "Are you all right?" I ask.

"I came down here to ask the same of you," he tells me.

"I'm *fine*." I approach him, studying his yellowed eyes, the sudden gauntness of his face. Something is wrong; something *is* happening. "You need to promise me one thing," I tell him.

"What's that, darling?"

"You're going to let me take care of you for a change."

He smiles. "I gather that I have no choice."

"Oh," I say, laughing a little bitterly, "we *always* have choices."

We embrace each other. "Yes, we do, darling," he says. "Yes, we do."

DEATH

Katie Haaglund was the first person I ever knew who died. She was a little girl with a flat face and freckles, whom I played with once or twice and who died when I was still just a little boy.

"Katie Haaglund has leukemia," my mother told me one rainy afternoon.

I stood there in our kitchen, shuffling my feet back and forth on the red-and-blue speckled linoleum floor. A rerun of *Gilligan's Island* was playing on the TV in the living room. I was on my way out to watch it when my mother gave me the news.

"She's in the hospital," my mother told me.

"Really?" I asked, betraying little concern. I was eight, maybe a little younger—but certainly at the age where showing concern for a neighborhood girl was considered silly.

"They're going to ask us to pray for her in church," my mother said.

That's what I'm telling Javitz now, trying to make him laugh as the nurse wheels him down the corridor of the hospital. I'd forgotten how bright hospitals are. So much artificial light. My eyes blink against the whiteness. "Don't worry," I say to Javitz, averting my eyes. "I'll have Father McMurphy pray for you in church."

But he says nothing in reply.

I try to goad him into laughing. Lloyd, walking on the other side of the wheelchair, looks over at me and scowls. He's not in the mood for levity. Javitz's sudden illness has scared him, thrown him for a loop. Javitz begins coughing.

"Here's your room, Mr. Javitz," the nurse says, abruptly turning him at an almost ninety-degree angle into a small, private room. He hacks in reply.

It's been some time since Javitz was in the hospital. The last time was several years ago, and we thought he was going to die. He didn't, of course, so I'm less frantic this time. But Lloyd hovers around Javitz like a nervous butterfly, and Javitz, of course, con-sumed by the pneumonia, is convinced this is the end.

And maybe it is. I look at him as the nurse and two orderlies settle him into the bed. He looks like a little old man, or a little boy. Or both. They've got him in one of those johnnies, and his legs look as spindly as a bird's sticking out from under the white cotton. Lloyd arranges the sheet up around him. Might this be it, then? Might this finally be the end of it all?

"Let us pray," the old priest had said, and that Sunday he had indeed prayed for Katie Haaglund. It seemed everyone in our neigh-borhood was Catholic, and we all went to the same church. When someone was prayed for from the pulpit, it was serious. It meant the person faced death—and usually, that it was imminent. Death was something dark and mysterious for me back then; I couldn't imagine ever knowing someone who'd died. All four of my grandparents were still living then; even Junebug was still a frisky kitten. I'm pretty sure that *Gilligan's Island* was effectively ruined for me that afternoon my mother told me Katie Haaglund had leukemia—even if it was the one where Mary Ann thinks she's Ginger or the one where a ghost haunts the island (my two all-time favorite episodes). I'm pretty sure all I did was think about Katie, lying there in that hospital bed, and the fact that they were going to *pray for her in church.*

When the annoying little cold Javitz developed right after Hal-loween was still hanging around a week later, he called and said, "I think I'm getting pneumonia again."

I hurried over to Cambridge, made him a big pot of steaming chicken soup (elbow macaroni and leftover Kentucky Fried Chicken), and ordered him to bed. "You're not getting pneumonia," I said. "We'll knock this out of you."

But by the next day he was too weak to even lift the spoon to his mouth, so I fed him. "Here," I said, wiping his chin. "Eat up. This is my magic recipe. It'll make you better."

"No, Cat," Lloyd said. "We've got to take him to the doctor."

So here we sit, each of us on one side of his bed, and he looks so weak, so drawn, so yellow. Like Gordon had in those last couple of weeks, that eerie shine that emanates from the skin just before death. Lloyd stands up, edgy, places his left hand just a fraction over

Javitz's forehead and begins to chant. He closes his eyes to hide the terror in them.

I close my eyes too. And I see Katie Haaglund, a stern little girl, the daughter of Swedish immigrants with blond hair and broad faces. Katie, however, was dark, with a flat face and freckles. Her death shocked the neighborhood. My mother and all the other ladies brought cakes and pies and casseroles to the Haaglund family the day Katie died. "How are they going to eat all that?" I asked, but I was merely shushed.

For some reason, my mother had thought Katie and I should play together. Once, she took me to Katie's house. She and Mrs. Haaglund drank coffee in the kitchen and watched Katie and me play in the backyard. I don't remember now what Katie and I played, but I'm pretty sure I told her that day a riddle my mother had once told me, a silly little ditty she must have heard on the radio. "A girl is put in a room with no windows and only one door . . ."

When my mother first told it to me, I thought and thought, determined to come up with the answer. "What happened to the girl?" my mother asked. *She slipped out when they opened the door. She was hiding in a secret passage. She drank an invisible potion.* But my mother just grinned.

"The radiator," she said. "Get it, Jeffy? The radiator! The radi *ate* her!"

I hated that answer. "No, no," I protested. "She was okay. She got out. She found a key and opened the door. . . ."

My mother just laughed.

Katie didn't like the answer any better than I did. "That doesn't make any sense," she said, frowning.

Funny how I'm thinking of Katie Haaglund, standing over Javitz's hospital bed, Lloyd trying to heal him with psychic energy. Javitz has fallen into a steady breathing rhythm. He licks his lips as if he's trying to say something. Lloyd stops chanting and bends down.

Javitz rasps, "What was the name of that guy in ACT UP, the one who had the cross tattooed on his forehead?"

"Why?" Lloyd asks.

"Just—what was his name?"

Lloyd looks over at me. "Wasn't that Todd?" I ask.

"Yeah," Javitz nods. He can barely speak. "Is he dead?"

"Why don't you just rest? Stop trying to talk," I tell him.

"He's dead," Javitz whispers, and closes his eyes.

Lloyd gets up and moves into the doorway, staring out into the hall. I come up behind him. "You okay?" I ask.

"This is absurd, you know. Nobody gets pneumonia anymore."

"That's not true. We just don't hear about it like we used to. Javitz just refused the Bactrim."

Lloyd hangs his head. "This is it for him, you know," he says, very, very quietly. "Last week, at my meditation group, I had a vision of Javitz. It was like he was an angel."

"Javitz?" I ask. "An *angel*?"

"It was like he was dead."

We're silent a minute. Behind us Javitz has drifted into sleep. His chest heaves in rattling snores. We step outside into the bright fluorescence of the hallway.

"It's hard for us to understand," Lloyd says, "but death has its place in life."

"Sure," I say. "At the end of it."

He grimaces. "No, I mean, death is a part of how we live. It has its purpose, its place. Death is not a bad thing, not something to fear."

"It sucks," I say plainly.

"That's the wrong attitude, Jeff," he scolds.

"How about if we just call it *my* attitude instead of 'wrong'?"

"Part of the reason I'm exploring my spiritual path is because of Javitz," Lloyd offers.

"As if I couldn't figure that out. Lloyd, you're scared shitless about him dying. Admit it."

"I'm not sure I'd say 'scared shitless.' "

"Well, then, whatever. All I know is death scares the hell out of *me*. It always has. Always will."

We hear Javitz coughing again inside the room. We both head back to his bedside.

"You want some water?" Lloyd asks. The fear is right there on his face, no matter how much he may try to deny it. I watch as he holds the cup of water to Javitz's lips, cradling his head in the crook of his arm. I watch Javitz's lips drink as if he were an invalid cat.

Then he starts barking again, spewing the water over his bedsheets.

And suddenly I wonder if they might be right, if this is indeed the end. I wonder if I too am denying my fear by the very act of acknowledging it. But how will I react the moment Javitz's eyes turn glassy, the second his cough stops, the first time I touch his hand and find it cold?

After Gordon died, I thought nothing could be more horrible than seeing his gray body exposed on the white sheets, his shriveled dick mocking the passion we once felt in the front seat of his mother's car. But seeing Stick was worse. The second of the Three Musketeers put up a longer fight: kicking and thrashing in his sheets, cursing me for coming before he lost his voice to the morphine. "Look at you," he spat. "Pitying me."

"I don't pity you," I said.

"Well, I pity you," he said. "I pity all of you who are left."

I tried to calm him but he was in pain, twisting under that thin film of sheets, the dark contours of his body clearly seen through the fabric. He had always been tall and thin—hence his nickname —but now he was something obscene, a sideshow attraction, the Living Skeleton. His sunken face stared at me with hatred, his eyes shining with the power of his pain. *This* was death. *This*. Not the beautiful death of Garbo in *Camille*, gently coughing into a lace handkerchief, propped up by pillows, her deathbed hair and makeup provided by the best MGM technicians. Not the noble sacrifice of Bette Davis at the end of *Dark Victory*, turning calmly to Geraldine Fitzgerald to say, "Is it getting dark?" No, death was Stick writhing in his bed. Death was poor Aunt Agatha rotting for days on her living-room couch. Death was little Katie Haaglund in her tiny white coffin.

I never went to Stick's funeral. I'm not even sure if he had one. But I went to Katie Haaglund's all those years ago. My mother thought it would be good for me, as Katie had been "my friend." I disputed the designation. "We only played together *once*," I said, dreading the idea of the church and the mourners and the baby casket, but I was taken anyway. I kept my eyes on the floor the whole time.

Actually, there was one other time Katie came over to play, and it's that time that catches me in the throat every time I think about it, even now. It was maybe a few months after she and I played in her backyard. This time, I was at my house with another friend, a boy, a faceless, nameless child lost in the swirls of memory. But for whatever reason—maybe because she was a girl and this is how boys behave, or maybe because I was a kid who did terrible, senseless things—I decided I didn't want Katie to join us.

"Katie's a baby! Katie's a baby!" we chanted gleefully, and whether she cried because we called her a baby or if we called her a baby because she cried, I can't remember. But we ran after her, and she cried buckets. *God,* how she cried. All the way back up the street, her little flat face spitting out tears right and left, while inside, unbeknownst to any of us, those little leukemia cells were doing their horrible handiwork. My buddy and I turned to each other like victorious warriors, having saved our precious little male games from the female intruder. We slapped our hands high over our heads, laughed at how hard we made Katie cry.

But by that night, I'd already begun feeling guilty. The worst horror came just weeks later, the day my mother told me about Katie's leukemia. Somehow those two events linked themselves forever in my mind: I was mean to her, and then she died.

"It makes no sense," Lloyd says, startling me.

"What makes no sense?"

"How he keeps asking if people he knows are dead."

"Nothing makes sense," I say.

Least of all death. When Katie died, I showed little emotion. But at night, in my bedroom, after Kevin had fallen asleep and would begin to snore, I'd cry my tears for Katie Haaglund. She *had* been my friend, even if for just one day, one day out of the thousands of my childhood. The neighbors all said things like "Poor little girl" and "Makes no sense at all" and "Here today, gone tomorrow." Leukemia became that dreaded harvester of children, and there was a part of me that waited alone in the dark for it to claim me, too. But more than that, I feared it would claim all the other children around me, and everyone in my family, and that I'd be left alone.

"Katie is with God now," my mother told me, but I wasn't sure if I believed her. After all, she had told me that riddle, too, that stupid, terrifying, goddamned—

"My cousin Howard," Javitz grates, pulling me back to him. "Is he dead?"

"I never knew you had a cousin Howard," I say.

He nods, but just closes his eyes. I look over at Lloyd, whose eyes are liquid in the light. He reaches down and takes Javitz's hand. Suddenly I'm overcome with a horrible sense of finality, that this is it, the beginning of the end. For all of us. I feel terribly weak, as if my knees will buckle.

"I—I'm going out to call Chanel and Melissa," I say. "Maybe they should—maybe they might want to come by and see him."

Lloyd nods.

At the end of the corridor there's a phone. I blink back the horrible brightness and press Chanel's number. When she answers, I start to cry.

"Jeff, what's the matter?" she asks.

I'm not thinking right. "Katie Haaglund's dead," I tell her.

And I start to cry harder, as hard as Katie did, all those years ago. Poor little girl. Made no sense, not then, not now. Here today, gone tomorrow. Where did she go? What happened to the girl?

I know.

The radiator.

It's the only answer that makes any sense at all.

Provincetown, April 1995

"Why didn't you tell us any of this before?" I'm asking Javitz. Lloyd is sitting next to me, right by my side.

"Darling, there was nothing to tell."

Lloyd stands, impatient. "What do you mean, 'nothing to tell'? This *fatigue*—"

"And the loss of vision," I add. "Javitz, why didn't you tell us before that you were having trouble seeing?"

He reaches across the table for his cigarettes, then thinks better of it. "I've made an appointment for next week at the clinic here," he says. "We'll just take it one step at a time." He looks back and forth between us. "All of us. We'll *all* take it one step at a time."

Lloyd kneels beside him suddenly. "I'm sorry I haven't been around."

Javitz caresses Lloyd's cheek. "Oh, but you have, darling. You never leave me. I've missed you, but I got over that. I knew you were never really far away."

They embrace. "I'm not going away from you again," Lloyd promises huskily.

I catch his eye. He can't promise me the same thing. When he came back, he found Javitz and me sitting here. I'd finally gotten Javitz to talk about the fatigue, and then he mentioned that he'd been steadily losing his vision. He'd be in the grocery store and he couldn't see to the end of the aisle. He scraped his car against the side of a house on one of the east end's narrow lanes.

Lloyd sat down beside me, listened to it all. His eyes came alive in a way I haven't seen them in a long time. As if this was what he'd been searching for all along—or running away from. Either way, there was no avoiding it now.

"Maybe you should get back on an antiviral," Lloyd says.

"There's something else coming out," I offer. "Tommy told me about it. Something called a pro—?" I can't remember the name.

Javitz nods. "They're called protease inhibitors. They're not widely available yet, and when they are, they're going to be outrageously expensive. You have to take them with an antiviral. The idea is that the protease will inhibit the replication of the virus, and then the antiviral will have an easier job attacking what's left."

"That's good news," Lloyd says.

Javitz shrugs. "Maybe. So was AZT ten years ago." He stands. "We'll just take it one step at a time."

"But you'll ask the doctor about them? These protease things?" I say.

He looks at me. "Darling, I'm going to die, and I'm going to die of AIDS. Maybe not right now, maybe not tomorrow. But I *am* going to die. It's sooner now, rather than later. And yes, I am going to let you take care of me." We hold each other's gaze for several seconds. Then he looks over at Lloyd. "And you, too."

Nobody says a word. He walks to the stairs. "I'm going up for a nap," he tells us. "Will you still be here when I get up, Lloyd?"

"Yes," he says.

"Good." Javitz smiles, then heads upstairs.

"Cat," Lloyd says.

I don't answer.

"Cat, we need to find some balance with each other. If Javitz gets sick—"

"If Javitz gets sick," I repeat, "we'll *have* balance. But right now, I don't feel very balanced, and I don't think I want to, either."

He's silent.

"I'm going for a walk," I tell him.

"Jeff." He comes to me, looks me square in the eyes. "I love you."

I turn away. Damn, why is it even now I can't stay angry at him? "I know you do, Lloyd," I say, pulling on my coat. "Listen, I won't be gone long."

Outside the sun is starting to set. The town glows with a reddish gold sheen. I head back to the beach, where the wind now swirls in mighty gusts. The waves are fiercer now as the tide comes in. This is why I moved here. These waves.

"Not yet," I whisper to the waves. "He can't die yet."

Then when? Next year? The year after that? It's sooner now, rather than later. After all those years, in and out of the hospital, back and forth—even long-term survivors die eventually.

Life without Javitz. I cannot bear to imagine. It is impossible. He has always been there, longer than any of the others. His move here was supposed to give him a new lease on life, a new beginning. Now he's going to die. He's going to *die*, and it's sooner now, rather than the ambiguous, comforting "later" that it's always been before. He's going to *die*, just as Lloyd has left me, and our happy family will forever be gone, and I'll be alone.

You're angry with me because you're afraid I'm not going to take care of you anymore.

"Not yet," I repeat. "Please, not yet."

I'm walking along the narrow strip of sand, moving in and out as the tide comes in, each time a little more aggressive than the last, each time claiming a little more of the shore. I find myself in the same spot where I'd met the painter earlier. His easel still stands there, forlorn and empty. I approach it, and follow with my eyes the windswept footprints that lead up to a small gray, barnacled cottage.

I see the painter inside, under the soft orange glow of a table lamp, eating his dinner. His long hair is slicked down now, as if from a shower, the bald top of his head shining under the glow of a single unshaded gold bulb.

"Hello?" I call, knocking gently on his screen door.

He squints. "Oh, hello. It's you, my portrait model. Come in."

I step inside hesitantly. The cottage smells of paint and turpentine. Dozens of canvases are stacked against the walls. An old black stove slumps to my left; in front of me the painter sits at a rusted linoleum table. "I don't mean to interrupt you, but as I thought about it, I really felt I should give you something for the painting."

He grunts at the idea. On the plate in front of him are the remains of a baked trout, its head and eye all that are left on the long, prickly skeleton. I think it odd that he's eating trout and not lobster or clams or any of the seafood native to Provincetown. A half-filled bottle of red wine sits beside an empty glass. He wipes his mouth with a paper napkin and shakes his head. "No, no. I gave that to you. I've long since stopped taking payment for my art."

"Well, then I thought maybe I could interview you. Do an article about you for the local paper."

"Whatever for?"

I'm not sure. "Maybe I just wanted to talk to you some more," I admit.

He pours himself some wine, then holds up the bottle to me. "No thank you," I say. He gestures for me to sit down.

"Is this about your lover?" he asks.

"Well, yes, partly. I—I guess I just wanted to hear more about Chester—*your* lover—and what you said about the wind and the waves and the gulls."

He sighs. "I'm not sure there's more to say. It's just part of the cycle of life. An ingenious cycle, really. Chester, he believed that he'd come back as a seagull. I think that's crap, if you ask me. But still, when those seagulls cry out there, I feel Chester's talking to me."

"So it's just you making yourself feel better."

"Perhaps. And what'd be so bad about that?" He takes a long sip of his wine. "But it's more than that. When Chester died, up in that Boston hospital, a lightning storm struck just at the moment I saw the light go out in his eyes. Some folks say it was just a coincidence. But I'll tell you. After living on this same beach for nearly thirty years, watching the seasons come and the seasons go, watching the gulls eat the sand crabs and the cats eat the gulls, there's only one thing I don't believe in anymore. And that's coincidence."

"My lover says the same thing," I tell him. "That there's no such thing as coincidence. That it's all part of something, something bigger, something connected."

The painter smiles at me gently. "He's dying, isn't he, your lover?"

I pause. I think about it. "Yes," I say. "Yes, he is. It's sooner now, rather than later."

He nods his head. "That's what I thought."

"I want to believe that he won't leave me. That's what scares me. That he'll leave me, and I'll be alone."

"Sometimes you will be. Other times—" He shrugs. "You just come out here and watch the waves."

He stands with some difficulty, bends down to hunt through an old wicker box. He finds a small book, its cover, cracked and faded, depicting a cottage among tall grass and sand dunes. "This is the book I told you about earlier. Take it. It's yours."

"Oh, I'll return it—"

"No, keep it. I know it all by heart anyway."

I thank him for the book and his words. I stand, reluctant to leave, yet again. I turn back to him. "You know, I want to say that I'll go back now, and I'll feel better, that I'll believe, that everything will be okay. But I'm not sure I can."

"Don't expect you to. We can only be in one place in life, and that's the place we're supposed to be. You'll get to where you need to go."

We bid each other good night. The sun has disappeared now. The darkness is rich and thick, a deep chilly violet. As I walk back out onto the beach, I realize I still don't know his name, or he mine. I turn, ready to ask him, but see that his light is already out and his cottage is in darkness. It's a curious sensation I feel: as if he was never really there at all. "People seem to come and go so fast here," I whisper, Dorothy in Oz. But I hold his book in my hands. That's proof of his existence. I imagine he rises pretty early in the mornings to paint. I won't disturb him again.

I wander along the beach all the way to the pier, and decide to walk out along its length and enjoy the coolness of the night. There's light here, a milky, hazy light from the lampposts above. Several tourists mingle about, pointing up at the monument, over at the lighthouse on Long Point. I look down at the book: *The Outermost House*. There's a bookmark in one page, and I open to it. "Whatever comes to pass in our human world," I read, listening to the waves crash ceaselessly against the pier, "there is no shadow of us cast upon the rising of the sun, no pause in the flowing of the winds or halt in the long rhythms of the breakers hastening ashore. On the outer beach of the Cape, the dunes still stand in their barrier wall, seemingly much the same, but to the remembering eye somewhat reshaped by wind and wave."

Someone calls my name. I'm startled out of my reading. "Jeff?" Even as I turn, I know who it is.

"Eduardo—isn't that your friend Jeff?"

It's Eduardo's father, and Eduardo is with him. They're walking down from the end of the wharf, where Eduardo's father keeps his boat. Eduardo wears cut-off denim shorts and a big blousy white shirt. Seeing him—and the way the wind catches under his shirt, billowing it up from his lithe brown body—stops my breath in my lungs for a second. But I manage to smile and wave.

"Hello, Jeff," his father greets me, shaking my hand heartily. His grip is as strong as I remember, his hands as big. "Back for another season?"

"Actually, I don't know. I've been here for the last month, staying with a friend." I turn to Eduardo. "Hi."

"Hi," Eduardo says.

"You didn't do your paper-in-the-hat trick again this year?" his father laughs.

"No," I say, smiling. "Not this year."

Eduardo seems uncomfortable that we've stumbled onto each other. Clearly he has not told his father about our problems. I wonder if he's brought Tommy home to meet his parents.

"Well," his father says, "you ought to come out for dinner some night. Eduardo's just up from Boston, and he's already bored."

"When do classes end?" I ask.

Eduardo nods. "In a couple of weeks. Then my internship starts."

"Oh," I say. "That's right. At a newspaper. Which one?"

He hedges, then tells me the name of a gay newspaper in Boston. I grin. And he can't suppress one of his own.

Eduardo's father moves off, talking with a couple of other fishermen at the wharf. Eduardo looks awkwardly from his feet up to the star-dotted sky. "So how are you?" he asks.

"Not great," I tell him. "I'm a little worried about Javitz." I decide not to say anything about Lloyd.

Eduardo's eyes dart to mine. "Is Javitz . . . ?"

"He's been suffering from a lot of fatigue, and some eyesight problems."

He sighs. "I felt so bad this past winter. Tommy told me he'd been in the hospital. I felt so bad that I didn't know."

I don't say anything. I don't have to. He was the one who didn't return phone calls.

"He was always so good to me," Eduardo is saying, looking at me. "I'll go see him this week."

"That would be good."

We stand awkwardly again. "Eduardo," I say finally.

He looks at me as if he knows what is about to come and dreads it. "Yes?"

"I wonder if we could have lunch, or coffee, or whatever."

He looks away.

"Even simply to put closure on what happened between us."

He looks directly at me. "Jeff, I've moved on. Can't you accept that? I have fond memories of last summer. But people change. Feelings change. That's just the way things happen."

"Fine," I say. "So let's have lunch."

His father is approaching us again. "Okay," Eduardo says quickly. "We can have lunch."

"When?"

"Uh—the day after tomorrow?"

"Fine. Where?"

"I'll come by Javitz's."

I give him the address, and he moves off toward his father, who waves a warm farewell to me. Eduardo doesn't look around. I'm left feeling neither elation nor disappointment, neither happy nor sad. I just stand there and watch the waves.

Boston, November 1994

Of course, it's my brother who takes charge the moment my father dies.

The afternoon we brought Javitz home from the hospital, the pneumonia having been vanquished yet again, my brother called to give me the news. "Jeff," he said directly, without any pause, "Dad died this morning."

So here we are now, Lloyd and I, driving to Connecticut, along a particularly monotonous stretch of the Mass Turnpike. I stare out the window, counting the mile markers as we pass. How quickly things happen; how quickly plans are changed. Today we had planned to rent movies and bake brownies, prop Javitz up on the couch and get lost in the camp of *The Women* and *All About Eve*.

"Do you feel like talking, Cat?" Lloyd asks.

I shake my head no.

"Well, I'm here in case you do."

We drive in silence. Of *course* it was my brother who called, who told me where the funeral was, what time, who had been called before me. Of course it would be him. The keeper of the flame, the caretaker of the family honor. I was sure, even in my grief, that he would be there when we arrived, consoling my mother, instructing the pallbearers, the funeral director, my sister, me. My brother comes alive only in moments of crisis. The rest of the time, he sits barely breathing in front of the television set, like the lizard I had when I was a kid. I didn't know it had died until weeks later, when I reached in to lift it from its branch and it was as hard as ice. But in crises, my brother animates himself. This is, after all, what a *man* should do.

"If your brother ever cracked," Lloyd has predicted, "he'd go *completely* off the deep end."

I haven't yet shed any tears. In Boston, upon getting the news, I obsessed about the matters of my life: how long we'd be gone, if Javitz would be all right, whether we should take Mr. Tompkins to Melissa and Rose. "I've left them enough food for a day," Lloyd assured me. "And Chanel will come in and feed them after that."

"And they'll all look in on Javitz?"

"Yes, Cat. Stop worrying. Everything is under control."

We were almost out the door when I remembered something. I stopped, bent down, pulled out the drawer in the little table in the hallway. I reached in with my hand, found my father's ring, rubbed the fake amethyst with my thumb. Did I think it would be gone? Yet I didn't take it out; I couldn't bear to look at it. Then my fingers brushed against the cracked glass of the ceramic dog, and along the smooth surface of the book Eduardo gave me last summer. I closed the drawer quickly. It has become impossible to look inside.

And of course I'm right: when we arrive, my brother is already directing things. He's in the driveway, just about the spot where Junebug was killed, where the man who is now dead dropped a shovel on my old friend's neck. My brother is telling my aunt to park her car up on the grass. He spots me. He's never met Lloyd, not after all these years.

"Kevin," I say, "this is Lloyd."

He barely nods at him. He looks instead at me as if to ask how I could so dishonor our father by bringing my homosexual lover to this house. "Jeff," he says, "Mom's going to need us more than ever now."

"How is she?"

"Go on in and see her," he instructs. He turns to Lloyd. "Park the car over there."

"I'm going into town to get us a room," Lloyd says.

"You're not staying with Mom?" Kevin asks.

"If you think we should . . ." I offer.

"I think *you* should," he says.

I level my eyes at my brother. "Lloyd stays with me."

"Look," Lloyd says, "I'll go get a room and then we can decide." That seems to settle things for now. Kevin moves off to embrace my aunt.

I watch as Lloyd leaves and my heart falls. I don't want to be here alone with these people. Not now. It's as if my father's death has made them all even more like strangers to me.

I turn, expecting for a moment that my father will be standing there on the step, holding open the door, saying "Jeffy, it's *good* to see you," a twenty-dollar bill rolled up in his palm. Instead, it's his cousin, my aunt Loretta. I haven't seen her in nearly a decade. Her eyes catch me and register discomfort. The gay son has arrived, I hear whispered in my head. That's the gay one.

Ann Marie embraces me, her hard, pregnant belly between us. "Oh, Jeffy," she cries. "Poor Daddy. Poor Daddy."

The house is filled with relatives. A couple of aunts kiss me. "Jeffy," says one, "you look so much like your father did at your age."

On the wall is a photograph of my father and me, back from a fishing trip. I'd forgotten about our little forays out in his boat. I hated the whole business: spearing the worms, cleaning the fish. And usually I'd sit there all day with never a bite, since most of the fish in our nearby pond were gone. But that time, the day this particular photo was taken, my father had driven me to a lake about twenty miles outside of town. Every ten minutes or so, I remember, he'd switch rods with me. Each time, I'd discover something nibbling at the end of my line, and we'd haul in a fish. "Gee, Dad," I said, "I'm having all the luck and you're not getting anything." Such a bright boy.

I smile despite myself. In the photo, I'm beaming, holding up my booty: thirteen good-sized trout. My father grins impishly behind me.

"Jeffy," my mother says when she sees me.

We don't say much. I hug her and she strokes my hair. Later, when Lloyd arrives, she thanks him for coming. We don't stay long. Ann Marie is here, and my aunt Loretta plans to spend the night. Kevin makes a face when we leave, but I don't care. We go back to the motel room, and still I don't cry. "Cat, don't hold back," Lloyd urges, but it's as if I used up all my tears crying about Javitz and little Katie Haaglund. We fall asleep in the breathing position, and I thank God for it.

At the wake, my father is laid out in the casket, surrounded by lilies, which strangely comfort me with their aroma. "He looks good," Aunt Loretta assesses.

I glare at her. "He looks *dead*," I tell her.

I think about Javitz back in Boston. He fought back the pneumonia enough to be allowed home, but he's still pretty down. When I called to tell him that my father had died, he asked how old he was.

"Sixty-seven," I replied.

"And he died in his sleep? Lucky man."

The funeral is agonizing. Back in the pews of my childhood, as the craggy old priest offers my father's soul to Jesus—the church hasn't changed much. The same old stained-glass windows, purple and blue and vivid red. The one of St. Boniface always intrigued me: the young, sissy-looking boy in a cassock fleeing a group of hooligans throwing stones at him.

I walk my mother out of the church, and her grip on my arm is unbearably weak. Kevin's on her other side, with his wife and his kids. Behind them is Ann Marie, very pregnant, heavy mascara smeared down her face by tears, walking with her long-haired fiancé, who up until Dad's death was just her boyfriend.

My mother surprises me. "Make sure Lloyd rides back in the limousine with the in-laws and the kids," she instructs. "If Ann Marie's boyfriend can be there, so should Lloyd."

I look at her for a moment. "All right, Ma. Thank you."

It's bright and sunny, not at all like the funerals in movies, where it's always raining, horrid torrential downpours. We stand under a warm autumn sky, and the new granite stone sparkles in the sunlight. Mom's name is already there, birth year and maiden name clearly etched, just her death date waiting to be chiseled in. And there's Dad's name: JEFFREY MICHAEL O'BRIEN 1927–1994. It looks so neat and tidy. As if that's all there is to say.

I realize, standing here listening to Father McMurphy intone his final blessing, that I'm Jeffrey Michael O'Brien, Junior. I haven't thought of that in years. Strange how I ended up being Junior, and not Kevin.

The sound of dirt thudding on top of metal hurts my ears.

Back at the house, my niece tells me that *The Wizard of Oz* was on the night before. She's singing: 'There's a place that I've heard of—'" She stops, grinning up at me. "Daddy says that was your favorite movie, that he used to make witch noises and scare you."

"It still *is* my favorite movie," I tell her.

Most of the people around us are gray-haired friends of my father. "He was a *good* man," they all keep saying to me, clasping my hands heartily, as if I needed to be convinced of the fact. I just smile.

My mother sits at the kitchen table, smoking with my aunt Loretta. "I loved him, Loretta," she's saying, in that raspy voice of hers. "I *really* loved him."

I sit down with them, just as I might have when I was a child. It was always Jeffy and the ladies in the kitchen. Already some of the men have gathered in the living room. Thank God for ESPN. In the old days, what would they have done on days when no sport was being televised? Even Kevin has found a seat there now, too. His work is done. My father is buried. He can return to his chair.

"I wish he'd lived to see Ann Marie get married," my mother says. "He wanted that so much."

"And to see the baby," I say.

"Yes, that too," she agrees.

"You doing okay?"

"For now." She puts her hand on mine. Funny how her hands have never changed. They looked old even when I was a kid, with their raised veins and brown spots. I look at mine. They look like hers.

Aunt Loretta gets up and leaves us alone. "I'm glad Lloyd came with you," my mother says. "I'm glad you have someone to be with you."

"That means a lot to hear you say that."

She shrugs. She's watching the grandchildren wrestle on the floor, seemingly already oblivious to the memory of the man who used to sit in the empty chair in the corner. "He always thought he'd failed, you know," she says at last. "We never got a bigger house. Look how crowded it is in here. We're still driving a 1983 Buick." She stops, collecting her energy to keep her voice from breaking. "But I loved him. And we were together for forty-three years."

"That's hardly a sign of failure, if you ask me."

She looks up at me and smiles. For the first time in more than ten years, my mother and I smile at each other.

Later, after most of the others have left, I walk with my niece through the yard. Ann Marie is with Lloyd. They've been talking for hours. Free psychology, I imagine.

The yard seems so much smaller. Yet the bushes are deeper and the trees tangle into each other over my head. I walk over to a part of the yard that's noticeably higher, a little grassy hill in the middle of nothing.

"This was Gramma's rock garden," I tell my niece.

"Rock garden? What's that?"

"Oh, she had pansies and petunias and Johnny-jump-ups and marigolds in here, surrounded by rocks. It was really neat."

"Yeah?"

"Yeah. And she let Ann Marie and me play in here." We stand on top of the little hill. Crabgrass has overtaken the garden. I feel very vulnerable all of a sudden. I think my niece senses this, and she moves away slowly, inching towards her brother, who's playing with a truck on the patio. I sit down on a patch of crabgrass. Lloyd looks up at me from his conversation with Ann Marie, as if somehow he senses I'm about to crack.

I look to my left, and there's Dad, in the same spot where he once stood, asking me why I'd taken the clothes off my G.I. Joe. "Because I like his hard chest," I admit finally, and he smiles.

Now I'm digging with my hands gently into the soil under the crabgrass. I think wildly that I'll find her—my little plastic orange witch. My heart begins to pound, and I'm a little kid again. It's like I'm digging inside of me, and it's my flesh that's being caked under my nails.

Of course I don't find anything. I stop digging. Lloyd stands over me now, looking down. I smile, get up, brush off my pants. "It's time to go," he says gently, and I nod. We make our way over to the others to say good-bye. As we walk, I understand finally why I could never find my witch all those years ago. She's not there. She's in a place that I've heard of—once, in a lullaby.

Provincetown, May 1995

It's Memorial Day weekend, and the town is packed. The boys have arrived in droves, hooting and hollering all through the streets in their little shorts and boots and open shirts. All winter long they've prepared for this very moment. They've bought all the accessories from *International Male.* They've pumped their pecs and popped their steroids. They've brought with them their stash of X and crystal meth. This afternoon, tea dance will spill out through the open doors all along the deck overlooking the bay. The boys will be happy, hopping, and horny.

"Jeffrey O'Brien, I can't believe your restraint," Chanel says, grinning, when I tell her I have no plans to join them.

"Oh, *please.* Once some friend of Joan Crawford's asked her to go out for dinner. This was near the end of her life. She said no way, there was no possible way she could do it. The friend asked why not. 'Well,' she said, 'it just takes too long to put Joan Crawford together these days.' "

Javitz sniffed. "That wasn't what she said. She said, 'Do you want me, or do you want Joan Crawford? If you want me, I'll be ready in a few minutes. If you want Joan Crawford, you'll have to wait a couple of hours.' "

We all laugh. "Same difference," I tell him.

He's in bed. He hasn't left his bed much this past month. He was sleeping all afternoon; I had to wake him to tell him that Chanel was here. The results of his tests were inconclusive. He'll have to go up to Beth Israel next week for some more. Meanwhile, all he wants to do is sleep.

Lloyd left this morning. We didn't speak much during the time he was here. On each of Lloyd's trips since Javitz first told us about the fatigue, I've managed to be distant. He sleeps on the couch. Today, he had to get back because he agreed to do the holiday shift at the hospital. It's the first time in six years that the three of us haven't been together on Memorial Day in Provincetown.

Now Chanel and I sit on either side of Javitz's bed trying to encourage him to get dressed and join us on the deck. "In a little while," he promises.

"You've been saying that all day," I tell him.

"I have some news for you guys," Chanel says. "I broke up with Kathryn."

"Really?" I'm surprised, looking over the bed at her. "Why didn't you call me?"

"Oh, because in the end it didn't seem all that important. She was sweet, she was nice. But there wasn't anything there ultimately."

"Not like with Wendy," Javitz says.

"Romantic love drags us down, I've concluded," Chanel says. "Distracts us from our goals in life. No more falling in love for me."

I just look at her. "You want to fall in love again so bad you can taste it."

She breaks into a broad grin.

"Go on, you two," Javitz says. "I'm going to sleep for just an hour more."

"Just an hour," Chanel says. "I came all the way down here to see you."

We head downstairs. We're quiet for a while, avoiding the topic. I start washing the dishes. She asks how Lloyd and I are doing. "Who knows?" I tell her. She asks if I've heard from Eduardo. "Yeah," I tell her, "when he called to cancel out of lunch a few weeks ago."

"We've really made a mess of our love lives, haven't we?" she says, laughing. "I *mean* it, Jeff. No more falling in love for me. That's my new rule."

I glance at her over my shoulder. "Even when we rewrite all the rules, even when we tell ourselves this is the way it's going to be, we'll never be able to stop falling in love. Or *wanting* to fall in love, for that matter."

Chanel grins. "You know, you're sounding more and more like Javitz all the time."

"Heaven forbid," I shudder, turning back to the dishes.

She stands, coming up behind me at the sink. "Jeff. What's wrong with him?"

I dry my hands, turn and face her. "We don't know," I say softly. "But he had a viral load test. He's off the scale."

"Which means . . . ?"

"He's got a whole shitload of the virus, and it's running pretty rampant."

"I brought him a magazine. He said he can't *read*."

I nod my head. "We'll be going up to Beth Israel next week. I'm worried about CMV."

She looks horrified. "Jeff, this all happened so quickly. He just moved here!"

"I know. But it hasn't been quick. Not really."

We wash the dishes together without speaking further, me washing, her drying. Finally she says: "How much more time do you think Javitz has left?"

In the past, in the not-so-distant past, I'd evade that question whenever it was posed. "Oh, he's not going anywhere," I'd say. "He's got more time than me," I'd josh. But such responses are no longer appropriate, if they ever were. I answer truthfully. "A year?" I guess. "Maybe less, a little more. But I think we're finally getting near the end."

I can't believe the words I've just articulated. I stand there with a dish in my hands, not moving, as if I had not been the one to speak, as if I had just heard the words for the first time myself. Chanel's reaction mirrors my own. It's not as if we didn't know, it's not as if we hadn't already thought this in our minds. But to hear the words, to say them . . .

"I'm going for a walk," she says. "I just need to get some air."

"Sure. I may go out, too. . . ."

"Tea dance?" she smiles weakly.

"No. Definitely not tea dance."

We agree to meet back here for dinner. I head up to Javitz's room, sit on his bed, and gently stir him awake. "I'm going out for a bit," I whisper. "Need anything?"

"No, thanks."

"I thought you were going to get up soon."

"I will."

I kiss him lightly on the forehead. I stand, turning to leave the room. "Oh, darling . . ." he says.

"Yes?"

"I just want you to know that you look great."

My heart melts. I know what he means. I'm unshaven, and I'm wearing a plain blue T-shirt, not something that hugs my pecs. Old jeans, sneakers—hardly the uniform of the season. There will be boys out there: it's Memorial Day, for God's sake.

"My year is up," I laugh. "Can't get away with it anymore. Might as well dress comfortably."

We both laugh.

The street is indeed mobbed. The shutters over the shop windows have all been opened. Vacancy signs sway from the shingles of guest houses, replacing the ones that had read: "Closed for the Season." People shout to each other from across the street, giddy after their long hibernations. The horse-drawn carriage is back for another season, clattering down the road, pulling its eager cargo of hets and their wide-eyed kids. The tourist trolley rattles by, an unwieldy monstrosity that veers awkwardly down the narrow streets. The tour director drones: "To your left, ladies and gentlemen, are original sea captains' homes, built in the late eighteenth century. . . ." One of the women on the trolley seems fascinated by me, watching me as I walk. She's a blue-haired lady in red stretch pants and a halter top. She stares directly at me, narrowing her eyes. In my mind, the tour director intones: "To your right, ladies and gentlemen, is an authentic homosexual of the late *twentieth* century." And they all turn and gawk, snapping photographs.

I decide to beat it out of town.

There's a rest stop right here on the Cape that I've never been to. Surely today it will be busy. It's all I really want today, and dinner later with Chanel. I hop into Javitz's car and head south. I miss

Lloyd terribly, but I refuse to think about it for very long. Before he left this morning, he gave me a card. It was a lovely image of a purple sky, with an old-fashioned man-in-the-moon surrounded by a host of stars. The verse read:

> *Every night we're apart,*
> *I look into the heavens toward the stars . . .*
> *I send their warmth to you*
> *And ask the boundless sky*
> *To wrap around you like a blanket . . .*
> *And the moon to kiss you goodnight.*

It made me pause. Its sickeningly sweet words seemed to miss their mark. I showed it to Javitz, who roused himself enough to read it. "He's *madly* in love with you," he said, rolling his eyes. "Sometimes I don't get the two of you at *all*."

I threw the card away. Somehow it made me angry. I didn't want to see it, didn't want it around. Did he expect I'd go all soft and gushy upon reading it? Did he expect it to *comfort* me?

And then there's Eduardo. Should I have been surprised that he called to cancel? No, nothing should surprise me anymore. But still, it did. He gave no reason, and I asked for none. So much for closure.

I pull into the rest stop. There are, as I'd hoped, quite a few cars. It's a pretty area, stretched along an inlet of the bay, not dirty and grimy like the stops on the way to Boston. I don't hesitate. I get out of the car, planning to head down the trail. But just then I see a police cruiser pull in behind me. I panic for the briefest of seconds, then relax, striding around to the front of the car and lifting the hood.

"Got a problem?" the cop asks, slowing down, pulling up alongside of me.

"No," I say in my butchest voice. "Just adding a little wiper fluid."

The cop nods and circles out of the rest stop. It's a good thing I'm dressed the way I am—the dumb cop probably believed I really knew how to add wiper fluid to a car.

That's when I look up and see a man staring at me from two cars over.

I let the hood drop. I clap my hands together to get rid of the grime. The man is approaching me. He's in his fifties, not unattractive, a full head of white hair, a bit of a paunch. Even from here I can see the sun playing with his gold wedding band. He saunters up to the car.

"Hi," he says.

"Hi," I say back.

We stand for a few seconds looking at each other. His skin is very pink, his hands plump and clean. Well-manicured nails, with a gold Rolex watch complementing his wedding ring. He's a rich man—I can tell from his shoes: brown wingtips buffed to a high gloss.

"I always figure, nothing ventured, nothing gained," he says, grinning. "You got a couple of minutes?"

I'm not sure what game he's playing, so I remain aloof. "What for?"

He winks. "I could show you a good time."

There's a buzz, some kind of unspoken communication between us. I know what his fantasy is. I'm a straight boy, stopping to fix his car. A dirty, white-trash kind of straight boy. So I respond in kind: *"What?"*

"Why not?" His voice gets a little breathy. "Give it a try. Nobody will ever know."

"Hey, man," I say, trying to sound like Marky Mark, "I don't do guys. I got a girl."

"That's good. I'll do you. You don't have to reciprocate."

I glance over my shoulder towards the trees. "In there, man?"

He nods. He's nearly salivating by now.

"Aw, I don't know. . . ."

He stares down at my crotch. "I bet you could do with getting your rocks off."

I look at him. "All right, man. But let's go fast."

He leads the way. We tramp over grass that's been matted down by hundreds of men before us. He heads straight for a little clearing near the water. He turns and faces me.

"You're a catch," he says. "You really are." He falls to his knees in front of me. "A real straight guy. I only do straight guys. I hate goddamn femmes. If I wanted a girl, I'd get a girl."

He unfastens my belt, pulls down the zipper. Suddenly I feel a little foolish, but I try not to let it interfere with my desire. The guy blows pretty well, getting me hard in a matter of seconds.

"Tell me about your girl," he says up at me, between swallows of my dick. "She got nice tits?"

I don't like this person, but still I play along. "Yeah, man," I say. "Nice big knockers."

"Think about them now, while I'm blowing you."

Hey, whatever floats your boat, guy. But something feels wrong now. Something feels really *off.*

"I never blow fags," the guy on his knees tells me. "I only blow straight guys."

Why does he have to keep talking? Just suck my dick, asshole. Knock off the gab.

"I'd rather go home without *any* action than blow a *fag*," he says again, his face up under my nuts. "I'm very particular about who I blow."

"Suck my dick," I snarl. The contempt in my voice is no longer an act.

He obeys. I shoot. He takes it all, swallows every last bit, drinking it fast like we used to do as kids at the garden faucet.

"Thank you," he sighs, wiping his mouth with the back of his hand. I catch the glint of his wedding band in the sun again.

I pull away, zip up. My head hurts. I push off down the path, but take a wrong turn somewhere and get lost. Round and round I go, up a hill, down the other side. This is crazy, I tell myself. This is just a small area. But I'm lost as if in a maze, stumbling along well-worn paths, in and out of bushes and under trees. I come upon two men fucking, and their eyes greet me with desire, but I turn and begin to walk faster. I finally stop near the water to catch my breath.

"This can't be happening," I whisper to myself. "This can't be real."

And then I know that none of it is. Not the sex here, not tricking at the bar, not standing on the steps of Spiritus, not the idyll of a perfect home, a happy marriage, a summer love.

The man who just blew me walks up again.

"Ready for round two?" he asks.

I turn around and face him. The pinkness of his scalp shows through his white hair. He looks at me wide-eyed and greedy, and I can see right through his skin. I can see his wife and four daughters and the large glass windows of his Hyannis Port home. I can see his BMW, his Labrador retriever, his gay porno magazines stuffed in the back of a drawer.

"I'm not straight," I snap at him, turning to walk away. But then I stop, surprising myself. "In fact," I tell him, "I'm as queer as they come." His pink face grows pale as my voice rises in intensity and speed. "I'm ACT UP. I'm Queer Nation. You should've seen me in drag a couple Halloweens ago. Very feminine, very pretty. No real straight guy would ever put on a *bra*. That's because straight guys are *boring*. I wouldn't be straight if you paid me a million dollars. *Ten* million dollars!"

I walk up close to him. "Look, I don't mean to ruin your fantasy. It's hot, if you don't think too much about the implications. But you need to get a grip, girl. Live in the real world. These guys you blow—they aren't straight. They're as gay as I am. As *you* are." I smile. "I'm just trying to do you a favor, mister. You can't have it only your way. Believe me when I tell you: the world doesn't always follow your lead."

I leave him flabbergasted in the bushes. Suddenly the way out is clear and obvious: why didn't I see it before? I return to Javitz's car, start it up, head home.

I drive to the beach at Herring Cove. There are hundreds of people here, gay men and lesbians and straight families with kids. They toss beach balls back and forth, they dip their toes timidly in the water, they blare their radios and portable CD players with everything from Bach to Blondie. But they make little impression on me as I walk. I stop to watch a seabird running ahead of the surf. It leaves little three-toed prints in the sand that keep getting washed away with every new lap of the tide. I think about Lloyd. I think about Eduardo. I think about Javitz.

This was all supposed to be much easier than it is. We were changing the rules, making our lives more authentic, honoring the love as it came, the friendships as they were made. We were fashioning new families out of whole cloth, tearing out the stitches that were tight, mismatched, weaving in only those that were beautiful and fitting. We were making our lives happier, more honest, more enduring.

Suddenly I'm alone on the beach. The people all have vanished, replaced only by the gulls and the steady beat of the surf. I feel myself settle into calm. I walk for miles, it seems. Occasionally the artificial world interrupts: a child's ball crossing my path, a dog barking, a shout of hello from someone I once knew. But it doesn't distract me from my course. I just keep walking, and at the end of the journey, I feel tired and good. I go back to the house as the sun begins to set, as the shouts and the whoops from the season's first big party night get carried along by the night breezes. Javitz is asleep; Chanel is in the kitchen, whipping up a spicy Spanish dish for dinner. I sit down in front of my computer and begin to write. I write about choices and fears, about passion and truth, about love and being alone, about everything—and everything in its season.

Boston, November 1994

Thanksgiving dinner: Lloyd and I, Javitz, Chanel, Tommy, Melissa and Rose.

"Pass the sweet potatoes," Lloyd calls out.

"I made them with cinnamon," Melissa tells him, sending over the bowl.

"Yummm."

"We've got rhubarb pie for later," I say. "Tommy made it."

"*Tommy* made it?"

"Hey, way to go, Tommy boy."

He blushes.

"Shouldn't we say grace?" Rose asks.

"Yes," Lloyd says. "We should. Look at all this food. We should be grateful."

"I'm grateful that Jeff and Javitz got up at five a.m. to baste the turkey," Chanel says. "I can't *imagine* Jeff getting up at five a.m."

"Well, I did," I tell her.

"And *me* just out of the hospital," Javitz says, hand over heart, batting his lashes like a simple southern Jewish belle.

"Instead of grace, how about if we all say what we're all thankful for?" Melissa suggests.

"All right."

"Okay."

"I already said I was thankful for Jeff and Javitz and this turkey," Chanel says. "That, and single lesbians."

Everybody laughs—except Melissa, I notice. Melissa must be thinking about Wendy, who last year sat with us around this table. This year, no one mentions her name.

"I'm thankful for my health, my heart, my soul, and the love of friends," Lloyd says.

"Aww . . ."

"I'm gonna cry."

"I'm thankful for Rose," Melissa says simply.

Rose reaches over and takes her hand. "I'm thankful that Javitz is sitting with us here today instead of lying in that musty old hospital bed."

We all nod. Tommy and Lloyd raise their water glasses and clink a toast.

"I'm thankful for every *day*," Javitz says, uncharacteristically subdued.

I smile at him.

"I'm thankful for being queer," Tommy says.

"Hey, hey."

"Hear, hear."

And me? What shall I be thankful for? I look over at Lloyd. His green eyes are still looking at me, as they have all day, as they have since last week, since the day he spoke those horrible words.

It began pleasantly, inauspiciously, enough. "It's going to be a nice day after all," I said just before he landed the bomb, watching through the skylight as the sun burned away the rainclouds.

It was a lazy late Sunday morning. Our room was still filled with flowers—daisies and white roses from Javitz, lilies from Chanel, chrysanthemums and irises from Melissa and Rose. We had come back from my father's funeral to find the house bedecked with flowers. Mr. Tompkins had started to eat the lilies, but otherwise they were fresh and fragrant. The flowers from our family made me cry for the first time. I sat down on the kitchen floor and Lloyd wrapped his arms around me. If only my father had once asked about my life today—if only he hadn't retreated behind the withering glare of my mother.

But on this Sunday morning, as we both slept in late, I felt much more alive than I had in weeks. Outside there was an excited chattering of birds, roused by the unexpected appearance of the sun. "Come on," I said to Lloyd, poking him softly. "Come on."

"Please," he murmured, "please don't—I don't want to . . ."

"Don't want to what? Make love?" I looked at him with big eyes. "Lloyd, it's been . . ."

He sat up, his eyes crusty with sleep, his face creased from the contours of the pillow. He looked at me. He spoke the words. "Jeff," he said, "there's no more passion."

In that moment, the world bumped a little as it turned on its axis. In that moment, a hole ripped through the fabric of time and space, and I became clairvoyant. I could see weeks, months, years, into the future. I could see myself alone on a beach, Javitz dead and Lloyd very far away. But I closed my eyes against it: I could not bear to look. I waited until the portal had closed, until the world began to turn smoothly once again. The anarchy of the present, however frightening, was preferable to the certainty of the future.

I looked at him queerly, and I made a little laugh in disbelief. "What do you mean? That's not true. What are you *talking* about?"

He buried his face in my lap, wrapping his arms around my waist. "Us. The passion between us."

"There's passion between us," I insisted. I touched his face. "Dog. Come on. Of *course* there's passion."

"Not like there was with Eduardo."

Lloyd's voice brings me back now, calling to me from across the table. "What about you, Cat? You haven't told us what *you're* thankful for."

Suddenly I feel very sad. Here we all are, gathered together in the home Lloyd and I have made, a fire in the wood-burning stove,

Mr. Tompkins under the table waiting for scraps. Everyone's laughing, carrying on. There's no call for sadness, not today, not when Javitz is home from the hospital and we're all together. But I feel sad nonetheless.

"Cat?" Lloyd asks. "Are you okay?"

"I'm fine," I lie. "I'm thankful for life. For my life. *Our* lives."

"How profound!" Chanel laughs.

"You always know *just* how to grab a guy, Jeff," Tommy says.

"I'm not going to *touch* that line," Javitz says, and guffaws—in that laugh of his that I'll never forget, not in a hundred years.

I'm still looking at Lloyd. He smiles. I smile back. But I'm remembering his words: will I ever forget them?

"Okay, let's eat," Rose says, digging into her plate.

Lloyd keeps looking at me. We hold our gaze for several seconds. Between us, at the head of the table, is Javitz. I realize he's looking at me, too, and at Lloyd. The three of us share a moment, a soft, silent look that passes around from each of us to the others. Then we blink back whatever it was and join in with the feast.

Provincetown, May 1995

When I walk in and see Eduardo sitting beside Javitz's bed, his hands dangling awkwardly between his legs, I know I would never have seen him again if not for this chance of fate.

"Hi," I say, coming into the room. Javitz had asked for root beer; I'd gone to the A&P to get some. Ernie had been here then. He must have let Eduardo in.

I set the root beer down beside Javitz's bed. "Hello, darling," he says to me. "Look who came by to pay his respects."

Eduardo smiles, looking up at me with those empty eyes. "Hi, Jeff."

"We've had a nice talk, haven't we?" Javitz says. "He's told me all about his new job."

"Well, it's an internship," Eduardo corrects.

"Whatever, darling. But now I'm ready for a nap again. It's all I seem to be doing these days."

"Okay," Eduardo says. "I just wanted to come by. I've—missed you." He stands, bending down to kiss Javitz good-bye.

"And I've missed *you*," Javitz tells him.

I walk with Eduardo down the stairs. We're quiet. I expect he'll leave quickly now, make some excuse, dodge out of here as fast as he can. But he turns to face me.

"What did the tests show?"

"What did he *tell* you they showed?"

"Nothing."

"He's right." I walk into the living room. "He's got to go up to Beth Israel. They need to do an MRI. Maybe a spinal tap."

"Is he going to be okay?"

"Eduardo, he has AIDS."

He sits down on the couch. I sit opposite him in a chair.

"How's Tommy?" I ask.

"He's good." Eduardo looks over at me. "I'm sorry you guys had that argument."

"Was that what it was?" I ask. "I couldn't quite figure out *what* that encounter was."

"He's going through a lot of shit, as I'm sure you can imagine."

"He hates me," I say simply.

Eduardo sighs. "He's just . . ."

"He hates me." I smile. "Do you?"

"No," he says, as if that were the silliest thing in the world. "I don't hate you."

"I'm glad about that, at least."

"Oh, Jeff. What do you want from me? What do you want me to say?"

"I'm not sure." I smile. "I guess I'm just trying to understand."

"Understand what?"

"What happened. With us, with you, with me. I don't think I *want* anything from you, Eduardo. I might have, just a few weeks ago. But now—now, I think I just want to understand." I look over at him. Such a small, thin child, sitting terrified on the edge of the seat. "Do you love Tommy?" I ask quietly.

"Yes," he says, gathering himself. "Yes, I do. He's been wonderful to me. When we first met, I was pretty scared, confused. I was starting school, feeling overwhelmed, intimidated. He gave me incredible support."

"Maybe he'll get you to move to the South End now that you work for a gay newspaper." I smile, trying to get him to do so as well.

Eduardo shifts a little uncomfortably. "It's just an internship. After school I want to get a job with Condé Nast."

"Of course," I say, and I can't help laughing.

"Jeff, it's *different* with Tommy."

"How is it different?"

"Tommy needs me."

"And I didn't. Is that it?"

"Tommy's my *best friend*. He's—so unlike any man I've ever known. We can be at a party together and we're just there, together. I can be off all night talking to someone, and he'll be off doing his thing, but then we leave together. Always. That's the way it is. It's very—"

"Very what?"

"He's my *best friend*," he repeats.

"So you don't have sex?"

"Not everything has to be about sex, Jeff."

"No," I agree. "But it's good when *some* things are."

Eduardo shakes his head, and there's a hint of a smile. "You'll never change."

"Oh, don't say that," I reply, and I mean it. "I hope I've changed *some* since you saw me last."

"I hope so, too." We hold each other's eyes for several seconds. He begins to smirk. "Yes, even though it's none of your business."

"Yes, what?"

"We *do* have sex."

I smile. "With or without your cock ring?"

Now he can't help smiling as well. "Jeff . . ." he warns.

"So tell me about school. How it went."

He looks at me a moment, as if he doesn't quite know what to make of me or my question. Then it appears he decides to trust me, for now. "My teachers really liked my stuff," he says, leaning back into the cushions of the couch. "You know those posters showing the guy looking up at the Hancock tower, plastered all over town?"

"Sure."

He grins. "That's my design."

"No way," I say, surprised at how proud I feel. How my chest expands and my heart just about breaks. Somehow seeing Eduardo as designer—as creator—turns me on in a radical new way. I watch him as he talks, using his hands to express himself, to shape the air as he describes how the poster came to be, how he put it all together.

"Now, for the newspaper, I'm redesigning their logo. The one they have is so tired, so seventies." He smiles over at me. "Sorry."

"No, no, it's time we embraced the nineties. Go on."

He pauses. "Jeff, I'm sorry I never sent you a note or anything when your father died."

I wasn't sure if he knew. "I understand."

"No, it was wrong of me."

"I'm sorry I wasn't around when you got your test. After all, I was the one—"

He stops me. "It all turned out okay."

"Did it?" I stand up, walking over to sit beside him on the couch. "Eduardo, are you happy?"

"Sure." He closes his eyes. "Sure, I'm happy. Why wouldn't I be? I *matter* in Tommy's life. I really make a difference. He makes me feel that I'm the most important person in his life."

"That's one of his gifts," I admit. "And I'm sure you *are* the most important person in his life." I pull back a little bit, giving him space. "But are you happy?"

His eyes open and move over to look at me. "Don't lecture me, Jeff."

"I'm not—"

"Because you can't do that anymore. I won't let you."

"All I'm suggesting is that we look at our lives, all of us." I lean in closer to him. "I know things were pretty unbalanced between us last summer, and I just want to say I'm sorry."

Eduardo turns his face. "Look, Tommy would be upset if he

knew I were here. He really flipped out when I told him you and I had been—together. He really has some issues with you."

"Not entirely unjustified," I admit.

He sighs. "Of course, I told him that it was just a summer affair, that you have lots of them." He faces me, cruelly. "Maybe this summer I'll meet the new boy, as Raphael met me."

From somewhere outside the foghorn calls, a low, hopeful sound. "That's not how it was," I tell him. "That's not how it turned out, and you know that." Damn the torpedoes, I'm thinking. I'm going straight ahead, whether I push his eyes back to emptiness or not. "Remember how you said you felt you were second in my life? I don't doubt you felt that way. I don't doubt I *treated* you that way. But you weren't. You were *first*, Eduardo. Almost from the very start, you were first."

He stands up. "Don't, Jeff."

"Lloyd saw it happening. Hell, that's part of the reason we are where we are right *now*. I can't explain it fully, but when I was with you, I felt so alive, so full of hope and challenge and affirmation. I couldn't wait to see you every time I got here, but of course I never told you that, never admitted it, because I wasn't really even admitting it to myself. That would have been too scary, too risky. To fall in love with a trick. To fall in love with someone who wasn't Lloyd. To fall in love, period."

I rise now too, coming up behind him. "I thought I was too old, that my days were numbered, that my time had passed. Not that I wasn't content with my lot, but I've learned that contentment is fleeting, that we have to be ready to grasp happiness wherever and whenever we find it. Well, I found it with you."

We're both quiet, as if we both know we've now passed the point of no return.

Finally he speaks. "Last summer, to hear you say those words would have made me very happy."

"But this summer?"

"They're far too scary. Last summer, you were safe. You had a lover. A lover we all assumed—you, me, Lloyd, everybody—that you'd be with for eternity. This summer you stand before me and say I'm first in your heart, or at least I was, and there's no Lloyd for you to go home to. Where does that put me?"

"Where do you *want* to be?"

He smiles. "Don't you see? I never wanted you and Lloyd to break up. That was never in my fantasy. You were role models for me. Proving to me that love can endure, that love can accommodate how we grow, how we change. I was devastated to hear you guys weren't living together. Hell, if Jeff and Lloyd couldn't make it, what hope was there for the rest of us?"

"I don't understand," I say. "Why did you get so angry at me all the time, then?"

"It wasn't Lloyd," he says, smiling, as if he's the patient parent now, explaining to a perplexed child the simple truths of living. "It was all the others. It was the sense that nothing was real, that nothing was ever solid. Even when you said you weren't tricking—and I believed you—there still remained that option. Who *was* I to you then? Not your lover, certainly. Not a trick. But just one of the many men you defined places for in your life."

"If you'd ever asked," I tell him, "if you'd ever asked me to stop tricking, I would have."

"Don't deceive yourself."

"I'm not. I would have. Do you have any idea how important you were to me? *Are* to me?"

I sense a retreat. He looks out over the bay. "You taught me that we can define our relationships, our lives, any way we choose. That's what I'm doing with Tommy, no matter what you think of it. But I'm not sure you and I could agree on what the definition of *us* would be."

I come up behind him, taking a chance. I slip my arms around his waist. He doesn't protest, doesn't tense. The smell of him quickens my pulse, gladdens and saddens me at the same time.

"Can't we see what happens?"

"I could never go back to the way it was," he says very quietly.

"Neither could I," I tell him, my lips near his ear. And I realize, for the first time, that I really *wouldn't* go back, no matter how much I lament the change of seasons. How much more exciting to create a future than recreate a past.

"Can you tell me," Eduardo asks, turning in my arms to face me, "right here and now, that you have given up on Lloyd, that you could embrace a monogamous relationship with me, and be happy about it?"

"No," I say simply. "Right here, right now, I couldn't say either of those things."

He grins widely, as if I've said the right answer. "And I can't say that I want that. And I can't say that I don't want a relationship with Tommy, because he's a dear, sweet, wonderful man who needs me as much as I need him, and I don't care how you define that."

"Then I should just forget you."

"I'll tell you one thing, buckaroo," Eduardo says, and his eyes suddenly come alive—his old eyes, the eyes from last summer, the eyes that loved me. "I've never felt more passionately about a man than I felt toward you."

That's when Ernie comes in, spying us standing there with our eyes locked together. He just smiles, as if he senses something, smells the sudden release of testosterone in the room. He heads upstairs to Javitz's room, and Eduardo and I go outside, to the little stretch of grass hidden from the road by a line of shrubbery.

"Jeff," Eduardo says, "it was very hard for me to see Javitz so sick."

"Because of Tommy?"

"Because of everyone. Everything." He looks at me, and his eyes are wide and wild. "Sometimes I worry I'm going to be the only one left."

I kiss him. Hard and deep, and it comes flowing right back up between us, burning up from our toes, careening up from our gut, exploding out of our hands and mouths and tongues. We fall to the grass on our knees, still locked together, fighting like dogs for supremacy on top. "Hey," I say, breaking free from hot, wet lips, "you've been working out, Brad Pitt." He pins me down, winning fair and square. He pulls off his shirt, and his chest has indeed tightened since last I saw it; his abs have most definitely defined themselves.

He takes a condom from his wallet and rolls it down along his shaft. It's been a long time since any man has entered me, so it takes some adjustment on my part. But he manages, lifting my ass with his hands, guiding his dick inside. Through it all, we remain locked in each other's gaze. We make love right there, oblivious of everything else in our lives but our shared passion. It's all still there, every last bit of it, and when we come, we come together, slicking our bodies as if the juice had simply been waiting for this moment, as if we hadn't climaxed in the entire nine months we'd been apart.

We make no plans to see each other. We talk no more of commitment or lovers or definitions. We part simply: a kiss, a touch, our eyes. He walks back home to his parents, and I try not to think, try not to live anywhere else but in this precious, blissful moment. But of course the phone rings then, and when I run inside to answer it, it's Lloyd on the other end of the line, telling me that Mr. Tompkins has finally had his stroke, that he might already be dead.

PASSION

Boston, December 1994

My mother loved me with all the passion she had for life, and she never let me forget that. That is, until the day I told her I was queer, and whatever passion there had been for me dissipated like the smoke of her cigarettes, exhaled into the air. My father used to say, "You're *passionate* about those kids," when she'd meet us at the bus stop, cookies in hand, when she'd sit in the dirt of her rock garden with us, planting marigolds. "Not every mother gets up at five o'clock in the morning to make lunches," she used to say, whenever she got angry with us. "Lots of mothers just give their kids money and tell 'em to buy a sandwich at school!"

Passionate. That was what my mother was. But for the last decade my mother has been anything but, instead becoming the dry, indifferent ghost of the woman I once loved.

Today, however, is one for the record books. My mother has come to visit me. My sister, Ann Marie, drove her to Boston in the '86 blue Camaro she bought with her income tax refund last year. "I'd never drive *my* car into Boston," my mother insisted, so Ann Marie did the honors. With them is Ann Marie's new baby boy, a ten-pound, blue-eyed tyke named Jeffrey Michael. Right after he was born, Ann Marie backed out of her proposed marriage to the fiancé whose name I cannot recall, a man whose hair was as long as his arrest record. "I've had enough disasters in my life," Ann Marie reasoned. "Why look for another?"

They were coming to Boston today, my mother said, so I could see the baby. "Who knows when *you'd* be coming back to see *us?*" she'd said on the phone. Besides, she added, there were a few things of my father's she wanted to give to me.

She knew I was likely not coming home for Christmas. I hadn't in several years, although this year, being the first without my father, I had considered going. I think my mother wanted to see me for the holidays, one way or another. Strange concept, my mother wanting to see me.

"How neat you keep this place," she comments, first thing, walking through the living room. "You should've seen how he *used* to keep his room," she says over her shoulder to Lloyd.

She lights up a cigarette. Lloyd looks at me. I don't say anything. She puffs up the room. What am I supposed to do: send my *mother* out to the deck? Good thing Javitz isn't here.

The baby is wide-eyed and fat. "Look how big he is!" I exclaim, taking the child into my arms.

"Not bigger than Mr. Tompkins," Lloyd says.

"He'll be six and he *still* won't be bigger than *that* cat," I quip.

Mr. Tompkins nips at my mother's hand when she replaces her cigarette case in her purse. "Hey," she scolds, shaking her finger at him. "You behave." He runs, and we don't see him the rest of the day. No one has ever before intimidated Mr. Tompkins into obedience.

"I hope that you don't mind that I named the baby Jeffrey Michael," Ann Marie says, as I place her son down on the couch for Lloyd and I to google over. "I mean, that should've been your right."

My mother harrumphs. "I told her not to be silly. I mean, *you're* not having any children."

"You never know, Mother," I say, smiling up from the gurgling creature on the couch. "Lloyd and I might surprise you."

She raises her eyebrows, the eyebrows she still pencils in carefully every morning in front of her mirror. She looks back and forth between Lloyd and me, then shrugs. "It's the nineties. I keep forgetting."

"I just love him *so* much," Ann Marie coos, picking the child up and holding him to her breast. "It's like I never loved anyone this much. All I can think about is him. He's my whole world. Like I never want any other man in my life but him."

"She's *passionate* about that child," my mother tells me.

"That's wonderful," I say. I've never seen my sister so happy, so content, so focused on anything other than herself.

"I told her, well, what does she need a husband for?" My mother exhales a cloud of smoke. "I know, I know. I've always been one to believe that a child needs two parents. And I still do. But that's the best scenario. There are others, maybe not perfect, but there *are* others."

She's walking around the room, inspecting photographs. Javitz and Lloyd and I in our Provincetown beads and boots and tank tops. Melissa and Rose kissing over an anniversary cake. She picks one up for closer inspection—the whole gang plus Eduardo at my birthday party last summer—but makes no comment. "Your father insisted that the child be born legitimately," she says. "But you know, I'd rather see her happy and that child raised well than have them stuck in some—what do you call it—defunctioning?—"

"Dysfunctional?" Lloyd offers.

"Yeah, that's it. One of those dysfunctional families just because it's the thing you're supposed to do."

I smile. "I'm proud of you, Ma."

"Yeah, well," she says, "your brother's not. Says she should be married. Says that child should have a father."

"He's got uncles," Ann Marie says in her defense. She hands the baby to Lloyd, whose face drops into the child's own.

"So is there any place we can have lunch around here?" my mother asks. "Like a Friendly's or a Wendy's or something like that?"

"There's a nice cafe right on Tremont Street," I suggest.

"I don't want any of those fancy city places. Just a grilled cheese or a tuna salad will be fine."

I laugh. "Mother, I'm sure we can find you something."

We end up piling into the car and heading out to the Big Boy. My mother's delighted to leave the city. "This is more like it," she says. "A place where you can actually park your car."

She carries a large shopping bag into the restaurant. I can see there are a couple of books inside. I'm not sure what they are. I don't ask, either. I imagine that's what she plans on giving me. I don't know what books my father owned. Maybe a Bible.

Little Jeffrey Michael sleeps contentedly in his seat between Ann Marie and me. "He looks like all you kids did," my mother says. "Bald and fat."

"I'm doomed to symmetry," I say, ordering a grilled-chicken sandwich, no skin, no cheese, hold the fries.

"I'll take his fries," says my mother, who just orders a bowl of soup. "Lloyd, how about if you and I split them?" Lloyd nods. What else could he do?

After we eat, my mother hauls out the books. "These are for you. I figured you should have them. Your father kept them for the last few years."

I look over at Ann Marie quizzically. She smiles. "Open them up, Jeff."

I do. They're scrapbooks. On the first page is a newspaper article pasted down, its corners frayed, the glue showing through the corners. I recognize it, but I'm not sure from where at first. Then I realize: *I* wrote this article. Five years ago. For an obscure newspaper in Michigan. A *gay* newspaper. It was one of the first pieces I did after I went freelance.

"How did he . . . ? How could he possibly . . . ?"

Lloyd has come around the table to stand over my shoulder and look. "Cat," he says, flipping ahead through the pages, "this is all your work. All of it."

I look up at my mother. "How did he *find* all this stuff?"

She shrugs. "You know your father. He had his ways. Didn't talk much about them. But what he set his mind to do, he did. Oh, he never got us a bigger house or got a job that lasted more than a couple years at a time. But he had his ways."

"Daddy could be very resourceful." Ann Marie tickles Jeffrey Michael's nose. "He had a lot of friends."

And he did, too. The house had been filled with them. Gray-haired men and women, all of whom said over and over again what a great guy old Jeff was. "He was a *good* man," as if to convince me. I'm struck with that idea now: what a good man my father was. I look like him. I walk like him. I have his name. But am I a good man? Will my friends someday say about me, "He was a good man"?

How had those friends of his reacted when they discovered he had a son who was queer? This scrapbook—had they helped him with it? Might one of them have had access to a library? Might one or two of them—surprise, surprise—have been gay themselves?

"It's all here," I say in wonderment. "Everything. From the littlest book review to my piece in the *Globe*'s Sunday magazine—it's all here." Even, I note, with some flushing of my skin, the pieces on public sex and whether HIV can be spread through sucking cock or nicks on the skin.

"That's incredible, Cat," Lloyd says.

I don't know what to say. Except "Thank you," of course, which I do tell my mother, who nods silently, self-contentedly. I'm not very present for the rest of the meal or on the ride back to the city. I'm thinking about my father, and how much I could've had with him, what a great, passionate friendship there might have been. If he was reading my stuff, damn it, why didn't he ever say anything? Like "Good job, Jeffy," or "Don't understand this rimming stuff, can you fill me in?" I'd have blushed ferociously, I'm sure, and stammered and stuttered. But we would've *talked*, goddamnit. We would've *talked*.

Lloyd helps Ann Marie strap the baby into the car as they prepare to leave. I walk my mother down the steps of our house. "Thank you for coming," I tell her. "It means an awful lot."

"He loved you, Jeffy," she says to me. "That's why I brought you those scrapbooks. He loved you very much."

My eyes start to sting. "Then why didn't he ever *say* anything, Ma? I'm glad he kept those books. I'm glad you gave them to me. But in some ways, they make me feel worse. They make me think about what's too late to have."

"It wasn't just him that wasn't saying anything, Jeffy. It was you, too. You had a hand in creating this. You had a hand in what happened."

I look at her. If she didn't pencil them, she'd have no eyebrows. When she was young, it hadn't mattered. She was blond and blue-eyed, voted Most Beautiful in her senior class. "Dear angel," the fellas had written near her photo in the high-school yearbook. I remember that photo, that girl with the soft face who became my mother, that girl I'd stare at for hours, trying to imagine what she was like. I look down at her now, standing here in front of me, hunched over, gray and wrinkled. I look at her still soft face, and I feel endlessly sad that she doesn't have any eyebrows. She'd started penciling them in after she got married, when her hair started turning brown. I remember watching her put on her makeup when I was a boy, watching her face come to life, watching her transform herself from a tired mother into the most beautiful woman in the world. How I loved her then. How beautiful she was to me. Once I took her eyebrow pencil to draw pictures with, and she smiled, telling me that it was Mommy's and not to touch. I remember taking it again, when I was fifteen, using it to darken my very first mustache, the hairs of which, like her eyebrows, were too blond to see.

I realize standing here that I am still that boy in so many ways, still that fifteen-year-old boy with the adolescent mustache. At heart, I am still just that boy from Juniper Lane, and therein lies the reason for most of what I do and say and feel.

"You're right, Ma," I tell her. "It was me, too. My own fear, I guess. Fear that he'd stop—*you'd* stop—loving me."

Now her eyes must sting her, for she blinks them several times. "We haven't been trying very hard, you and I," she says. "It's been easier just to be, not to question how things are." She looks at me, and smiles the way she once did, after she'd put on her makeup and looked to me for my reaction. "But Jeffy, he would never have stopped loving you. No matter what. And neither will I."

She hugs me. *My mother hugs me.* All is not right between us, and maybe will never be. But this day, on the front step of the home I share with my lover, Lloyd, my mother hugs me. And that is all that matters right now.

Provincetown, May 1995

I once promised Mr. Tompkins that I would never leave him. I know he's just a cat, and maybe a slightly unbalanced one at that. But he's *mine.* Lloyd and I picked him out together, chose him from among all the others, brought him home, made him a part of our family.

He's always been a very frightened cat. He's always pounced on Javitz from countertops or nipped at the hands that fed him, but it's been merely a charade, an elaborate game of bully's bluff. It's as if his whole life had to be lived raging against a world determined to prevent him from eating, to keep him from comfort, to throw him back onto the dark, oil-slicked streets from which he came. That's where they found him, those stalwart crusaders at the Humane Society. Covered in grime in a garbage bin, abandoned by his mother, two dead brothers and a flea-infested sister mewling at his side.

In his first weeks with us, Mr. Tompkins followed me around everywhere. I'd be sitting on the toilet and he'd crouch down in front of me, a tiny fluff of a creature, two big round kitten eyes staring up at me. He began his neck trick early, pawing on my throat to wake me up in the morning. "He thinks you're his mother," Lloyd said often. "He thinks he can suckle."

"Don't be so *scared* all the time," I tried to comfort him. "I'm not going to leave you."

Of course, sitting here with Javitz now, I realize I left him often: dropping him with Melissa and Rose every time I wanted to come here and trick, every time I wanted a week or more of the Provincetown scene, my boots, my shorts, my boys. "He'd always cry like a child," I tell Javitz. "Every time he saw that traveling case."

"Stop it," Javitz says. "In the morning you can call Lloyd. If you need to go up to Boston, you will."

"He can't have died," I say. "He can't have died without me there."

Just like Junebug. I turned my back on him too, leaving him with my parents when they hadn't even wanted him. "Why don't you take this damn cat?" my father said, many times. "He was *yours*."

I don't sleep. How could I? Eduardo's scent lingers on my skin. I long for him, long for his arms around me, holding me the way he did the night Junebug died. This morning I had begun to feel more resolved, more accepting, of whatever path I found myself upon. But tonight I wrestle with my sheets. It's too hot to sleep, too horrible.

At five-thirty, as soon as the sun edges the dunes, I call Lloyd. No, Mr. Tompkins has not yet died. He's still at the vet's. His back legs appear to be paralyzed. I tell him I'll be there in under two hours.

I pass the rest stop. Even at this early hour, there are cars—a couple I think I recognize. I think fleetingly of the games, the deceits—same there as anywhere else, despite what I once had thought. It starts to rain.

I'm the reason Mr. Tompkins is so fat. He ate for security, for comfort, because I didn't keep my word. I *wasn't* always there for him. I came and went as I pleased. So he ate and ate and ate, because that was his only constant, and who knew when even that would be taken away as well?

I meet Lloyd at Naomi's. Naomi's made breakfast for us—scrambled eggs and muffins—but I can't eat. "Let's go," I say. "I want to see him."

"The vet's office isn't even open yet," Lloyd says.

I pick at a blueberry muffin. I look down the hallway, notice Lloyd's Rollerblades and helmet, the shoulders of his sport coats hanging in the closet. I notice too that his hair has begun growing back in, and he's shaved the goatee. He just sits there, across the table, staring at me with those damn green eyes of his.

I insist we leave. The vet's office is just a couple of blocks to the east. I'm about two steps ahead of Lloyd the whole way.

Dr. Hanley is expecting us. "He's in here," she says gently.

We pass through a door and enter a room lined with cages. I recoil. *He's in a cage?* Several cats rush to the front of their pens, push their fuzzy noses through the grating at us. One old tom utters a deep, guttural moan. The smell in the room is foul, thick with cat piss. Somewhere from another room several dogs start barking, all at once.

Dr. Hanley opens a cage at the far end of the room. She reaches in and extracts Mr. Tompkins, all twenty-plus pounds of him. Immediately I see something is wrong: his back legs fall limply below him. His eyes look glassy.

"Let me have him," I say, putting out my arms.

She gently settles him with me. All his rage seems gone, replaced by a deadened acceptance of fate. His eyes seem to know me, but I can't be sure. Dr. Hanley strokes his head. "He's regained some use of his right leg," she tells me. "That's a good sign."

"Regained some use . . . ?" I lift my head, suddenly filled with hope. "Does that mean . . . ?"

"It's far too early to tell," she says, continuing to stroke his head. "But this might reverse itself. I've seen it happen before. We've got him on medication now. The likelihood is that he won't recover. You need to understand that. But I'd advise against making any decision until we see how things develop."

Mr. Tompkins looks up at me. Yes, yes, I'm *certain* now that he knows me.

"Why don't you take him in there?" Dr. Hanley says, pointing to a private room. "Talk to him. He needs those who love him more than any medicine right now."

It's a small room, two chairs, nothing on the walls. A metal examining table, reflecting distorted images of myself and the cat in my arms. Lloyd appears over my shoulder, brushing his lips against Mr. Tompkins's fur.

"Maybe he's going to pull out of this," he says.

I look down at Mr. Tompkins. Come on, you little monster. Come on, let me see that old spirit. Bite my hand.

"Jeff," Lloyd asks, "did you open my card?"

Mr. Tompkins nuzzles my hand in front of his face. I actually feel his tongue, like warm, damp sandpaper. He's licking me. I don't think he's ever licked me before in his life.

"It was very sweet," I say, looking up at Lloyd.

He pulls close to us. "I had a nightmare on the night Mr. Tompkins had the stroke," he says. "It was awful. I was trapped in a house on the edge of a cliff, and there was an earthquake, and the house was shaking. It was going to fall right off the cliff. . . ." He pauses. "I woke up petrified. I reached over for you, but you weren't there."

A few seconds of silence pass. "I appreciated the sentiment of the card," I say, "but the stars and the moon are poor substitutes for the real thing."

"Jeff, I do miss you. I miss our family. With Javitz being sick, everything's changed. I don't know, it feels as if—as if things are getting clearer for me."

"What things?"

"Things that matter." He stands, reaches over to stroke Mr. Tompkins's fur.

The cat shifts in my arms. I notice a hopeful twitch in his right leg. "Lloyd," I say, "I think he's going to get better."

"Jeff, don't get your hopes up. This could be just a—"

I look at him. "Don't I *always* get my hopes up? Why stop now?"

We bring Mr. Tompkins back to Dr. Hanley, who takes him gingerly from us and promises to keep us informed. We return to Naomi's, less frantic now. We sit around the table, gratefully devouring her blueberry muffins. She's gone off to work, and Lloyd needs to get ready himself. He's going to be late.

"Cat," he says, standing up from the table. "You were right. For all my talk about death, for all my past life regressions and séances, I'm terrified of Javitz dying."

He starts to cry. It startles me, how he could move so quickly from relief about Mr. Tompkins and the neutral observation that he might be late for work to this sudden catharsis of tears. I stand, pulling him into me. He just sobs harder, his chest heaving in my arms, his head pressed under my chin. I rock him softly, saying nothing.

"I wasn't there for him," Lloyd says. "I walked out on both of you."

"Don't, Dog. Don't."

He looks up at me, his face red and shiny. "Do you remember the day we rented that boat? You were so scared we'd capsize. I wanted to have sex out there, do you remember?"

"Of course I do. I was a wimp."

"No, you weren't. I was scared, too. Only I didn't show it."

I stroke his face. "I'm here, Lloyd. We're going to go through this together."

He kisses me. On the mouth. It startles me more than his tears. He turns and heads into the bathroom. I hear the shower faucets squeak, the bang of water pressure being released. I hear him step into the stream of water, making a little "yow" when he discovers it's too hot, or too cold.

Everything's changed. It feels as if things are getting clearer for me. Things that matter.

And what the hell does *that* mean?

There's a rap at the front door. I look up. I can see through the screen door that it's Drake. For some reason, I'm not surprised. But still I'm not sure what to do. Knock on the bathroom door and tell Lloyd? Answer it myself and be civil? Ignore him and hope he goes away?

But options are eliminated when Drake walks in on his own,

stepping tentatively through the living room. "Hi, Jeff," he says, leaning in the doorway of the kitchen.

He looks the same as I remember: tall and icily handsome, those steely eyes and thick wavy hair, high cheekbones and chiseled jaw. Sitting here with my eyes reddened by tears, my face unshaven and unwashed, I imagine the picture I must present. But I look up at him anyway.

"Hello, Drake."

"I just wanted to check and see if Mr. Thompson was okay."

"Tompkins," I correct him. "Yes. He's going to get better."

"Well, that's great news. I said a mantra for him this morning."

I feel generous. "Thank you. Maybe that's what helped him."

"I hope so."

"Lloyd's in the shower," I tell him.

"Oh. Well, then, you can just tell him I dropped by. I'll see him at the hospital."

"Sure thing."

He seems to have something that he wants to say. We hear the shower shut off; he doesn't have much time. "Jeff," he says, "I want you to know that I never meant to cause you any pain by buying the apartment."

"Do you like it?" I ask him. "Is it everything you hoped it would be?"

He looks at me squarely. "No. I had hoped Lloyd would be there."

His honesty catches me by surprise.

"I know you don't like me, and I suppose I don't blame you. If I were you, I wouldn't like me much either. You're right if you think I love Lloyd. I even dared to imagine he might love me." He laughs. "I'm used to getting what I want. That's been my way. I admit that. But I didn't get Lloyd. It wasn't as easy as I imagined, replacing you. That caused me considerable disappointment."

"Well," I say, "another discovery by the Brahmins that there is no right to ease."

"I'm learning that. Yes, things have come easily for me in my life. But I don't think they will anymore. Not when you start going after things that are real, that matter."

"Why are you telling me all this?"

"I still love him," he says plainly. "He taught me a great deal. About inner strength, about exploring our paths. I want him to be happy. But I'm afraid Lloyd is destined for a rather lonely road." We hear the electric razor start to buzz from the bathroom.

"Really now?"

"I believe we must all take our leaps through life, follow our own paths. But there is no need to do it alone, not when there are others who are willing to leap with us." He looks directly at me. "Don't give up on him, Jeff. If you do, I'll be there, ready and waiting."

Drake turns, walks back through the living room and out the door. I hear his BMW start in the driveway. I hear the electric razor click off in the bathroom. I hear Lloyd clear his throat, slap his cheeks.

I'm standing there in the doorframe when he opens the door. He wears nothing but a towel wrapped around his waist. It's his turn to be startled, stunned. I gently push him back into the steamy, damp room. I close the door with my foot. I begin to kiss him hard upon the mouth, my tongue exploring places it had long since forgotten. He resists a little at first, but it's as if I were a stranger, a burglar who's just broken into the house and stumbled upon this near-naked man stepping out of the shower. I push him against the sink and pull the towel from his waist, his dick springing into full hardness. I unfasten my belt, pull down my jeans. His eyes look at me with fear and wonder. I rest his butt on the sink, tilt his legs up into the air. He tips his head back, his breath catching in his throat.

I press my dick up against his hole, but I don't enter him. Instead I kiss him again, long and slow and hard. His arms reach up around me, his hands pressing against the back of my head, pulling me closer to him. I can hear his heart now in my own ears, and the passion that burns between us is as raw and exciting as it was that first time, the night he drew for me that bath and I brought him those daisies—even though no fucking follows our kiss, even though our dicks eventually subside and soften. But our eyes continue to grip each other with a ferocity we'd both forgotten lived between our souls. We say not a word—not about sex, not about passion, not about the future. We just smile into each other's eyes, listening to our hearts beat high in our ears. That's the way it stays, for the rest of the day.

Boston, December 1994

I wish I'd never told Javitz that Lloyd said there was no more passion between us. But I did, so I have to live with the fact that he's going to bring it up every now and then, and try to get me to talk about it. But I won't.

He's feeling better. He's still taking it easy, letting us bring him dinner in bed tonight. Chanel's whipped up a Philippine spicy rice dish. "An old family recipe?" I ask.

She smiles. "Kind of. It was in Cook's family for generations."

Lloyd is exhausted. He's flopped down on Javitz's couch, worn out from a long day at the hospital. "Some patient flipped out in the ER," he told us. "Went after her girlfriend with a syringe. Chased some kid down the hall."

"Poor Lloyd," Chanel says, bringing him a plate of rice and feeding him his first bite. He accepts it gladly. I cover him up with a blanket.

"It's just that I'm so tired of always being the one who has to take care of everyone else. Is that what I was put on this earth for?" I soothe him with my hand on his forehead, a soft sympathetic hum in his ear. Within minutes, he's asleep.

Chanel brings in a plate to Javitz. She sits on the edge of his bed as he tries it and asks him if it's too spicy.

"Nothing can ever be too spicy," he says.

"Just be careful," I urge. "You're still a little delicate."

He frowns. "Not a word I've often heard in conjunction with myself."

"Well, get used to it."

Chanel says, "You'd better get your strength back soon because you have to check out my new girlfriend."

"A name?"

"Kathryn. She's very cute."

"As cute as Wendy?" I ask.

She makes a face. "In a different way." She looks up at Javitz. "You've got to meet her, Javitz. I need to know what you think. She's cute, she's smart, she's nice, but—"

"No passion," Javitz finishes for her.

"No, not really."

"Darling, without passion, there's not much else."

"Ah," I interject, "but define *passion*."

"You shut up," Javitz says. "Don't confuse the issue. Passion, my dear, is the bottom line. Whenever a student comes out to me, they always want to know how to be queer. The tricks of the trade, so to speak."

"So what are some of these tricks that you teach them?"

"That there *are* no absolutes or definites. Except one." He smiles. "Passion. Passion tells the *truth*."

"Ah, but we still haven't come up with a definition for that," I remind him. I laugh to myself. There he goes again. Making these great proclamations like the pope issuing encyclicals. I look at my friend, my lover, my mentor, in the bed below me. I have learned much from him and will learn more. But now I wonder: how much fear and indecision are cloaked by his magnificent pronouncements? Javitz, our fearless leader. Might he be as confused as we are? Might the teacher make up an answer when he really has no clue? I reach down and stroke his hair, something I don't often do. He looks up at me with suspicious eyes. I just blow him a kiss.

Chanel smiles, then shrugs. "I guess we'll just have to see what develops." She taps his plate of food. "Come on now, eat up. I'm going out to the kitchen to load the dishwasher and when I come back your plate had better be empty."

After she's gone, he looks up at me. "I've been coughing again."

"Then I don't want to catch you smoking. I mean it."

"In a couple more days, it'll be gone." He sighs. "How you doing?"

"Fine. I don't want to talk about it."

"All right." He takes another spoonful of the rice, then pushes the plate away from him. "I'm not very hungry."

"If you don't like it, I can get you something else."

"I'm not hungry."

"You've got to eat."

He sneers. "You know, my mother wasn't even as bad as you are. And she was Jewish."

I laugh. "It's entirely selfish of me. It's a shorter T ride to Cambridge than schlepping up to Beth Israel."

He finishes off his ginger ale, the ice tinkling in the glass. "You know, I'm getting tired of this place. I think maybe I want to move."

I can't imagine. "Javitz, you've been here for *seventeen years.*"

"Precisely." He looks up at me, all eyes.

"What's wrong with this place?"

"Nothing's wrong with it," he says. "It just feels as if it stopped growing with me. Like I've gotten beyond it somehow."

I look around. The bookshelves crammed with volumes. Obscure titles of Greek philosophy. Thick texts that look as ancient as the history they tell about. The odd frayed envelope here and there, stuck between the bindings of books like a leaf sprouting from a crack in concrete. The posters: "Workers of the World Unite," "Josephine Baker in Paris," "Eugene McCarthy for President." The dusty photos on the walls: Javitz with me, with Lloyd. With Reginald.

"How come you never talk about Reginald?" I ask suddenly.

Reginald was the one man besides me that Javitz ever dated longer than a few months. If I remember correctly, Reginald was around in the early seventies, just before Javitz left New York for Boston. In all our time together, he's barely mentioned Reginald's name. Probably he hasn't brought him up in six years now. But still his photograph hangs on the wall.

"No particular reason," Javitz says. "It's just that there's nothing to say."

"You must have loved him."

"Why must I have?"

"You were together—what? Three years?"

"Three and a half." He pushes away the tray. "Jeff, I'm just not hungry."

"Do you ever think of trying to contact him?"

"Whatever for?"

"You were *lovers.*"

"Do you ever think of contacting *Robert?*"

I scoff at this. "Robert wasn't a lover. He just filled in the space between you and Lloyd."

"Well, Reginald was certainly a lover. You're right. I *did* love him. And he loved me. But that was that. Then we were done."

"I don't believe love can just fade away like that."

"It doesn't. I suppose it's still there, down deep in my heart. But he wasn't political enough. He didn't make the connections, between homophobia and racism and sexism and all of that. Actually, he was pretty conservative, now that I think about it. So what would I have to talk with him about today? And besides, he didn't want to move to Boston when I got the job here. So that was that."

"But if you really loved him . . ."

He laughs. "Oh, Jeff. How wonderfully romantic you are. Don't change."

"Do you ever think he might be dead? Is that why you don't try to find him?"

Javitz considers. "Yes, I suspect he might be dead at that." He smiles. "Don't get me going asking about people who are dead."

"Right." I take away the tray. "How silly of me."

In the kitchen, Chanel and I stack the dishes in the dishwasher. "What did you think of Kathryn when you met her?" she asks.

"She was nice," I say, trying to mask my lack of impression. "It was so quick, we were at the bar, I didn't have time to—"

"It's not like with Wendy. With Wendy we were mad for each other, always wet, always hot and horny for each other."

"So call her. It's not too late."

She brushes me away. "Jeff, stop. It *is* too late."

"Passion tells the truth," I remind her.

Lloyd has just woken up. He stumbles over to us, rubbing his eyes. "Can I hitch a ride back with you?" he asks Chanel. "I'm so beat."

"Sure," she says.

I tell them I'll take the T back after Javitz falls asleep. Lloyd goes in to kiss him good-bye.

Chanel pulls on her coat. She calls in good night to Javitz. He thanks her for the meal. I walk with her to the door, and she looks up at me. "I know you and Lloyd are having a rough time right now," she says. "I'm not really sure what's going on for you, but I know you guys will get through it."

I smile, but it pisses me off. Then Lloyd comes out, gives me a kiss. "I'll be waiting in the breathing position when you get home," he whispers.

After they're gone, I stand there for a few minutes wondering why I feel pissed. Then I return to Javitz's bedroom.

"I admit it *was* hard," he says when I walk in. What's he talking about? Oh, right: Reginald. "I *will* admit that. It was hard leaving him. Thinking he didn't care enough to come with me, to fight for me. I'll admit it took a while to get over him."

"But you did."

He nods. "Oh, yes. We always do. You get over one struggle only to start the next."

"Do you know what Chanel just said to me about Lloyd? That we'd 'get through' it."

"Don't you hate that?" Javitz says.

"I can't *stand* that!"

"Of *course* we'll get through it," Javitz says, with one of his patented long sighs. "People can get through *anything*." He gestures to himself spread out in the bed. "Take this fucking virus, for example." He pauses. "*Please!*" I laugh. "I went back into the hospital. Sure, I got better. That's the damn problem! It's not a question of survival. I've been surviving so long with this thing they'll have to write a book about me. It just *sucks* that we have to keep going through it over and over and over again."

"And just when you think, Okay, I've been through the fire—"

"Something else flares up and you've got to *get through* it again," he finishes.

"But we do," I add.

"And you will."

I look at him. "He said he missed the limerance."

Javitz has lit up a cigarette. Whenever he gets agitated he reaches for those damn things.

"Hey, I told you—" I start, but he ignores me.

"Limerance," he spits, as he exhales into my face. And he tells me to go read a paperback with Fabio on the cover if I want limerance.

He stubs the cigarette out in the ashtray on the side of the bed. "I'm sorry. I just get angry. Angry at the both of you. I'll tell you what passion is. It's what makes the two of you rush home to each other. It's what sets your heart racing when you hear his key in the lock. It's how he laughs when you do Bette Davis. It's how the two of you can get into the car and head off into western Massachusetts and find pumpkin stands as if by instinct. And Big Boy restaurants and cider mills and old musty bookstores and come home telling me what a marvelous day you had." He pauses. "Maybe you're not fucking on the kitchen table, but you're doing something far more important."

"And what's that?"

"Don't ask questions you already know the answer to." He settles back into his pillows. "But I'll tell you one thing. When the three of us are together, when we're sitting around the wood stove at your place, or up on the deck in Provincetown, and we're talking, talking about the world and what it means and how we could make it better—when we're like that, and Lloyd settles back into my arms and you come out with hot chocolates for all of us, when we get so tired we begin to fall asleep on each other's shoulders—in those moments I have the greatest passion of my life. And sometimes it's hard—I'll admit it's hard—when the two of you then stagger off to your room, and fall asleep in each other's arms, and I go back to my room, and fall asleep alone."

"Javitz—"

"Don't say anything. There's nothing to say. Nothing that should be said."

I just look at him.

"Go on. Get out of here. I'm tired and need to sleep. And Lloyd will be home soon. Don't make him wait."

I kiss him.

"I love you, you know." I don't often say it, but it's always there, close to my lips.

"I know, darling." He smiles up at me. "I know."

Provincetown, June 1995

We're out in the dunes, where once we made love, where once I lost the star he gave to me on a chain. It's a spot far away from the center of town, far away from tourists and the make-believe of summer. It takes a good hour to walk to this spot, but it's worth it. Here, the sun beats warm against your skin and the only sound is the steady rush of waves far below you. I come here quite a bit these days. I meditate, sitting on top of the highest dune I can find, and I go places I never imagined I could go.

"I'm glad you came down this weekend," I tell Eduardo.

"Are you?"

"Yes." I give him a grin, but no smile. "Even if you *did* come with Tommy."

"I told him I wanted to spend some time with you."

I raise my eyebrows. "And what did he say about that?"

"I can't say he was happy."

"Does he know about the other day, at Javitz's?"

Eduardo looks up at the sun. "I can't tell him that. It would hurt him too much. If he asks, I won't lie. But . . ." His words trail off.

"Do what you need to do. Just be honest with yourself about what it is you need."

He frowns at me. "You're sounding more like Javitz all the time."

"Ah," I sigh, "youth is only a moment in time when we are—when we—when—" I can't remember how it goes. "Damn it. The point is, you've got to find your own way, but there are other people who can help you when they can."

We laugh. Today his soul bewitches me. His eyes reveal more truth than any spoken words he might have said.

"Passion tells the truth," he whispers to me. "Isn't that what you told me once?"

"Yes," I say. "And now you're telling me."

"I keep thinking about that," he says. "Jeff, I don't know where you think all this might lead. . . ."

"Maybe nowhere."

He nods, as if that were the answer he hoped for. "Yes. Maybe nowhere. Maybe that's the best." But he's unsure. "Still, passion—"

"—tells the truth." I touch his cheek. "And that's as good a starting place as any. The best, actually."

"Starting place for what?" Eduardo asks, suspicious.

"To move forward. To grow. To take chances." I smile at him. "I assume you want to grow, take risks, reap rewards."

"I suppose." But he seems reluctant.

"Every time we make love—and I don't necessarily mean just you and I, I mean the 'we' of the world—we're taking a chance on life. In the end, that's all we can do. If I've learned anything, that's it." I grin. "Sometimes things can get just a little too comfortable."

"How can anything be *too* comfortable?" he says.

"Don't sell yourself short, Eduardo. Get as much out of this life as you can, because it goes so fast, and nothing lasts forever."

We lean against each other as the sun reaches midday.

"I'm not sure when we'll see each other again," he says.

"Then I should give this to you now." I pull my backpack through the sand, unzip the top, fish around inside. "Here," I say, presenting him with a scroll of paper, tied with a bright purple ribbon.

"What's this?" he asks, taking it from me.

"A belated birthday gift. A *very* belated birthday gift."

"Jeff—"

"Unroll it," I say.

He does. "It's a *story*," he says.

"From me to you. Happy birthday."

He's touched. He hugs me. "That is *so* sweet. What's it about?"

"Actually, it's part of the novel I'm writing. It's a dream sequence—kind of. I haven't figured that out yet. But it can stand on its own as a story. It's about this guy who has a dream about a magician. And this magician gives him a star, a magic star that grants three wishes."

"Oh, yeah?" Eduardo says, smiling. "And did this magic star happen to have four points?"

"How'd you *know*?" I ask in mock disbelief. "Anyway, that's the story."

"Well, what are the three wishes?"

"I'm not going to ruin the story for you," I say coyly. "Read it."

He grins. "Thank you. This is one of the nicest gifts I've ever been given."

I smile over at him. "How did you ever come to be so important to me?"

"I don't know."

"I do. You just started loving me. I wasn't looking for it, wasn't even particularly open for it. You just did. Despite everything."

He brushes my hair back from my face. I'm letting it grow longer now, no matter if the length does expose how thin it's gotten in front. "Oh, Jeff," Eduardo says, "you talk as if no one else has ever loved you, as if there has never been any other love in your life."

"Oh, no, no, not at all," I protest. "I've had great love in my life. Great passion." I smile, looking out over the sea. "More than I ever knew was possible."

I lean back into the sand, and my hands find their way into the softness beneath me. The sand is warm, comforting, enveloping. "Jeff," Eduardo says, "I wanted to see you for a reason. What happened the other day—"

The fingers on my right hand suddenly catch something: a twig maybe, or a piece of dried seaweed. Or—a chain. Yes, it feels like a chain—

"—it can't happen again. Jeff, do you understand?"

A chain. I follow it along under the sand.

"Jeff," Eduardo whispers intently, "do you *understand*?"

"No," I say, looking at him. "I'm not sure I do." I pull the chain through the sand. Something's attached at the end—

"Jeff, you've *got* to understand. *Please* try. It's just too difficult— I'm not *you*, Jeff. Oh, maybe I will be, ten years from now, but sitting here today, I can't do what you do. I can't take the risk of Tommy finding out. I know you say taking risks is how we should live our lives, but things are *good* with Tommy, don't you understand? I just can't—"

He seems near tears. It's at that moment—just as my fingers settle around a piece of metal attached to the chain—that it all makes sense. "Of course," I say, touching his face with my free hand. "Of *course*. We can only be in one place at a time, the place we're supposed to be. You'll get to where you need to go." I smile. "I *do* understand, Eduardo. I'm sorry that I didn't before."

He stands, brushes the sand off his shorts. "I'll call you," he promises. "Or you can call me. . . ."

I smile up at him. "We'll call each other."

"Yes," he agrees. "We'll call each other."

Our eyes hold.

At last I say, "I love you, Eduardo."

And he doesn't even need to say it back, because it's there, it's there in the way he hears me say the words, it's there in the way his lips close and his hands move, it's there as he turns gently from me and walks away, heading back to town. He's got a long walk ahead of him. I watch him until he rounds the top of the farthest dune and passes out of sight.

Only then do I decide not to pull the chain from the sand. I sit there by myself for more than an hour, holding whatever it is that I've found in the palm of my hand, letting the sun wash over me, the sound of the waves in my ears. Maybe it really is the star that I lost so long ago, and maybe it's nothing more than a dried coil of seaweed and an old bottle cap. Whatever its truth, it doesn't matter. I push it back far down into the sand, as deep as I can. Standing, I stretch, and start my own walk home.

Boston, December 1994

It's Javitz's second time in the hospital in two months. The pneumonia came back, as we feared it would. He's better now, slightly, and they may let him go home tomorrow. That would be good. It's almost Christmas. Almost a new year, with the calendar spread out before us blankly, awaiting whatever marks we will make upon it.

"Jeff?" Javitz asks.

"Yeah?"

"What was the name of the guy we met in the hospital last month? He had AIDS. We met him in the hallway. He was short, chubby, black."

"That was Alfred."

"Is he . . . ?"

"Javitz, I'm happy to report he's still alive."

He settles into his pillows. "Good."

Lloyd couldn't come tonight. That damn beeper. "Oh," I remember, smirking. "Lloyd told me to tell you not to die or anything while he's not here."

"I should, just to spite him."

"Not until after Christmas, okay? We're going this weekend to chop down our tree."

"I can't understand why you go to all that trouble. Driving all the way out of the city and then crawling around in snowbanks. . . . I'll never understand Christians."

"It's a tradition," I say, as if that explains everything.

"And the two of you *thrive* on tradition."

We do. Out will come the ornaments, the little nativity scene, Rose's tattered old angel for the top of the tree. "Hey, you're part of that tradition, too," I tell Javitz. "You always put the angel on the highest branch."

"The two of you have given me a great deal, you know. Vegetarian burgers. Tofu bacon. *Christmas.*" He rolls his eyes. "If my grandfather the Hebrew cantor ever knew . . ."

"If you don't want to come to Christmas, you don't have to."

He gives me a serious look. "I can never thank you and Lloyd enough for giving me Christmas. And all the other things, too."

How much I want him to be home for Christmas. And Hanukkah. And New Year's and Lloyd's birthday and Valentine's Day and all the rest. I think of the three of us, the passion with which we laugh, pontificate, promulgate, carry on. I think of Lloyd and Javitz tickling each other on the couch, Javitz jumping naked into Provincetown harbor in the middle of March, the three of us smashing into the surf as we tried to water-ski. I think of Lloyd asleep in the crook of Javitz's arm on New Year's Eve, me at their feet finishing off the last of the brownies we've made—I think of these things and know Lloyd was wrong when he said the passion was gone.

Outside, it's begun to snow lightly. "I've been thinking about Eduardo," I say.

"*He's* still alive, I take it."

"Who knows? Haven't talked with him in months."

Javitz closes his eyes. "Wasn't he some absurd age?"

"Twenty-two. Twenty-three, now."

"Are there even such things as—"

"Yes, Javitz, there are."

He grins with his eyes closed. "So why were you thinking about him? I hope you're not still *pining* for him."

It's begun to snow harder. We hear the wind rattle the window ever so slightly.

"No, it's something else. I feel as if—as if there's something there I'm supposed to understand."

Javitz opens both eyes. "Tell me more."

"I don't know what else there is to say. I do miss him. I miss the way he made me feel. I guess I really messed up that whole relationship. There was so much more I could have shared with him. . . ."

"That's the nature of these things. I think that way every time one of my best students graduates." Javitz sighs. "I'll watch him or her as they walk down that aisle and accept that diploma, and I'll think, I forgot to tell them this, or I forgot to prepare them for that. And I imagine they'll hate me for it for the rest of their lives."

"I think Eduardo hates me."

"Oh, no. Maybe at first. But he won't, not forever. You may think you messed up—and darling, I was there. I *know* you weren't perfect. But you made a difference in that boy's life. He'll see that eventually."

"That's hard for me to believe right now."

"That's because you don't see yourself that way. You still see yourself as the boy waiting to be taught yourself." He grins. "Hate to tell you, Jeff, but that ain't the case no more."

I laugh. "What would I ever do without you to keep me in line?"

"One of these days you'll have to make some arrangements."

I squint my eyes at him. "Don't get melodramatic. You may be going home tomorrow."

"But eventually, none of us are going to be around anymore. I'm talking about me, my generation. Your much-reviled baby boomers. *Then* what happens?"

I grin. "Oh, right. It becomes my job to connect with the children, to tell them about what came before." I shake my head. "I had my chance last summer, and I blew it."

"I don't think so, darling. I think you're going to surprise yourself. I think you're going to do just fine."

I look over at him.

"But here's the secret," he says, motioning for me to come closer.

"No," I say, thinking all this silly. "Just tell me from there."

He grimaces, and says very loud, just to teach me a lesson, "A teacher always learns more from his student than the other way around."

"So what did you learn from me, then? All those years ago?"

"Everything, darling. Everything that I then turned around and taught you in turn." He grins. "You taught me the tricks of the trade."

Provincetown, June 1995

We're on the breakwater, Lloyd and I, waiting for Javitz.

It's a beautiful, warm, sunny day, and for the first time in weeks Javitz is out of the house. It took some doing, and he's still a little shaky, but he was determined to meet us here.

"You go on," he instructed us. "I want to wander a bit first."

The failing eyesight turned out to be cataracts, which can be operated on—but there's still no definite answer on the fatigue. He took a few halting steps out into the sunlight and passed judgment on the day: "Glorious." We kept turning around as we walked on ahead, worried that he was going to get too tired on his own. But he just gave us those Javitz eyes and said, *"Go."*

So we did, and here we are. There's an edge of humidity, but nothing we can't live with, nothing like the grueling days of last August. On our way here, a gaggle of boys in a convertible Saab had driven past us on Commercial Street, Mariah Carey blaring from the stereo, the boys dancing in the backseat, waving their beads and their butts.

We couldn't wait to get out here, away from all that.

"Mr. Tompkins seemed happy to see you," Lloyd says to me now.

"Yeah," I agree. "Took a chunk right out my hand when I went to pet him." I grin. Lloyd brought him down from Boston yesterday. He still has little use of his back left leg, but he gets around pretty ferociously on the other three. He even jumped off the dresser at Javitz this morning. *"That'll* get you up," I said. For however long I'm here, I want Mr. Tompkins with me.

Of course, the risk is still there. The vet said it was perhaps even more likely now that a second stroke would kill him. "He just needs his mother," Lloyd said, and I suspect maybe he's right.

"I've missed this," Lloyd says, stretching his arms out over the sea. The tide is going out. We can hear the trickle of water running between the rocks below us.

"It's missed you," I tell him.

"I could live here year round," he muses.

"Thinking of trying it? The winters are pretty rough."

He smiles. "Jeff, I quit my job."

I look over at him. "Well, it's about time." We embrace.

"I don't know what I'm going to do," he says. "I've got a few leads for private practice, and I may do some per-diem work. But suddenly, a whole new set of options opens up for me."

"Like Provincetown?"

"Maybe. My family's here."

I smile. "Think about it, Dog. Think about it long and hard. Because I can't promise anything for sure anymore either."

He sighs. "Sometimes I feel I should just go, get in my car and drive away. But that's how I've always felt. Now, I think about Javitz, how much time he has left, how much time all of us have left." He stops, looking deliberately over at me. "I'm sorry our plans to move back together haven't materialized."

"You can only be in one place at a time," I tell him.

He rests his head on my shoulder. "I love you, Cat."

"Oh, Dog, I know that."

"I wish I could say I knew what was ahead for us. I still don't know if we're meant to be together. But things are starting to make more sense. I just can't promise beyond that." He lifts his head to look at me. "But I haven't given up hope. Have you?"

"You know me. I'm always the one with the high hopes."

"That's what I love about you."

"But see those waves out there, Lloyd? See the tide going out and the sun going down? The tide's going to be back in a few hours, and at dawn the sun will rise again, over there. Whatever it is that we end up doing, those things will never change."

Lloyd just looks at me for several seconds, in a way he's never looked at me before. Then he smiles, singing very softly: "When you take you gotta give, so live and let live. . . ."

I laugh, joining in. "Or let go-wo-wo-wo-wo—I beg your pardon, I never promised you a rose garden."

We laugh together, arms encircling each other's waists.

"Cat," he says.

I look over at him.

"This is passion."

We hear a long sigh. "Darling, I wish one of you had realized that a *long* time ago," Javitz says, suddenly behind us, a little winded, a little flushed, but nonetheless *here*. "Would've saved us *all* a lot of misery."

Lloyd laughs. So do I.

Javitz sits down. We make room, easing him between us.

"So where did you wander?" Lloyd asks.

"Oh, the beach in the east end, out through the meadow near the cemetery. Such a glorious day." He sighs. "And what a *magnificent* sunset. Did you know—?"

"Yes," we say in unison, "we know."

"It's just that such things *matter*," he says softly.

"They sure do," I agree. "Isn't that why you moved here?"

Lloyd and I snake our arms around Javitz's waist. He purrs. "How *good* it is to be together again," he whispers.

None of us has to say what we're all thinking, what's on our minds as we watch the sun melt into muddy colors over the surface of the ocean and the dunes. Javitz reads our minds, as he's always been able to do, and takes in a long breath, almost as if he were dragging on a cigarette.

"I live in a world in which the overriding principle is ambiguity," he says. "Tomorrow I may get sick again. Or I may not. That's what we live with today. Maybe that's what people have always lived with. Maybe we just like to believe it's different today, because it's all so much more apparent. The fear and the confusion is not nearly so hidden. But in the end, that's all we have: the knowledge that ultimately we know nothing at all."

"Not a very good conclusion," I say.

"Yeah, come on," Lloyd says, laughing. "We can do better than that."

Javitz shrugs. "Maybe you'll come up with a better one for your novel."

"I doubt it," I tell him. "Living by a script was easy. Confining and predictable, perhaps, but *easy*. And comforting. But the damn script kept changing. I couldn't memorize my lines anymore." I hunch down, bringing my face in close to theirs. "But you know what? There's a certain beauty to ambiguity. It's only then that we take control over our lives."

I look at Javitz. "How was that?"

"Very profound, darling."

"Yes, Cat," Lloyd says, smiling. "I'm impressed."

I laugh. "But really. I think we can't know all the time what it is we're supposed to do. There's no way—not anymore—for us to think *anything* is ever going to stay the same. But we *can* trust that we'll do the best we can, and I like to think there will be people who love us who will help." I laugh self-consciously. "Javitz, this is supposed to be your job."

"Not anymore, darling. You're doing fine."

He puts his arms around both of us. We sit there like the three wise men, or the three stooges, or the father, son, and holy ghost. Whatever works. We sit there, the three of us, and look out over the waves.

William J. Mann is an award-winning journalist whose work has appeared in numerous publications including *The Boston Phoenix*, *The Advocate*, *Frontiers*, and *Architectural Digest*. A contributor to more than a dozen anthologies, including *Men on Men 6*, he is also the author of *Wisecracker*, the biography of William Haines, an openly gay Hollywood star of the 1920s (forthcoming from Viking). He is a recipient of a 1996 grant for fiction writing from the Massachusetts Cultural Council, and divides his time between Northampton and Provincetown. This is his first novel.

· A NOTE ON THE TYPE ·

The typeface used in this book is a version of Janson, a seventeenth-century Dutch style revived by Merganthaler Linotype in 1937. Long attributed to one Anton Janson through a mistake by the owners of the originals, the typeface was actually designed by a Hungarian, Nicholas Kis (1650–1702), in his time considered the finest punchcutter in Europe. Kis took religious orders as a young man, gaining a reputation as a classical scholar. As was the custom, he then traveled; because knowledge of typography was sorely lacking in Hungary, Kis decided to go to Holland, where he quickly mastered the trade. He soon had offers from all over Europe—including one from Cosimo de Medici—but kept to his original plan, returning to Hungary to help promote learning. Unfortunately, his last years were embittered by the frustration of his ambitions caused by the political upheavals of the 1690s.